DOONATA

DOONATA

WALT OXER

JanWal Publications

DOONATA

A JanWal Publications book
First published in Great Britain in 2022

JanWal Publications
Lancashire, Great Britain

ISBN: 978-1-9160819-8-7

To my wife,

Jan Lorraine ... like rainbows

ACKNOWLEDGMENTS

An enormous thank you to my editor and right hand, Alan Whelan.

www.alanwhelan.co.uk

Also thank you to my cover designer Birgit Guetier for a brilliant job.

BG-Coverdesign

1
HIDE AND SEEK

'Ninety-eight, ninety-nine, a hundred... coming, ready or not!'

Her brother Teddy's call sounded as if it came from the kitchen, where their mother was preparing some treats for Mari's seventh birthday party—piles of sandwiches and mountains of scones lay out on the table, a large bowl of trifle chilled in the fridge. Her father was lighting the barbecue in the back garden.

Mari raced along the hall and ducked into the cupboard under the stairs, wedging herself behind a large suitcase. Peering through the lattice door she saw Teddy scamper past.

'I'm coming to find you!' his voice trailed into the back room.

She planned to give him a few minutes to open doors and look behind curtains before revealing her hiding place, as she always did. Then she would roar like a lion as he opened the door and run screaming to Mum. But not this time.

As the house descended into something close to silence, Mari heard the front door open. Then a strangled scream.

Teddy? Then an echoey plosive sound not unlike the pop of a champagne bottle, immediately followed by her little brother falling back against the cupboard door with blood pooling from a hole in his head.

Her instinct was to rush out and help her brother, but the sound of heavy, unfamiliar footsteps made her retreat deeper inside the cupboard. Squinting through the lattice door, she saw a hand reach down and touch Teddy's bloodied neck. The man's arm was inked with the image of a wolf's head underscored by the word "Nayka", a word she would later learn means 'Pack' in Russian.

More footfalls—two men, both wearing leathers and motorcycle helmets with dark visors.

One of them spoke. 'Why the boy, Andre?'

'Two reasons, my brother: one, the boy becomes a man, his cap pistol becomes a Glock, his aim to seek out the killers of his family; two, our contract is to leave no witnesses, four Bambellas to be eliminated.'

Mari heard her mother come into the hallway.

'What have you done, what's broken, let me see?'

Two more pops were followed by the heavy sound of Gianna Bambella's body crashing to the floor.

The man called Andre said, 'The garden, Hugo, find the girl, Mari.'

Mari hardly breathed. Strange men, motorcycle clothing, guns. Where was her father? Her brother?

The front door must have been left open; a car approached.

The man called Andre said, 'Shit, we have visitors, Hugo. Quickly, Bambella is in the garden, see to him while I see to the visitors.'

Mari was frozen in fear. She heard the combined voices of Aunt Sarah, Uncle Jimmy and cousins Fiona and Harry sing Happy Birthday as they stepped into the hallway. She wanted to shout out to warn them, but her voice died in her throat. The desire to remain hidden overcame her wish to save the rest of her family.

Moments later she heard the pop-popping sound coming from both the front and rear of the house. Then all was silent again except for the two men breathing heavily.

'Is it done, Hugo? Are we all finished here?'

'No, my brother, Mario and two others are sorted but I can't find the girl.'

Andre breathed a long sigh. 'Okay, forget the girl, let's get the fuck out of here. God only knows how many more may arrive. They asked for four, we give them nine. We ask for more dollars, brother. The girl, she so lucky.'

Mari heard steps retreating and crunch down the gravel drive. A motorcycle fired up and skidded off. She was left with buzzing in her ears but she couldn't tell if it was ringing from the shots or the blow flies beginning to feast on the blood pools that flowed slowly down the hallway.

Then the tick-tick of a taxi—more killers or a late arrival for the party? Mari manoeuvred her position so she could once again see clearly through the lattice door. It was Aunt Sophia. A scream, the sound of something dropped and smashing, a shout to the taxi driver to call the police.

'Oh my God, Teddy and my Gianna too?'

Barely able to move but finally finding her voice, Mari let out a yell. Moments later her aunt opened the cupboard door and reached into her niece.

Sophia and Mari held onto each other amidst the bloody scene of carnage and debris of her seventh birthday party.

On that day Mari wanted to die too.

The murders remained unsolved. With indecent haste the police threw them in the cold case file—until and unless some new evidence showed up.

But there *was* new evidence to share, evidence Mari withheld. Despite numerous police interviews and gentle coaxing from various female officers, Mari never spoke of the man with the wolf's head tattoo or shared the names of the killers, for fear of them returning to finish the job.

She carried her secret into adulthood.

2
Special Intelligence Service

Spinster Aunt Sophia became Mari's guardian, and put the house of horror on the market at a giveaway price. The money from the sale went into the girl's educational fund and they both moved to Sophia's house in the Yorkshire Dales. She put Mari into an exclusive boarding school for girls where, in time, she seemed to put the trauma of her seventh birthday behind her. She threw herself into her school work, which gained her a place at Cambridge University where she excelled in everything she chose to undertake, gaining degrees in languages, art and science. She was known as a polymath on campus and became fluent in French, German, Italian, Russian and Chinese.

This may give the impression that Mari was somewhat nerdish, stuck in the library most of the day. But that was far from the case. In fact, she found her desk work a bore because she was blessed with an uncanny memory. Once read, never forgotten. Her aunt told her that her photographic memory reminded her of Mario, the girl's father, adding that it was a special gift given to only a few, and that she should use it wisely.

Another gift she inherited from her father was a natural athleticism. At 5' 10", slim yet muscular, she had a body most women her age would die for. She was a living Venus de Milo. She became European Taekwondo champion, and went on to study the art of Brazilian Jiu-Jitsu, Kendo and Kyudo before mastering the deadly Krav Maga. Her college friends marvelled at her overachievements, and often wondered where it was all leading. While they had their eyes on lucrative jobs in the city or entering one of the highly paid professions, Mari seemed to be mastering these disciplines for their own sake. She never shared that the remaking of Mari Bambella was aimed at a cause that would soon become apparent.

On her twenty-sixth birthday she found herself quite alone. Sophia had taken off on one of her many expeditions, having dashed to Siberia to view the recent discovery of a baby woolly mammoth in the permafrost. What some people find interesting!

The silence of the house always unnerved her; she half-expected to hear a taxi's diesel engine ticking over on the drive, a recurring trace of that awful day. The chime of the doorbell broke her reverie. She opened the door to a young motorcycle courier, which took her aback. She was relieved to see the man was clutching not a gun but a letter that required a signature.

The envelope was addressed to her with "Private and Confidential" stamped in red. The courier asked for identification before handing her the letter, which bore no postmark.

Although brief, the headed notepaper was laid out formally:

Colonel Harry Oliver Windrush
85 Albert Embankment
Vauxhall
London SE11 5AW

Dear Miss Mari Bambella,

I would very much like to invite you down to interview for a position in our government services. If you could kindly telephone my secretary at a time suitable for you, she will give you further details.

If you have no interest in such an offer, then please accept my sincere apology.

HO Windrush, Colonel

Was this a wind-up? She Googled the colonel. Her eyes scanned the first page of results... "Colonel Windrush... MI6 head of administration... Secret Intelligence Service... top spook".

The only thing she knew about MI6 was Ian Fleming's fictional character James Bond. Why would some spy out of the blue offer her an interview for a job?

She had heard about Oxbridge graduates being recruited into the intelligence services but even so this approach seemed especially random. There was only one response to such an invitation. She called the number at the top of the letter.

A week later she was walking down Frith Street in London's Soho district, heading for a lunch date with the mysterious colonel, a date she had been asked to keep secret. It gave the meeting a frisson of adventure, wherever it may lead.

In a small Italian restaurant, seated at a corner table, a man in his early sixties was wearing a Harris Tweed jacket over a country check red shirt that was tucked into a pair of light brown corduroys. His feet were shod in highly polished Kerridge brogues. The ex-Scots Guards officer was 6' 2" with a full head of silver hair, and bore a small but noticeable scar over his left eye.

Sitting alongside him was an athletic and handsome man who was soon introduced as Major Joe Delph. The major, who Mari guessed to be in his thirties, was dressed in complete contrast to the colonel: black sweatshirt, black slimline Armani jeans and black trainers. A black leather jacket hung on a nearby coat stand. Even his hair was black, short cropped. He reminded Mari of the dashing man in the Cadbury's Milk Tray advert. Despite his sombre appearance, when he started to talk, Mari was comforted with an accent she had grown to love. He was Yorkshire through and through.

The restaurant was empty but for a waiter and the owner, standing patiently a little way back, waiting to be called.

The colonel finally waved him over. 'We're ready to dine, Gino, what do you recommend, my man?'

Gino smiled, nodded. 'I have the mussels in a cream sauce for a starter, followed by a beautiful baked salmon steak for main, and to finish a palate-cleansing lemon cheesecake, or if you prefer, a homemade Italian trifle. Of course we also have fine wine from the vineyards of Tuscany. So fruity, so full of sunshine.'

'Sounds good, Gino. I'll have what you suggest, with the trifle to finish.'

He turned to his guests. 'Mari, Joe?'

They both nodded. Joe gave a thumbs-up.

'Make that three, Gino. But first let's be sampling your Italian bottle of sunshine.'

Gino bowed and walked proudly to the kitchen.

Mari said, ‘Business can't be that good, the place is empty.'

Windrush laughed, slapping his knee. 'That's because it's been pre-booked by me. I didn’t want to be disturbed.’

He pointed at a menu on the table.

‘Opening time is seven-thirty.’ He looked to his watch. 'Its only five o’clock.' He winked. ‘Gino knows that I tip well.'

Joe held up a hand. ‘Normally this restaurant would be jammed to the doors, it’s always booked months in advance, such is the quality of the food. I do believe the P.M. himself is a regular visitor, along with members from all political parties. Stars of screen and sport are frequently seen at Gino’s.’

Mari whistled. 'Must be expensive.'

Joe nodded. 'You want the best then you have to pay, it’s the way of the world, I’m afraid.’

It didn’t take long for Mari to find truth in Joe’s comments. The food was simply the best, a feast fit to set before the gods—accompanied by a wonderful bottle of reserve Barolo.

Once the plates were cleared, the colonel turned with a smile. 'So, Mari, time to get down to business. Thank you for coming today.'

'What can I say, sir, it’s been a pleasure to dine with such fine company and enjoy a meal that I will never forget.'

Windrush turned to Joe and nodded for him to continue.

‘I hope you will forgive us, Mari, but for the past year we’ve been like big brother—we’ve been watching you.'

She gave them a suspicious look.

Joe held up a hand as if to say ‘Hear me out’.

‘We have been watching your most excellent and outstanding progress, through your schooling and athletic achievements. In short, you have all the qualities required to enter the service.’

Mari's frown relaxed and her eyes widened. 'Service?'

'That is, the Special Intelligence Service.'

She mouthed the words but made no sound.

'What used to be known as MI6.'

She got a flash memory of a scene from a James Bond film. She had to force herself not to laugh.

Major Delph continued. 'A woman with your abilities and talents has all the markings of a fine government agent. One that—assuming you remain standing after a strenuous two-year training course—could make a valuable contribution to the security of this country.'

The colonel caught her eye. 'Think you can make it through the course, Mari? People like yourself are hard to come by in our line of work, protecting the nation against ever growing threats, international terrorism, you name it.'

He looked to Joe to continue.

'But first, the service course, one I have christened Storm. You are one of seven candidates we have identified. Not all of you will sail through it, believe me.'

'Two years?' exclaimed Mari.

Colonel Windrush answered, 'And it's far from easy, believe me. There's so much to learn, techniques about how to stay alive... to avoid getting caught by the enemy... or how to escape if such an unfortunate event should happen.'

Joe explained that she would be taught how to lie and deceive adversaries in situations when her life was on the line, where death is the result of being broken by the enemy. He went on to warn her of two years in which she would face many heartbreaking situations. After doing his best to put her off the whole idea, Joe added that despite the obstacles, he believed she will be one of the few who will come through the Storm.

It was as if her whole life had been preparing for this moment. She had been searching for something that now, at a stroke, was being made solid. Was this the thing that would help her move on from the trauma of her childhood—or the means by which she could avenge her family's murders?

Mari smiled. 'Thank you for believing in me. I want this MI6 offer. Whatever is asked of me, you can be sure I will give my all.'

The colonel tapped the table top. 'Storm will begin very soon with a full medical. You must say nothing about this meeting, the Service, or your inclusion on the course. One thing more: you will be assigned a new name. If you accept, your past, your name Mari Bambella, will be no more.'

The major took his cue. 'From the moment you leave here for your journey back to Yorkshire you will carry the new name Ryona Steel.'

'When do we start?' she said.

3
STORM

On the train journey home, Mari's thoughts were a jumble—the MI6 surveillance, keeping silent on the forthcoming training course, her change of name. Ryona Steel. It sounded more impressive than her Italian birth name. She would need a plausible excuse for Aunt Sophia to explain her upcoming two-year absence. Perhaps she could take a 'sabbatical' to Japan, knowing that Sophia would be going away again on some archaeological dig. Nevertheless she would want Mari to phone and write regularly. She would ask Colonel Windrush to cover her tracks; she felt sure he would come up with something plausible.

Once her thoughts about the meeting settled, she began thinking in more concrete terms about how passing Storm and joining the service could eventually bring her closer to finding the killers of her family. This she wanted more than anything. To put a bullet between the eyes of the killers called Andre and Hugo, but not before they gave her the name of whoever issued the contract.

And then there was her mentor, the handsome Major Joe Delph. What more could a girl want than to have her own James Bond alongside her.

Mari returned to the empty house in Yorkshire and immediately set about packing for the SIS training course and mentally withdrawing from her old life. She soon learned that she would be relocated to Porton Down, the government military science park in Wiltshire, to begin the training programme.

There was little preparation for the course. She was thrown into torturous mind games, and learning the art of deception from brilliant instructors. She impressed her instructors with her physical capabilities. She not only survived but thrived on testing the physical limits of her body—midnight manoeuvres, strength-sapping, pack-carrying, twenty-mile hikes and regular cross country runs—which only improved her 5' 10" frame. The no-makeup looks of Venus de Milo took nothing away from her beauty.

The course moved on to weapons training. Having mastered the firing range in both rifle and small arms, she gained knowledge of search and kill operations that were staged in what looked like a Hollywood film set, complete with human-sized cut-outs. Her mission was to differentiate between gun toting terrorists and peaceful town citizens.

She was one of seven trainees that began the course, but after nine weeks only three remained: herself, a rugged and muscular ex-paratrooper, Chris Peterson, from Bristol, and a baby-faced Scot, David Carter, a marine from Dundee. The three completed the first year before a serious back injury eliminated Peterson, leaving David and Ryona to finish the course. The final two triumphantly passed out with high marks and formed a sort of brother–sister relationship.

After graduation, and bestowal of their new titles as SIS intelligence officers, the two warriors treated themselves to a celebration at a country pub. David was congratulating Ryona on her high scores on all the different sections of the course.

'You are one hell of a lady, Ryona Steel—if that's your name. I hope we get the chance to work together at some time in the future.'

'That would be nice, but who knows what tomorrow might bring. What does SIS have planned for us?'

David shrugged. 'Yes, suppose you're right. I'm not too keen on my name: David Carter. They should have given me a Scottish one, don't you think, especially with my accent?'

'I'll call you Davie if you like.'

He put up a thumb, then asked, 'Where did they dig out your name from? Sounds a bit Baltic does Ryona. Bet your real name was better, mine was Jason.'

She looked around the bar before whispering, 'You're not supposed to tell anyone.'

He shrugged again. 'Come on, Ryona.' He peered at her over the top of his pint, winked, and whispered, 'What's your real label? You afraid to tell me?'

'It's Juliette.'

He tapped her gently on the wrist. 'Now that name I like. Tell you what, you call me Davie, I'll call you Julie. How's that for frog's eggs?'

She laughed. 'Our secret, Davie.'

'Now that we've got the important stuff out of the way, I should tell you that I have already received my assignment. I'm to report to agent Stacy Kilmer in Berlin.'

She told him that she was going on a mission with Major Delph, concerning some problem at the World Health Organisation offices in Geneva.

David gave her a nudge. 'Out with the boss, are we?'

'Well you shouldn't complain, you have a woman looking after you.'

'Ain't I had a woman for these last two years? Can't see another's going to change things.'

She leant into him. 'Snap.'

4

FIRST MISSION

Colonel Windrush and Major Joe Delph sat in the colonel's office discussing the outcome of the latest Storm course.

The colonel shook his head. 'So out of our magnificent seven we finish with two. I would have thought we'd have got at least four. How wrong can one be.'

Joe sighed. 'Ah, but didn't you say that Ryona and David were the most likely to come through?' Putting up a finger, he added, 'You said that to me, Harry, at the outset.'

'Yes, I did.'

'I know one thing, Joe, Mario Bambella would have been so proud of his daughter. Mario was undoubtedly one of the best, if not the best agent that ever walked these corridors.'

Joe held out a palm. 'I didn't know that, Harry, I would have probably been in short pants at the time.'

Harry smiled. 'I was just starting out at that time. Still had my L plates on. A long way from sitting in this chair.'

'So you're saying that, if he had survived, Ryona's father would be sitting in that chair, Harry?'

The colonel laughed. 'No way! Mario was a field operative like you, Joe. If he'd been office-bound, he'd have been upstairs. He would have made head and that's for certain. He was everything that I wanted to be.'

'So Ryona never knew of her father's involvement with SIS?'

'Nothing. Nor does she know of Sophia, her mother's sister, who is also an old hand from these parts. Sophia worked here in administration. Sir Bernard Higgins was chief at the time, I was a mere foot soldier. Sophia put the brakes on with regard to leakage, gagging the press and TV media following the Bambella family's horrific deaths. You know something, Joe? That girl reminds me so much of Mario. She seems to have inherited her father's super memory. Her scores on the course were off the charts.' He gave an assuring smile. 'Mario was so good... sadly that super brain of his cost him his life.'

'How come?'

'He was murdered before he could share with us a list of traitors that had infiltrated the service. He carried it in his head, a list of double agents, spies that were running all across Europe and America. He had called for a meeting with all the department heads, he was ready to disclose what he knew.'

'You're telling me that he didn't write the list down or even tape record it? Such important information, I can't believe the guy was that dumb.'

'We've always believed that a list *was* put down, whether written or taped. Could well have been left with someone in safekeeping. I'm thinking that's why almost the whole family was assassinated. If a list is still out there, it would be worth a lot of money to the people whose names are on it.'

Windrush help up a hand. 'Sad times, Joe. Sophia retired not long after, but she remains useful when it comes to safeguarding her niece. Ryona knows nothing. Best we keep it that way.'

Joe came away from the meeting in complete agreement with Windrush's opinion of their protégé. The first time he met Ryona Steel he regarded her as one special lady, a lioness that stood out in the pride. A woman to be feared, who would not think twice to kill the enemy if necessary. The final report on her training had been rated outstanding. She had a fire inside her that wasn't likely to burn out.

In some ways she reminded him of his own path into the service. The son of a South Yorkshire miner, Joe was born Joseph Turner. Delph was his SIS cover. Much like Ryona he had grown up with a great love of sports. He became schoolboy boxing champ before moving up to the seniors and becoming ABA middleweight champion. He gained a place in the English team that fought against Romania in Budapest; the team lost nine bouts to one, Joe being the team's only winner.

A further year of convincing knockouts brought offers to turn professional, which he declined. Instead, with the dream of one day joining the SAS, he enlisted in the army—at the same time as his close friend, Anton Spicer.

Like his boxing career, he succeeded in everything the Army threw at him. He was talent spotted and joined the elite Pathfinder Platoon, a squad of some forty top-of-the-tree soldiers and given the rank of major. He played a significant part in the Pathfinder missions in Kosovo, Sierra Leone, Afghanistan and Iraq, before being poached by MI6.

His friend Anton Spicer had joined the service before him and was already controlling head of overseas operations in Europe—effectively, Joe's boss.

Elsewhere in Yorkshire, a fresh sea breeze blew over Oliver's Mount, the perfect spot to view Scarborough's motorcycle race circuit. Ryona sat with Aunt Sophia on the infamous Farm Bends, her aunt surprising her by how enthralled she was by the speeding stallions that came roaring around the bends. It was Ryona's treat for her bike-loving aunt, before her mission to Geneva with Major Delph. Sophia seemed to accept Ryona's cover of taking a long sabbatical to Japan. She in turn replied that she was going to a New York archaeological conference followed by some Mexican adventure.

Two days later Ryona found herself with Joe Delph walking along a Zurich street, having just left a meeting with Swiss Intelligence. They were both somewhat puzzled by the lack of interest from their Swiss counterparts in the fates of two missing Chinese chemists.

She turned to Joe. 'What gives with these people, that they show no interest at all in this case? Do they think we're here for the fun of it?'

Joe stopped. 'They were more interested in the money laundering, the millions of dollars going into Swiss accounts.' He pointed back at the Swiss SIS building. 'That office needs a good clear-out, it needs Anton to shake them up. Why is money more important than people's lives?'

Ryona scoffed. 'Jesus, Joe, the Swiss have been at it for years, centuries, it wouldn't surprise me if they've still got Nazi gold in their vaults.'

Joe nodded. 'We know these two Chinese chemists are important, Anton wouldn't ask me to take the case without good reason.'

'Next stop World Health Organisation?'

'You've hit the nail on the head, girl, because if they don't know why we need to find them, who does.'

Simultaneously, the agent known as David Carter entered the reception of Berlin's Hotel Prestige. He wore a neat, dark blue Italian suit over a RAF blue shirt open at the neck. In his hand he carried a large carpet bag.

'Mr Carter?'

He acknowledged the attractive woman who was waving him over.

She said, 'Miss Kilmer is in the diner taking coffee, she asked that you join her. If you'd like to leave your bag with me?'

He looked around. She pointed to a set of double doors.

'Your bag?'

David handed it over.

'I'll have the porter take it to your room, sir, room twenty-eight.'

She handed him his room key. 'Enjoy your stay.'

He entered the diner where there were two occupants, both women. One was in her late sixties, reading a magazine and eating chocolate cake. He turned to the other, sitting at the bar and already sizing him up. Could this young woman be Agent Kilmer? He had expected to see a woman in her late thirties and was somewhat taken back by the woman with Tomboy looks: ice blue jeans, a Ben Sherman western-style shirt, high laced boots, hair cropped as an American G.I. She was barely twenty-eight, if she was a day.

The woman stepped off the stool and held out a hand. 'Looks like Joe's sent me a choir boy. What do I call my Michelangelo's David? It is David?'

He nodded. 'You're not looking too bad yourself. Do I call you Stacy?'

She pinched his shoulder. 'If you like.'

'You can call me Cart.'

She led him to a corner table, then called to the waiter.

As soon as the coffee was on the table, she briefed him on the job at hand: the CIA-led undercover operation was one of record-and-report. They are both to stake out a warehouse on the outskirts of Berlin. They have the midnight to 8 a.m. shift.

She patted him on his arm. 'You got my drift, choir boy?'

'You're driving the train, Stacy. Yeh, I've got you.'

'Cool, my man, me and you are going to get along fine.'

Meanwhile in Geneva. Joe and Ryona were trying to get something useful out of the World Health Organisation representative, Professor Greta Nostrum. The two agents had a list of questions about the missing chemists, but it was clear she was holding back. What does she have to gain by not playing ball with British Intelligence?

After thirty minutes of obfuscation, Ryona lost patience. 'Look, professor, let's cut the bullshit, shall we? We have not come all this way to be fobbed off. You either want these chemists found or we pack up and head home.'

Joe interrupted. 'Professor, you come clean with us or, as my partner says, we leave... and believe me, we have never been more serious.'

Nostrum picked up her desk phone and dialled a number. 'Hello, it's Nostrum. Professor, I've got MI6 London here. Could you share a few moments of your time and answer some questions they have... Yes sir... I don't think I'm authorised, sir... You will? Thank you, I will tell them.'

'My boss Professor Edmonton will be along shortly.'

'We do hope so, Professor Nostrum,' said Joe, 'we do hope so.'

The following day, agents Steel and Delph were in London to report back to Colonel Windrush.

After the briefing Windrush looked quite concerned. 'When two top Chinese chemists go awol, God only knows they're not on some bloody walkabout, leaving no clues, telling no one. We're looking at a possible kidnapping. These two are high-profile individuals that have been working on hazardous viruses, contagious diseases and chemical warfare gasses... and they just disappear into thin air. Can someone tell me what the hell's going on?'

Joe had little to add. 'I have a funny feeling about this, Harry.'

'Well I for one ain't laughing,' said Windrush.

He then turned to Ryona for her thoughts.

'I'm thinking it's a kidnapping, sir, these chemists have been abducted for one of two reasons.'

'Enlighten me.'

'First, someone may have a problem that only these two chemists can solve. Or second, someone has something planned that they *don't* want these men to solve. If it's the second option, then my best guess is that they are already dead.'

Joe concurred. 'Ryona could well be right, Harry, we've got to hope and pray it's one, because if it's two, we have a problem.'

'Then we have to get out there, find out what's going on, don't you think?'

The colonel took a moment to gather his thoughts, his fingers drumming rhythmically on the desk. He seemed to make up his mind.

'Okay, here's what we do, we continue the search for these chemists, dead or alive. Contact their family, friends, last sightings of the pair, go through their history, find out their work schedules. Throw a few dollars at the dregs of society. See if you can find someone who knows anything, maybe some rat will crawl from the sewer, who knows.'

He took another moment's thought and shook his head at the ceiling. 'I'm getting a whole lot of flak from upstairs, Joe, even the Home Secretary is on our case.' He stabbed out a finger. 'I'm telling you both, whoever they are and whatever they've done, these chemists are important guys.'

'Do I take it that we both remain on the case?' asked Joe.

'Take it to the wire. Let's move on this.'

5
A FOREST SOUTHEAST OF BERLIN

Two rangers looked down the old hauling track scarred by heavy horses that once dragged cut timber down to the river. The deciduous forest was overgrown and still, except for the mosquitoes that danced their own private rhythm.

Karl Shotzner—bearded, solidly built, six-two, beanie hat, camouflaged weatherproofs, leggings tucked into high weather-sealed boots—cradled a Blaser R8 rifle in his arms. Alongside, stood his eighteen year-old son Jon, a younger version of his father, who held a 12 bore shotgun.

The rangers both experienced a stab of nostalgia for the abandoned sawmill up ahead, with its double doors hanging askew on buckled hinges, and corrugated roof falling in on itself. It now housed a monstrous secret within.

Above, the cathedral-like interlocking canopy of beech and oak took on a quasi-religious significance as it allowed spears of sunlight like theatre spots through to the ground below.

The moment was broken by a vehicle that slowly headed towards them. They chuckled at the driver who was fighting to keep control, the car's engine straining on the furrowed track.

'Looks like our company have arrived, son.'

'How quick was that, father?' He looked at his watch. 'It's taken them just over an hour since we phoned it in, they've made excellent time.'

Karl spat.

Jon asked, 'What if it ain't them, that it's the killers returning?'

The car came fully into view, its engine shutting off.

'Not in a police patrol car, son.'

Two uniformed officers stepped out and remained standing behind the two open doors. The passenger flipped open his identification badge over the door.

'My name is Officer Eric Van Braun, please lay down your weapons, gentlemen.'

With no reply, the driver called, 'Please do as Officer Braun asks.'

Karl showed his side arm to the rangers, then nodded to his son before they both laid down their firearms.

Braun came from behind his door and walked towards them.

'You the guy's that called in a homicide?'

Karl nodded.

The senior officer looked down at the R8.

'Bet you could drop an elephant with that fire stick.'

Karl shrugged. Jon answered, 'Well it ain't for shooting pheasant that's for sure, we have a catapult for them.'

'Our report says you saw bodies in the old mill?'

'Hope you guys ain't had breakfast, because you sure as hell are going to bring it back up.'

The two police officers shared a glance. The senior pointed to the mill. 'After you.'

Karl and Jon both lifted a neckerchief over their nose and mouth. Karl suggested the two officers do likewise. All four men took a deep breath and stepped through a curtain of blow flies into the dimly lit mill.

Before them, hanging from four meat hooks, appeared to be a collection of poorly butchered meat. More hacked than butchered. Karl could see the two officers trying to make sense of the body parts. They stepped closer. Blood from the meat had coagulated on a steel bench below, that served as a cutting surface for a 36-inch circular saw, the blade streaked dark purple, and a bubbly ooze seeping through the centre slot. Flies gorged on the machine.

As their eyes became accustomed to the dark, the realisation hit the officers simultaneously. They stood with mouth's agape, shocked at the macabre scene. The younger began retching and ran out of the mill.

Karl looked to the remaining officer and shrugged. 'There goes breakfast.'

The officer tried to piece together in his mind the constituent parts hanging from the meat hooks: Two bodies, one female, one male, both decapitated, all limbs amputated. The female sliced open from neck to vagina, with great holes that once bore her breasts. She had been hung in two parts. The male treated likewise, genitals missing.

Karl felt he had to say something. 'Drawn and quartered, they used to call it.'

From outside, the younger officer yelled, 'I'm calling this one in, you sort the shit out, we have to get the biggies here to see this fucking house of horror.'

Karl said, 'You think this is bad, wait till you see what's in the barrel and the bowls.'

He pointed at a side table on which sat two large bowls. Alongside were two open oil drums.

'Do I have to, or are you going to tell me?' He pointed at the horror on the meat hooks. 'Fuck, if this isn't enough. What's in the containers?'

'The barrels contain arms and legs, heads; the bowls their eyes, ears, teeth. Her tits and fanny, his cock and balls. Believe me, officer, you don't need to look at them.'

'You know what, Mr Shotzner? I don't think I will, I'll take your word on that.'

The officer visibly shuddered, and asked, 'How are you so nonchalant about it all?'

'Not nonchalant at all, but I've seen enough killing and butchering in these woods that the sight of blood and a bit of cut-up meat is not going to—'

'Okay, enough. I know it's probably difficult to tell but are the two heads recognisable? Have you seen them before?'

'Even their mothers wouldn't recognise them.'

6
ZURICH

Back in Vauxhall, agents Ryona Steel and Joe Delph had their phones on the go, making arrangements for their mission: to find the two missing Chinese chemists. Ryona was booking an early morning flight out of Heathrow to Zurich; Joe was trying to break through some Chinese bureaucratic barriers, who for some unknown reason seemed to have little trust in the British police. The British consul had already sent an agent to the appropriate department in Beijing to see if he could pull a few strings. He had returned with zilch. However, Hong Kong was a different kettle of fish where there were enough old hands prepared to give whatever help was required to their ex-colonial colleagues.

After some digging, Ryona found a useful contact in Zurich, a retired Chinese chemist who had worked with the two missing men. Luckily Professor Woo Tsang spoke excellent English. Joe had put a call into his old pal Anton Spicer in Berlin, asking that he put some heavy security around Tsang until their arrival.

Joe and Ryona took the opportunity of a hasty meal and a drink or two across the Thames. Before they had finished their first drink, Joe's phone rang. It was on crimson, the SIS hot line communications channel. It was Anton. Joe listened intently. It was a long call; the news was not good.

When he killed the call, Ryona asked, 'What's up?'

'Everything. Cancel the Zurich flight, we're going to Berlin.'

'The chemists?'

'If only.'

He took a final gulp of tequila, then called for the bill. They headed for Vauxhall Bridge to return to the office.

Ryona asked, 'If not the chemists, then why Berlin?'

Joe turned to her. 'Maybe I should let you go to Zurich and sort out those chemists. Me, I've got to be in Berlin and take on a job I thought I'd never have to.'

'What is it?'

'That call was from Anton Spicer, head of SIS Europe. He also happens to be my closest friend, we've journeyed through the services together.'

His eyes watered and she tugged at his sleeve. 'Share?'

Joe slowed his pace and swallowed a sob. 'His message concerned a dear friend of mine who has been brutally murdered along with her partner.'

Ryona interrupted, 'A woman?'

He stopped and gripped the bridge parapet, then took a deep breath. 'Yes, Stacy Kilmer, a woman I loved dearly and hoped to marry. She was one of us.'

Ryona placed her hand on Joe's arm and gave a deep swallow. 'Stacy Kilmer! Oh, dear God no, that was David's contact in Germany. He was my partner on the Storm course. Tell me he isn't the other victim.'

Joe sighed. 'Yes, Ryona, I'm afraid it is David.'

Her eyes filled. 'His first assignment... after only a few weeks in the service, he's dead. Now I'm all fired up, Joe, let's go get the bastards.'

Joe composed himself. 'Good to know we both have a score to settle, but be warned. Stacy was a first class agent, one to be feared. How they got to her makes me think these killers are good, they'd have to be to take her.'

With a dry throated whisper, she said, 'But we're good too, Joe, ain't we the best?'

A smile replaced the sadness in his eyes. 'You were the best trainee I've ever had, why, you cut down our best judo fighting instructor. Let me tell you, girl, he was steaming. He will never live that down.'

By lunchtime the following day they were in the Hotel Prestige, Berlin.

In reception Joe noticed a lone man in a window seat holding a newspaper and showing an obvious interest in the English visitors. Joe looked away. Thirty seconds later he surreptitiously looked back. The newspaper was now lying on a table, its reader gone.

Joe asked the receptionist, 'The man who was sitting in the window seat. Do you know him, is he a guest?'

'He is not a resident, he said he was waiting for someone. I guess they didn't arrive.'

Joe whispered to Ryona. 'I think they did.'

Turning back to the receptionist, he asked, 'We have friends who are staying here. I wonder if they have arrived, a Miss Kilmer and a Mr Carter?'

'Yes, rooms twenty-six and twenty-eight.'

Ryona asked hopefully, 'They're here?'

The receptionist looked back at the pigeonhole.

'No. They still have their keys, although I've not seen them for over a week. The last time was when they left with two men, in quite a hurry if I remember.'

'Did it look like they were being forced to leave?'

'I was busy with a guest at the time, but yes, they did look like they were being hustled. Come to think, the man reading the newspaper—'

'Yes?'

'He looked like one of the men who rushed your friends out the door.'

Joe grimaced. 'Let me know if he reappears, phone mine or Miss Steel's room, day or night, it's important.'

The piano bar at Prestige was full to bursting. The pianist's classic jazz and blues numbers were being killed by the raucous laughter and chatter coming from an unappreciative audience. Waiters seemed to be dancing with their beer-laden trays held aloft while working their way through the ever growing mass of revellers.

Ryona and Joe did their best to blend in with the hip crowd. Their entrance drew more than a few idle glances. Ryona was wearing a black trouser suit over a deep purple blouse, black high boots with matching Chanel shoulder bag. Joe was in a Chelsea blue sport shirt and white chinos over a pair of dark blue Zara casuals. Around his neck was a cross on a gold chain, on his wrist a gold Omega.

A doorman in evening suit and bow tie, bent down from his six-two, and confided, 'Two stools going begging in the far corner of the bar, sir, if you're quick.'

A few gentle pushes and body swerves got them through the crowd. There were three men working the bar, Joe gave one a wave.

Joe shouted to Ryona above the noise of the boisterous crowd. 'What's your poison?'

'Beer!'

Before the drinks came the pianist gave up, and his mellow vibe was replaced by a thumping German polka booming out of the PA.

Ryona's face screwed up, half in a smile, half in grimace.

She shouted, 'It's fun but I couldn't go all night with it.'

Joe agreed, 'Me neither, I'm for one, then we blow.'

The barman arrived with two steins of beer.

Joe suddenly became aware that they were being watched. He looked into the mirror that ran the length of the bar and saw the newspaper man standing alongside the bouncer.

Joe nudged Ryona. 'Don't look now, girl, but we've got a Peeping Tom... our newspaper boy, he's over by the entrance.'

She raised her eyes to the mirror. 'You sure, Joe? I can only see the bouncer.'

Joe looked again. The man was gone.

Ryona said, 'This place is beginning to give me the creeps, let's drink up. We'll take dinner in my room.'

They took the lift to the second floor and stopped outside Joe's room. Before using the key card he ran his fingers around the door frame.

'It's as I thought. The tape seal I put on is broken, which can only mean someone's been in my room.'

'You sure, Joe? Could have been a cleaner.'

'At quarter past seven? No, someone's checking us out.'

Ryona lifted a pistol out of her handbag and handed it to him. 'Let's be sure that whoever broke in has already left.'

Joe swiped the key card and quickly swung open the door and rolled into the room. Nothing. He got to his feet and put on the light. He checked the bathroom before calling Ryona in.

She was holding a piece of broken tape. 'I found it on the hallway carpet, must have stuck to their shoe.'

'They've been through my luggage.' He checked under the bed. 'My Glock is still there. Any SIS agent would have discovered it. Amateurs. Let's check your room.

'Are you telling me you taped that too?'

He winked. 'Didn't they teach you anything on that Storm course?'

Ryona's room had also been checked out.

'We've got an enemy we don't yet know,' said Ryona.

'We have to move on this, get to grips with any upcoming situation. Tomorrow we meet up with Anton, he will tell us what's gone down in Berlin.'

Ryona took a moment to get up to speed with the fast moving situation. 'Not that I'm grumbling, but aren't I supposed to start my career off with an easy case?'

'Nothing is easy in our line of work. Look at David, Stacy, they were on what they thought was a straightforward stakeout, both end up cut to pieces on a Berlin mortuary slab. Like I say, nothing's easy, you better get real to that.'

'Guess when you put it like that, you're right.'

Later that evening Joe put in a code crimson call to Anton Spicer.

The call found Anton in pyjamas pacing the floor of his penthouse apartment in Charlottenburg, west of Berlin. In one hand he was swirling a tumbler of Johnny Walker Black, in the other he held the phone away from his ear. Joe was shouting.

'What the fuck happened, Anton? Give it to me straight, no bullshit.'

Ryona entered the room with coffee, so Joe put the phone on speaker. There was no response from Spicer.

'Anton!'

'I'm here, Joe.' There was an audible sigh down the line. 'Stacy, well she took this last minute contract, some joint

SIS–CIA operation, a job that had originally been marked down for you.'

'Do go on.'

'General Porter, the CIA's top man in Berlin, was asking for you. I was in Oslo on some Norwegian–Russian matter. So Doug Elliott's office ran it through Vauxhall. Stacy took it on voluntary.'

Anton stretched out on his recliner and drank the last measure of whisky. 'London offered them Gordon Kelly, but they declined. Windrush told them that you were employed on the missing chemists. So Stacy volunteered, and took the new recruit Carter. She thought it would be a nice opener for him. A no-thrills surveillance job.'

Joe snarled. 'How fucking nice and steady that turned out to be.'

Anton got up and refilled his tumbler. 'The CIA had Frank Bitten on board, who was supposed to accompany Stacy. All I can say is he let Carter in.'

'Who was responsible for the briefing?'

'Believe me, Joe, I was kept in the dark on this.'

Joe could no longer hold back his anger, which came out as bitter sarcasm.

'Kept in the dark? Anton Spicer head of SIS Europe? Where nothing goes without his say? Come on, Ant, don't you dare shit me with that.'

Now it was Anton's turn to shout. 'Yes, Joe, if you want someone to blame, blame me. Forget about me being tied up in Norway, forget about Doug Elliot running it through London. You can even forget Stacy volunteered for the job.' He hurled his glass into the fireplace. 'I have made enquires, only to find the Yanks have shut the job down, that they had a leak. All I know for sure is that SIS was *not* involved.'

'So what was initially called a routine surveillance has put two agents in the fucking morgue?'

Anton reached for another glass. 'Sure looks that way. They murdered Bitten too, found him floating in the Spree two days ago.'

Joe. 'What about Stacy and David? Don't spare the details.'

'Their dismembered bodies were found hanging like beef half-cuts in an abandoned sawmill southeast of Berlin.'

The line went silent.

Spicer continued. 'I have a meeting with General Porter tomorrow, Panza Platz. I've already informed him that you and Ryona will be there. Let's wait to hear what he has to say.'

Joe had a bad night. He dreamt of Stacy in her nakedness being savagely tortured by butchers in bloody aprons clenching choppers. He woke with his body soaked in sweat. He looked at his watch: 8.45 a.m. He phoned room forty-two. A rather fresh sounding Ryona answered. She had foregone her usual early morning jog due to Joe's warning about the Peeping Tom, and was already looking forward to breakfast at Café Vienna and their meeting with Anton. Not many apprentices would get to breakfast with the MI6 top man in Europe.

The café consisted of three tables, each with four chairs. Two had already been occupied by chattering elderly ladies sampling the black forest gateau with cream and Amaretto. Joe chose a table at the rear of the café away from eavesdroppers. He ordered coffee but decided to wait for Anton before ordering breakfast. Spicer arrived bang on the minute, looking a little apprehensive. He was carrying a leather document holder.

He greeted them both, then addressed Ryona. 'Miss Steel, I've heard so much about you from Harry Windrush.'

'Only good I'm hoping, sir.'

He puts up a thumb. 'Most excellent, I can assure you.'

They all ordered breakfast.

Spicer turned to Joe. 'No need to ask how my dearest friend Joe Delph is feeling. I'm deeply sorry for your loss, Joe... sad, sad days indeed. Stacy was the best.'

He turned his attention to Ryona. 'David Carter too, such talent I'm told. Much like yourself, he was regarded as someone with so much promise. God knows how much we want to catch these bastards.'

Anton put the folder on the table. Addressing Joe, he whispered, 'I received some photographs, they're not nice, but I knew you would want to see them. They were taken by the *Kripo* at the scene of the murders.'

'*Kripo*, that's the German criminal investigators, right?' said Ryona.

'You've done your homework.'

Anton gave a deep sigh and shook his head.

'There're also some pictures from the coroner's office, so horrific, disturbing. Jesus, Joe, they're fucking bad.'

Joe said firmly, 'I need to look, Anton, if you'll allow me.'

The waitress approached with a laden tray.

'Let's have breakfast first.'

Joe asked if it was possible to check out Stacy and David's hotel rooms. Surely their belongings would still be there, and they may have left some sort of clue to their fate.

'We know two men hustled them out of the hotel, this we got from the receptionist. One of the men was the Peeping Tom who spied our arrival.'

Anton nodded. 'Gordon Kelly is making enquiries. Soon as I know, you'll know.'

Ryona joined the conversation. 'I'm surprised that this so-called routine surveillance is a cause of so much death. Shouldn't we be sitting at the CIA table, getting to know what the hell's going on?'

Joe clapped hands. 'She's right, I hope this meeting with Porter is going to reveal all and the Yanks don't fob us off.'

Anton smiled weakly. 'This afternoon we meet with Porter.' He wagged a finger. 'We don't come away without some answers.'

He held up the folder. 'I want someone to explain to me what's in here, for Christ's sake, why these animals would need to go to such fucking lengths. This isn't just agent assassination, it's almost satanic.'

He slapped the folder down on the table. The conversation at the other tables abruptly ended. Anton realised he was in a public place and apologised to everyone.

Joe tapped the folder. 'Okay, boss, let's have a look at the horror show.'

'Consider yourself warned... but here they are.'

Joe opened the folder and took out the photographs, blown up to A4. His eyes began to fill as he slowly sifted through the horrific images. He passed them to Ryona who, with hand over her mouth, cried 'Oh, sweet Mary, mother of God.'

Joe steeled himself. 'I want this job, Anton, for Stacy and David, so you better tell our friends at CIA or whoever is pulling the strings there, that Joe Delph goes with or without their blessing. I'll go it alone if I have to. I can't risk Ryona on this, it's too heavy duty.'

She put her hand over his. 'You're going to need help, Joe, and you've got it: me.'

Ryona gave a vague smile of encouragement, and added, 'The Lone Ranger is going to need his Tonto. Besides, I'm not in MI6 to sharpen pencils, so think again.'

7
GENERAL PORTER

That afternoon, Anton, Joe and Ryona entered CIA headquarters on Panza Plaza. An escort met them at the security desk before taking them up to the general's office. 'Go right on in, the general is expecting you.'

The first thing they all noticed was a pool table that doubled as a desk with six chairs in attendance. Another desk, large, oak, with a captain's armchair seemed to be the only item that seemed out of place, all the other furniture looked like it had come from Ikea.

Sixty-year-old General Norbert Porter had seen action in Vietnam and fought in the Gulf wars and had developed a lazy stride that reminded Joe of Robert Mitchum.

'Anton, welcome to my new abode.' He waved his hand at nothing and everything. 'Bloody awful don't you think?'

'Bit of a mis-match if you ask me. That desk and chair are the only two office items I'd keep, the rest are cold additives. If it was me, I'd dump the lot.' He held out his arms in a forgive-me gesture. 'Well you did ask! What happened to the old oak and walnut office?'

The general laughed. 'Progress defeats us all in the end, Anton.'

'Good to see you, Norbert, you never seem to get any older.'

'And you need glasses, but thank you for that.'

He turned to Joe and Ryona. 'Your people, Anton?'

'Ryona Steel and Joe Delph.'

'Miss Steel, welcome.'

She took his hand. 'Honoured to meet you, General.'

Norbert turned to Joe. 'Here's a man who needs no introduction, Major Joe Delph. It's a pleasure to meet you.'

'No, sir, the pleasure is mine. Your work in the Gulf is legendary.'

Norbert shook his head at the memory. 'We've paid a high price. Nine-eleven, how we came to allow that I'll never know. We didn't catch the signs, Joe, they were there, we missed the fuckers at such cost. But let's not go down that road, let me try and answer your questions on what's been happening in this crazy world of ours.'

He lifted the receiver of his desk phone, and spoke into it. 'Send in Roberto.'

One handsome, 5' 11" Italian stallion of some thirty-five years entered the office. CIA operative Roberto Veneto was fashionably stylish in his dress. He had jet black hair and skin the colour of an Italian sunset. He smelled like a bottle of Jean Paul Gaultier eau de cologne. Ryona thought him too good looking for the CIA, more of a catwalk model stepping out for Armani, or maybe a Hollywood heart throb.

After introductions, Ryona innocently enquired about his background.

'My ancestors came out of Sicily, mafioso or so I'm told. My father Piero protected the family's past from my two brothers and me. Whatever it held, he took to his grave, he never revealed the details.'

He sighed. Ryona asked him to go on.

'It was my grandfather, Francesco. He made the crossing of the water to America. He was a fine carpenter with samples of his work in the Basilica of Saint Patrick's, New York City.'

She smiled. 'You must be so proud of him, to bring the family away from the crime fields of the Mafia?'

'I am. I had two brothers, the eldest, Stefano, is a priest. He's in Botswana. My brother Giovanni was NYPD and was shot dead on the streets of Fort Greene Brooklyn.'

After that sobering thought settled, General Porter said that one more agent, a woman, would be joining them in a couple of days.

'She is nonactive. Pat Taylor comes out of administration. She will be my voice, your voice, in all further conversations. What you might call our Postman Pat.'

Ryona giggled. 'With a black and white cat, sir.'

In a more serious tone, Spicer cut in, 'So you're saying that this operation will be carried out from an American window?'

Norbert put a hand on Spicer's shoulder 'No, my dear friend, what started as CIA will now become a CIA–SIS ploy, possibly with others. It all depends on putting out a candle before it becomes a fire.'

Joe said, 'It would be a good idea to put us in the picture, sir. Who lit this candle?'

General Porter nodded. 'Best I get on with it, there's quite a lot to go through.'

He pulled open a desk draw and picked out a file with the photographs of the forest murders. He then distributed them to each.

'I know you've already viewed the horror show; Agent Veneto has not. It was not only MI6 that got it, but our agent Frank Bitten was pulled from the river with fifty-nine bullet holes in his body. Christ almighty they could have made it fucking sixty. I ask you, who the fuck are we dealing with?'

Norbert slammed his fist on the desk. 'Who the fuck are these people? Russian, Armenian, Middle Eastern? You tell me.'

Joe said, 'It's not the Russians. Serbians or Armenians more likely. These gangs are spreading their power across the globe with Central Europe getting heavy hits. You yourself know, General, they're digging their claws deep into the USA.'

Ryona said, 'There has to be a reason they would use such methods. This is more than assassination; someone is trying to send a message.'

'Well, this is what we have so far.' General Porter settled into his armchair. 'Last December in an American government location—let's say Washington—we lost a shipment of five hundred drones. Cutting edge technology, little flying birds that can soar over two hundred miles on battery power, at speeds exceeding fifty miles an hour, with an undercarriage designed to carry a pound in weight, including a long-range zoom camera with auto playback to a master monitoring system.'

'Sounds like a top piece of kit,' said Joe.

'You're not kidding. This new generation of super drones can drop pellets with astonishing accuracy anywhere on the planet. And they're virtually undetectable. They're sprayed with some kind of carbonated paint that deflects radar.'

Spicer interrupted. 'Those little flying bees they're calling the flying spy?'

General Porter wagged a finger. 'Not little flying honey bees, Anton, but fucking deadly, stinging wasps.'

He pointed out the window. 'Out there in this crazy world are these killers, terrorists being led by someone called the

Dragonfly. This Dragonfly has five hundred of our drones armed and ready to sting.'

Ryona asked, 'Armed with what, sir?'

'With a deadly bacterial germ, Miss Steel. A deadly airborne virus that could wipe out millions, potentially threatening every country on the planet.'

Joe gasped. 'That's it, Ryona, the chemists! This Dragonfly has kidnapped the chemists, got them to develop the virus. If we could get Woo Tsang here then we'd know more, he's the only one who can tell us what we're up against.'

Spicer said, 'They may already have got to Tsang. By God, we've got to move on this.'

The general furrowed his brow. 'Chemists, Joe? What's with these chemists?'

'Ryona and I got an assignment from Colonel Windrush to find two missing Chinese chemists. Before their disappearance they had been working on germ warfare, viruses and tropical diseases. Don't you see—our problem, sir, the drones, the chemists. It all ties in, it's on the same carousel.'

Spicer said, 'Joe's right, we've got to protect this guy Woo Tsang. Where is he?'

Ryona answered. 'He's retired, living in Zurich. Joe asked a friend to look him up, but he doesn't know the danger he might be in. We've got to warn him.'

General Porter lifted the phone receiver and put in a call. 'Hi, George, Norbert here. Need a favour, yes it's urgent, and George I do mean fucking urgent. Life and death situation. Yes, in Zurich, in your city. George, listen to me. I need you to pick someone up. Man's name is Woo Tsang, Chinese national, in his sixties, professor of chemistry. Yes, yes, keep it hush. Give him top security and get him on a plane, boat, or train to me pronto. What's that? If he won't come, cuff him for God's sake, just get me him here.'

Joe handed Porter the address on a slip of paper.

'George, the address I've got is on the eastern bank of the River Limmet. Yes, Niederdorf. His place is above Café Schurter. That's all I've got. Get back to me today.'

Spicer asked, 'This Dragonfly, what does he or she want, exactly?'

The general exhaled heavily. 'I was coming to that. The bastard is asking for ten billion dollars and that's just from us, the USA. The rest of the world, God only knows.'

Joe asked, 'What do we know about the virus?'

'Not too much. It's a mutated virus known as ZX-971, classed as a deadly air pollutant germ warfare agent that originated in North Korea, invented by a chemist called Sung Ho. As far as we can tell, its formula was never made up, that it had been destroyed. Now it seems these two missing chemists have brought it back to life. If this is true then we have a fucking big problem because there's no known antidote.'

The office fell silent, each was left with their own thoughts.

Joe broke the silence. 'I'm wondering if this is what Stacy, David and Frank Bitten were on. Did Frank go beyond the surveillance by trying to get more details which resulted in him getting caught? Could it be that Frank was executed before Stacy and David?'

The implication stirred General Porter. 'Now hang fire there, Joe, what are you getting at? You saying that Frank grassed on them?'

'No disrespect, sir, but Stacy and David were taken by force from their hotel. If what I'm thinking is right then maybe there's a chance that Stacy could have left notes, a report of some kind. She was a diary person.'

Ryona said, 'Whatever they knew, it was important enough to be tortured for it. To die like that they must have held out the distance. That's probably why our rooms were gone over. They, whoever they are, were looking to see if anything had been passed to us.'

Spicer said, 'I hope you don't mind me asking, Norbert, but how many people knew of this operation?'

Porter blinked furiously. 'Six, three if you don't include the surveillance team. Me of course, Roberto here and Pat.'

At that moment the phone rang. It was a call for Spicer.

'Anton Spicer speaking... can't it wait?... okay, let's have it... What! When was this? Put Tom Dixon on it and get me a report.'

'More trouble?' asked Joe.

'They've just pulled Kelly out of the River Spree. He's been garrotted.'

'Kelly?' asked Porter.

'One of our guys, I'd put him on the two heavies who picked up Stacy and David.'

Veneto said, 'Seems they want us to know of the killings, they're not hiding the bodies, they wanted us to find them.'

Ryona asked, 'Isn't there anything we can do?'

'Lots,' said Porter. 'If the virus is ZX-971, and I'm hoping to God it isn't, then we're dependant on Woo Tsang to do the science. I'll phone three of our best people. We have Sir William McKenzie in Edinburgh, Professor Frank Faulkner in Oxford, and from New York Professor Ray Dodds. They're all eminent scientists with profound knowledge on viruses and tropical diseases. We get them here to Berlin, pronto.'

The phone rang again.

'Yes, George.'

Porter put up a thumb and smiled. He placed his palm over the receiver and whispered to the others in the room,

'Our Mister Woo has been found, they have him in a safe house.'

He returned to the call. 'Put him on a train for God's sake, man. Put four of your best agents with him, yes, yes all the fucking way, let's get him here. What's that?' Porter listened. 'Yes, brother, we can do that, best keep it to ourselves. You'll speak with me later. George, you're a diamond. Regards to Mary Ann, bye.'

'Apparently Mister Woo refuses to fly, so he's arriving by train. George is boarding him tonight, twenty-hundred hours non-stop express. Gets into Berlin zero-four-thirty—assuming he makes it. The way things are panning out there's a possibility he won't.'

Spicer brought the conversation back to his two lost agents. 'Stacy was smart, not one for making silly mistakes like getting caught cold, which brings me to my question. Are you sure you don't have a leak in your plumbing?'

Porter looked like he just lost a dollar and found a cent.

'No! As you well know, in our kind of work there are always leaks in the system, that goes across the board. We won't ever eliminate them, but some agents can bend to temptation when cash is king. I remember agents Sewel and Watson. Putting a pistol to their family's heads was enough to make them crumble. That outfit gained an early warning call into that French drug shipping episode. Wasn't that an MI6 leak?'

Spicer nodded. 'I take your point, it cost us dear.'

'Here in Berlin, a banker's home was taken over by the Slavic Wolves, a gang that made him open his safe, and cleared it of some twenty million euros. That money helped the Wolves terrorise Berlin for years.'

The mention of the Wolves struck Ryona like an icicle in the heart. She was returned to the seven-year-old's birthday party and the tattoo on the killer's hand.

Joe noticed the shiver, and whispered, 'You okay?'

She nodded vaguely, then turned to the general. 'These Wolves, are they still active, sir?'

'I'm afraid so, Miss Steel, and with twenty million they will only get stronger.'

Veneto added, 'I've investigated quite a few incidents in which they were involved, high stakes robbery and murder. It's like old-time Chicago out there. The Slavics are one of the many biker gangs that are part of a new brotherhood that's infiltrated Europe.'

Porter agreed. 'It's one long ongoing battle with these gangs. The Hell's Angels, the Freeway Riders, the Bandidos, and now a new, predominantly Iraqi mob called Al-Salam 313 are entering the arena.'

He pressed his palms down on the desktop in an action of resolution.

'They're holed up in the Neukölln and Moabit neighbourhoods. The Wolves are easy to spot in their black Mercedes-Benzes. These gangs fight each other for control of the arms, prostitution, drug and human trafficking rackets. They're not fussy about who they recruit, so there are Germans, Russians, Albanians, Turk–Romanian, you name a nation and they have some involvement. Some believe the Russian government finances them.'

Joe said, 'So where does this Dragonfly sit in all this, sir?'

The general was pleased to answer a direct question. 'We can't confirm, but we're getting reports from our North American office that a Wolves cell is being set up in Toronto, Canada. As you will by now be aware, we are not dealing with common criminals, but a highly organised network that's eating into every major city in the world. It's boiling over, it's going to take a team of supermen to deal with this situation.' He apologised to Ryona. 'Ladies too. Soon most of your billionaires will be no more. Those who remain will become the new crime lords.'

Veneto asked, 'This Dragonfly, sir, do you think he's bluffing? That he'd go so far as to release a deadly poison on the world?'

'To answer that, Roberto, a possible bluff would not be my call. It would be for the President, his advisors. Would you risk millions of lives on a maybe? I certainly couldn't go on calling it a bluff.'

Spicer said, 'My best guess would be that this Fly's not bluffing, we've got to swat it.'

Joe got up to pour himself a drink. Ryona joined him at the coffee station.

She whispered, 'We want this Fly job, Joe. You have to get it, or like you once said, I go alone.'

Joe nearly spilled his coffee, and whispered back, 'You out of your mind or what? Go it alone, are you fucking serious?'

'Never been more so in my life.'

'I'll talk with you later, there's something you're not telling me.'

General Porter joined them. 'Coffee good, Joe? Or would you prefer something stronger?'

He lifted up a bottle of fine Kentucky bourbon. They all declined his offer.

'Before this battle is over, you'll all be drinking this!'

Porter poured himself two fingers. 'This Dragonfly is putting us under immense pressure so we need to buy some time to allow Woo Tsang and the professors to develop a vaccine. We have to find them a safe house with laboratory facilities. Not here in Berlin.'

Spicer said, 'I was given to understand that your friend George was bringing him to Berlin?'

'He is. I may have an answer to that problem. I have a holiday villa in Cottbus, it's ideal.'

Spicer said, 'Okay, consider that sorted. But whoever we put out there chasing this Dragonfly will also need time.'

Joe cleared his throat. 'Ryona, Roberto and myself will, as you put it, be out there. We will chase this Fly.'

Anton acknowledged Joe's gung-ho attitude and nodded his assent to Porter, who added, 'The Fly has given us four days to come up with the dollars, it's not enough. Okay, Joe, what's your plan?'

'Do I take it the same time limit has been given to other nations?'

'It's all up in the clouds. What we have is an international stalemate: the Russians are blaming the United States, saying it's an American set-up. London thinks it's a Russian ploy. Now it's everybody at each other's throats. All the world's major players have their banks on red alert. It's one hell of a mess.'

'Four days, whatever, we've got to move quickly,' said Joe. 'We need to bring in a couple of Wolves.' He gave Anton and Norbert a fist. 'We probably have no more than a day to catch and interrogate, break them. We'll need motorcycle gear, a black Mercedes, and small arms. We go in tonight.'

Porter picked up the phone receiver. 'Consider it done.'

Joe leant forward in his seat and placed his elbows on his knees. 'Here's what I'm thinking: firstly we enter their patch, take out one Mercedes and its occupants, and bring them in for some serious questioning. We make it look like a Bandido play, we leave a bandana behind with the sombrero emblem. If it means leaving bodies then so be it.'

He turned to Veneto. 'Roberto knows these gangs, he can bring us up to speed on dress, vehicles. Everything must be spot on, we cannot afford any mistakes.'

'Worry not, my friend, the Wolves use bikes and 4x4s, and dress as most biker groups except for the wolf on their back.'

Spicer turned to Joe. 'Seems you have a giant task on your hands. Whatever happens, these killers must be able to point out the Dragonfly. Barring that, a name would be useful.'

'Easier said than done,' said Veneto. 'Their code of silence means death to anyone who breaks it. They like to give the impression that they're modern-day Robin Hoods, the poor man's saviour, but behind the masks they're trained assassins.'

He went on, 'Their leader is Russian who stands alone and is the most feared leader of the Russian Bratva. Known as the Pakham, he is the most feared crime lord, the supreme Godfather. My hunch is that if anyone is this Dragonfly, then it's him. But in saying that, this is not the way of the Pakham. He's loyal to an eighteen-part code, known as the Thieves Code. To break it would mean death to the offender.'

Ryona said, 'I'm a little puzzled, Roberto, are they told by this Pakham to butcher in the way they savaged Stacy and David?'

'They will do what the contract calls for. They'd butcher the President of the United States if the money was right.'

Spicer added, 'Roberto's right, last year a Saudi Prince was assassinated in Medina. The killers escaped during Saudi National Day celebrations. An insider source said it was carried out by the Wolves, the Russian Bratva.'

'When did the Wolves first come to notice?'

Porter answered for Veneto. 'They've been showing up in our reports for the past thirty years, so it's time we got around to ending it. Trouble is, it's going to cost, and no fucker wants that bill.'

Ryona sensed Joe watching her, particularly on her questions about the Russian Wolves. But he will have to wait for answers.

As the meeting wrapped up Joe confirmed his need for a black Mercedes, the Bandido leathers, three Taser X26P stun guns, and their automatic Glock pistols with suppressor attachments. Porter said he would have it all within the hour.

General Porter said, 'That all, Joe?'

'I could murder a currywurst and a cold beer,

8

BIKERS' DOMAIN, BERLIN

Two a.m. A full moon peeked out from behind some heavy cloud. A black Mercedes with tinted windows cruised the quiet street up to the Crazy Sexy, an all-night dive and hangout for the Slavic Wolves. Roberto was behind the wheel, Ryona and Joe in the back. All three were dressed in Bandido leathers, their faces masked with the distinctive Bandido bandanas. The three simultaneously checked their Glocks and X26P tasers.

Ryona asked, 'What goes, Joe?'

'I'm going on walkabout, we need to know who's in that den. If it's light then we go in and take them. We taser two and kill the rest except one, hopefully a woman, she's to be our witness. Make sure she sees the emblems. Roberto will drop his bandana. We take the two who we taser, bound and gagged, in their own vehicle. Roberto drives ours.'

'You make it sound too easy, Joe.'

Roberto pulled down his bandana. 'Best remember, Ryona Steel, these men are killing machines. It's you or them. Watch how you go.'

Joe opened the passenger door. 'Stay in the vehicle and await my signal.' He held up a pocket torch. 'One flash for go.'

Joe stepped cautiously away from the car and searched the street, his eyes looking for any movement, his ears for any sound. All clear as far as he could tell. In a crouched position he headed for the entrance to the Crazy Sexy, occasionally stopping and taking a moment to peer into the shadows. The bar door opened and light flooded the dark street. Three bikers emerged, a wolf on each jacket, drunk and singing in Russian. Joe ducked into a doorway and, shielding his torch from the bikers, gave a quick flash back to the car.

Ryona and Roberto exited the Mercedes, playing their part of a couple of well-oiled lovers with one arm wrapped around the other. In their free hands the tasers.

The moon disappeared behind cloud, which allowed Joe to come out from cover and silently cross the street. His taser was aimed at its target—the wolf on the back of the nearest biker jacket.

The two lovers staggered towards the Wolves, who stopped singing as they tried to work out the approaching pair's colours. They could tell the couple were wearing leathers, but were they from a rival gang? They were within ten feet when the moon reappeared and the Bandido sombreros became visible. The three tasers aimed and fired simultaneously. The Wolves fell. They were quickly gagged and cuffed before being dragged to the Mercedes. Each were searched, the motor key found and handed to Ryona.

Joe said, 'You've got the wheel, girl, let's get out of here. Roberto will lead.'

The CIA agent threw a Bandido bandana onto the Crazy Sexy threshold and ran to the Merc. The two drivers hit the gas, but not before Joe blew out one of the windows of the den with two shots.

Ryona seems surprised at the action.

‘Makes the play more realistic, don’t you think?’

Spicer and Porter had been kept informed of events at the biker den. A little after 5 a.m. they returned to Porter’s office.

‘Seems it went down without a hitch, Anton.’

‘End of part one, still a mountain to climb, I’m afraid.’

‘Is your man Delph up to the task?’

Anton shrugged. 'I’ll be surprised if he isn’t. He’s the king of persuasion when it comes to mental torture—and he’s seen what they did to his girl Stacy.'

‘How could a man ever forget such fucking horror.'

‘You remember telling us about the banker Schultz, how they used his family to get him to open the safe?’

‘I see where you’re going with this, surely one of the three captives has a family that comes before his loyalty to the Wolves.’

‘Such as a lovely old mother, a son or daughter, a wife he loves.'

‘If he has, then Joe will get to him. I believe Ryona has found documentation that two of the Wolves have families. They foolishly left keepsakes of kin in their wallets. One thing is for sure, the mind will weaken when threats to your family become a life or death ultimatum. Unless these killers carry a love of the pack, and their work is worth more than their families.'

An exhausted Wolf—Boris Vladimir by name—sat with his wrists manacled to the arms of a chair that was bolted to the floor. A bright spotlight was directed into his face, bright enough so he could not see the three agents.

Joe addressed him in German. 'Hello, Boris, do you know why you are here?'

Boris spat into the shadow in Joe's direction. Joe leaned over the table and slapped him across the face. 'Naughty, naughty, Boris, shall we try again?'

The biker spat again, for which he was rewarded with another, harder slap that split his lip.

Roberto placed a pair of nut crackers on the table.

'You're making me angry, Boris, so fucking angry that I'm considering doing to you what you did to my people in that forest sawmill. You do remember, don't you?'

Boris snarled, his mouth releasing fresh blood. 'You know you're all gonna fucking die, you're messing with powerful people, you stupid shits. That forest job ain't nothing to what's gonna happen to you three sicks.'

Joe hammered his fist on the table. 'Oh, we all have to some time Boris, die that is.'

Out of the shadow a hand placed a photograph of a young girl on the table. Boris gasped.

Joe passed it to Ryona who read the back. 'Anichka Vladimir... and a house address in Repino Village, Saint Petersburg. We even have a phone contact number. We could have someone there inside the hour.'

Boris strained against the restraints on his wrists.

Joe shouted, 'You want to fucking spit now, you foul bastard? Do I make a call to Saint Petersburg? You want to see a photo of your daughter hung like a piece of meat in a butcher's shop? The Wolves or your daughter, Boris, the choice is yours.'

Joe punched a number into his cellphone.

It's too much for Boris. 'Stop! Stop! You don't phone and I will tell what I know. My daughter, no, you don't hurt, agreed?' His body slumped as he began to sob. 'She's all I've got, I should be there with them, my family, home. You will have to kill me, you or them. With you my family are safe. With them they die.'

Ryona asked, 'Who are *they* Boris? Who's responsible for all this killing, the carnage. Who are the leaders in your pack? If we can stop them, your family will be safe and you can go home.'

'And my comrades, Viktor, Alexander? They will know I talked.'

Roberto answered, 'We can put them away for a long time. You'll never hear of them again. They're as good as dead. You owe them nothing, it's your family that you want to be thinking about, seeing that daughter of yours grow up to be a woman.'

Joe said, 'We're on a mission to save millions of lives. We have to do whatever it takes to get a result. Your Dragonfly is holding the world to ransom, threatening to drop a deadly poison on the world's major cities, including Saint Petersburg. You have to help us stop him.'

Boris composed himself. 'I know nothing of any poison. Our orders come from a source here in Berlin. We get a newspaper advertisement, in it a coded message. Viktor, he breaks it down.'

'Tell us about the adverts, Boris, which newspaper, who places the ad?'

Boris hesitated. 'I'm finished, to give you what you ask, they will know, I'm a dead man.' He screamed, 'My daughter, I see no more.'

Joe softened his voice. 'Boris, if you help us, we could possibly get you and your family away. A new life, new identity in North America, South America, somewhere safe.'

Boris was torn. Ryona leaned in. 'Do you want your daughter to one day know that her father was a hired killer? That blood money was used to feed and educate her? I don't think so.'

He slowly nodded. 'The *Berliner Morganpost*, always the *Post*, always on Saturday. It comes as a coded love message, Sergei to Anya. From *Doonata*, they send it. Viktor, he has code book, he always has it with him, he either carries it or it's in the trunk of his vehicle under the spare.'

Boris broke down. Roberto offered him a cigarette, which he eagerly accepted.

Joe put a hand on the Wolf's shoulder and squeezed it. 'I'm going now to check, I hope that's the truth and I don't have to put that call into Russia.'

Boris drew heavily on the cigarette.

Joe asked Ryona to check Viktor's papers. Joe had noticed a small diary when they turned out their pockets.

'Was the code book a little black book?'

Boris nodded in recognition.

Ryona then asked, 'Boris, there are two Wolves who work as a team, aged mid-forties, names Andre and Hugo. Do you know of them?'

'Yes I know them, friends of Viktor. Black Angels.'

She couldn't believe her luck. Joe gave her an enquiring shrug. Roberto also looked a little puzzled.

Boris said, 'I have given you a lot for my daughter's life, endangering my own. It is now time for you to honour your part. You ask too many questions of dangerous men. I can only give you what I know of my involvement. Other groups are for you to find out. I have given you much, too much.'

Ryona said, 'Where do we find these Wolves, Andre and Hugo?'

'You will not get near them; these men are active, born killers.'

Joe turned to her. 'Where are you going with this? I think we need to have words later. I'm not one for keeping in the dark, girl.'

'I was going to explain to you both anyway.'

Joe turned back to Boris. 'We need to put you away, but you know it's for your own good until it's decided by those above us about your future.'

Boris mumbled, 'What happens to Viktor, Alexander?'

'Not your concern, they won't come back on you. One final question: who did the forest job?'

'I thought you already knew that. Your woman there, asking about Andre and Hugo.'

'You're saying Andre and Hugo did the forest killings?' asked Ryona.

Boris said, 'I thought you knew of the Black Angels. Sergei, Andre, Hugo, the Kovac brothers. They together with an Iraqi called Abbas Sarrat the lionhearted, it was their doing. Viktor pointed them to the hotel where the two British agents were staying, the Prestige.'

Joe angrily said, 'Who told Viktor which hotel?'

Boris shrugged, which infuriated Joe, who stabbed a finger at him. 'Our people were highly skilled in their work.'

Boris gave a sick smile. 'You think our people are not? You underestimate our power, Mr English, the strength of the pack. The super leadership, the Dragonfly, you would be foolish to ignore this power.'

Ryona asked, 'Are they still here in Berlin?'

The prisoner smirked. 'Who knows. Viktor he was with them, their companion while in Berlin. He has been back for over a week. Now they're long gone. Don't ask me where, better you ask Viktor.'

Joe walked to the door and shouted, 'Guard!'

In the corridor outside the cell, Joe turned to Ryona. 'Let's get one thing clear, Miss Steel, you don't hold out information to do with our work. You will explain to Roberto and me your actions in there. I don't ever want to have important information kept from our team again. Do you understand?'

The use of her surname took Ryona aback. Joe strode off towards the cell that contained Viktor Ivanov.

Roberto wagged a finger at her. 'You're a naughty girl, try not to get the wrong side of him.'

All three agents reached Ivanov's cell. Before entering, Joe said, 'Let's not give this bastard too much of what we already know. We hit him with a family threat and keep him thinking that his comrades, Boris andAlexander, have told us nothing.'

The guard opened the cell door and they all entered.

Like Boris, Ivanov was clamped to a chair under a powerful spotlight. The three agents remained in shadow.

A brief mention of his wife and mother was enough to stir him out of his smirking arrogance.

The tiger soon became a mouse.

Joe baited him and enjoyed seeing him get rattled. Ivanov's eyes bulged with fear as he followed voices from either side of the table like a tennis ball over a net.

'What the fuck you want, you no good bastards, yer evil cunts.'

Joe punched Ivanov in the face.

'Evil? After what you did to our people in that forest? You barbaric piece of shite. Shall we call Dimitri and tell him how you butchered his young brother, then sent him to call on Zahanna, and tell him it was her husband that murdered his brother? Well shall I?'

Roberto opened his cell phone and keyed in a bogus number and spoke to no one. 'Dimitri, it's Samuel here, how are you? Good. I have some news for you, no, no, it's relating to the death of your brother, it's—'

Viktor screamed. 'Okay, you stop now, put down your phone. What is it you want from me? You no involve my family.'

‘I will end the call, but if you don’t give, I redial. You fucking understand?’

The sweat pouring out of Ivanov was answer enough for Agent Veneto.

He wanted to tell as little about his part in the butchering as possible, the assistance that he gave to the Kovac brothers, operating the bench saw, the dissection of the bodies, how he supplied the wire to garrotte the Englishman Gordon Kelly. The interfering American Frank Bitten’s laughter as they emptied their Springfield XD-M’s into him.

Yes, he must answer only what is asked of him and ensure he keep that psychopath Dimitri from his family.

Joe took over from Roberto. ‘Let’s start with these killers you helped set up against my people. I want their names and where they are.’

Viktor shook his head. He was trying to give a reply that would keep him from extradition to America and death row.

‘I don’t know where they are, they completed their mission and left. Their names I don’t know, some Syrian brothers.'

Joe snarled. ‘I’ve heard enough of this man’s bullshit. Get Dimitri on that phone. Tell him the wife, the mother.'

Viktor strained against his bondage, and shouted, ‘The Kovac brothers! Andre, Hugo, Sergei, they along with the Iraqi Abbas Sarrat. They have returned to Marseilles, then they go to Paris.'

‘Who was the butcher? Was it you? We have it on good authority that you were once a master butcher. Forensics will tell if it’s you, and if it is, I will personally chop your fucking head off.'

Ivanov gave out a nervous laugh. 'Who tells you all this shit? Let them tell Viktor to his face.'

Ryona said, ‘Maybe the *Morning Post* can tell us, but then, of course, you know nothing of this. Your last chance...

who is Dragonfly? You protect a potential mass murderer, a dog, whatever the sex, the devil's spawn.'

'Who says this shit of me? You fucking tell me, I kill the lying dog.'

She shook her head and slapped a hand hard onto the table.

'That's not what we want.'

Joe interrupted. 'Let's take the butcher to his abattoir, show him what we found in the forest—a portable generator that could power a thirty-six-inch bench saw, items of jewellery, automatics with ID markings belonging to Federal agents, and of course the bodies.'

He leant into Ivanov's ear, and shouted, 'Do I need to go on, you lying, murdering bastard?'

Joe walked away and sat tapping his finger on the cell wall.

'Should we tell this piece of shite that this interview was recorded, if he does not give us what we ask?'

Joe returned to the prisoner. 'Tell us what we want, or I will hand this tape over to one Armenian Wolf, soon to be released, name of Tigran Grigoryan.'

Ivanov was now leaking sweat out of every pore.

'I think you know this man, Viktor, once a top dog that was higher on the ladder than you. Didn't some loose words from you, put him away for five years?'

Roberto leant into Ivanov's other side. 'We know all about you. We have a file on you a mile long about your cutting skills. That your father taught you in his slaughterhouse in Yaroslavl. Pity you didn't stick to the livestock. Moving to the executions and dismembering of humans, well that's brought you down. You're one piece of sick shit, you're not fit to live amongst human beings.'

Roberto stabbed a finger at him. 'Does your wife, your mother know what you do, how you earn your money? Best you give us what we want, cooperate now because you're finished.'

Ivanov's face momentarily relaxed and with a knowing wink, said, 'If you want to get to the top man, maybe you should look in your own backyard.'

9
FAMILIES FIRST

The following evening the three agents submitted their report on the escapade to the Crazy Sexy to General Porter; Spicer and Pat Taylor were in attendance. They booked a quiet table in a discreet restaurant to discuss the finer details, and to bring Pat up to speed on the global virus and the ransom demand of $10 billion.

Pat Taylor, thirty-eight, single, athletic build, long hair tamed into a horse's tail, was a great addition to the team. Although she was on non-active duty, she had been a fighter of crime all of her adult active life, having lost her father, an LAPD officer, after he entered one dark alley too many.

Porter turned to Joe. 'Do you think Viktor Ivanov would give you the location of our Fly?'

'I'm quite sure he doesn't know, sir. '

'These killers who work for this Fly are all coming out of the Baltic states, so surely it's a Russian or some other Slavic, Armenian, Romanian who runs the show?'

Veneto said, 'There's only one man in control of that part of the Eastern bloc, sir, and that's the Russian Pakham. Whether he's our boy, who knows?'

The team allowed a silence to develop. The time had come for Ryona to tell her story. She told them everything: her seventh birthday party, the game of hide and seek, her murdered family, adoption by Aunt Sophia. For a moment all the events of that dreadful day flooded back. She took a large pull on her glass of schnapps.

'They never knew I was still in the house, hidden under the stairs, so the killers let down their guards and addressed each other by their names: Andre and Hugo.'

She took a little more schnapps, draining the glass. Pat refilled her glass.

'One thing I never told the police, or anyone else for that matter, was the tattoo of a wolf's head on the arm of the one called Andre, and the word "Nayka" that I later learned was Russian for The Pack. You know what's fucking funny? It's taken nineteen years before I heard those names mentioned once more when Ivanov told us the killers in the forest were Andre and Hugo Kovac.'

General Porter said, 'Why not tell the police at the time?'

'Fear on my part, you understand, a fear that those men would return for my aunt and me.'

She left a pause as if wishing to change the subject. 'Now please answer a question that has been puzzling me: how did you not know this when Anton and Colonel Windrush first checked me out for the service?'

Anton Spicer replied with a lie. 'It wasn't in your record, it was missing, not reported.'

Porter was getting a little confused with what he deemed were British side issues. What with Ryona's story, the whole biker scene, the interrogations and missing chemists, his mind was made up. He suggested that Anton return Joe and

Ryona to Windrush in London and work the British garden. Roberto Veneto would stay in Berlin and work on the Chinese chemists. Besides, Roberto's knowledge on the gangs of Berlin would be best served in Germany.

'It's your call, Norbert,' said Spicer. 'I think it's a good one, but we've got to move at speed on this. I'm hoping that Tsang and the professors can work up a vaccine.'

Joe said, 'No disrespect to General Porter, but I'm pleased we're going back to the UK. We know our own garden. When Ivanov alluded to the problem being in our own backyard, it's not Ireland, because if it's there then we have a problem.'

Ryona put up a hand. 'I have a feeling it's some off-shore island, outer, inner Hebrides, west of Scotland. Could be either Lewis, Harris on the outer, or Skye, Mull, Islay on the inner, or one of those uninhabited islands, there are hundreds.'

Spicer said, 'That seems a fair assessment. I'll inform our contacts in the Royal Navy and see if we can get a team up in Scottish waters asap.'

Joe looked at them, smiled. 'One thing's for sure when we leave here, I'm going to miss my currywurst with fries.'

10
LONDON

Windrush was soon brought up to speed on developments in Germany.

He wagged a finger. ‘Okay, let me give Admiral Mathews a call, he's got naval commandos in Scottish waters on manoeuvres with the Norwegians.’

Joe said, ‘Harry, tell the admiral it's a life threatening situation with no time to lose.’

It took a full day before Admiral House got back to them with news that a naval team had stormed a cave on Bird Island, where two Russian Wolves had been guarding a large store of food supplies. After a fiercely fought gun battle, one Russian remained with a fourteen-year-old orphan who had been snatched from the streets of Budapest.

Captain Tony Ford had taken the captured Russian to Shotts high security prison on the Glasgow to Edinburgh road. The girl, who had be subjected to a series of rapes, had been taken into care.

Joe immediately booked a flight to Glasgow for himself and Ryona to meet Captain Ford, and hopefully interrogate the Russian.

Meanwhile, reports continued to come in from all over the world for ridiculous demands for ransom money. The UK had already been given a week to come up with £10 million.

Windrush said, 'Could this Dragonfly be bluffing?'

'Hard to know,' said Joe. 'But in my opinion it is most unlikely, and anyway it's a hell of a risk to take with billions of lives.'

'In which case, how do we proceed?'

'Ryona's assessment could be correct in wanting complete security, a castle with a moat, as it were.'

'That's why you were right in thinking he was holed up in the Hebrides.'

'Thank you, sir,' said Ryona modestly.

Ryona was not only concerned with her professional life. How she missed the smiling face of Roberto. She had hoped for his call after he'd promised to keep in touch with news of the Kovac brothers and if all was running smoothly with the professors in Cottbus.

She smiled at the way he trusted her by sharing his family history. He wasn't anything like Joe, who by contrast was a deep thinker. Maybe losing Stacy wasn't helping him, that was understandable. Come to think of it she had never asked anything personal about Joe Delph, he always seemed so career driven. He had told her of his love for Stacy, and their plans, but when it came down to it, could he settle down in another softer environment?

Then what of herself? What was a life when you did not know your own family's history. Aunt Sophia had never taken the time to sit down with her and tell her about her mother, her upbringing, or her father. Or even how her parents had come to meet and marry. But in their absence,

Ryona could not wish for a more loving aunt, even though she always carried an air of mystery about her. She had never spoken of marriage, and whenever Ryona raised the subject she would be fobbed off with a feeble excuse. Ryona was left with the strange feeling that her aunt had once loved but had also suffered.

Joe too was deep in thought. He had been thinking how one moment in time could change a man's life forever. But maybe that was just life in the services. Take Stacy's execution, and the fact that she took on an assignment that was intended for him. His training the new recruits over two years, after which David Carter would only serve two weeks. If that wasn't bad luck then what was.

He was finding it hard to understand how the Kovac brothers could take Stacy out. If only he'd taken that job. Would he have fared any better? Stacy had smashed the Romerrios' cartel. What a feat that was. Now she was no more. He had shed many a tear in private. There had been words he'd wanted to say, words that she'd never get to hear.

The Kovac brothers and the Iraqi would die. It was only a matter of time. As for the butcher Ivanov. Joe had already given him ricin; he would die a horrible death.

The name Captain Tony Ford rang a bell in Joe Delph's mind, but wasn't he a sergeant at the time? Harry Windrush said that Ford had made his way up through the ranks—paratroopers into SAS before moving into RN Marines.

Joe, holding the rank of major, could only reflect on his own similar progression from SAS to MI6. Joining the service gave him the chance to be his own man and have the freedom to make decisions and take whatever action was required. But it also meant a life of few friends, some of whom may not make it to retirement. He found that being a loner suited him, especially following the horrific loss of Stacy.

Joe and Ryona were met at Glasgow Airport by a smiling Captain Ford.

'Been a long time, Major Joe Delph, the Black Sea, Constanta. Remember?'

'Yes, I remember, we lost Freddy Hook on that one, good to see you.'

Tony Ford shook his head. 'Someone fucked us on Freddy. Joe.'

He sighed. 'You going to tell me what the gunfight was all about, Joe?' He held up a hand. 'What's going down?'

Joe was remembering an operation involving the kidnapping of a British diplomat's daughter. Although she was eventually returned to her father, the whole operation had been blighted by the death of Commander Freddy Hook. Joe thought that six years was too long to allow a worm to enter the wood.

He shrugged off the memory. 'We have a date with a killer, let's get this interrogation over with... Shotts prison if you please, Tony.'

11

A FLY IN THE SOUP

In a large villa in Agrigento, Sicily, a group of six men—three on each side of a large table—waited for the arrival of the Pakhams' General Angelo Rossiano. They gathered as one but under each hat sat an individual, each responsible for a part of the crime world under the Pakhams' powerful control.

Angelo Rossiano, sixty-five, silver haired, heavy framed, approached the table at which sat the Silent Ones. They all rose, he waved them to sit. He remained standing, hands pressed down onto the tabletop, his head shaking.

'Seems we have a Fly in our soup, gentlemen.' He hunched his shoulders. 'But this little gnat, this so-called Dragonfly, doesn't know what happens to annoying insects that fall in the Pakhams' soup.'

He shook his fist and laughed. 'This imbecile wants to hold our world to ransom. This crazy nutcase wants billions of dollars, sterling, euros from every country.' His fist came down on the table. 'Or he will send a plague that will kill us all. Gentlemen, he wants our fucking money.'

There was a murmur of assent.

'This Dragonfly must be a super fucking being or stupid to dare venture into our playground and take us on.'

He called on the Turkish member, Ercan, who stood and bowed in respect to Angelo, before turning to his colleagues in crime.

'What *Il Padrino* is saying through Angelo is this Dragonfly has had the audacity to take us on. Our Pakham in Moscow wants the Fly found and executed.'

He threw a wave, 'This Fly is a lunatic.'

Next, Angelo called on Jose Garcia, a Mexican crime boss, better known as the Gringo Killer.

'Thank you, Angelo, Dragonfly has already hit the North American banks, it has a sting in its tail, we need to spin a web, brothers.'

Moroccan Jacques Hardie stood, all six-four of him. 'Major General, members, this first I hear of this Dragonfly, maybe it's better that it fears Hardie. If he enters my wood then it's a dead fly.'

Angelo acknowledged that Baltic member Igor Kutnezov wished to speak. 'Excuse me asking, Angelo, but are we talking of this Dragonfly as a man or a woman?'

Angelo looked to Ercan, who held out his arms. 'I don't know, Angelo.'

'We must fucking know. Are we using an automatic or a broom to confront the enemy? Get your soldiers out, let's get a fucking grip on the situation, someone must know.'

He turned to Apollo Lopez. 'My Colombian friend, you have nothing to say?'

The man from Bogotá stood with skin the colour of gold and a matching tooth.

'I have a bad feeling. This Fly is dangerous and most powerful. For it to take on the Pakham, maybe it is not crazy. It thinks it can win. Ask yourselves, brothers of the table, who would take us on? A fool, yes maybe, but this Dragonfly I feel is no fool. Male or female this Fly is a killer bee.'

The last man to speak was the European representative, Ryker Meier, the Finisher. 'What has already been said of this Dragonfly is alarming. Ask yourselves, how strong is its army to dare take on the Pakham? We weave the biggest net on the planet. If we cannot swat this intruder, then no one can.'

12
HM PRISON SHOTTS

They entered the windowless cell, nicknamed the Cupboard.

Sergey Yahontov's arms were shackled to his chair. 'The three musketeers, I presume,' he mocked.

Joe Delph, Ryona Steel and Captain Tony took their places opposite the prisoner.

Joe turned to Ryona, then Tony. 'Did you hear the Pig, he asks what we want. We want some no-lie information, no fucking bullshit, oh, should have said pigshit. '

Joe walked up to his face, stared. Quietly, in a low voice, he said, 'We've been doing some digging into your family. We know your mother Olga resides off Alexsleeva Street, with your sister Anastasia, and let's not forget your boy Maxim. Do they all know that you're a child shagger, a murderer?'

Sergey screamed, 'Okay, English, you make your point. Say what you want, my family no, you don't hurt you leave alone.'

Joe threatened Yahontov with retribution via his family.

Joe shouted, 'No lies, do you understand?'

He put a hand to his ear as if holding a phone, while pointing to Ryona.

The lion was turning into a mouse.

'Question one, where are the drones?'

'They have them on the yacht *Doonata*.'

Next question, where's this *Doonata*?'

'It could be anywhere, they use desolate islands to anchor and take on supplies. The Gulf, the Pacific, Indian waters, who knows?'

'So why were you in a cave on Bird Island guarding crates of food?'

'The cave is only a survival warehouse, we have many more around the world.'

Joe turned to Ryona. 'It looks like they're getting ready to drop the virus. The survival stores are meant to sustain them till the air clears.'

Ryona leant towards Yahontov. 'Where are the Kovac brothers?'

The prisoner shook his head. 'They are bad people, they protect the Dragonfly, where the Fly is, they are not far away. On the yacht, maybe.'

Joe said, 'Who is Dragonfly?'

A shrug. 'You will have to catch a Kovac to find that out. I tell you, English, I'm thinking it can only be a man, no woman rules in Russia, then again it could be anyone.' He laughed. 'Maybe the Fly is British.'

Ryona asked, 'So this Fly, the Kovac brothers, they were in Berlin some weeks ago, you know of this?'

'I have told you what I know, Berlin I cannot say, I was not there. If there were killings, then the Kovac brothers were involved.'

The three interrogators stepped outside to compare mental notes.

Joe said, 'We have to find that yacht, the *Doonata*. We find that then it could be game over.'

Tony nodded. 'I'm for the Pacific.'

Joe said, 'Where would you take a yacht that would not look suspicious?'

Tony said, 'I would mix in with countless others. A zebra hides in the herd. Somewhere like the Marina Grande in Capri, the most expensive berth in the world.'

Joe said, 'That makes sense.'

'Sardinia, St Tropez, Abu Dhabi, Barcelona, want me to go on, Joe?'

Ryona said, 'Stick a pin in the map, Tony, it could be any of those.'

Tony said, 'Give me a couple of hours and I'll make up a shortlist.'

Joe, 'Great. In the meantime Ryona can drive us back to Menwith Hill and get us a little help to spot the *Doonata*.'

Tony had a thoughtful look. 'Perhaps the name *Doonata* might give us a clue. How did it get the name?'

Joe smiled. 'I'm ahead of you. It may be a coincidence but *Doonata* is an anagram of the word Odonata, an order of flying insects that includes the dragonfly.'

13
BITTER SICILIAN WINE

Angelo Rossario was disturbed by the sound of cars on the gravel outside his Agrigento mansion. Visitors only arrived by invitation. Who would arrive without an appointment?

He looked out of his library window to see the Silent Ones stepping out of their luxury vehicles.

In the reception hall, the six brothers were confused to hear that Angelo had not summoned them to a meeting.

Ryker Meier asked, 'Permission to speak, Major General? You are saying that you did not send out these urgent requests for the meeting today?'

'You have all received this message?'

They all produced a cablegram inviting them to the meeting.

'I sent no such message. Who dares to play games with us, what the fuck is going on?'

Jacques Hardie stood. 'Forgive me, but I have been doing as you asked, putting my soldiers out, asking of this Fly. As yet I have nothing, but my captain informs me of the sin, a breaking of our code, that some of our members are leaving their families. Leaving to pledge their alliance to a new godfather, that the Moscow Pakham will be no more, that he is finished.'

'His name, Jacques, this new godfather?'

'The Dragonfly.'

Angelo put a hand to his brow. 'Where were these cablegrams posted?'

Ercan the Turk spoke for all. 'They were posted from this town, Agrigento.'

'Sent from my own backyard... then I have a traitor in my family. Someone who works for this Fly. '

He pressed a call bell. 'I ask my man servant, Sergio Romano, he will know.'

Igor the Russian asked, 'But your servant could be the traitor.'

Angelo snarled at his suggestion. 'Are you fucking serious, Sergio has been with me these last thirty years. We grew up together. No, no, you must look elsewhere for our traitor.'

Sergio entered the room. The Silent Ones went quiet.

Angelo said, 'We have a problem, Sergio. I want you to run a check on our family discretely, see if there has been anyone absent from their duties or who is carrying a big fat fucking wallet of euros. Do this now, it's most urgent.'

'I will start this hour, Angelo, is that all?'

Angelo smiled. 'No, bring me four bottles of my finest Bruno Ciacosa, I need to cheer up my brothers.'

14
BIG BROTHER

Menwith Hill, Yorkshire. Ground Station for US and UK satellites.

They were expected: entry permits and lodgings for an unlimited time period were already arranged. Colonel Windrush arrived for a briefing on the mission in Scotland, now referred to as Labyrinth. Joe, Ryona and Captain Tony Ford marvelled at the facility's capabilities, the ears and eyes of the world, whose surveillance equipment was said to spot a flea on an elephant's back. Hopefully all this equipment would help them find the *Doonata*.

Windrush invited them to dine with administration officer John Barnes and himself, but his visit was cut short after being called back to London in the hope he could soothe a worried Home Secretary.

Another urgent piece of news arrived courtesy of the BBC. A news flash reported that members of the Mafia organisation known as the Silent Ones had been permanently silenced. The top seven crime bosses were poisoned in Sicily and now lay in the city morgue. The state police were now seeking Rossiano's man servant Sergio Romano for questioning. The news report ended with one curious detail: the apparent poisoner left a note at the site of the killings that simply read "*Doonata*".

Ryona's phone rang. It was Roberto Veneto. He asked her if they had heard the news of the murders, and said, 'General Porter has informed me that a note has been left at State Police Headquarters. He's asked me to send it to you. Sounds important.'

Ryona said, 'We've just seen the news headlines. What was on the note?'

'I'll read it to you, is Joe there with you?'

'Sure. I'll put you on speaker.'

'It reads "So you thought Angelo Rossiano and your Silent Ones were the kings of crime. I laugh at you, why your kings lie with you dead, all kings of nothing, your powers no more. But then you are dead too, so I send this message to your Pakham in Moscow. You feel my breath Ivor Stravenski, heed my warning, this is a warning from the Dragonfly, it's I who controls your destiny, you are finished, I'm coming for you, Arrivederci."'

Joe took the phone from Ryona. 'We'll take that as a warning. How's it going with you?'

'Woo and the professors came through with what they believe is an effective vaccine, but it's not tested. I'm hoping to God we haven't got to use it.'

There followed a moment's silence before Roberto continued. 'Joe, I think we have a leak in the office. I'm sure we have a double in there, I'm trusting no one. I can feel it, you three take care.'

'Thanks for the warning, *arrivederci*.'

Ryona took back the phone. 'Bye, Roberto, miss you.'

Roberto could be heard to sigh. 'Miss you too, girl, stay safe.' Then he killed the call.

Tony said, 'You think your man's right about the mole in the hole? The question is, is it their house or ours?'

'Harry Windrush? I can't see it. The colonel runs a pretty tight ship, then again you could say the same about Anton Spicer in Europe, he's solid gold, came through the military together. I've known him all my life, kids to men.'

Ryona asked, 'What about the Americans? They seem to be solid gold, I know Roberto is.'

Joe smiled. 'What's this, you getting feelings for Roberto?'

'Could be, couldn't wish for a nicer guy, don't you think?'

'Totally agree, but let me say in the nicest of ways, it's not good to carry those feelings in our line of business. Take it from someone who's tried.'

15
SEARCH

Earlier, on the drive to Menwith Hill, Ryona had been thinking of Aunt Sophia, whose house was in the nearby Yorkshire Dales. Was her aunt safe? Now she worried about Roberto's theory that there may be a mole. Did anyone else share these thoughts? Now was the time to test the rumours.

Joe put in a brief crimson coded report to Pat Taylor. He didn't mention the possibility of a mole in their midst. All the time the Fly's deadline loomed. Joe knew they would need instruction from Woo Tsang on using germ warfare protective clothing, but wondered if such protection would be enough.

Next morning they were met by Chief Master Sergeant Chris Troon, crew-cut, mid-thirties, five-ten, with a cleft chin, which reminded Ryona of the movie star Kirk Douglas.

'Okay, sirs, and ma'am, I'm here at your beck and call. Tell me what's required, where you wish to visit and I'll try to make it happen.'

Joe smiled. 'I can't be doing with the sirs when we're not in uniform.'

'I can live with that.'

Tony asked, 'Can you give us a satellite view of some exclusive marinas around the world, we need to get a close view of the moored yachts.'

'Let's go find out.' He gave an overhand wave.

Troon led the way to another building. Once security was dealt with, the doors slid open and they entered a large room with scores of screens in front of which was a control operator. Feeds were coming in from every major city.

Tony gasped. 'So here lives big brother.'

Troon said, 'We'll find what you're looking for then transfer the feed to a private viewing room.'

He led the agents out of the main core of the building into a side room that contained a theatre row of chairs, a large screen and an operator.

'Your baby, Tony, you handle it.'

Tony said. 'Let's start by bringing up Capri, the Grande Marina, close up on the yachts, we're looking for the name *Doonata*.'

The operator tapped in some coordinates and seconds later they were looking at the Grande Marina.

Tony said, 'Zoom into the names of the yachts.'

Every berth was taken, but no luck.

Next, the Virgin Isles. Then Montenegro. It was tiresome peering at the screen for hours on end, so they decided to leave it to the expert and be notified if he struck it lucky.

They ate and retired to their rooms. Ryona read a few pages of Heart of Darkness before falling asleep.

At 5.56 a.m. there was a knock on her door.

Joe was shouting. 'Breakfast, Ryona, they've found our yacht, meet you down in the restaurant.'

Joe and Tony were already dipping cornbread into eggs when Ryona reached the mess.

'So where's the *Doonata,* Joe?'

'Not where we thought, it's anchored off one of the Lakshadweep islands.'

Tony added helpfully, 'That's the Arabian Sea.'

Joe said, 'It's off the west coast of India, takes two days travelling from the mainland.'

'What's our next move?'

'I'm thinking Ryona and I enter as tourists. Tony comes in by NIS Minicoy, the nearest Indian Navy submarine base.'

Ryona said, 'So if the Fly doesn't play ball then we send him to Davy Jones via a couple of torpedoes.'

'Something like that, we need to be sure that he's on board with the drones.'

Tony asked, 'What's Windrush had to say on this?'

Joe smiled. 'He won't know. Why? Because we ain't going to tell him.'

Tony and Ryona were taken back. Tony asked, 'You sure on this, not informing the colonel?'

'I'm sure, didn't Roberto warn us about a mole in the office? We've no idea who this mole is and until we do I suggest we keep it to ourselves. We don't want no fuck up.'

Ryona raised a hand of caution. 'So Tony, the Indian Navy, tell me how we're going to get all that's required to set this up. We're going to need help on this operation. And where's the funding going to come from?'

'I'm hoping Tony can engage Admiral Mathews to get him into the NIS, fix it with the Indian Naval Command, and that the admiral can keep a secret. You and I, Ryona, have the funding, more than enough to supply our needs.'

Tony said, 'The admiral won't be a problem, I've never told you because of protocol, but I'm married to his daughter. He's my father-in-law.'

Joe blinked rapidly. 'Come on guys, you know the rules, no revealing family names.'

Tony shrugged. ‘It shows how much I trust you both.'

Joe tapped him on the back. ‘So let’s get to work.'

Ryona said, ‘What’s with this tourist plan?’

Joe said, 'The plan is to take a crew member when they come ashore and find out who and what’s on board the yacht.'

'That’s asking a lot, Joe.’

'Then it’s plan B, we do an underwater dive, place a limpet, transmitter–receiver on her iron and listen in.'

Joe said, ‘Once we know the Fly is aboard, we can take it from there.'

16

LAKSHADWEEP ISLANDS

Joe and Ryona's flight from Heathrow via Mumbai to Agatti Island took most of the following day. All expenses came out of Joe's personal account to keep their movements under the radar.

Meanwhile Tony was making headway with the Indian Navy on Minicoy Island, thanks to his father-in-law Admiral Mathews.

The Indian sub would only be called upon to play its part if all else failed. If anything should happen to his new friends, he'd blow that yacht to kingdom come.

In London, Colonel Windrush believed he was being kept up to speed on the mission by Pat Taylor in Berlin. He informed her that time was running out. The Home Office, screaming in his ear, was becoming a full blown headache.

Spicer and General Porter had heard nothing. What the hell was going on? He asked the eyes and ears at Menwith Hill if everybody was dead. On Joe's instruction they had said it seemed so and that the radar had lost Joe's team. The truth being the eye in the sky was still vigilant of the *Doonata*.

In Berlin, Anton Spicer too was anxious for news. Windrush had informed him of Roberto's involvement and that he'd heard that Joe's team was close to getting results. What he could not understand was Windrush being kept out of the loop.

Spicer had deployed agents on full alert, seeking the Fly's whereabouts. SIS Europe had nothing. Agents in every major country were pulling known criminals off the streets. Police cells were full to overflowing. The world was going crazy.

On Agatti Island, Joe and Ryona looked for all the world like honeymooners on a scuba diving holiday. With satellite pictures and a map of the island, Joe felt sure he could pinpoint *Doonata*'s anchorage. They had two days to get aboard and make the virus safe.

They settled into their reed hut before going to the beach bar and squeezing onto a couple of bar stools.

Joe said, 'Keep your eyes and ears wide open, we may learn something.'

The barman approached. 'What's your poison, guys, a Monday white or a Friday black? Choice is yours.'

'Give us a couple of Buds. '

'Names Coco, Coco Bond, shaken not stirred Bond.'

'Nice to meet you, Coco.' He pointed to Ryona. 'She's Bonnie, I'm Clyde shoot-first-ask-after Barrow.'

'You're two cool dudes. Two hot-leaded Buds coming up.'

Coco looked down at the gold Omega on Joe's wrist. 'That's some clock you've got there, brother, you come off the big boat?'

'We got money, but not enough to run that big baby.'

Coco put two Buds on the bar. 'Got fuck for a name. *Doonata*! Fancy giving a few million dollars to call a yacht that. Me, I'd want something like Dream Baby, but then she's fucking Russian.'

Joe asked, 'How come you know she's Russian?'

Coco looked around the room, and leant over.

'We get a few of her crew in from time to time.'

'Could be they're not your usual sandcastle builders?'

'If it wasn't for being Russian, I'd have said Hollywood film star.'

Joe winked. 'I think your first shot hit the target: Russian.'

Coco said, 'Hey, they keep spending those dollar bills, they can be from the planet Venus. Say, is Clyde Barrow your real handle, man?'

'That's what's written in my passport.'

Coco laughed and went to serve another customer.

He soon returned. 'Say, you guys here for the scuba? If you are, stay clear of the big yacht, they don't like visitors in their water.'

Joe asked, 'The big girl, Coco, been here long?'

'Three weeks. Seems to like it here, keeps coming back.' He scratched his beard. 'What's strange about that yacht is nobody scubas, don't fish, don't do nothing but sits there. If they take in the sun then they lounge away from port. Strange, don't you think?'

Joe said, 'Maybe they return to see you, Coco.'

'Crew they come ashore for my smoke.' He waggled two fingers. 'You want a quarter?'

'Maybe later.'

Coco was about to respond when the bar door sprang open and two rugged, middle-aged men entered.

Coco whispered to Joe, 'Speak of the devil and he's sure to arrive.'

Coco opened his arms in greeting. 'Welcome, my brothers, Abbas, Sergei. So you are back.'

Joe wondered if one was a Kovac along with the Iraqi. He gave a reassuring glance to Ryona.

The men nodded and ordered in English. 'Give us whisky, Walker Black.'

'I have some good skunk, Abbas. Blow a man's mind, like my friends Abbas and Sergei, it is powerful.'

Abbas smiled. 'You have a pound for me?'

'I have quarter, more tomorrow. You will be here tomorrow?'

'If I'm not then you give to a crew member.'

Coco nodded. 'You are leaving us, Abbas?'

The Iraqi looked down the bar at Ryona and Joe, then back at the barman. 'You ask too many questions, be careful what you ask.'

'So sorry, I did not mean to enter your privacy.'

Sergei spoke for the first time. 'We will sit at the window. Bring us pretzels.'

The men intimidated a young couple in the window seat into moving.

Moments later Coco was back with Joe and Ryona. 'You see what I mean, stay clear of the yacht. They are not good men. Abbas and Sergei are two of many.'

Ryona asked, 'How many?'

'I know of ten that visit here. But there's more.'

Joe asked, 'What else can you tell us about the yacht?'

Coco nervously said, 'I have witnessed strange goings on whilst *Doonata* sits in the bay. Young people have gone missing. Always when the yacht is here, two weeks ago a young girl of seventeen years scuba diving disappears, always a young girl.'

Ryona asked, 'The police, they were informed?'

'They are corrupt, we have no police.'

Coco left for another customer.

Joe whispered to Ryona, 'If one man can take down seven of the world's top crime bosses, then that kind of power would make for an impossible task.'

Coco returned with two Buds—'On the house'—and left the two strangers to their private conversation.

Ryona looked over her shoulder at the window seat. 'Are you thinking what I'm thinking, Joe?'

'One has to take opportunities when they arise.'

They had decided to take these two killers out of the game.

'We're going to do this tonight,' said Joe. Under his breath, he uttered, 'Enjoy your drink, boys, it's your fucking last.'

Their once full bottle of whisky was now showing a quarter. They were drinking it neat, shouting and swearing, clearing the joint.

It was getting late, time for them to leave the bar which was down to two with heads on the table, half a stub of a joint in the ashtray. They headed for the exit. Joe didn't look up but could feel the eyes of the killers following their every step as they exited the bar. The drunken voice of Abbas rang out.

'*Ty pozvolish ' mne trakhnut'eye.*'

The killers laughed.

Ryona shouted back in Russian. '*Vai a compare in Camelot*. Go fuck a camel.'

The two drunk men were silenced. Both stared at them through the bar window.

'Let's make for the palms,' said Joe. 'They're bound to follow. We take them out there. Suppressors on pistols.'

Joe and Ryona headed for a clump of palm trees on the beach. They selected what looked to be an ideal spot half hidden by a sand dune. Close by was the walkway that led to the jetty, a dark area that one wouldn't venture into at this time of night. Some 1000 metres from any snorkelling community beach party area.

They heard the approach of their prey stumbling, laughing, singing some Russian nonsense. With their arms wrapped around each other's shoulders, they were oblivious to everything else around them. Ryona held her pistol a yard from the Iraqi's head. Joe took Sergei.

Ryona uttered, 'Goodbye, camel fucker,' and fired two rounds. Joe stood over Sergei who collapsed onto his knees, and put two shots into his skull.

'That felt good,' said Ryona.

Joe dragged their bodies under the palms, and with a piece of driftwood scooped out two graves. They were history.

17
DOONATA

Later, in one of the beach shacks, they planned their next move when the rest of the yacht crew realise they are missing two.

Breathing heavily, Joe said, ‘How soon do you think before the cavalry arrive?’

Ryona said, ‘Whatever. We take out whoever comes looking. They’re sure to think it’s retaliation for the Sicilian murders.'

Joe put up a finger. 'Abbas asked Coco for a pound of grass, and told him to give it to one of the crew, meaning he was expected back on board.'

Ryona said, ‘We’ll need to stand watch. You take the bed for a few hours then relieve me.'

Joe wagged a finger. 'Don’t let me sleep through your time, you need to rest too, we have so much to complete.'

Six a.m. Ryona was feeling the effect of too many Buds, and was pleased it was time to wake Joe for the changeover.

'Anything happen, Bonnie?’

‘All quiet, Clyde.'

Joe shook himself awake. 'Things can be too quiet, like there's not a breath of air then, before you know it, lightning strikes and it's a whole new ballgame.'

Ryona stretched her tired limbs and climbed into the warm bed, fully clothed. Joe sat with his back to the door, in a defensive position and holding a fully loaded Glock with its safety catch off.

Eight a.m. Four figures made their way along the beach front from the direction of the bar. As they came fully into view Joe could see they all carried AK-47s.

He gave Ryona a gentle shake. 'We have visitors, four, and armed to the teeth.'

Joe passed her a pistol, armed and ready. She placed their backpacks on the bed and threw a sheet over them. Using the bed for cover, Ryona aimed her weapon at the door. Joe stood at the ready behind it.

'Ready, Bonnie?'

'You bet.'

He unlocked the door and motioned to her to duck down. The sound of combat boots approached. A loud knock, the door opened. A male voice shouted '*Prosypaysya*.' He walked over to the bed, a big man with a Mongolian face. Ryona popped up and put a bullet in it. Another entered the shack; Joe shot him in the back of his head. Ryona and Joe raced out onto the patio, where the other two crew members were standing with mouths agape. The agents rushed at them with their pistols firing. They make mostly head shots and they fall.

Plan B was now imminent. They would need to board the *Doonata* and fit the radio transmitting limpet. Come nightfall they could use the Russians' inflatable to get aboard.

Joe sent Tony a message that they were green for go, and that he was to torpedo the *Doonata* if the operation backfired. No way would they allow the yacht to pull anchor or let the drones fly. Better to send all to the ocean bed.

For her part, Ryona's thoughts were on the fourteen-year-old girl from the streets of Budapest. She was hoping the *Doonata* was not holding any violated young girls. If there were, how could they send innocent lives to an early grave? She couldn't live with that.

Later that evening, as the light began to fade they prepared to push out the dinghy. They would paddle out to the yacht; the outboard motor would only be used in an emergency. Joe would swim the last 100 metres and attach the magnetic unit. Using the listening device, Ryona would translate whatever language was being used.

They paddled out as far as they dared and checked for life on deck. There was none. Joe swam up to the stern and fitted the limpet, and returned unseen. Ryona tuned in the receiver and fitted earpieces to listen in.

'Sounds like the crew are playing cards. They're not Russian, they're French. Sounds like four players.' After a few moments' concentration, she said, 'Wait. There's a new voice. He's asking after the missing crew. He says they should up anchor and sail back to Sardinia.'

'Why Sardinia? It's got to be their base. Maybe the yacht is registered there.'

'Shush, Joe, he's talking about a woman in Alghero, saying she's with child.'

The conversation around the card table turns to the intended drone attacks. One is thinking seriously of his family's safety in Marseilles. The others tell him not to question the Fly's intentions.

The man was shouting, 'How can you sit there playing fucking cards, Henri, when something is wrong? Those

Russians, that search party have not returned. Our comrades along with those Baltic madmen are still on that island.'

A new much younger voice said, 'Louis is right, something is not right, they should have returned hours ago.'

'We should up anchor and fucking get home. '

'When our orders are to stay here? Are you going to ignore the Fly?'

'If it means my life, then yes. The Fly, who we've never met, who's never even been on board, who the fuck are we working for?'

'Someone who pays us big dollars, money it would take us years to make. You take it up with the boss. But you're on your own, do not involve us.'

Joe turned to Ryona. 'I've heard enough to know the Fly's not onboard, but the drones are. Let's get back to dry land and plan how we sort this out.'

Back on the island they leave the Fast Cat at its berth. The dunes around the palms had been disturbed. The bodies gone. She felt a chill. Abbas was her first kill, maybe it happens to all first-timers.

They returned to the beach shack. Joe seemed thoughtful. As the senior officer, he was left with two options: to board the yacht with Ryona and take out the crew, or let Tony hit her with a couple of torpedos.

'What's our next move, Joe?'

'I'm thinking we could take that yacht, there can't be many crew remaining with six already down. A vessel that size would take on no more than sixteen.'

'I'll go with that, we have few other options and I was thinking along similar lines. Tomorrow is our deadline. Everyone's deadline!'

'Okay, we take the yacht under cover of darkness, with our night views and SA80s we hit the wheelhouse and radio room. We only have tonight.'

'I'll contact Tony and tell him to board with a raiding party.' He shook the finger. 'But we take the skipper alive, he's the one who'll know the whereabouts of the Fly.'

'Of course.'

'Our part is to board and secure, we leave Tony and the INS to take the *Doonata* into Minicoy and disable those drones. They'll need someone like Professor Woo to handle the virus. That's not our play.'

Ryona said, 'And then we—'

'Then we go for the Kovac brothers, the Fly.'

He took the words out of her mouth.

Joe was soon on crimson telling Tony that they will hit the yacht at twenty-three-hundred hours.

Half an hour before the agreed rendezvous, Joe and Ryona were on the return trip to the *Doonata*. The music coming from a beach barbecue faded to be replaced by the gentle slapping of waves against the dinghy.

Less than 200 metres away, the *Doonata* seemed to be on filter power, its lights a dull yellow. The bridge was in monitor lighting, emitting a glow from a bank of monitors flashing in two-second intervals. Joe held up a hand, slowly decking his paddle. Turning to Ryona he pointed at the glow of a lantern that was moving around the yacht's promenade. They followed its progress through their night viewers, not daring to move.

On board the captain and radio operator lay asleep in chairs. On the deck a bottle containing the dregs of Stumbras Lithuanian vodka.

The watch was light, only one Romanian watchman looking at pornography under the light of his lantern. He didn't hear Joe come aboard or the pop of the pistol that put a hole in his brain or felt being dragged to the side of the boat and rolled into the sea.

Ryona pointed to the wheelhouse two decks above. Joe motioned for her to take the gangway to the upper deck. Joe followed, covering her back.

He pointed up to the next level as a door opened on the port side. A man exited, staggered to the ship's rail and vomited over the side. Joe calmly popped him from behind. Lifting him by his ankles, he let him slip into a watery grave. Ryona pointed up. Joe shook his head, pointing to the door that the man had come through. She nodded and followed Joe through another door into a cabin with two beds. One was occupied by two sleeping males. Ryona made the shots to their heads. Pop, pop. She took a good look at their faces. They were not the Kovacs.

'I make that ten in all,' said Joe, 'you still think there are six more?'

'We'll soon find out.'

They searched the deck through night vision goggles. They came to the second to last cabin when they heard snoring. Joe carefully opened the door, and saw two king-size beds, each occupied by two people: two men and two girls, young teenagers. Without hesitation, Joe shot both men from close range. Horrified, the girls sat up. One of them pleaded in Turkish, '*Lutfen, Lutfen.*'

Joe said, 'Tell them to dress and wait in the next cabin. Say it's dangerous to venture out, and we will come back for them soon.'

Rhona translated. The girls clambered out of their beds and punched the faces of the dead men, then spat on them.

'Ask the girls if they know how many men are on board.'

Ryona translated.

They counted on their fingers. '*On yedi,*' said one.

'Seventeen, Joe.'

'Tell them to get warm clothes, because they're going home.'

The girls hugged Ryona and cried out a smattering of whimpers.

'They say they have no home, they're orphans. They want to come to the UK. What do I tell them?'

Joe knew they were not going anywhere if they don't keep quiet until they have taken control of the vessel.

'Tell them they can come only if they stay hidden in that cabin and wait for us.'

Ryona translated. The two girls erupted with joy. '*Senden data bay Joe, sender data.*'

'That doesn't need translating,' said Joe, as he led them out to a safer cabin.

Then the two agents headed for the bridge. The girls had said there were seventeen on board. The kill count had reached twelve. Five to go, including one to be kept alive for interrogation. The most likely candidate was the guy on the bridge.

Proceeding with utmost caution, they reached the door of the bridge. Joe crept along a wall and took a peek through a window. He mouthed to Ryona that there were two in the bridge, both asleep. They both silently entered. A man was sitting in a swivel chair: the captain. The other was slumped over the radio. Joe pointed his weapon at the captain; Ryona pointed at the other.

Joe whispered, 'I want our captain to know we mean business when I wake him.'

Ryona popped the radioman, which was enough to bring the captain around.

His eyes flashed open and he felt Joe's cold barrel against his cheek. He clocked the figure of his communication officer sprawled on his seat with a hole in his forehead.

In French he stammered, 'What, what, you've murdered Rene! What you doing on my yacht? Who the fuck are you?'

Joe said, 'We are the retribution squad, this yacht, its cargo, and you belong to us now. Last of the Silent Ones, the mob, the Mafia.'

The captain looked terrified. Outside, the sound of heavy boots were climbing the steps to the bridge. The door opened, a man appeared. Ryona popped him another clean, accurate head shot. The man fell back down the stairs he had just ascended.

The captain is wide awake now.

'Okay, what is it you fucking want that spares my life? I've a family, a wife, daughter, son, for God's sake.'

'Your daughter, how old is she?'

'Maria, she's thirteen years of age.'

Ryona spat at him. 'Like the girls you have on board, you bastard. How would you like your Maria to be constantly raped, you piece of shite?'

She brings her mouth down to his ear and shouts, 'Well, would you?'

'It's not my doing, those girls, they did it, the Russians, it was them that brought them aboard.'

Joe tapped his pistol on his shoulder. 'Let me, first of all, warn you, my friend, that if you give me one lying answer, you will never see your family again. That clear?' Joe shouted, 'I asked you, is that fucking clear?'

'Okay, ask your questions. I will endeavour to answer them.'

'Let me tell you this, my little French cockroach, you *will* fucking answer them. Who and where is the Fly?'

'The Fly, no one knows its name. I have never met the Fly, man or woman. All I know is what I have gathered, coming from overheard conversations. The Russians say it lives in the United Kingdom. This, I swear on my children's lives, is all I know.'

Ryona squeezed his shoulder. 'The Kovac brothers, Andre and Hugo, where are they?' She sternly added, 'Don't make me angrier than I am now.'

'This I know, their brother Sergei was on board, he went ashore with his associate Abbas, they don't return. The others are in Paris, they are close to this Fly. They're contract killers.'

'Paris is a big city.'

'They have an apartment in Marx Dormoy, eighteenth arrondissement.'

'You're doing fine, now let's talk about this yacht, *Doonata*. Who owns it, who do you work for?'

A little uneasily, the captain realised he had to spill the beans. 'This is what happens, I work for a French company, Sea Recruitment. It's in Nice, you can check me out, my name is Maurice Aliard, captain first class, I've worked many cruise vessels in my past. We are assigned these jobs. The owner? That you must ask through the office. The crew are French, the Russian members were already aboard. The young girls also. You don't know what I've had to go through this past month. The Russian element on here is not to be messed with, they are not nice men.' He began to sob. 'The young girls, yes, I knew that they were being raped. Don't you believe me? If you don't, then shoot me now.'

Joe asked, 'How many crew do you carry?'

'Eight French crew plus myself, eight Russian.'

Joe turned to Ryona. 'Think he's telling the truth?'

'He better be or he's a dead man.'

Joe asked, 'Those drones, are they armed?'

The captain nodded. 'They're carrying some kind of attachment on their undercarriage. What it contains I don't know. I was warned to keep off, no enquiries. They are all in the pool, now empty of water.

Satisfied with the intel they gleaned from the captain, they rounded up the rest of the French crew and locked them in the storeroom until the INS special squad boarded.

18
THE GINGER CAT

After the yacht was brought in to port, responsibility for the drones was passed on to US Naval Command. Joe updated Vauxhall with the state of play. They would need to get Woo Tsang and his professors as soon as possible.

Tony was pleased to hear that Joe had asked Admiral Mathews to allow him to remain with them as part of his team that would also include Roberto. The CIA were not to be left out of such a mission. A team of four would now continue to flush out the Fly. Once Tony had cleaned up in Mumbai, he was to join them in Paris where Anton Spicer had secured a safe house. The SIS acting British chief in Europe was asked to say nothing of their assignment, due to the report that they could have a mole in the hole. Only Spicer would know of the operation because of Joe's lifetime friendship, the one man he could completely trust.

The Foreign Office released the good news through secure channels to the world's banks, but also to be aware of repercussions. If it was to strike again, next time there would be no warning. It could be armageddon.

Agents Joe Delph, Ryona Steel, Captain Tony Ford and Roberto Veneto gathered in a detached house in Croissy-sur-Seine. The house was bequeathed to the service by a high ranking MI6 officer in his will. It was larger than the usual safe houses, set well back from a secondary road and surrounded by open countryside, with six luxurious bedrooms.

Spicer had already stocked up the house for a long stay: a fridge and freezer full of food, and two cases of red and white wine.

Knowing the Kovacs were in the city less than an hour away, Ryona didn't sleep. She was itching to get at them. She imagined Joe feeling the same way. The photographs of Stacy's execution must still haunt him. The traumas of both her childhood and adult life were coming to a head. It was payback time for the brutal murders of David Carter and Stacy Kilmer, the killings of Frank Bitten and Gordon Kelly. Then, of course, the seven members of her family murdered in cold blood. Retribution was long overdue.

Next morning Joe insisted on an early assault on the brothers. They were to be taken alive as he had plans to loosen their tongues. Roberto suggested they cuff and gag and inject them with a rape drug to get them in for interrogation, even if it meant breaking the Geneva Convention. Ryona said she wanted her pound of flesh, and to remind them why they were going to die.

Joe said, 'You will have your wish as I will have mine. They will suffer for their crimes.' He turned to the others. 'A bullet to the brain is too good for these satanic bastards, with Ryona and me it's personal. We're not asking you to be involved after their interrogations, and we will not hold it against you if you stand down.'

Captain Ford scoffed. 'I'm in this team. Count me in, chief.'

Roberto added, 'You lot trying to drum me out? There's no need to doubt me. I'm in.'

After naming their off-the-record operation Fly Spray, they laid out a street map of Paris on the lounge table and focused their attention on the area around Marx Dormoy in the eighteenth.

Their intel, as usual, was useful but disjointed. They knew the location, which apartment was in use, that the brothers were at home to visitors, and that they were heavy drinkers at a bar called Le Chat Roux (the Ginger Cat) 300 metres away.

The operation had not been registered through the normal channel and would remain off the record. Joe was to make a crimson call after making contact if the cleaners were required.

They had two options: hit them on the way back to their apartment from the Ginger Cat, or wait at the apartment for them to arrive home, which could well mean a shooting gallery. Captain Ford suggested they wait another day.

Ryona had other ideas. 'I'm inclined to go for the hit and run. Get them hog tied into the back of the van and away to the woods. Okay, there could be witnesses, but I assume we will be masked and the van dumped later. Afterwards a pop-pop and goodbye Kovacs.'

Joe agreed. 'Okay, we go with Ryona's option, we take them from behind on their way from the bar, into the van, tied and gagged and away into the forest, which is appropriate considering what they did to agents Carter and Kilmer.'

Two a.m. A Ford Transit pulled into an off-road parking spot 200 metres from the Ginger Cat. The area was free of night owls. Joe and Ryona were in the back seat, Roberto Veneto was behind the wheel, Tony beside him. Roberto squinted into the wing mirror. 'It's them, the brothers are coming towards us—and they've had a skinful. Shall we give them a lift?'

Tony and Ryona slipped out of the van as Ryona wheeled out the spare and positioned herself at the front driver's side wheel arch. Tony laid flat with his back on the tarmac as if inspecting the underside of the van. The stumbling, singing pair were now within twenty metres.

Inside the van, Joe whispered, 'Come on you bastards, a few steps more.'

The brothers obliged by moving up to Ryona. 'You broken down, lady?'

Despite the years, Ryona recognised the voice that returned her to the claustrophobia of hiding in the cupboard under the stairs as a child. There and then she had an overwhelming urge to empty her pistol into his brain.

'My brother can help, he good mechanic, he help fix for you.'

One of the men bent down trying to look at the man under the van. Tony was laying with his pistol in his hand, ready to use if required.

Ryona allowed the spare wheel to drop, the signal for Joe and Roberto to exit the van.

The two bodies hit the pavement. Tony emerged from under the vehicle to see Joe and Roberto holding coshes at shoulder height.

The unconscious brothers were cable-tied around wrists and ankles and bundled unceremoniously into the back of the Transit. They were soon on the highway heading towards the safe house.

‘You know I nearly shot that fucker, Andre, back there? I recognised his voice.’

'Truth is, if we didn’t need the information, I’d have shot them too.'

Roberto turned onto an overgrown path that circuited the edge of a wood.

‘This is as good a place as any,’ said Joe. 'Sit them at the bottom of those pines. We give them one hour to share what they know, then it’s goodbye Kovac brothers.'

The brothers were still unconscious.

Joe said, ‘Turn away while we wake them Mafia style.’

Joe, Tony and Roberto unzipped their flies and pissed on their heads. The men woke, now wet and stinking with fire in their eyes.

Joe squatted in front of Hugo, pulling off the gag. 'I am going to ask you only once, brother Hugo, your answer will determine whether your brother lives or dies.’

Andre shouted, 'Tell them to go fuck themselves, brother, you say nothing.'

Joe asked Hugo, 'Who is this Fly, and where does it reside?’

Hugo looked to his brother.

Joe warned him, ‘One chance, Hugo. You lie to me then Andre dies.'

‘My brother knows nothing, I know nothing, we are contracted. We do our work, we get paid. The Fly, buzz buzz, who knows.'

Joe nodded to Ryona, 'Andre Kovac is all yours.'

Hugo started panicking. 'The Fly is English. That’s what we’ve been told, but who knows.'

Roberto said, 'Who says the Fly is English?’

‘A Romanian biker wolf, a human trafficking head out of Salina, he tells us.'

He looked on as Ryona put a length of piano wire around his brother's neck. She tightened it.

'Andre, I want you to go back twenty years, to a time when you called on the Mario Bambella family in Norwich, England.'

Andre gave a shrug of indifference.

'After twenty years I can understand you being a little forgetful.' She pulled on the wire. Blood started to flow from the ring around his neck.

'Maybe Hugo remembers?'

Hugo shook his head. 'Twenty years is long time back, lots of waters flow since then.'

Ryona jagged the wire to turn Andre around to face his brother. 'Let me remind you both of that day.'

She doesn't miss out any details.

'Still don't remember?'

Hugo had a moment of realisation. 'She's the girl, Andre, the one we missed. Oh, fuck man, it's her.'

Andre was straining, nearly choking as the wire tightened. 'Shut up, fool, you and your fucking mouth.'

She smiled a wicked smile. 'I've waited a long, long time for this. And don't forget my friend Joe over there. The butchered agents in that forest in Berlin. Don't say you can't remember the saw mill.'

She gripped the piano wire tighter and dragged Andre behind her, his eyes bulging in their sockets. She lifted his head then let go. The man dropped dead at his brother's feet.

Joe patted Ryona on the shoulder before uttering, 'Three down, one to go.'

Which is enough to send Hugo wailing.

'Oh we didn't tell you?'

Hugo, 'Didn't tell me what?'

'That you're the last of the gang to die.'

'Andre, Sergei, Abbas, all gone, only you left.'

'We'll cut you up last.'

Hugo gasped. 'Cut?'

Ryona stepped up. 'That's right, we're going to do a Berlin forest job on you, this time with a teeny weeny chainsaw, never been tried on bone before.'

'It wasn't me that cut them, it was the butcher Smirnoff. Yes they were alive when he cut them. The young man, he didn't last long, the girl she was different. He cut her bit by bit. Him and Abbas had raped her. She was strong right to the end.' He started shaking uncontrollably. 'I tell you we knew they were watching us, the others, the American, the British they call Kelly. We knew about them. But not about you.'

Joe was furious. 'How did you know, who told you about the others?'

'We have an agent that works for the Fly in the London office. The name I do not know. This is the truth I tell you. Look, I've told you all that I know, please shoot me.'

He turned to Ryona.

'My brother always said leave a witness and they'll come back to haunt you, now I know we should have searched and found you that day twenty years ago.'

He looked down at the slumped body of his brother. 'You were right all along, my brother, I should have looked for her. She has gained her revenge, she's taken your life, now she will take mine. *Au revoir mon frere*.'

He got down on his knees and prayed furiously.

Joe said, 'Let's get this over with, I have the cleaners waiting.'

Ryona asked, 'How do you want to do this, Joe?'

'I'm a man of my word, he dies like I'd promised myself if I ever caught the people who murdered Stacy and Daniel. You heard what he said. That they butchered them alive.'

Roberto stepped up and put a long plastic apron over Joe’s head, and tied it behind. He did the same for Ryona. He then brought the handheld chainsaw.

It was a messy scene. Once it was over, nobody felt revenged, or clean, or even human. But the deed was done.

Tony passed around the extra strong black garbage bags, which they fill with body parts.

Roberto took out his cell and made a call. He didn’t speak, just listened, then shut it off.

He said, ‘The cleaners are on their way.'

Joe said, 'They know where to come?’

Roberto produced a small location bug, which he taped to one of the bags. 'They do now.'

19
GOD'S COUNTRY

The information from Kovac, that he believed the Fly to be English, was not shared with the higher-ups. Joe told his team that the information was for their ears only. He was sure that this was not the last they would hear of the Fly, and that whoever and wherever this person was would be greatly hurt at the loss of the *Doonata* and its cargo. He asked Anton Spicer to request that General Porter put SAS or SEAL guards on the yacht until its final handover back in the United States.

Spicer called back to say that General Porter was pleased that he'd requested a stay-on for Roberto, and happy that he was keeping the Americans involved. With Tony Ford, Anton had bypassed Windrush by going directly to Naval Command's Admiral Mathews, who said there was no problem. He said to inform Tony that there had been no movement on Bird Island. Tony had suggested, through Anton, that his man Frazier should keep on with his other duties, but to keep a guard on the island.

Spicer said that Windrush was not happy, Pat Taylor having not heard from him. Consequently no reports were being passed to Vauxhall. Spicer had had to lie that he wasn't getting much from Joe either.

Consequently Joe decided to move his team to South Yorkshire, his old stomping ground.

They touched down in Manchester. Their weapons would arrive through RAF Lyneham in Wiltshire, then taken overnight to be picked up at Menwith Hill when needed. Each team member was assigned a duty: Ryona on communications; Tony and Roberto on surveillance; Joe would investigate the theory of a British mole.

Tony's Jeep was fuelled up and waiting for him at a friend's location in a Manchester suburb. He picked up the keys from a pre-arranged spot and headed over the Pennines into God's country—Yorkshire.

It was early morning when they arrived in the village of High Melton, a few miles out of Doncaster. Joe was slightly taken aback by the sight of giant wind turbines erected on the field close to his uncle's house. His mother's unmarried brother had died some years earlier and the house had passed to Joe's mother. It had since been used as the family holiday home, and would now be used as an SIS safe house.

The team settled in and it was time to get to work. The bit that was nagging at Joe was that if the Kovac brothers had been getting information from the office, then so must the Fly. Forget the possibility that it could be a European mole, this was a British leak. Anton Spicer, and indeed General Porter, had known about the *Doonata* episode, but the fact that the yacht was not moved or better protected seemed to prove that there was no leak from Berlin. But who was running the show in Vauxhall? Who had set up the murders? How long had these murders been going on? Could it go as far back as the murders of Ryona's family and beyond?

He shared his thoughts with his team. It appeared that the only person who could pinpoint the Fly was this mole. So he put it to them. How do we bring the Fly out into the open?

Ryona spoke first. ‘I’m thinking that this person is one who comes out of the office of our Colonel Windrush, or someone who Windrush trusts enough to feel safe enough to speak openly. A close and trusted friend. We have one thing to remember, this mole has been working a long time, giving out information on agents in the field. Perhaps over twenty years. And been paid well for the service.

Roberto said, 'Ryona is right, this person must have quite a large bank account. We should look into this, they could have been paid into a Swiss account or the Cayman Isles. They wouldn’t necessarily be spending it... more like saving for a nice retirement.’

Tony added, 'Could be it’s been put into property, a fine house somewhere out in the sticks. Shares. They could well dabble in the stock market. It’s certainly worth a thought. I have to agree with Ryona and Roberto. This mole’s got money.'

Roberto said, ‘I hate to be the one to say it, but what if it’s the colonel himself, what if he’s the mole?’

Joe slowly nodded. ‘That’s got to be worth taking a look at. Leave that with me.'

Ryona said, 'Is there *anyone* in that office we can trust?’

Joe shrugged. ‘On balance, no.'

‘If the mole has been active for at least twenty years that means she or he must have a long service record with SIS.'

Joe paced, deep in thought. ‘So it’s someone of longstanding who has a fat bank account. That should narrow it down.’

Roberto said, 'Can we get this information without setting off an alarm?’

'We can get anything if we go through the right door, not one in Vauxhall if suspicion is to be avoided. I was thinking of going through Tony's chief, Admiral Mathews at Naval headquarters.'

Tony scratched his chin. 'You think?'

Yes, in our recent escapade that involved the INS he kept our operation away from our office. The man supported us and furthermore we had no leak. Yes, I'm thinking Admiral Mathews may be able to open a few doors, that's always assuming Tony can get his father-in-law on a one-to-one?'

Tony smiled. 'One can only try.'

Joe said, 'Good, that'll be Tony's baby.'

Turning to Ryona and Roberto, he said, 'You two are together on this. Work from past to present who we had, and still have, working through MI5 and 6, go back the full twenty years.'

With open arms, Ryona asked, 'How're we going to get into the archives, Joe? I mean, without causing suspicion?'

Joe smiled. 'An old partner of mine, sadly got caught with a land mine in Afghanistan. He's now office-bound, works down in the archives. He'll give us all the help he can.'

Roberto asks. 'You sure, Joe?'

'Yes, I'm sure. I once saved his life!'

Joe, with a more serious look, said, 'I don't like asking you to do this, but I'd like you to go through your father's execution and the murders of your family. In those archives will be a record of his work and his death. See if you can find anything relating to why he would have been targeted by the Kovacs, what he was working on at the time. According to Windrush, your father Mario was a super agent with a computer brain and a brilliant memory. A man who knew too much and was marked to die. In that last job will be a clue.'

He looked at her sadly. 'You have to find that clue, girl. Roberto, you've got to help her.'

He held out a hand. 'Me, I've got our Colonel Windrush to investigate. If he sways a little, then I'll feel it, I'll know.'

'It goes without saying that everything must be kept tight, in-house. Don't leave anything written, unless it's absolutely necessary. If the Fly gets a smell of the operation the mole will be exterminated—assuming that this mole isn't the Fly.'

A week passed and Tony returned to the team after a sit-down with his chief, Admiral Mathews. Joe was relieved to hear that the admiral was going to help in any way he could. He had told Tony that he knew a few top faces in the Foreign Office who would give him what was required, including the wage structures and possible earnings of staff for the last twenty years.

Ryona and Roberto reported that the meet with Joe's friend in the archives, John Barlow, had been nothing but a pleasure—and he turned out to be a human encyclopaedia: names, dates, actions, he could recite it all.

They had learned that over sixty agents had been lost in the past twenty years, most were lying in the cold case files. There had been only five agents who could have been involved in all of the registered deaths. Colonel Windrush was one of the five. The others were listed as Peter Wardle, Norman Aimes, Jenny Dilcox and Martin Shawnley. Only Windrush, Aimes and Shawnley were still active, Dilcox and Wardle having recently retired.

Ryona had unearthed some useful information about her father's activities. Not long before his death, he had infiltrated a nest of human traffickers with known drug cartel connections. In the bottom of a file was a handwritten note that her father's last vocal message was one of "Not proved, dismiss all enquiries". This seemed unlikely. This wasn't her father's way of doing things. Such a message would never have come from him by phone, and if it was, who received the message? John Barlow thought the handwriting—a light touch with a whirling flow—was unlikely to be a man's hand, more a woman's.

Ryona thought this credible.

Joe said, 'That leaves us with one name in that list of five that is female: Jenny Dilcox. Check her out.'

Tony said, 'But she's a retired agent. How would she get information out if she's out of the office?'

'Fair point, Tony. You've got me thinking, what if there were two, one on the inside, one out?'

Roberto added, 'The note on Ryona's father's file had to have been written a long time ago. Somewhere there's got to be a sample of Jenny Dilcox's handwriting.'

'Roberto's right. I'll get John to pull something from the files.'

Ryona said, 'If it's a woman, she had to be in love with this partner... sixty fucking murders! She's some evil, satanic bitch.'

Joe said, 'I'll get John Barlow to supply us with everything on Jenny Dilcox and whether she had something going with either Colonel Windrush, Norman Aimes or Martin Shawley.'

20

A MOLE IN THE HOLE

Having set up base in Joe's South Yorkshire retreat, time had come for the team to return to Vauxhall to interview the five likely candidates in the hope of unveiling the mole. Tony had retrieved their weapons from RAF Lyneham and was asked by Joe to drive the team to London.

Later that evening John Barlow forwarded a report to them, which stated that Jenny Dilcox had no file in the archives, and no document or computer records in the library. Joe's take was not that Jenny Dilcox had no files, but that they were missing. Why? Who had taken them? The difficulties of holding the investigation was compounded by the fact that one of the five was Colonel Windrush, his commander.

He asked Admiral Mathews for his views on how he should approach this delicate matter. Mathews advised that Joe should go a step up the ladder and consult the head of SIS. Mathews would discretely arrange a face to face with its Director-General, Sir Alister Cummings. The meeting took place that evening at Sir Alister's country residence in Hampshire. Cummings listened carefully to Joe's report on the Fly and how far the investigation had come. Cummings was especially concerned about the list of sixty agents who had been eliminated over the last two decades, and of its five suspects, one of whom was Colonel Windrush. Sir Alister granted Joe an open book to root out the killer mole. He was to refer back to Cummings if his investigation met any resistance.

Joe returned to Vauxhall to interview Colonel Windrush. Ryona acted as witness to the meeting in the colonel's office. For his part, Windrush brought in a young secretary to sit in and take notes.

'Well now, Joe. What's this all about?'

Joe remained impassive in reply to the smirk on the colonel's face.

'Jenny Dilcox, does the name ring any bells with you, sir?'

The Colonel answered with a question. 'Why do you ask?'

Joe held out a palm. 'Her name has come to the top of our enquiry into the Fly, sir.' Joe lied, 'Came up in a recent interrogation of a witness, sir.'

Windrush wore an expression that couldn't have looked more disinterested. But Joe could sense the Colonel was worried at the mention of her name.

'We think that this agent may be able to help us with a few important issues that have surfaced.'

'What issues?' He shrugged and left a pause as if recalling a distant memory. 'The woman in question retired after many years of good service to our department. Furthermore, I see no reason for me to disturb her well-earned rest. You know the rules, Agent Delph. On retirement, agents' names change, a relocated address gives protection to them and their families.' He tapped his desktop. 'Maybe if you were to tell me what this is all about, then I could ask her if she was willing to come back into the fold and help you guys out.'

With a shake of the head, Joe said, 'This I can't do, sir, reason being it's regarding the Fly. We need her to clarify something for us.'

The colonel became a little heated. He snarled, 'Something, Delph, something? What the fuck are you talking about?'

Joe sensed that he'd got the old guy going. Joe pushed a little harder.

'You know that anything that refers to our ongoing operation has to be kept in-house to prevent leaks. No mole in the hole. Not like some departments who have been feeding this mole for the last twenty or so years, resulting in a death toll of scores of agents. That's three murders a year, sir.'

He acknowledged Ryona's presence, who had been admiring Joe's handling of Windrush.

'Maybe going back further than her family murders.'

The colonel suddenly stood and pointed a finger at Joe. 'I hope you're not implying that Jenny Dilcox was involved in these murders, that she's this damn mole, Delph?'

Joe decided to ease off.

'Oh, no way, sir, but you must understand our position. Everyone's a suspect until it's sorted.'

With a suspicious look, Windrush said, 'You know, Joe Delph, I've never heard such a load of bollocks in my life, you're so fucking false.'

He looked at the silent Ryona. 'That goes for you too. Why don't you come clean and let me know what's happening? I'm in fucking charge here, you work for me.'

Joe shook his head. 'I'm afraid that's not true. The team and I are working under the command of the Director-General, Sir Alister Cummings. We are closing this office down until further notice, to such a time as this mole and the murders have been resolved.'

Windrush fumed. 'You mean to tell me you went over my head with this?'

'Yes. But first you will take immediate leave. Outside your door are two RMP redcaps waiting to escort you to your residence until this operation is closed. Anton Spicer will be flying in from Berlin to occupy your chair.'

Windrush lost his tongue.

'I'm sorry, sir,' said Joe, 'but this office seems to be at the heart of our troubles. Your refusal to give us valuable information on a former agent has been noted. If you'd be so kind as to gather your personal belongings... This meeting is now called to a close.'

Windrush stood with open mouth. He looked about the room with something close to a fierce resolve. 'You fucking cannot be serious, man, you know who you're fucking talking to?'

'I hope you're clean, colonel, because if you're not, for what happened to Stacy, David and the Bambella family, along with the sixty or so other murders, I will see that you pay, you better believe me.'

Windrush screamed, 'You can't order me, major!'

Joe raised his voice even louder. 'Guard!'

Two redcaps entered the office and stood either side of Windrush.

'Take him where he's wanting to go,' said Joe. 'He's not a prisoner, he's an officer under house arrest till further notice. Give him a little respect, treat the operation as one of protection.'

The senior of the two policemen said, 'If you'll be so kind as to follow us, colonel.'

Windrush smiled. ‘If I am under house arrest, I choose to go to my retreat up in Inverness. Are you going to escort me there?’

The sergeant replied, ‘Yes, if that's where you’re heading, sir.’

Joe said, ‘I’m sure when you calm down, sir, you will understand that we have to do this to shut down the factory that produces nothing but murdered agents.'

Windrush waved a hand. 'Fuck you, Delph, you're going to be sorry. You’ll be down to private by the time I've finished with you.'

‘Before you go, colonel, where is Jenny Dilcox?’

‘I can't bloody well remember. And anyway,’ Windrush raised a middle finger, ‘I’m on leave.’

Later that day Colonel Windrush boarded the Inverness train at Kings Cross, accompanied by the two redcaps. Expected time of arrival: 1 a.m. Boarding in the next carriage was a middle-aged woman, dressed in black mourning clothes, a pill-box hat, with a veil obscuring her face. She was accompanied by an athletic-looking man of around thirty years, also dressed in black.

In the meantime, Captain Tony Ford had given instructions to the redcaps to hand over protection of Colonel Windrush to two of his men, thus enabling the redcaps to return to their London base.

Joe guessed that Windrush would find a way to contact Jenny Dilcox, to ask her to come out of the woods or give her a warning that she was on the investigation’s most wanted list. Even so, he was hoping that he was wrong about the colonel. As for the rest of his team, they felt Windrush was deeply involved in the murders.

The other suspects still had to be eliminated from the enquiry, namely Aimes, Wardle and Shawnley, three men in their twilight years. Could it be that one of them carried a heavy wallet? This had to be the starting point. No agent was going to risk imprisonment for treason without being paid a substantial fee.

Ryona's father Mario had carried a list in his head. That unwritten list had cost him his and his family their lives. But for a game of hide and seek, Ryona would have joined them in the cemetery. Could one of the three agents that Joe was investigating be the one who had given up her father to the killers?

With Windrush apparently secure in Scotland, they would begin the interviews in earnest the following morning. First to arrive was Martin Shawnee. He looked a little nervous as he entered the room to face the team of four.

Joe fired his first question, route one. 'What do you know of Jenny Dilcox?'

Shawnee was clearly nonplussed by the question.

Joe rephrased the question. 'How many times have you had correspondence with her, worked with her in the last twenty-five years?'

Martin shook his head. 'Jenny Dilcox... that takes me back. I didn't think you'd be asking me about her, we were never that close. She was a highly rated agent. As you probably know, we were both MI5 at one time. We did a few jobs here and there, Beirut, the kidnappings of American and British workers, that kind of thing.'

Joe nodded. 'What about now, Martin? Do you have any idea where she moved to after her retirement?'

'Your guess would be as good as mine. I do know she wasn't keen on city life, more of a rural girl I would say.'

'One final question: What have been your assignments for the last year?'

'Not a lot, I've been on extended leave due to my wife's breast cancer, basically trying to keep the family happy in some turbulent times. So apart from a surveillance job with the Swedish government—a bit of the old Soviet Union making a nuisance of themselves in Swedish waters—I'm on part-time.'

The atmosphere of the interview could not have been more different than that with Colonel Windrush. It was clear to everyone in attendance that Shawnee was not their man.

Norman Aimes was next.

'I know Aimes,' said Joe. 'He's a front-liner, nerves of steel. A man you'd be glad to have in a shoot-out. I worked with him one time in Bosnia, and he's been in the field virtually ever since. He's barely been in the office in all the years I've known him. Nevertheless, I'd be interested to hear what he's got to say.'

Norman Aimes entered. A forty-five-year-old veteran looking like a man ten years younger.

'What's eating you?' He put his hand to his heart and crossed it. 'If I can assist you in any way then I will, brother.'

'Jenny Dilcox,' Joe stated baldly. 'That name mean anything to you?'

'The Dancing Queen? Sure I've had the pleasure, been in a few wars with that gal. She's retired, isn't she?'

'When you say a few wars, what are you saying?'

Norman replied, 'She had to have her way, not always the right one, sad to say. We had a stake-out in a desolate stone ranch house on one case, near the Mexican–American border. That's what she got us to believe, anyway. I'd been told that the ranch was being used as a meth lab by a Mexican cartel. I told Dancing Queen we had to hit it. You know me, Joe, I'm a shoot first, ask after sort of guy. She said we were to wait. She had the shout, Joe, so we waited. I had Dave Dunning and Barry Green with me as support. She ordered them into no-man's land. Once in, there was no way out without a fight. Those chemists had an eight-man protection block on the lab. Dave and Barry walked into an almighty ambush. After that I told her I'd never work with her again.' He shook his head at the painful memory. 'And I never did.'

'You think she knew what was waiting for them?'

He tried to create a form of words to describe the situation.

'You know, Joe, it was such a stupid command. You or I would never have given it to those men. She was so high and mighty that, on balance, I'd have to say she knew. No team leader would have sent them in in broad daylight. We had night goggles so we could have taken a couple of grenades into that shed then picked them off one by one as they came out.' Another shake of his head. 'That's how you and me would have played it. I couldn't trust her judgment after that.'

By now the team were getting a clearer picture of the missing Jenny Dilcox.

'Any idea where she's spending her time now?' asked Joe.

'I would have thought you could have got that off her dancing partner.'

'Who might that be?'

'Harry Windrush, of course. They were thick as thieves.'

Joe, held up a palm. 'When you say "old dancing partner"?'

Aimes smiled. 'You didn't know? You must have been asleep, Joe. It was common knowledge. Once they took a week off and went to Blackpool. According to what I heard, they were never off that Tower Ballroom dance floor.'

'Which explains the Dancing Queen tag?'

'Now you're catching on. Fucking Fred Astaire and Ginger Rogers they were.'

'That close?'

'You've got to believe it.' Aimes crossed two fingers and held them before the team. 'That close.'

'Which would allow a lot of possibilities as far as passing sensitive information was concerned.'

'You can say that again. You think Windrush was the chief? Well think again, Dilcox was *his* mentor. She was unofficially above him.'

Ryona couldn't help interrupting. 'Was there something more than a professional relationship? Perhaps they were in love.'

Aimes said, 'You'd think that wouldn't you? But far from the truth. That woman had a heart of stone, only thing she loved was herself. But he was smitten... couldn't see, didn't want to. It was all a game to her.'

'To what end?'

'Power, Joe, for its own ends. She wore the trousers on the top floor.'

'Any idea where she might be, Norm?'

'You want to see the bitch, Joe?'

'You bet, like Astaire wants Rogers.'

'I take it Windrush pleads ignorance? I for one would want to know why.'

'He's running the official line... retired agents have to be left to live their new life, free of any involvement in the office.'

Aimes laughed. 'You and I know that's bullshit, you don't need their residence to ask them to come in.'

The meeting was suddenly interrupted by Tony's cellphone. He glanced at the screen. 'It's my man in Inverness.'

Joe said, 'Go ahead, could be important.'

The rest of the room listened to the one-sided conversation. 'You're sure about that... Okay, check the next one in. Let me check out this end... You're saying there's been three in? Still no show? No hold ups. Keep looking, I'll get back to you.'

Tony ended the call. 'You're not going to believe this. Windrush has not shown his face in Inverness. He should have been up in the Highlands hours ago, half a day at least.'

Joe said, 'Nothing from the redcaps?'

'No, it's like they've all vanished from the face of the earth. My man has checked right down the line with British Rail. There have been no delays. We should make sure they got on a train.'

Joe said, 'That means checking the cameras at Kings Cross.'

Roberto said, 'But surely the redcaps would have reported any problems.'

'That's what I'm worried about,' said Joe.

Aimes became part of the search. 'You want help with this search, Joe? I have the time at the moment.'

Joe knew what an asset he could be. 'Why not, Norm, welcome aboard.'

Ryona said, 'If they did board the train, something has happened on that journey, perhaps they got off en route—Peterborough, Doncaster, York?'

'And probably a dozen others.'

But first they had to acquire the video of the previous evening's activities on platform 7 at Kings Cross. Which they did in double quick time. The video confirmed that Windrush and the redcaps *had* boarded the Inverness train. But where did they get off? Joe and Ryona also took note of two other passengers, a man and a woman dressed for a funeral, who seemed to show more than a casual interest in Windrush and his escorts.

The team now had the laborious task of checking video footage from every station along the way: fifteen in all. Joe told them that while they were at it they should not only check the movements of Windrush and his guards but also the mysterious couple in black.

21

KINGS CROSS TO INVERNESS

Joe found it curious, but perhaps not surprising, that Jenny Dilcox's work record, her actions in the field, had been scrupulously removed from the archives. And now her dancing partner had gone awol. Tony's men had checked the route between Inverness and Edinburgh. There had been no sightings of Windrush at any Scottish stations. Wherever they were, they were south of the border.

Joe gathered the team. 'It would be a bonus if they left the train at Doncaster because Donny is our base. So, any further thoughts on the little we know, guys?'

Roberto Veneto said, 'I'm thinking you Brits have a bad chief on the Vauxhall reservation. Colonel Windrush has a few ghosts in his locker. The man's not truth.'

'You're saying he's lying to us, Roberto?'

'One hundred per cent. He's protecting Dilcox. He's our mole.'

Joe asked, 'Anyone else think Windrush could be the leak?'

Norman Aimes said, 'All these years, all those murders... I'd be hard to convince he was clean. Tell me if you think differently, but he's top of my list.'

Ryona said, 'What about this Ginger Dilcox Rogers, surely you can't rule her out. Like Norm was saying, she's a glory seeker that the boyfriend Windrush was probably feeding these past twenty or so years.'

Joe said, 'Tony, do you want to say something?'

'I'm with the team on this, Joe. It seems these dancers have been getting away with murder for years, I'd like to take a peek at their bank accounts.'

Joe clapped his hands. 'So let's bring in the suspects. Let's go ride that train and find him if we can, but I have a bad feeling that something has happened to the escorts.'

Ryona said, 'If he can dispose of sixty agents, then two redcaps would be no problem to him. I'm thinking they're dead.'

'Ryona is right. He's running to the queen then, who knows, possibly leaving the country, to Russia, to the paymaster. They will have made withdrawal plans in case something happened like this.'

Tony said, 'I'll get onto customs and airports, and alert border control.'

It came as no surprise to hear that the Royal Military Police were already investigating the disappearance of the two redcaps. Joe contacted Captain Wilfred Grey, the acting officer in charge of the police operation. Joe insisted on complete secrecy regarding its ongoing SIS operation. Captain Grey promised his full cooperation on Joe's play, offering to have his men take over the camera surveillance work at the rail stations.

Meanwhile Joe and his team would return to their Doncaster base and wait for news. Anton Spicer, having arrived in London, had already established himself in the Windrush office. He had informed Interpol and his other contacts of the wanted couple, Windrush and Dilcox. Their code word was The Dancers.

The following morning Joe and the team got the news they were dreading. A work party of railway plate-layers had found three bodies by the side of the track between Doncaster and York, each shot with a single bullet to the head. They were lying a quarter of a mile from each other, indicating that they were tossed out of a moving train.

They could understand the redcaps being executed by Windrush in an escape attempt. This he could, would do. But his death? That didn't fit. As they sat contemplating their next move, Joe's phone rang. It was Captain Grey. The couple in black were seen on camera leaving the train at York and taking a taxi, a Toyota Avensis. Destination unknown.

Joe urged the captain to acquire video footage from city cameras that might pick up the taxi's route.

'Will do, Joe,' said Captain Grey. 'Now that I've lost two good men, it's personal.'

Joe said, 'We're on our way to York, we will take it from there.'

Joe ended the call and the team reflected on the news.

'The body count's gone to three more,' said Ryona. 'Let's go get them.'

Tony said, 'What I can't get my head around is them taking out Windrush. Why do that?'

Roberto had a ready answer. 'Because he had become of no further use to them. His cover was blown, he'd become a liability.'

The bodies of Windrush and the two redcaps were taken to Worsley Barracks for examination, so the team headed to

York in the Jeep, fully loaded; their weapons stashed in the boot.

The medical officer reported that the redcaps had both sustained blows to the head, severe enough to render them unconscious, after which they were each shot with a 9 mm pistol at point blank range. There was other bruising, which was consistent with being tossed out of the train.

Windrush was also killed with a 9 mm pistol, the bullet going in from the back of his head and coming out through the forehead, fired from such short range the pistol barrel could have parted his hair. The medic mentioned one other notable finding. His jacket, a Harris Tweed, carried the distinctive aroma of a woman's perfume. The jacket had already been taken to a professional perfumer and had been identified as A Goodnight Kiss by Roja, a perfume costing over £1000 per 100ml.

Joe turned to Ryona. ‘Have you heard of this?’

She laughed. 'At over a grand a dab, that's way out of my price zone.’

The medic said, ‘There you have it, guys. If the lady that hugged him was anything like that perfume, then she must carry a gold pistol in her purse.'

‘Colonel Gaddafi had one.'

Tony said, 'Yes he did, but he smelt like a camel!’

Joe wondered out loud, ‘How many shops sell such a high-priced item? Harrods, Selfridges maybe? Or Roja may have their own outlets. They could have a customer list.’

Ryona said, ‘I’ll check that out.’

'It's worth a try. The couple in black boarded in London. Take that into consideration. They got off at York then took a taxi, perhaps to another car park where they had a vehicle of their own waiting. I can't see them being dropped at an address in the city. They're much too smart for that.’

Roberto said, 'We need to find the taxi driver.'

Tony said, 'The RMP are on it.'

As soon as they were on the move again, Joe called Captain Gray. 'Have you got anything for me, captain?'

'I was about to phone you, Joe. Not good news. The taxi driver has been found—burnt to a cinder. His taxi too.'

Joe exclaimed, 'Who the fuck *are* these people?'

Norman Aimes said, 'They remind me of some Algerians that once crossed my path. They left nothing to talk about. They were called 'Acid Rain' because that's what they caused: corrosion. Turned gold into rust.'

'Anyway, back to the issue at hand,' said Joe. 'Looks like we're left with the perfume, let's hope we don't find the nose dead.'

'It wouldn't surprise me if she was.'

Joe made a special effort to remind the team to be extra vigilant, carry a weapon at all times, and do not be afraid to use it. This was mainly for Ryona's benefit, as the baby of the party, although she had shown no hesitation proving her mettle on the *Doonata*. If he couldn't be by her side 24/7, then he'd have a private word with Norman to keep a close eye.

Norman Aimes was a double 0 agent, licence to kill, but who had always been a little wayward when it came to playing by the rules. The words Geneva Convention meant nothing to Norm. He lived, and survived, by the phrase *every man for himself*. Joe respected him. Norm was the man you'd always want in your corner.

Roberto Veneto was another agent who was judged by his actions. He had shown bravery beyond the call of duty in the aftermath of the terrorist attack on the World Trade Center. He worked relentlessly to bring out survivors while floors were collapsing around him. Many of the injured owed their lives to Roberto. For his selfless courage he received a citation with the Medal of Honour. The report on his recent actions by General Porter meant he was ready for a senior command in the womb of the CIA.

Another irreplaceable member of the team, Captain Tony Ford, served with Joe in the Pioneer Special Forces, a premier search and rescue unit. For so long he thought he was cursed by his association with a man who had been the cause of the squad's commanding officer Freddy Hook's death. Thank God Joe had supported him and not Barry Warren.

That incident came to transform Tony into a more dedicated soldier, making Captain, before flitting over to the Royal Marine Commandos. Although his work was important, the testing of the new armed landing crafts, work that was being shared with the Norwegian Navy, he had come to miss the more active side of his role as commando. This new association with Joe Delph was like a dream come true. Tony was more than happy to give the lead to Joe, the more experienced double o agent. Joe was a man, he respected and admired.

The team arrived at the scene of the burnt out taxi. The assassins had chosen a desolate spot near the River Derwent, set back from the road. The farm track led to three derelict buildings that encircled a yard. The Toyota was a blackened shell, with the body of the taxi driver lying across the back seat. They noted fresh tyre tracks that led from an old repair shop and stable.

They were met by an RMP sergeant and two of his constables. The sergeant said they had found two empty fuel cans that had been thrown in with the body. The result would have been like a bomb going off. Any occupied dwelling inside a mile could not have failed to hear it.

Joe could now piece together the mole's plan to murder Windrush: the assassinations on the train, alighting at York, the taxi, the car parked in the barn in readiness for their escape. Colonel Windrush had known everyone who had been involved, so he would have to be silenced. What Joe couldn't understand was the Fly's connection. The Fly had emerged into the light only recently, but the murders had occurred over a number of years. Was the goal the simple annihilation of agents? Joe didn't think so. Was it that the Fly was having a final curtain? One last big shot at the money?

Aimes questioned the agents' deaths. 'If it was a God almighty clear-out, then why haven't you and I been targeted?'

'Good question,' said Joe. 'But I think we're getting closer to finding an answer.'

It was a puzzle to be solved. The money angle. Hadn't they acquired enough over twenty years of contract killings? Money was at the heart of it all, the mobster having met this new invisible force. Losing an empire. A new breed was moving into their domain—international crime, money laundering, human and drug trafficking, prostitution, computer fraud. The world's new breed of Mafia, springing up everywhere, with a new godfather perched on the throne, the Fly.

Roberto thought that throne was being contested by its known champion, Moscow's Rakham, Ivor Stravenski, fighting the new contender, the Fly.

Two hours later the team had returned to their Doncaster base, which allowed time for the new information to percolate.

After treating everyone to fish and chips, Tony said, 'Why did they kill Windrush around York, Joe? Was it random or does it have some meaning?'

Norman said, 'One, they know the area; two, they feel safe there.'

Joe, cutting in, said, 'Norm's right. Why get off the train and take a taxi up to the farm? Remember, it's night time. The cabbie's murder, I can understand that, but the firing of his cab?' He shrugged. 'No use in stabbing in the dark. These killers have made an error along the line. We have to get something on the perfume. So far, it's the only mistake of the woman in black.'

Norm said, 'And the Fly is going to be angry with her.'

Roberto added, 'I've got to agree with Norm, that Fly's going to be livid. Far from finished with us, losing *Doonata*, that would hurt.'

Later that evening the RMP sergeant called to say he had spoken to a witness to the burning taxi. The car that left the scene was a BMW saloon, colour dark blue. The sergeant had followed the car's tracks and viewed CCTV footage that confirmed the BMW had taken on fuel at a nearby garage. The shop assistant remembered the man dressed in black paid with cash—and whose clothes had a distinctive smell of smoke. He had also purchased bread and milk.

With an urgent edge in his voice, Joe said, 'Tomorrow we go to York, we follow their trail, CCTV cameras, locals, and hope they're still in the country. We need to get something out on this. Anton Spicer says there's no news from the ports. I've told him to concentrate on the east coast ports and Leeds Bradford Airport.'

With all the intel gathered, their morning drive took them north towards Pickering.

'Next stop Middleton,' said Joe.

Ryona reacted with some alarm. 'Middleton? That's heading north onto the moors.' She held up a hand to her face and gasped. 'That's not far from my Aunt Sophia's cottage.'

'Where exactly is it?'

'G-G-Goathland Moor, it's a beautiful spot, outskirts of Beck Hole. I don't understand. My aunt lives alone. She wouldn't have a younger man there without my knowing.'

The car fell silent. Joe broke it.

'Look, Ryona, did you not know your aunt's past life, her work, what she did?'

She shook her head with a cross between bewilderment and anger.

'She never talked much. Of course, I'd asked her a few times but she always said she would tell me later.'

Joe reached over and took her hands.

'Ryona, your Aunt Sophia was one of us. MI6 admin, similar job to what Pat Taylor does.'

She gasped. 'Oh my God, she worked for Windrush! She's not, is she, Jenny Dilcox?'

'I'm afraid it's true. She did twenty or so years up to her retirement. While you were away at boarding school, she was still at work, sort of semi-retired. She didn't want you to know.'

She stared at him as if for the first time. As if stung by something, she pulled her hands away from his.

'How come you know all this and haven't told me?'

He looked to the others who were all silent and looking a little confused.

'I was told by Windrush that Sophia did not, under any circumstance, want you to know of her past. Now the situation has changed. You want the truth from me? I never gave it a thought that your aunt could become a suspect. Not until now, anyway. What with you coming from the Yorkshire Dales, the name Jenny Dilcox... it's been there in front of me all along. I'm fucking stupid not to have seen it.'

Joe looked at her with pleading in his eyes, and put his hands together in prayer.

'I'm so sorry, Ryona, I should have told you.'

Roberto put his arm around her. 'You know that Joe did what your aunt wished. Sure it was something Windrush should have kept to himself, if anyone should have told you it was him. Joe, like all of us here—except Norm—have never met this Jenny Dilcox. He's the only one who can recognise her.'

He gave her a gentle squeeze. 'Let's wait and see before we pre-judge. If it *is* your aunt, then why did she let you come into the service? That's what's got me thinking.'

Tony said, 'What aunt would put her niece into a dangerous situation?'

Norm sighed. 'That woman Jenny Dilcox for all the world is a devil of a lady. I know what she looks like even though I've not seen her for quite a few years. Ryona, if you've got a photograph of your aunt, I can tell you.'

Ryona shook her head.

'Come to think of it, that's another thing that worries me. I always thought it a little odd that she never had photographs of herself or anyone else in the cottage—except one of an elegant young man around twenty-five years old with a moustache. I remember asking her once who it was. "Just a friend" she said.'

The remainder of the drive north to Middleton was conducted mostly in silence. Just when Ryona thought she had the plot, the mole, the Fly all worked out, and she was dealing with the murders of her family and her own part in the elimination of hardened criminals, she was hit with a family secret that threw everything into turmoil.

Surely her loving aunt couldn't be associated with these assassins.

She looked out over God's country and prayed to that same God that the woman known as Jenny Dilcox was *not* Aunt Sophia. All those good times that were part of her growing up, holidays shared, had in a stroke become meaningless. She was coming to understand why Windrush had kept it all away from her. By instructing Joe to follow Sophia's wishes, Aunt Sophia did not want her, Mari, to know.

Would the garage video reveal her identity? And what of the man? Would she know him? She felt her automatic hanging down from the holster under her jacket. It suddenly felt heavier. If it *was* Sophia, Ryona would empty its load into her lying, deceitful body. The Geneva Convention could go to hell.

22
THE CHASE

They all crowded into a tiny space in the garage's back office to view the CCTV recording, which had been paused at the point a blue BMW entered the garage forecourt. The RMP captain pressed play. A man wearing dark glasses got out of the front passenger door; evidently the woman was driving. The man walked around the car to fill up. The woman wound down her window and seemed to speak to him. Whatever she said, caused him to glance up at the camera and quickly turn his back on it.

The forecourt attendant told them the man had put twenty litres into the tank. He entered the store where another camera showed him selecting bread and milk before walking to the counter to pay in cash. The only words he spoke were a polite 'Thank you', which the cashier thought had a foreign accent. Maybe French? He wasn't sure. He also said the man's skin tone was Mediterranean yellow-gold. He then returned to the car, which drove north towards the A169, fifteen miles from Beck Hole—Aunt Sophia's home village.

Joe said, ‘It looks like Aunt Sophia could be involved, girl.'

Ryona tried to contain her emotions and concentrate on the team’s next move. 'How are you going to play it, Joe?’

Joe turned to the whole team. 'We get up there to Beck Hole, see if the BMW’s there. If it is, then we wait till nightfall, make sure the motor doesn’t move. If it does then we take out the tyres, give the driver the chance to surrender.'

Norman nodded. 'If it stays put, we go in after lights out?’

‘Yes, that’s the only way to do this, attack when unexpected.'

Ryona was ambivalent about the operation. She said, 'Can I go in first, Joe? See what she’s got to say?’

'Only if that BMW isn’t there and the lights are on. If that becomes the scenario, then you phone her first, tell her that you and I are in the area working a case. Don’t mention anything about Windrush or that you know she worked for us. Act as any niece visiting an aunt would. She’s smart, she’ll search us out for any cracks.' He left a pause. ‘Be ready to kill if necessary. If you don’t, she’ll kill you.'

Roberto Veneto said, 'There’s no way anyone is leaving. On two feet or carried out, makes no difference, they’re going down.'

Joe said, 'Let’s hope it won’t come to that.'

'You guys don’t think of anything other than they’re the enemy killers,’ said Ryona. ‘Forget that’s my auntie in the cottage. Come the end of the day, I want all my friends safe. It’s time to draw the final curtain.'

Tony said, ‘Sorry, Ryona, your aunt ain’t my aunt... to me she’s just a killer. Now let’s get up to Beck Hole. Don’t let’s give them time to run.’

In her heart of hearts she knew Tony was right. This was not the time to be sentimental. Ryona turned her attention to how best to approach the house.

'Close to the cottage is an old water mill. It's not been used for over a hundred years; I used to read there as a child. It's got a loft, that was probably used for storing the corn. It's still got a chute that leads to a granite wheel. There's plenty of space for us all in that loft, ideal to view the front of the cottage. We can enter through a back archway which leads to the old stables, I used to keep my pony there.'

They drove out towards Beck Hole and left the Jeep in an overnight car park full of motor homes and caravans. They stashed their weapons in a zip-up hold-all and headed for what Ryona estimated was a good mile hike across fields and woodland.

Joe had arranged with the RMP to be ready if required to set up road blocks on all routes out of Beck Hole, and to move into action on his call. The team reached a small wood copse that looked down on the cottage frontage. Night was falling and the time had come to fix their night views over their black balaclavas.

Ryona pointed out their approach path to the water mill, a thick hedgerow that ran down to the rear archway.

Joe was thinking, *So far so good.* They paused for a moment as the cottage came into view; its lights were on. Somebody was home but there was no sign of the BMW.

Joe whispered, 'Go take a look, Norm, see if you can spot the car. Take care.'

Norm gave a mock salute and took out his automatic rifle. In a crouched position he skirted around the rear of the mill and crept towards the garage. The BMW was not parked outside or on the road leading up to the house.

Meanwhile the rest of the team entered the mill. Ryona pointed out the wooden steps that led to the loft, and they all ascended.

Joe said, 'Great place to read a book, girl.'

Tony remarked, 'Mill on the Floss?'

Ryona was less interested in literature. 'Can you see Norm? Will he be okay?'

Joe said, 'Norm will be fine. He's used to these ops. He could brush your hair and you wouldn't know it. He was our sniper, he could shoot off your eyebrows from a quarter of a mile away.'

Joe turned to Tony. 'You've worked with Norm, haven't you?'

'I was in an SAS patrol in Iraq. Norm was in a forward elite Pioneers group, but everybody knew of him, of his courage.'

Moments later Norm returned silently into the mill, and climbed the ladder into the loft space.

Joe asked, 'What you got for us?'

Norm told them that there was no BMW on the premises, but that the garage held the aunt's Saab. The cottage had one female occupant wearing a red sweatshirt and jeans: Jenny Dilcox, although somewhat older than Norman remembered her.

Joe pressed. 'You're sure she's alone?'

'Sure.'

'Ryona, you knock on the door. Remember, that woman inside is a multi-killer. Try and hold it together. Let's see if we can't get her to tell us who her partner is, where he's vanished to.'

She shook her head in disbelief. 'My aunt Sophia, fucking Jenny Dilcox, a mole, a traitor of longstanding, the fucking killer of my family, her family too.'

She pondered the significance of the next few moments, then, through gritted teeth, said, 'Let's get this done.'

Norm said, 'I'll have you covered, the back has a set of floor-to-ceiling French windows. I'll be on the outside patio.'

Joe addressed Roberto and Tony. 'You watch the approach road for our missing friend's return. If he does come back, take out his tyres, and him too if you need to. I don't want him getting away.'

A little puzzled, Roberto said, 'You're going to arrive at her door without a vehicle? Don't you think she'll think that strange?'

Tony said, 'I can bring the Jeep to the top of the driveway.'

'Roberto's right,' said Ryona, 'we've got to have a vehicle. Remember, she's smart.'

Joe suddenly came to a decision. 'Tony, give me your keys. Ryona and I will collect the car and go in through the front. If while we're gone anything unexpected happens you know what to do. They don't leave here, okay?'

'Stay safe. '

Norman looked at his watch. 'Expect to see you in, let's say twenty minutes.'

Joe smiled. 'What you think we are, fucking greyhounds?'

Thirty minutes had passed when Norm, Roberto and Tony heard the sound of a vehicle approaching. Through their night views, they could see Joe at the wheel and Ryona in the passenger seat of the Jeep. It stopped outside the cottage's front porch as one of the curtains in a window twitched. They got out and walked to the door, which opened as they approached. Sophia stepped out and greeted them both. The first thing Ryona noticed was the perfume Sophia was wearing: A Goodnight Kiss by Roja.

'Well I must say, Mari, what a surprise seeing you. I thought you were in Japan. Who's this good looking man you've brought with you?'

Joe answered for her. 'Joe Delph. It's so nice to meet you.'

He wasn't lying. He was more than pleased to meet the woman responsible for Stacy Kilmer's death.

Sophia nodded a greeting. 'Let's all get inside, I have a fire going. I'll put on the kettle.'

In complete contrast to the reason for their call, the cottage was warm and welcoming.

'Take a seat, Joe Delph,' said Aunt Sophia, with a flirtatious giggle.

She walked towards the small kitchen and called back to Ryona, 'You must tell me about Japan, Mari, those letters you sent, they told me little of its history.'

'It's like this, Aunt Sophia, I don't like lying but I have been told to keep my work mostly undercover.'

She played along that she was sorry for not telling her about MI6. As if the evil cow didn't know.

Sophia acted shocked. 'Your work... What's this "undercover"... And why are you here?'

'You see, aunt, I've been working for the government, special sort of police work, MI6. You've probably heard of it?'

'Sort of James Bond?'

'You could say that. 007!'

'Joe is my boss, my mentor.'

'Oh I see, so what brings you to the Dales? You're not on business, are you?'

Joe said, 'We've been following a murder of one of our chiefs. Happened in York. With us being up this way, Ryona wanted me to meet her Aunt Sophia.' He spread out his arms. 'So here we are.'

Holding out a palm, he said, 'I do hope we're not putting you out?'

'Ryona, Mr Delph, who is Ryona?'

'That's me. When you join the service, they change your name, for family protection. I'm called Ryona Steel.'

Sophia looked at the clock on the mantelpiece. It was the first time that she looked a little agitated.

She tried a smile and, turning to Ryona, said, 'You should have phoned, Mari. You should have let me know that you were coming.'

'I thought it better to surprise you, auntie. There's no problem, is there?'

Sophia gave a deep sigh. 'Yes, I'm sorry, dearest, what with there being only the two bedrooms and the fact that I'm expecting the son of an old friend arriving any minute... well, it puts me in a bit of a dilemma.'

'No problem, auntie, we can book rooms at the pub in the village.'

Sophia looked again at the mantel clock. 'Yes, the pub, that's best. He'll be gone in the morning, then you can visit. You can tell me all about this secret service job—if you're allowed.'

As Ryona and Joe turned for the door, a vehicle pulled up outside. They went to the window to see the blue BMW do a U-turn. Then the bullets began to fly. The car was hit from a volley of shots coming from the watermill. The driver's door opened and a man exited and ran across the open field towards a copse. Ryona and Joe turned back to Sophia, who was now pointing a pistol at them.

She was smiling. 'Don't you think I don't know about you, Joe Delph? Why you are here? I was in your kind of work when you were still in nappies.'

Joe said, 'Twenty years a killer, that's not our kind of work, Miss Dilcox.'

'You're ten years out of date, Delph.'

Ryona couldn't hold back any longer. 'You had your sister, her whole family, my family, murdered, you fucking evil bitch.'

'Yes, they should have searched a little more to find you. I wanted you dead too, Mari Bambella. The lot of you.'

'Why? What have we ever done that would cause you to have us murdered?'

'Why? You should have asked your father, how he, commanding a drug operation, killed the only man I ever loved.'

She stabbed her finger at Ryona. 'Henri, like me, a double, bloody triple agent if you like... shot down like a dog, with me carrying his child inside me. A son, Francois, who he never got to see.'

Joe said, 'That doesn't give you the right to continue thirty fucking years of killings, including Stacy Kilmer, the love of my life, you bastard, you cut her and young David up.'

'Oh, I enjoyed seeing the pictures. Know what I did? Why, I paid them a bonus.'

She waved the pistol. 'Now you better tell the rest of the losers in my mill to fuck off, while you two drive me to a little place I know. Where my son will be heading, waiting for me.'

Ryona snarled, 'Your son... the Fly?'

Sophia slowly shook her head. 'They told me you were good, Mari, how wrong can they be. You're as far off as the planet Mars.'

Joe said, 'I don't know about that, Dilcox, we got to you easily enough.' He pointed to the BMW, its engine still running. 'That son of yours, he's running. He's not going to get far before he gets cut down. You know what? I hope your bastard lives long enough for me to squeeze out of him what you didn't get by squeezing Stacy Kilmer. Giving him the same treatment. Would he talk to me? I leave it to you,

you're the expert. How long would he last? An arm, a leg, two arms, two legs? You tell me.'

Sophia laughed with a maniacal edge, and waved the pistol. 'You're forgetting who's holding the gun, Delph. Now tell them to get the fuck out of my mill, or I take Mari now, you hear?'

Joe held his hands at shoulder height. 'Call them yourself. You can use my cell.'

'You think I was born yesterday?'

She clicked back the hammer on the pistol, and snarled at Ryona, 'Take out his phone. Any hanky panky, your heads get blown off. Nice and easy lay the phone down on that table.'

There was a sudden shattering of glass as a high-velocity bullet smashed through the window striking Sophia in the shoulder. She spun around with the impact, losing her grip on the pistol. It clattered to the floor and Joe grabbed it.

Sophia was knocked into the television, both of them now a sorry broken sight. Blood pumped from the wound in her shoulder.

In the space of three seconds the roles had been reversed. Joe now stood over her with pistol in hand. Blood spread over her sweatshirt. Sophia cursed the pain and demanded an ambulance.

Ryona said, 'Say please, you evil cow.'

'Never, go get fucked.'

'Then bleed to death.'

The door flew open and Norman Aimes rushed in, lifting his balaclava.

Sophia looked up. 'Fucking glory seeker, Aimes, shooting a woman in the back!'

'Want me to put one in the front too? Better not, I'll leave that to Ryona and Joe.'

Sophia cried out in agony, 'Get me to a hospital, you've got your prisoner.'

Ryona took out her pistol and aimed it at her.

Sophia taunted her, 'You wouldn't dare.'

Ryona aimed the barrel at the other shoulder and pulled the trigger.

'Aaagh!'

'That's for the neighbours.'

She fired again, this time into her aunt's right leg. 'That's for my good Aunt Sarah.'

Again the pistol barked, the bullet taking out the left knee. 'That's for Uncle Jimmy.'

Tony and Roberto joined the scene.

Sophia screamed, 'You're fucking mad, the lot of you, you can't do this, transgressing a prisoner's rights!'

Ryona invited Joe to join her. She uttered under her breath, 'For Stacy, Daniel, my mum and dad, brother Teddy... let's do this together.'

Roberto pulled out his Glock. 'I'll join you, for Frank Bitten and the countless others.'

Ryona, Joe and Roberto all emptied their magazines into the heart and head of Aunt Sophia–Jenny Dilcox.

When their ears stopped ringing, Sophia was a bloody mess.

Joe said, 'We had to do this, guys, there's no way she was going to prison.'

Norm turned to Tony. 'See what? I didn't see anything. You Tony?'

Tony shrugged. 'Just a man running across the field away from this terrible deed.'

Joe smiled a thank you. 'That man is her son, let's go get the devil's spawn. I'll call in the cleaners for her.'

Ryona looked to the ceiling, and whispered, 'We got her, Daddy.'

23
HUNT FOR THE SON OF A DANCING QUEEN

A few miles down the main road, on foot, was the lone figure of Francois Dupont. He approached a house with its lights shining onto a white Mercedes-Benz. He rapped on the door and moments later the middle-aged owner of the car was lying dead in his own hallway. Francois took the car keys from the hall table. He was no longer a pedestrian.

The petrol tank showed close to red. He would need to fill up within ten miles. He knew that in this part of the world, at this time of night, only a major highway would have an open station. That meant driving back down the A169 to Pickering. From there he would need to decide on the best option for getting back to London, to a mews home in Little Venice.

With alarm bells already sounding, and with his mother probably under arrest, he began to assess his predicament.

He had a pistol, money, and a car, so his chances of avoiding capture were better than good.

The colonel, the redcaps, the taxi driver, all easy kills. He had proven he could deal with the pushback from the SIS. On the downside, his mother was out of action—for now. But whatever prison tried to hold her, he'd get her out and back to Algiers, to their Mediterranean home. Then they could relax for a while, until the Fly called once again for their services.

He would return to London where he had connections.

And what connections they were.

The O'Neils, lead family of a runt IRA unit, were the kind of associates one relied on to do their worst in all situations. They were not people one would want to count as enemies. Judiciously, the Fly had made substantial deposits into their Cayman Islands account, so—for the time being—they were the closest thing Francois had to an ally.

Francois Dupont had been born twenty-eight years earlier in Algiers. The father, Sophia's loving partner of five years, Henri Dupont, had been gunned down in an ambush in Piedras Negras on the US–Mexican border. The French drug runner died in a CIA-led raid on his meth lab that was producing a mind-blowing concoction and importing it into North America's major cities.

The raid was led by Mari's father, Mario Bambella, brother-in-law to Sophia Grazadei by virtue of marrying her sister, Gianna. The two sisters had hitched their wagons to two very different horses. Henri's death would drive Sophia, a double agent, into killing all connections to the MI6 Vauxhall office and its office in Langley, Virginia, home of the CIA.

Mario later discovered he was related to a traitor to the realm. Sophia, in an attempt to keep her status as a double agent secret, was to give Mario a list of other doubles, and moles, both British and American. Colonel Harry Windrush was one of the big fish she handed over to him.

Of course she could not let Mario live. He had to die along with his family; it was the price for the death of her beloved Henri. She brought up her son alone, and her deceitful life continued with her newfound partnership with Colonel Windrush, who escaped detection on the death of Mario Bambella.

Aside from the colonel, Sophia met up with a most remarkable man. Both had suffered devastating loss—she with Henri's father, he with his wife. The man that the authorities were calling the Dragonfly, the new found hero of organised crime. A man he knew must be traumatised after the loss of the yacht *Doonata*. But he would rise again, next time stronger than before.

Francois was on a secret visit that his mother had planned, with Mari Bambella nicely tucked away on MI6 duties. They had received a call from Windrush of his arrest and that he needed to be rescued from a two-handed redcap escort to his retreat in Inverness. He had supplied the train and its departure time out of Kings Cross, asking that Sophia board the train at York and carry out the rescue. The only thing they rescued was their own secrecy. They murdered both Windrush and the two escorts, and tossed them from the train.

Meanwhile, at a house on Goathland Moor, a woman returned to find her husband had been murdered and the family saloon stolen. She contacted the police who put out an all points on the stolen vehicle, a white Mercedes-Benz.

There was a delay before the message reached the RMP, who immediately relayed it to Joe. They also told him that their men had been told to watch out for a blue BMW, with male and female occupants. But now the runner could be anywhere.

Then the team were blessed with a stroke of luck. The petrol garage that had provided the CCTV footage of the blue BMW, confirmed that a white Merc had filled up—and then headed south.

Francois was indeed heading south on the A1 and planned to ditch the Mercedes as soon as possible.

Joe and the team climbed into the Jeep and followed. Tony took the wheel.

Roberto said, 'Our man must be at least an hour ahead of us... with his foot to the floor, the Mercedes could do 160 miles per hour, whereas this old Jeep can barely muster a hundred and ten.'

Norm suggested that the runner would probably ditch the Mercedes at the first opportunity, then take another route by jumping on a train or coach.

Roberto thought back to the time Sophia and her son first boarded the train out of Kings Cross. 'A taxi must have taken them to the station, from some London address. If we could find the taxi through CCTV, the driver is unlikely to forget such an unusual pick up. Best bet is Kings Cross taxi rank.'

Joe agreed. 'Take us to Kings Cross, Tony, let's re-check their CCTV and find that London cabbie.'

Ryona said, 'Of course, we could well see him on screen on his arrival. Or he may come in by coach.'

'Okay, Ryona, Roberto and myself will take Kings Cross. Tony with Norm goes to the coach station.'

One crew was dropped at Kings Cross station; the other continued on to Victoria Coach Station.

Ryona, Roberto and Joe headed for the rail communications office. Joe showed his MI6 identity card and explained their requirements. A technician was put at their disposal who found the file of the date and approximate time they were looking for.

It was not long before they were looking at grainy images of Sophia and Francois getting out of a “Fast Taxi Services” cab with a helpful phone number on the door, which Joe called. The dispatcher said that the driver was at that moment in her regular pick up spot outside Kings Cross. They couldn’t believe their luck.

‘Call her on the radio and tell her to wait for me. It’s government business.’

They showed the driver the footage of her dropping the couple in black.

‘Do you remember them?’

The driver curled a lip. 'I won't give them any future pleasure, that's for sure.'

Ryona asked, 'Why is that?’

'Why, you may well ask. I pick them up from some million-pound mews in Little Venice, dressed like they’re going to a funeral. Pricks never tipped. I heard them sniggering, laughing. Funeral my arse.’

Joe said, 'Mews house you say?’

‘Thats right, must be worth three or four million, off Bloomfield Road.'

Roberto asked, ‘Has the house got a name, a number?’

‘My duty sheet is in the car.’ She gave him a questionable look. 'They do something terrible?’

Joe gave a nod. 'You could say that, they're not good people.'

Opening up the glove compartment, she took out a duty sheet and handed it to Ryona.

‘There, at the bottom,’ she said, pointing to the address. “The Summit”.

24
PADDY FIELD

The cobbled approach to The Summit was straight out of a Dickens novel. A forgotten street in old London that awaited a horse-drawn carriage, hooves clip-clopping and wooden wheels creaking over a brown and gold cushion of fallen leaves. Despite the yesteryear-look gas lamps, the whole area stank of money, money, money.

Francois had managed to call his contact before he arrived in London. He was told to drive to an address in St Albans and leave it there. From there he would be given a safe ride to Little Venice. The car was most likely already stripped and resprayed in preparation for an overseas buyer. All part of the O'Neil service.

Billy O'Neil, veteran of 'The Troubles'—the inverted commas always bothered Billy; to him it was a war—was nobody's friend. He had fought the good fight without a blemish. His grandfather fought alongside Michael Collins. He was from good stock, and soared through the ranks to become chief organiser of the New Irish Republican Army, English section. A bad man to get the wrong side of. The explosive expert was not called the Widow Maker for nothing. He trusted only his family. It was an arrangement he was happy with. The only reason he was still in the game was because he relied on the trust of his family—his twenty-five-year-old twins, Brendan and Charlie, his twenty-year-old daughter Cathy, and wife Mary, an active bomb-maker in her own right.

A business associate who would certainly not fall into the category of friend—known to authorities and national crime agencies throughout the world as the Fly—recently contacted O'Neil to say that a wingman of his was in a tight spot and could he give Francois the help he required. O'Neil knew when to stoke goodwill with someone so powerful and took on the responsibility.

The Fly badly needed information on Sophia, the man's mother. A contact in the Royal Military Police had said Sophia had disappeared from the face of the earth. A search was being conducted to find her, but so far there had been no trace.

O'Neil had arranged that night to slip Francois out of the country in a cargo vessel out of Tilbury Docks. *The Black Seagull* would take him to Algeria and home. There was one problem, Francois was reluctant to go. He told O'Neil there was no way he was leaving without his mother. This, of course, was a forlorn hope. Sophia was dead many times over. Joe Delph's cleaners had ensured no trace of her body would ever materialise. The farm incinerator had seen to that. Whatever was left was buried in quicklime.

Meanwhile both the Fly and O'Neil had their faces out in a countrywide search for the woman, while her worried son sat waiting in O'Neil's luxurious mews house for news. O'Neil tried to cheer him with a bottle of Egan's Reserve Legacy whiskey. He was forever giving him the 'Leave it to the Man' speech, which was getting on the younger man's nerves. So much so that he was gulping down the Irish classic like he was putting out a fire.

The Fly had other issues. Surely with the best information pipeline in the criminal world they ought to have heard of her whereabouts by now. How could they keep her in custody without him knowing? It was worrying. Recent events were considered: the loss of his prized yacht *Doonata*; the cargo of death, the virus. Could he be losing his power, his control?

If that were to happen, Billy O'Neil would want the seat at the head of the table. While his expertise lay in explosives, his NIRA activities stretched to money laundering, human trafficking, robbery, fraud and prostitution. Being the top dog IRA hit man in England, if O'Neil wanted you gone, then you'd go, without trace. Many a special agent wanted the man dead. But if they were to nail him and lock him up, what of the reprisals? One man for twenty, fifty? All things considered, it would not make for a prudent operation. The war would return to the streets of mainland Britain and Northern Ireland. And anyway, such a powerful man would have the run of the prison in no time at all. Probably with a frightened warden under his thumb.

If The Summit was Billy O'Neil's hearth and home, the Five Leaf Clover bar and restaurant was his place of business. Run by the pragmatic and amenable Thomas Coyne, it was effectively a gangsters' meeting house—convivial drinks and food downstairs; office and boardroom upstairs. The permanent two-man guard at the entrance was a reminder that the Five Leaf was members only. It was not listed on any online review sites.

Hardly a Saturday night went by without finding the O'Neils tucking into free plates of food and drink. Like every business that had dealings with O'Neil, they paid monthly protection for a quiet life. Rather to one of his own kind than any one of the foreign-run rackets in northwest London.

For all his menace and guile, Billy O'Neil was afflicted by one fatal flaw: vanity. He liked to show-off. Which was why Joe was sure his new house guest—the runner, Francois DuPont—would be sat at O'Neil's table come Saturday night.

The cabbie was soon hailed by another fare outside Kings Cross and Ryona and Roberto returned to Joe with the address. Joe's face turned to stone.

'You okay, Joe?'

'The Summit.'

'Yeh. Something wrong with that, Joe?'

'It's not good, let's get back to Vauxhall and get Norman and Tony back. We've got a problem.'

Twenty minutes later the team were gathered in Windrush's old office, now taken by Anton Spicer. He listened to the report of the incident at Beck Hole and the death of Sophia. After a raging gun battle, while trying to escape, Sophia DuPont–Jenny Dilcox had been burnt beyond recognition after her car's petrol tank exploded. Her remains were thrown into a quick-lime pit. Spicer accepted this line without question. There was no way he would contradict his lifelong friend. His mind flitted back to Joe surprising him when he said he had fallen in love with Stacy Kilmer, his partner. But he had never seen two people more suited. Her death must had left a hole in Joe, a hole where his heart used to be. If the elimination of this double agent helped ease the pain, then so be it.

Joe explained to his team why he had become concerned by the address Ryona got from the cabbie. It belonged to the one and only Billy O'Neil.

The name caused Norm to sigh like air leaving a tyre. 'IRA,' he declaimed. 'A man to be feared. The address in

Little Venice is family, to be avoided. Two agents were executed there last year just for crossing the threshold. They went to question him on the robbery of a Picasso from a house in Mayfair.'

He looked at each in turn.

'The agents' bodies were later recovered from the Thames.'

He shook his head.

'If our runner is there, he's safe for now. We could do a surveillance on the chance that he makes a move. In this situation we have to take him, strike while the iron's hot.'

Joe was deep in thought. 'Norm's right, if we decide to take them down... and I'm stressing *if* we do this, then we take two birds with one stone, or four, if we include our friend O'Neil and his sons. We have to make it look like other parties are involved.'

Tony asked, 'How?'

Joe said, 'We select a group of killers that have been making progress in the underworld. The kingpin I have in mind is an Albanian called the Monster, believed to be part of a Colombian cartel—and he's in London. I bet O'Neil's boys would find him for us. He's no lover of the IRA, after the Irish fleeced him out of a two million drug deal two years ago.'

Spicer said 'I believe I like it.'

'We leave clues, his distinctive DNA, and wait for O'Neil to take the bait.'

Spicer was up for it. 'We can do this but we have to have no mishaps, it's got to be a clean operation.'

Roberto Veneto said, 'We know of the so-called Monster on the other side of the pond. He's on both the FBI and CIA European office most wanted lists. He escaped from police custody several times. I always thought bribery was involved, once in Saudi Arabia, another time in North Africa. He's one slippery item.'

Joe added, 'I chased him from Turkey into Russia and was only minutes away from an arrest in a hotel when he slid down the laundry chute and shot a woman dead in the car park. Rather conveniently he left behind a number of items—clothing, a suitcase, toiletries. So we have his DNA.'

Norman said, 'But not his name?'

'We can't be sure. We found a name—Abdulselam—written on the inside cover of a memo pad. We're not sure if it's our man.'

Spicer said, 'There were also plans for an oil production plant. The writings came from the pen of one Osama bin Laden.' He said the name with dread. 'Joe forwarded them to me prior to the death of Agent Kilmer. Bin Laden was already dead, but the terrorist group didn't die. In fact they tried to penetrate that plant with the intention of blowing up the wells. But for Joe and his intel, they would have successfully completed their work.'

Joe said, 'It was a close run thing, sure enough.'

'Joe had a joint mission of SAS and SEALS waiting for them,' said Spicer, 'they terminated twenty-six of them.'

Joe added, 'Anton is going back a few years, but those cells are still out in Pakistan, training the next intake of killers under the noses of a government, that to be honest, do not want to know.'

Spicer said, 'Sounds like O'Neil and the Albanian were made for each other!'

The interjection released the tension in the room and the team refocused their attention on the O'Neils.

Tony said, 'So you're saying we take out O'Neil and his two sons, Joe?'

Joe nodded. 'Remember, they work for daddy, they do what O'Neil tells them—robbery, rape and murder is your starter for ten, so yes, they come as a package'

Ryona added, 'Some family.'

Joe smiled. 'This is what we do.'

'Before you start, please allow me to take my leave,' said Spicer. 'I wouldn't want to cramp your style.'

Once Anton Spicer had left the safe house, and Joe was released from SIS standards and practices, he laid out his plan and briefed the team on responsibilities, weapons and tactics. 'We go in late Saturday, and you know what Elton John sang... Saturday night's all right for fighting.'

Three a.m. Sunday morning. The team were masked up in a black Ford Transit that pulled up to the kitchen door of the Five Leaf Clover. One hundred yards away stood the box van belonging to the cleaners, who would move in to clean up on Joe's given signal.

Instruction to the team: shoot on sight, no witnesses, take the runner alive—if possible. Norm, Joe and Tony would take down the O'Neils, after first silencing the kitchen staff and restaurant owner Thomas Coyne. Ryona and Roberto would neutralise the two door guards and come in through the front, then secure the restaurant by bolting its entrance door. Joe was not expecting too much resistance at this time of the night; the O'Neils should be well intoxicated.

The kitchen door opened. A kitchen porter appeared in a white smock and lit up a cigarette. Let the show begin. Norm lowered the window, took out his pistol with its screw-on suppressor and carefully put the man's head into the sights and fired. The man slumped to the ground. As one, the team left the vehicle. Ryona and Roberto raced around to the front; Joe, Tony, and Norman headed for the open kitchen door. Joe entered first, quickly followed by Tony and

Norman. They fired at will, taking down three remaining staff that caused a clattering of plates and pans as they hit the floor.

A shout came from the main restaurant: 'Fucking clumsy bastard!'

The three agents burst into the dining room with pistols at arm's-length.

The only occupants were a group of men with mouths agape in a half-moon booth. Pop, pop, pop, pop, pop, pop, like champagne corks. All head shots; all men. The runner was covered in other men's blood and seemed astonished that he had not been hit. He stood up and automatically raised his hands. Joe pulled him to the floor and cuffed him. Then the front doors flew open and Ryona and Roberto came racing in. The job was not finished. Ryona faced the women and shot them all at point blank range.

Joe took out a picture of a dragonfly and placed it with Abdulselam's memo pad on the bloodstained table.

On Joe's say-so, the cleaners arrived. He told them to leave the placed items in view.

By daybreak the restaurant had been cleaned of visible evidence of the twelve murders that had taken place.

The news on the street was that Billy O'Neil and his family were missing. Paddington's Little Venice and Kilburn's Irish community were awash with rumours. The missing guards, kitchen staff, Thomas Coyne, all gone without a trace. The police switchboard was overloaded with enquiries. But the police were just as dumbfounded, and anyway, to put it politely, they were pleased to see the back of the troublesome Irish family.

25
INTO THE LIME PIT

Joe and his team drove DuPont gagged, bound and blindfolded back to Joe's family home in High Melton, South Yorkshire. They relished the idea of interrogating the man partly responsible for so many deaths. To Joe and Ryona it was personal. Joe began to take a fresh view of his protégé. She was becoming what was known in the service as a field assassin. He knew that the discovery of her mother's sister being involved in the murders of her family would cut deep. The gagged and blindfolded man was her cousin. But it would mean nothing if she was to execute him now.

He compared Ryona to Stacy. Two agents cut from different cloth. Stacy, a prudent planner, had been so like Joe in many ways, who gave a play much thought before entering the arena. Ryona had already showed that she went into situations much like Norman Aimes: shoot first, ask questions later.

He missed Stacy badly. She was to be his future wife, which was only one of the many reasons that the Dragonfly would suffer once caught. Surely now it was only a matter of time.

Joe escorted the terrified, hooded man out of the Jeep around the house to a rear yard and stables. The house was surrounded by dense woodland, and a concealed inner pond had been a haven for wildfowl that had at one time been the nesting site of pheasant and partridge. Joe could remember his father having a thriving little business delivering the birds to local butchers. The stable once housed a pair of cobs and a carriage. The abandoned chair with its shafts pointing roofwards reared in a corner like elephants tusks. They sat the prisoner down with his back against a water trough but did not remove the hood. They would use the green slimy liquid to rouse him if he passed out.

Joe started the interrogation. 'I'm going to ask you questions that you will know the answers to. Give me a wrong answer and you will lose a limb. Do you understand?'

The man didn't answer.

'Do you understand?'

The hood nodded.

'See, it's easy.'

'What is your name?'

The man hesitated before shakily replying, 'My name is Francois DuPont.'

'Where are you from, Francois DuPont?'

'I'm from Paris, France.'

Joe put a hand on his shoulder. The hood shuddered.

'You sure about that? Because we will check you out.'

'I know that, I'm sure. Paris, France.'

'Why did you murder five people, with the woman Sophia?'

'I do as I'm told. '

Joe could feel the change, the bastard was gaining confidence. Time to put the pressure on.

'Who the fuck tells you what to do? Who's the commander? Who's giving the orders?' Joe tapped him on the head. 'Remember what I've told you would happen if you give a shit answer, Francois.'

Under the cover of the hood they heard DuPont breathe heavily. The hood was being sucked in and out.

Joe snarled. 'I'm waiting.'

He stammered, 'I don't, don't know, it's passed on to us. Sophia, she gets it, she knows who, I fucking don't know. You have her. Why don't you ask her?'

Joe tapped Francois again. 'We already have. She says to ask you. We think after losing her legs she's telling us the truth.'

The team smiled at Joe's turning of the screw. DuPont says nothing.

'Okay, have it your way. Get the chain saw!'

Norm walked to the door, opened and closed it, but remained in the room.

Joe told Ryona to spread some plastic sheeting down, that he didn't want blood on the stable floor.

DuPont shuffled as best he could and suddenly cried out, 'Okay, it's a man. He lives in Algiers, but he's in London. He's the Fly. I don't know his name.'

He sounded disgusted at his own weakness.

'Nobody knows his name. We met him only twice, each time behind a tinted screen, like blacked-out car windows. He can see you, but you can't see him. His voice was distorted into a rough sounding vocal with no clue to accent.'

Joe pressed, 'Where did these meets take place?'

DuPont was quick to answer, knowing the damage had already been done. With the O'Neils dead, his mother presumably in some English prison cell or hospital, the thought of her being legless... his options were running out.

'One time in Paris, and once in London.'

'Where in Paris, where in London?'

Roberto was ready with pen and notebook.

Joe repeated his question.

'About six months ago Sophia and I were taken blindfolded to a meeting at night in some warehouse. I could smell oil, gasoline, as if we were in some large garage.'

'What was the meeting about, why meet, why not get instructions by e-mail, telephone?'

He shuffled again. 'It was about the money. With Sophia it was always about the money.'

'What money?'

'Payments that Sophia wanted. Unaccountable sums of cash that she needed to pay out to agents, chiefs... others she had to blackmail to get what she wanted.'

Joe said, 'Which was... what did she want?'

'Numerous things, shipping schedules, gold bullion, paper money—dollars, sterling, euros—route movements. Money, always the money. Distribution heads, their families. She needed to know if they could be bought or blackmailed.'

Joe was nodding with all this new intel.

'What about Windrush? Why kill him?'

DuPont laughed. 'Because he was weak. The double o agent Joe Delph was on his back, he was ready to crack, to tell all. Sophia couldn't take the risk, so she had to exterminate him.'

'And the taxi driver, for fuck's sake, why him?'

'You don't know how Sophia works. She has a rule she always abides by, leave no witnesses that may one day come back to haunt you.'

Joe bent down and whispered in his ear.

'You have saved your right leg, now save your left. Tell me about the meeting in London.'

'What is there to tell? Only that Sophia went to collect a case containing fifty thousand pounds sterling. Like I've already told you, it was always about the fucking money.'

'Tell me about the place where the meeting with the Fly was held?'

DuPont hesitated, then uttered, 'Two weeks back, we had to wear the blindfold again. Another night meeting. We were taken by car somewhere, I don't know where.'

'Taken by car from where?'

'From the O'Neils' place. We were driven for a good half hour, bit of a shit hole of a place.'

'How was that?'

He again hesitated; Joe poked him.

'Like I said, we were blindfolded. But the smell was overpowering, like rotting meat, blood.'

'Sounds like a place you'd crawl out of, you murdering fucker.'

He slapped DuPont on the back of his head.

'I do what I'm fucking told, man, I've no say.'

'Okay, go on.'

'Where was I... oh, like I say a shit house, close to the sounds of trains speeding past, same distorted voice, like it was coming at you from underwater. This time he'd promised Sophia an enormous sum of five hundred thousand dollars in cash, laundered, probably out of the Caymans or some Swiss account. Sophia received a part-payment of one hundred thousand dollars, which she put into an old joint account.'

'Who else was named on the account?'

DuPont took a moment to gather his thoughts, and realised there was no benefit to withholding. 'What the Fuck. I'm finished. We're finished.'

'The account was one of my father's old Swiss accounts.'

Joe was slightly thrown by this. 'Your father? Why have you not mentioned his involvement before?'

'Because a set of SAS and SEAL agents shot him dead. He died before I was born, shot in an ambush in Mexico.'

'Your father was a notorious drug runner shot while making crystal methamphetamine, big blue, blue magic, whatever you want to name it.'

Joe stepped away and gathered the team. 'It all adds up now, she certainly had more than her revenge, all those fucking good men and women she helped send to their graves. What a pair of evil bastards they were.'

Ryona said, 'Have we got all that we came for?

'Guess so.'

Ryona drew her pistol walked to the hooded figure and fired it into the hood. Francois DuPont was no more. The body slumped to the ground and a slow flow of blood emerged from under the hood.

'We've caught the workers, now let's have the queen,' said Joe with a note of satisfaction. 'I'll get the cleaners in. We're certainly keeping them busy.'

Joe could not believe what Francois had told them, that this Fly, now thought to be male, was so high on the SIS ladder. How high remained to be seen.

Joe believed their target must be in the top five. MI5 or MI6, toss a coin, take your pick. He couldn't believe it was Sir Kenneth Boblington, top drawer in the Foreign Office, second only to the Foreign Secretary. The man had distinguished himself in Irish affairs as well as the capture of Saddam Hussein. Did Windrush know who he was? Had he tried to get help from him after Joe's suspicions? Whose boots had the colonel been polishing?

Norm broke into his thoughts.

'What are you thinking? Maybe we can help out.'

'What am I thinking?'

He clapped his hand to his forehead.

'My thoughts are who the fuck is pulling the strings, our strings, who's been sitting back watching our every move? Perhaps listening to our conversations?'

Ryona said, 'Whoever it is must have made one mistake somewhere along the line, something that we've missed.'

Tony said, 'I don't see how we could have missed anything. But, you know what? This has been running for over twenty years, but not with the Fly, who I believe is a recent addition. The clue lies in a recent operation. There's no way he's been around the last twenty years.'

Norm shook his head. 'I don't know, Tony, Jenny Dilcox/ Sophia has been all around the clock. She'd have been still ticking if we hadn't stopped her. So although you could be right about a new face, we must not turn our backs on the old.'

Tony raised a hand to Norm. 'Yes, there's many a good tune played on an old fiddle.'

Joe said, 'Lets face it, it could be any one of them upstairs, anyone who has the privilege to go into files, reports, operations without suspicion.'

He put up a finger and wagged it.

'We leave nobody out, no stone unturned, and we watch each other's back. We stay safe, trusting only ourselves.'

Roberto said, 'You know, DuPont could have been lying. We all heard him say "What the fuck, I'm finished". He could have been having us chasing our tails by diverting our investigation away from the Fly, knowing he was finished.'

The team considered this new angle.

Roberto said, 'There's one way of checking. Whoever met Sophia and son in Paris—if it was someone from Vauxhall—had to have had a flight booked around that time.'

Joe said, 'There will be some kind of record, likely in expenses. If there is then we'll find it.'

Ryona warned, 'Wouldn't it be better to keep it in house? Use our man in archives, John Barlow?'

Joe put up a thumb. 'Yes, it's in-house. I can sense the rat sliding back into his sewer, till he's ready to strike again.'

Roberto agreed. 'It's like the feelings I sometimes have since the horror of nine eleven... the feeling that they'll be back to hit America again, only harder next time.'

26

THROW THE DOGS A BONE

The Kilburn Irish community wanted answers over the disappearance of the O'Neil family, their guards, Thomas Coyne and all his staff at the Five Leaf Clover. The Metropolitan Police were bombarded with calls. New Scotland Yard joined the search, sharing control with MI5. The whole situation was getting out of hand.

There were rumours of a rival gang takeover, of foreign incursions, even kidnapping for ransom. The national newspapers and TV channels were reporting every possible scenario, no matter how unlikely, to keep the story going. One said the family had been seen holidaying in Bermuda; others said they were back in Ireland. All stabs in the dark. Only some Irish newspapers—that had the inside track on O'Neil activities—were saying that the O'Neils were most likely dead.

Two weeks after their disappearance, the New IRA were as clueless as everybody else, but feared the worst. They also feared the backlash from their brothers in arms. The disappearance of twelve people—the O'Neils, no less—was embarrassing to say the least. The extended O'Neil family in Castlebar, County Mayo, decided to take matters into their own hands, and sent Billy's brother, Peter John, across the water to bash some heads and discover the truth. What Peter John found was that Uncle Billy's chair had already been taken by a commander named Sean Nolan.

'Who voted you top dog?' said Peter John. It came out as a threat. Everything from Peter John came out as a threat.

'Get the fuck out of my brother's chair or suffer the consequences,' he said.

Nolan, after stammering out apologies, got out of the chair—and suffered the consequences anyway. He was never seen again.

As NIRA's west coast commander, Peter John was one iron-fisted ruler. A hard bastard by any other name. Many said he was more intimidating than younger brother Billy. Despite this, Peter John was a master tactician in the art of fundraising for the cause. That meant drugs, money laundering and his personal favourites, bank robbery and house raids in which he divested the wealthy of their art and antiques and dispersed them to willing buyers throughout Europe and North America.

Back in the day, he was the first to be offered the London job, which he declined. The committee then offered it to Billy, who justified their decision by consolidating the London crew and streamlining the operation. Peter John loved the hurling and the smell of peat fires too much to leave the west of Ireland, and had no intention of living with the fucking Brits. He even turned down regular offers of fundraising trips over the pond to New York City. This he gave to his great friend Brendan Murphy, the one man he trusted, their friendship going back to Bloody Sunday 1972 when the two unarmed men watched the British paras shoot and kill twenty-six demonstrators. Peter John would never forgive or forget that day.

Peter John always felt anxious in London, a feeling that he was on the enemy's patch, so passed on the Billy O'Neil investigation to a trusted comrade. Liam O'Brian, currently in a joint command in Cork, had family in Liverpool, so Peter John sold the job to him on the basis that he would be closer to his family for the duration. Liam could also take his personal soldier, the 'undertaker' Kevin Quinn. Liam's lieutenants would be Peter John's own sons, Ryan and Patrick. Their mission? To find Billy, and to get a result, even if it meant burning down the city of London.

Joe and the team arrived back in London. He was proud of how the team had worked in the Five Leaf Clover job, and they all took pleasure in the speculative news reports. Joe would do his best to stoke any and all media suppositions.

Meanwhile the team had two promising angles to investigate.

1 If the Fly was an MI6 mole, he would have had to travel from London for the meetings with DuPont and son. Action: check the expense claims.

2 One of the meetings was held within the stench of rotting meat and the sound of a railway line. Action: search abattoirs near railways.

Joe arranged with John Barlow for Ryona to go through the expense files, with a chance that something would come to light about the trip to Paris. It was tedious old-fashioned police work, but if there was anything to be found, John would help them find it.

Meanwhile Joe would take a look at the European possibilities with Roberto—recent visits to London from the continent, including all SIS involvement. Tony and Norman would do the rounds on the known abattoirs within a thirty mile radius of the city.

Before they all set off in different directions, Joe reminded them that the operation was in-house, closed shop. Even away from Anton Spicer.

Joe and Roberto managed to find the names of three agents and officer personnel that had made a trip from various European locations into London in the past month. Tony and Norman added that another six had flown London–Paris six months ago. Ryona and John Barlow produced half a page of names who had claimed expenses from jaunts to France.

Joe arranged a bug-free interrogation room to be put at their disposal—bars on the window, minimal furniture, which gave a certain urgency to the job in hand. Their first meeting was to share intel and plan the next move.

Tony stood next to a display board on which a map of the South of England had been pinned. With a small cane, he pointed in the general direction of Essex.

'It took Norm and me three hours to cover all the slaughterhouses within our catchment area and came across one that we both thought to be the most likely DuPont was referring to. It's situated in a rural position with an express rail track cutting across open grassland to its rear. It's called the Davidson Meat Company.'

Joe looked surprised at the swiftness of the assignment.

Norm added, 'There were a couple more likely candidates, but too far out of London. DuPont had said it was within a half hour drive.'

Tony continued, 'So if you're looking for the favourite then'—he tapped the cane over the map—'this ticks all the boxes.'

Joe said, 'Okay, go pay them a visit. Best you call as health inspectors, say you've had a report on their meat being unfit for human consumption. I'll get Vernon Sykes to run us a couple of fake IDs and the necessary inspection warrants.'

Ryona went next. 'Barlow and I went through the expense sheets on flights taken by Vauxhall's elite during the last six months, mainly Heathrow–Charles de Gaulle. We have come up with a list of five names who surrendered expense requests. These five were whittled down to two that could possibly have been in Paris six months ago.'

'You've got our attention,' said Joe. The others laughed.

'One was Jenny Dilcox, the other was the SIS foreign office representative, Miles Cawthorn.'

Nobody was familiar with the name. Ryona filled them in.

'Cawthorn is a thirty-seven-year-old who has moved quickly up the executive ladder. The type who wants to be king of the castle.'

Joe thought this most interesting and asked Ryona to get to know more about the man, why he had taken that flight, and whether he had accompanied Jenny Dilcox.

Roberto was up next. His role was to check the flights from Europe and North America into Heathrow during the last month by either SIS or CIA. He had discreetly asked General Porter in Berlin to go through the necessary channels to get the information to him. He produced names and dates of nine possibles, which they had cut down to three names of the most likely candidates.

One was Anton Spicer who Joe had asked to take over Colonel Windrush's old office while their operation was ongoing. Without any hesitation Joe took his name off the list. Of the other two, Pat Taylor had been sent by the general to represent him at a SIS–CIA convention that had taken place at the Grosvenor Hotel. The general absence was due to some urgent matter in relation to the Pentagon.

Last of the three was another up-and-coming CIA agent, a thirty-four-year-old out of San Francisco: Tyrone Williams. He'd been having some success apprehending several operatives of the Mexican drug cartel, and had been sent over the pond to discuss the rapidly developing situation in worldwide drug trafficking.

'So, anyone got any ideas on these characters? Who's your money on?'

Norman said, 'Mine's on the favourite, Joe, at an odds-on starting price.'

Joe smiled. 'Who might that be?'

'This new guy, this San Francisco whirlwind. The golden boy whose gone flying up the America rankings.'

In answer to some questionable looks, he continued.

'Okay, he's not been around for thirty years, but that doesn't mean he ain't the Fly. Thirty years ago we were not getting these heavy duty ransom demands. These have come most recently. Sorry guys, but he's my man, he's young, fresh and ambitious—in all the wrong ways.'

Joe gently shook his head. 'Here's me thinking this guy is your all-American dreamer.'

Roberto said, 'Can't believe that you Brits are going all-American on this, especially after the Sophia–Francois, mother and son partnership. For me, I don't think so. I'll tell you for why. I know this guy, he's new, an ambitious, hardworking career freak. I'm thinking he's had about five years with the CIA. He comes out of Langley, his father's one of the high-ranking officers there. Tyrone, he's racing up the charts, making his father proud.'

He turned to Norman. 'No, Norm, you're out, not even making first base on Williams.'

Norman defended his choice. 'No disrespect, Roberto, but who else could it be?'

Ryona put in her two pennies' worth. 'I think Roberto could be right, that we should look elsewhere. Williams reminds me of David Carter. He wanted to make his family proud.'

Norman shrugged. 'Maybe you're right, but if it's not Williams, then who?'

Joe tried a different tack. 'Let's put aside these killings for a moment and consider the money angle. Remember what DuPont told us about his mother? It was always about the money. This Fly has been demanding a ransom amounting to billions of dollars, pounds, euros. Don't you fuckers see? It's all about the money.'

Ryona nodded. 'Joe's right, Sophia is gone, out of the game. But when she was active she was buying information on gold bullion runs, pickups of large bank cash transfers. Yes, it is about the money. I'm going to take a closer look at Miles Cawthorn.'

Joe nodded and turned to Tony.

'Do you remember Operation Fortress two years back? The big robbery that went down in Guildford with forty million stolen, of which only a few thousand pounds was recovered? What do we know about that?'

Norman said, 'I was called in on it, we caught and convicted two of the gang. They got ten years, eight to go. They didn't grass on the others, who are probably living the good life in South America, Cyprus or Spain. The prisoners meanwhile are having their families looked after. The price paid for their silence.'

Joe said, 'Yes, makes sense. So how come they haven't been eliminated? Why are they still receiving these benefits that could well be avoided if the receivers were no more?'

Ryona suggested, 'That's because these prisoners have something on them—documents, videos put away in safety deposit boxes, or in some solicitor's office.'

Norman asked, 'So are we saying that the Fly was involved in the Fortress robbery, and that he's been running for over two years?'

Joe said, 'Could well have been. The drone robbery in the States, the kidnapping of the chemists, this wasn't a two-minute job, this was a well planned operation that required plenty of cash.'

Roberto said, 'So we could be taking on an army?'

Joe said, 'Let's face it, guys, the Fly ain't doing this alone —the yacht, crew, plus bringing in the Wolf cartel. It all had to be bought and paid for with cash and promises. This is bigger than we thought.'

Tony said what they were all thinking. 'We're going to need help on this.'

Joe said, 'We've got to go beyond our five likely candidates. We have to give some serious thought to a plan, a plan that gives us the chance of a favourable result.'

Norman asked, 'Who can we bring in? We don't know who the fuck is who in that office of ours.'

Joe smiled. 'That's why we bring in an outside force.'

'Who did you have in mind?' said Norm, with a coffee in hand.

Joe smiled. 'The New IRA!'

Norman nearly choked. 'You are joking, Joe. You're seriously thinking of bringing in the IRA to *help* us? You've got to be losing it.'

Tony added, 'Surely that's taking one hell of a risk.'

'Not such a risk when you think they're already out there looking for the O'Neils.' He winked at his own audacity. 'We throw the dogs a bone.'

Ryona said, 'We set them up against each other?'

'That's not all, we give those two doing the ten-year stretch something to worry about, letting them know that the

IRA are looking into their missing people, that they happen to know who may have them.'

Ryona cottoned on. 'That being the Fly and his bullion robbers. They take the blame. Nice, I like it.'

Roberto said, 'Of course they start to panic, knowing we could give their names to the Irish and knowing what will happen if we did. It's a humdinger of a play.'

Joe said, 'Cawthorn, Williams, it's possible, but would these young bucks be able to take on the old establishment?'

Norman chirped up. 'This Fly exterminated top mobsters, along with Stacy Kilmer, Frank Bitten, George Kelly and God knows how many more.'

He turned to Ryona. 'I'm not leaving out David, Ryona. Okay? Poor guy's first job, but he wasn't a dead brain. Come on, guys, this Fly's no flash in the pan, I'm thinking he's young and energetic, he's ambitious, he's fucking smart.'

Tony said, 'So let's go find out. What you say you and me go take a look at Davidson's slaughterhouse?'

Joe, clapped his hands to signify the end of the meeting.

'Yes, we've all got a job to do. Anything of interest you phone, on crimson, but only if it's urgent. We meet tonight eight sharp. Let's hope somebody gets a green light.'

After an hour's briefing from a retired meat hygiene inspector, Tony and Norman found themselves dressed in white coveralls walking into the yard of Davidson Meat Company. On their chests were pinned identification tags, showing their photographs, names and "Inspector British Meat Marketing Board". They approached a teenager who was looking at a holiday brochure, smoking a cigarette under a sign that read "Reception. No Smoking".

In the presence of two strangers with name tags and clipboards he stood to attention. Norman told him to put the cigarette out and to fetch someone in authority sharpish.

He made a quick call to his boss who came to the office. Tony informed him that they had received a report that contaminated meat had been sold by Davidson's and consequently they had come to inspect their storage freezers and take meat samples for testing. With the threat of closure hanging over him, the manager was eager to help in any way he could.

Norman took cuts from various packs of beef, pork, lamb and venison for 'laboratory testing'. He then suggested they went to his office and finish signing the documentation and issue receipts. As they took the stairs the windows shook from a passing express train. The two agents did not have to say out loud what they were both thinking.

They entered the office. Tony scanned the room for the chairs that Francois and Sophia must have used. Norman signed the report sheet and casually asked if customers would be allowed into this office. The manager, somewhat caught out by the question, replied that it was used only by him and his staff.

'Why would you want to know that?'

'In case someone from outside had brought something in on their shoes or clothing.'

The manager seemed satisfied with the answer.

Norman asked, 'What happens when you're not here?'

The manager was quick to reply that only he and his foreman had a key.

With that, Norman gave him a temporary all clear to continue production.

Once back in the Jeep, Norm asked, 'What did you think of our manager?'

Tony said, 'I think he's okay, more concerned about his job. But this foreman, now I'd like a look at him. He could be the doorman that let in the Fly.'

'Let's chew it over during dinner with those meat samples. You must have thirty steaks there, brother.'

'All the perks of being a meat marketing inspector!'

Ryona went once more to meet up with John Barlow to try to make a connection between Jenny Dilcox and Miles Hawthorn with regards to flights taken to Paris. John ventured up from his basement domain to greet Ryona. He was becoming quietly attached to this striking young woman. Her intelligence and attitude reminded him of his daughters, someone he could trust. John had already been briefed on what she was looking for and had searched the expense claims for the month that would match the Paris meeting. He already had the results, which he handed to her.

'It's the best I could do in the time, but I'll continue checking.'

'Thanks, John,' said Ryona, and kissed him his cheek.

She returned to Vauxhall with the list firmly stashed in her shoulder bag.

Joe and Roberto high-tailed it to HMP Whitemoor in Cambridgeshire. They were given permission to interview the two men convicted of the bullion heist. They were allowed two one-hour sessions. The warden had put aside the prison officers' games room for the interviews.

One would be with Mouse Moran, of Irish heritage, known as Cheese; the other was Toby Henderson. Both were former employees of Fortress Securities, who were the insiders in the heist.

Mouse Moran was up first. He was brought in and sat at a card table. Joe and Roberto sat opposite. Moran seemed unconcerned by their unusual interruption to his day, his eyes looking everywhere except at the two agents. He turned to look at the prison officer who had positioned himself at the door.

'So who the fuck's the Everly Brothers, Pearson?' said Mouse. 'What the fuck they want?'

Joe leant over and grabbed Moran by his shirt and pulled him face to face. He gave Moran the Glasgow kiss, a sharp head butt.

'Listen, you fucking little piece of shite. You fucking talk to me, not Pearson.'

Roberto called to the guard, 'Go take a coffee break, Pearson. Give us half an hour, okay?'

The guard left the room. Moran, his nose showing a trickle of blood, shouted to the departing guard, 'Hey man, you can't leave me with these sick bastards, I want to see the fucking warden, now.'

Joe snarled, 'See what you did, Moran, you fucking head butted me.' Then turning to Roberto, 'You see what he tried to do to me, brother?'

'What the fuck you guys want?'

Moran leaned his head back and padded his nose with a handkerchief.

Joe, pleased with the effect of his blunt intervention, said, 'Oh, now we're listening. I'm here to ask you one question, Mouse, and you give me the right answer, then we're gone, you'll never see us again. But give us the wrong one, then your family, wife Janet, son Jack, daughter Wendy and eleven-month-old baby Monica... well, they ain't going to be too pleased with you.'

Moran's face turned a ghastly pale.

'What... you... trying to tell me? If it's the money, I know fuck all where it is.'

'That's not my question, did I ask you that?'

'Then what?'

Joe asked, 'Who set the job up? Who was the mastermind behind the heist?'

Moran. 'I don't—'

Joe interrupted. 'Don't tell me you don't know, Mouse, don't you dare say that, because if you fucking do... your family will be getting a call from the Undertaker. You've heard of him, haven't you, Mouse? He's looking for a family that your past employer has taken out, but then you being in here, you wouldn't know that, or would you?'

Roberto leant forward. 'Billy O'Neil, Mouse.'

Moran was clearly unnerved by the mention of the name.

'What the fuck's that got to do with me, man? I'm locked up for ten fucking years. I'm not with that crew anymore.'

Joe stood and nodded to Roberto. 'Okay, he's had his chance, let's get the fuck out of here. Tell the Undertaker Kevin Quinn to pay the Morans a visit, you've got the address in South Norwood, Croydon.'

Moran was now in a panic. 'We was called to meetings, we never got to see him, he came masked, like yer Ku Klux Klan, long white mask.'

Roberto asked, 'Where did these meetings take place?'

'Every fucking week he was at us. He wanted to know everything... timing, he was obsessed with time, synchronised watches, that kind of thing. We met in a large community hall, always after midnight, you had to be there on time. The man was fucking obsessed with it.'

'Where was this hall?'

Mouse replied, 'Always a different address, never the same, one time Walford, then Brent. All over fucking London.'

He looked at Joe, then Roberto, as if to say, *You've got to believe me.*

'Always these small halls, one time in a Chiswick Salvation Army place. But the guy in here with me, Henderson, he's sure to know more, he was a key holder.'

Joe asked, 'What's this key holder?'

'You know, man, a special, a fortunate, he had keys to the money holds, he was a selector, a distributor. Ask *him*, threaten *his* fucking family.'

Roberto smiled. 'Oh, we will.'

'Okay, Mouse, you keep that mouth of yours shut. If the other cons ask why we had you in, say we were after the money.'

Mouse nodded gratefully.

As a final reminder, Joe jabbed a finger at him. 'Think of your family, Mouse.'

Toby Henderson's body language gave the impression that he had pre-knowledge of why Joe and Roberto had asked for the interview. He was brought limping into the room. He sat on the chair like he'd walked a marathon, like it was an effort, or maybe due to the fact that he was overweight. He sat staring at the two. The guard didn't need telling to leave the room.

Joe gave a smile. 'So here we have Toby Henderson, the great bullion robber.'

He didn't get a reply. 'Didn't get to spend any of the forty million though did we, Toby?'

'So I'm a poor man, you here to buy me an ice cream?'

Joe looked to Roberto. 'Hear that? Man wants a fucking ice cream.'

Roberto said, 'The guy's wanting something to cool him.'

Henderson, with a sick, smile nodded.

Joe said, 'Know what, brother, let's get one of our guys to pay a visit to his wife and kids with a whole carton of fucking Cornettos. Or does he favour Miser Softy?'

Roberto played along. 'It's got to be Mister Softy, why don't we send our friend Kevin Quinn around? The Undertaker, he likes his ice creams. You know Kevin, don't you, Toby?'

Henderson's eyes flashed on hearing the name. The smile left his face. Joe let the silence linger.

Henderson finally broke the silence. 'Okay, you're here with threats to my family, so what the fuck you want?'

Joe said, 'You gone off the ice cream, Toby? Don't want Kevin to call on 129 Sutton Drive?'

Toby was in a corner.

'I'm going to ask you one question,' said Joe, 'and you my friend better give me the fucking right answer, that's if you ever want to see your family again. You got me, ice cream man?'

Henderson, chin on chest, nodded.

Joe leant in close. 'Who planned the bullion heist?'

Henderson shook his head. 'Names I don't know, like I don't know yours.'

'Tell me what you know about them: features, ages, hair, skin colour, anything.'

Henderson said, 'When they called a meeting, they came masked, but he couldn't disguise his voice, though he tried. He put on a Scottish accent, but he was English as the Tower of London. She would bring him to the meetings in a dark blue Jaguar. Beautiful motor. Always wearing a headscarf and dark glasses. She would drop him off, then when the talk was over, pick him up.'

'She?'

'His wife maybe, your guess is as good as mine. She could well have been the boss, number one. He was a good six foot, athletic-looking guy.'

Henderson pointed at Roberto. 'About his age, not too unlike him, come to think, mask him up he'd sure as hell look like him.'

'Go on.'

'What I can tell you is that I have an idea of where they were living.'

Joe was now all ears. He eased his tone to gain Toby's confidence. 'How come, Toby?'

'Trouble was, no one wanted to take the risk of getting caught.'

Roberto caught Joe's eye and shrugged. 'Understandably.'

'So one of the lads suggested we put a tracer on the Jag, which we did.'

'So where did it lead you, the Jag?'

'Grosvenor Road, Pimlico apartments. Oh, and here's a thing, I have the registration number. Nothing was left out. Well you want to be sure, like I said. When there's forty mill at stake you have to know which bank, who're the bankers.'

Joe was jumping cartwheels inside but remained calm in case Toby clammed up. 'You sure do, Toby. The number?'

'We okay on this Quinn the undertaker? I'm needing your word... my family mean everything to me.'

Joe nodded. Toby hesitated before recalling the registration number. 'WH68 WBO.'

Roberto scratched his chin. 'How come you remember the reg?'

Henderson smiled. 'WH, I got as Working Horse... 68 was the year Martin Luther King was assassinated... WBO is for World Boxing Organisation. Simple when you've got a system.'

Toby Henderson's eyes darted between them both. 'My family... are they good now, no Kevin Quinn?'

Roberto winked. 'For now.'

27

WHEAT FROM THE CHAFF

The team travelled the three and a half hours back to Doncaster, their comfortable Yorkshire base camp, where they could debrief on progress in all the strands of the investigation.

For her part, Ryona was glad to be back in the company of Roberto Veneto. He brought a unique perspective to the traditional MI6 approach to the work. She was becoming quite interested in the man, but then she knew little about him. Perhaps that was part of the attraction. It wasn't a situation where people could get close to colleagues with regards to a serious relationship. She was still painfully aware of how Joe was suffering, still grieving over the loss of Stacy Kilmer. She could not take what he was going through.

Joe was pleased with confirmation that Davidson's was almost certainly the location of the meeting with the Fly, so he suggested Tony and Norman continue working on the meat factory. Go for the night foreman. Put some Irish pressure on him. Discover who he allowed in for that meeting two years ago. Use the tried and trusted family threat routine.

The new information gleaned from Toby Henderson needed to be followed up: the Grosvenor Road address and the Jaguar was a major breakthrough. Joe was looking for anything that could ostensibly tie the Fly to the O'Neil disappearance. What he was coming to realise was the team would need the Irish when it came to bringing down the final curtain. What he didn't want was a bloodbath on the streets of Little Venice. He needed to lure the two parties out into the countryside, away from the city. His ploy was to inform the NIRA that the Fly had exterminated Billy and his family, that they'd butchered them in the Davidson factory, and that they were planning another heist, for sixty million in paper money.

The Fly and his entourage would have to be tempted back into their domain, like the 2013 Cannes Carlton Hotel jewel heist where he got away with $136 million. Not bad for a job that took only a few minutes from start to finish. He also thought of The Hague Museum diamond heist eleven years before, a haul of another $12 million. Roberto also recalled the 2007 Dar es Salaam Bank heist in Baghdad—another $182 million. Whoever the Fly was, he was a class above any thief Joe had ever heard of.

But then most thieves that Joe knew about did not lower themselves to sadistic murders. The Fly and his kind had to be annihilated. They were the devil's soldiers. It would be no easy task.

But like a queen bee, this insect would always be safely protected and constantly fed by the workers. One thing Joe was sure of, the Fly was not Ivor Stravenski, the Moscow Pakham. He'd been in many violent situations with the Bratva king. Ransoming the world with a virus was not his style. The deaths of his brigadiers told Joe that he, too, was frightened for probably the first time in his life.

Joe was up against a master operator and had to lure him into a trap with clever bait. As Francois DuPont had said under interrogation, 'With them, it was always about the money.'

Joe presented Ryona with a set of car keys.

Taken aback, she said, 'I've got a car?'

She looked at the Saab key fob.

'Same make as that aunt of mine.'

Joe smiled. 'Same make, same colour, same car. You're her family, it's yours, you being the only known relative. Come to think of it, you get the cottage too.'

'I suppose it will come in useful.'

'You and Roberto can use the Saab for the Pimlico apartment investigation.'

Norman asked, 'What about you, chief, what are you going to use?'

'A Range Rover courtesy of Terry Grainger out of SIS vehicle distribution. Once owned by our good friend Colonel Windrush. It's waiting for me in the Vauxhall parking bay.'

'All right for some,' said Norm.

Joe looked at all their cynical expressions, before adding, 'I know what you're all thinking, but I can assure you I'm *not* the fucking mole.'

They all laughed.

Norman joked, 'Hey, I need to swap my partner, I'm beginning to worry about the man.'

He winked at Joe before turning to Roberto. 'You're a lucky man too, Roberto, having a swell chick like Ryona for a partner. Let me know if you fancy a swap.'

Ryona cut in. 'You know something, Norm, why don't you get yourself a *Readers Wives* magazine. Could be something in there to please such a lovesick man.'

Norman nodded. 'I've got a few, but nothing in them interests me. I wish I'd stuck to reading the *Dandy*.'

Tony and Norman arrived at the abattoir shortly before the 10 p.m. night shift was due to start. They waited in a side street watching the night crew arriving. They were about to drive into the yard when a white Ford Transit turned in. Through high-powered binoculars the agents could see two men get out and open the back doors of the van for an approaching fork-lift truck that was carrying three large pallets of pre-packed beef.

Tony took a camera with a long-range lens and photographed the whole operation. They could see a stocky man receiving a package from the van driver, who he slapped on the back. The men closed the doors and left. The overweight man scanned the yard before re-entering the factory.

Tony jotted down the van's registration. 'Looks like our foreman is stealing from the company. We can't allow that now can we?'

'We can twist a knife into those flabby ribs,' said Norm.

Tony drove up to the door the man had entered. They both checked their holstered Glock 19 and exited the vehicle.

In the yard they were met by a youth coming out of the factory door with cigarette in hand. They put the fear of God into him and he took off out of the yard. The two agents entered the packing room, crammed with a line of wrapping machines and folded cardboard boxes, but empty of staff.

The forklift driver had locked the door behind him and disappeared through a hard plastic curtain into another section. They let him go and headed towards the office light shining onto the stairs. A faint sound of country music drifted from the office. Tony took to the stairs, Norman close behind providing cover. The glass in the office window shuddered as they heard and felt the force coming from an express train thundering by.

Having reached the top of the stairs, Tony stopped for a moment. The only sound was that dreadful music. Tony pointed down to a short landing where the office door stood ajar. They both bent down and silently crept along the passage towards the door. Tony bobbed up for a quick glance through the internal window into the room. He could see the foreman sitting in the manager's chair, chin on chest, apparently asleep. On the desk, a monitor display of different sections of the factory. The two agents quickly scanned the four images on screen: the butchery, packaging, reception, gate and car park. They returned their attention to the feed from the butchery and looked closer. In between two sides of beef, three men in overalls were hanging from meat hooks.

'What the fuck's gone down here, Norm?'

Norm raised his weapon and walked over to the sleeping foreman, then lifted his chin with the barrel of the Glock. 'Not sleeping. He's a goner.'

A puncture to his neck was seeping blood onto his white shirt collar.

They both raced back down the stairs, crossed the factory floor and pushed through the plastic strip curtain into the chiller, surrounded by carcases, both animal and human. The forklift driver was huddled in a corner, sobbing. The young man pointed to one of the bodies on a hook. 'That's my brother. Why kill them for a few lousy pounds of meat?'

Tony patted him on the shoulder. 'That's what we aim to find out.'

Two hours later, after taking the man home and pulling rank on the local police, they headed back to London.

In the car, Norman said, 'The killers must know what's been going down, that we are on to them. The man wants all possible holes in the bucket sealed. No leaks make for fewer problems, Tony.'

'How did they knew we were picking out Davidsons?'

'They must have been alerted on our first visit, someone from inside the factory.'

'Who was probably one of the poor souls hanging on that meat hook.'

Norman said, 'That was only the night shift. We have the day workers to consider, too.'

Having dropped Joe at the Vauxhall headquarters, Ryona and Roberto continued to Pimlico Apartments. On the way, Joe updated them on the abattoir murders, which had been called in.

Joe warned them to watch their backs. Perhaps the Fly had been tempted out of hiding earlier than expected.

The apartment building concierge was in his early fifties and, to the agents' good fortune, was the epitome of a nosey doorman. He accepted their false names and fake IDs without really looking. Ryona questioned him about how long he'd been in the job and passed him a list of dates and people who were either residents or renters, and she described the dark blue Jaguar saloon.

The concierge recognised some of the descriptions and told them that there had been a couple in their early forties who rented a third floor apartment for two months. The concierge was a curious fellow who then went on to compare the couple to movie stars.

'The woman had an Italian appearance; Claude Cardinale springs to mind. The man had the rugged look of Charles Bronson. The pair of them could have walked out of the movie *Once Upon a Time in the West*. They rented under the names Thomas and Greta Dorsey. They stayed two months before they and the Jag were gone. During that time they did not receive or bring a single visitor to the apartment. Spoke hardly a word to anyone... with one exception: old Barry Woodward in apartment thirty-two. Nice old guy, mid-eighties, retired, used to work in aerodynamics. Barry told me how he missed their friendship. Told me he wanted to drop them a line or call them. Of course they didn't leave one, or any forwarding address. People come, people go in my work.'

When Ryona could get a word in, she asked if they could see Barry in thirty-two.

'I'll give him a tinkle,' said the eagerly helpful concierge.

The phone rang and rang. 'That's strange, I've not seen Barry go out,' he said. 'When he leaves he always stops for a natter, usually about cricket.'

Roberto suggested that he go check on the old guy as he may have had a fall or a heart attack. The concierge beckoned the two agents to follow him into the lift.

A minute later he was tapping on Barry's door. No answer, but they could hear a TV or radio.

Ryona asked, 'You got a pass key?'

'Of course, dear.'

Roberto urged, 'Well come on, man, let's get in there.'

The small apartment was soon searched. Roberto found the old man, fully clothed, submerged in a bath full of bloody water.

The concierge broke down.

'Looks like our friend is leaving no witnesses,' said Ryona. 'They're cleaning out their lockers, Roberto. What's next?'

28
FOOL'S GOLD

The view over the Thames from Anton Spicer's Vauxhall office always reminded Joe Delph of the Great Sphinx of Giza with its outstretched paws. Joe and Spicer had their chairs turned to the large window between the two bullet-nosed towers from where they somehow felt part of the non-stop river traffic.

Joe gazed towards Westminster. 'They're out there, Anton, fucking laughing at us.'

Spicer nodded like a sage. 'I still believe we are missing out on something, Joe, it's right in front of our noses and we can't see it.'

'You think *it* is right here in this building? Another mole?'

Spicer rubbed his chin. 'I do. He, or she, still has a source of information coming out of here. Who's telling teacher out of class?'

Joe gave a light shrug. 'In-house security is tight, Ant. My team have been together for quite a while, so it's not them. The only others privy to all the shenanigans are the cleaners, and you know they're hand-picked by Harry Parker, so you can bank your granny on them.'

Anton gave something close to a smile. 'Guess that leaves me, Joe. I'm the only fucker left.'

'You know something, Anton, I don't have a closer friend here than you. If I thought you were the Fly you would have been dead by now.'

Joe turned his attention to the sting. He discreetly requested the use of a bullion cargo house. Gatwick Airport had obliged. A series of large steel containers had been parcelled together to form a convincing looking bullion vault to give the impression that the hangar was a temporary hold, a short-term deposit box. Encircled by a tall electrified fence, it had been positioned a quarter mile away from the nearest runway, close to a B-road which led eventually to the M23.

The news of its whereabouts and contents of $65 million in gold and paper money could now be fed to the underworld. A slip of the tongue by super-nark Lenny Jameson on the street was all that was required. The bullion and cash were awaiting shipment, destination Berlin, scheduled to leave in the coming month of August, three weeks away.

The hoard was held in a central position 200 metres from the double gates that stood inside a fenced yard. The area was patrolled by four armed guards. What the raiders didn't know was that the crates contained lead blocks, with the top layers spray-painted gold.

Roberto Veneto brought in ten CIA agents from Europe as extra muscle, who were oblivious to the fake switch; their role was to act as airport security staff. Joe was hoping that it wouldn't come down to a bloodbath, that the Fly would have been caught by the remaining members of the O'Neil family well before a raid on the airport.

The loss of the yacht and its load would have hit the Fly hard. The virus drop was abandoned, the drones back in the USA, the *Doonata* in a secure Navy dockyard, and its crew dead or locked away awaiting trial. He would want some kind of rebate, wanting to show his strength, regain respect for his recent embarrassments. And he would need some cold hard cash to sponsor any new undertaking.

Joe was unsure of the couple who had rented the Pimlico apartment. His sense was that the man who had presided over the meetings, hooded as he may have been, could not have been the Fly—close to him, perhaps, a servant but not the puppet master. Joe could not reconcile the image of the Fly that he had created in his own mind with the couple renting an apartment in central London. And killing the old man in a bathtub? Not his style. Perhaps it was fanciful on his part that he saw the Fly living in a large house high on a hill, overlooking a grand estate. On the other hand, he had been involved in enough episodes to know that missions were not always made successful by logic alone. Sometimes he had to trust his instincts. Still, their investigation had brought them closer to the mysterious couple and a step higher up the ladder.

Was the Fly involved somehow with SIS? He was still privy to information from Vauxhall despite the demise of both Sophia DuPont and Colonel Windrush. So who was the mole?

Meanwhile they prepared for an assault at the Gatwick from players unknown.

Their informer, Lenny Jameson, knew of one safe breaker who would be called for if the raid was on. His name was Ugly Bennet, the underworld's master peterman. Ugly had been used in some of Europe's biggest heists. Consequently his luck ran out and he'd done time, care of Her Majesty's Prison Service. After his release he'd moved his family to

Northern Cyprus and bought a villa on the outskirts of Girne. He had also changed his name and was now known to a few as Harry Gibbs, Lenny being one of the few. Ugly no longer walked the floor, but was an in-demand consultant. His expertise was highly regarded throughout Europe, which had attracted a new moniker: the Opener.

'If there is to be a raid, Harry Gibbs will know about it,' said Lenny.

He had heard that Albanian gangsters had entered the UK. Gangs in London, Birmingham, Liverpool and Manchester, Newcastle and Glasgow were all on high alert. Lenny Jameson said the Albanian killers had already entered the country through the fishing port of Deal in Kent, and split into two mobs: one headed for the capital; the other travelled to a pre-booked holiday house near Crawley. Joe had some experience with such murderous Eastern Europeans. On occasions he'd fought face-to-face and was lucky to come out without a scratch, but not before putting a few six-feet under.

It was difficult to keep up with all the players, but one thing was certain: the Irish would not take kindly to receiving orders from anyone, least of all the Albanians. There was a rumble going down the corridors of UK organised crime and there was all to play for.

The house that could accommodate twelve people sat in a rural setting, its nearest neighbour three quarters of a mile away. A perfect hideaway for the Albanian gangsters led by the recently released Tigran Grigoryan after a five-year prison term for a casino heist in Monte Carlo. He had with him ten other individuals wanted for robbery, rape and murder. Grigoryan spread out a map on a large breakfast table and explained the operation and issued responsibilities to his crew.

One to drive the box van into the compound; another to assist. They will bulldoze the gates down.

'We have four guards to take out, then we take the gold.'

A trusted lieutenant shook his head.

'What gives? You not like what I'm saying?'

'There is nothing wrong with your plans, brother, but the prize of sixty million dollars in gold and paper, should come home with us. Why we hand over to this Fly? We take all the risks, he takes the money.'

Grigoryan looked to each of his men and could see there was strong support for keeping the haul. This new suggestion made sense. They had agreed to accept $1 million each on completion of the heist, which seemed fair payment when it was first offered. But now, why give this Fly some $50 million? Why not take it all back to Tirana? The initial plan was to take the haul to a plane waiting on a small airfield in Sussex. The fishing boat was no longer needed. They would sail away none the wiser. The waiting pilot was not one of their own, so he would need to be persuaded to change the flight plans. No problem; he will do as he's told. Besides, didn't his man, Arctur, have a pilot's licence. Yes, Arctur would fly them home.

He turned to his men with a wolfish smile. 'Okay, brothers, I go with your thoughts—mine too, I might add. We keep the heist, it goes home with us to Albania.'

The men gave a low cheer and patted Grigoryan on the back. His lieutenant said, 'You are right to do this, boss, you are greater than a Fly, you are a killer bee.'

In the mews house in Little Venice, Liam O'Brian and Kevin Quinn were having a briefing with the O'Neil brothers, Ryan and Patrick, together with six other soldiers of the NIRA.

The clan had given O'Brian complete control of the reprisal. It seemed simple to Liam: the complete wipeout of the Albanians using rocket launchers followed by automatic gunfire. The grapevine had told them that the Albanians were planning to hit a new holding vault in a hangar at Gatwick. The retaliation would act as a warning to others with thoughts of moving in on the Irish stable position in the UK.

The $60 million heist would also be there for the taking if the opportunity arose.

Peter John, on his Castlebar estate, had received a full report on O'Brian's plan of attack. He learned that the word on the street was that the Fly was involved in his brother's disappearance, that Billy O'Neil could well have been taken prisoner or worse. O'Brian would fuck up these Albanians then go after the Fly. Success of the double operation would confirm his new position as NIRA Commander in London.

Peter John's sons were not yet experienced in the killing games, so O'Brian had promised to keep a firm hold on the operation by instructing Kevin Quinn to keep them safe from harm. Knowing this, Peter John would sleep more easily.

The Coast Guard control centre confirmed the Albanians had entered the UK, after leaving the Belgian port of Blankenberge and landing at Deal.

Tony put down the phone. 'The Coast Guard say there was a people carrier waiting, last seen heading down the Dover road.'

Joe said, 'If they take the toll we should get them on CCTV. We know where they're heading but I'm interested in the vehicle to see if we can get a registration number.'

Norman said, 'Wouldn't think that it was rented, more like it was stolen.'

Roberto agreed. 'We ain't going to catch a Fly on a vehicle check, we need his address, we need to knock on his door.'

Joe said, 'Point taken, but we did follow a blue BMW and got Sophia and son, if you remember? Didn't we follow the Jaguar and get a hit on the apartment couple?'

The team knew he had made his point. 'Don't leave anything to chance. If it's buried, dig it out.'

Roberto, Norman and Tony drove to Gatwick to meet up with the ten agents who had flown in earlier that evening. The plan was that Ryona and Joe would remain outside the perimeter fence to observe the expected Irish intervention, and also to watch the Albanians' escape route back to the coast—if it came to that. Taking all options into account, Joe couldn't see that they would escape the same way they arrived. He was sure they would fly, especially with a cargo of gold bullion. There was one motorway out, but the channel tunnel was an unlikely possibility. They would need a transporter such as a cargo van with a false floor or removable side panels. Then again it was possible they had a hideaway, a storage unit that would hold the gold until things cooled down.

Joe asked for the team's thoughts. They all agreed that a flight was more likely.

But before that, a fierce battle was expected on two fronts. The first hit would be the compound attack, followed by an Irish onslaught. Such a loss would weaken the Fly and damage his reputation. The walls of his stronghold could then crumble into ruins. *Here's hoping*, thought Joe.

The night held the promise of rain and dark clouds drifted over Gatwick Airport as they drove the Jeep through the gates at Hangar 3. The gate man appeared in military camouflage carrying an MK 46 machine gun. He briefly checked in on Roberto, Norman and Tony, then waved the Jeep forward and pointed to a parking area beside the closed hangar doors. Tony waved to acknowledge him, but he was already gone. The man then faded into the night.

Norm said, 'You sure he's CIA, Roberto? Looked like a Ranger or Delta Force to me, MK 46 is not a CIA weapon, is it?'

'Let's go in and find out, Norm, I'm a little puzzled myself.'

They entered the hanger. Four men were sitting at a large table drinking coffee and eating bacon rolls. A man in battle dress—six foot, forty years of age, solid looking athletic frame—greeted Roberto.

'You must be Roberto? CIA? I'm Commander Barney Young, US Rangers Elite.'

Roberto took the commander's hand. 'Pleased to meet you, Commander. You said Rangers? Ain't I got no CIA agents?'

'You sure have, you got ten, along with six Rangers including myself. Your General Porter asked me to assist, said you could well need a little extra help. Those being his exact words.'

Roberto smiled. 'Welcome to our crazy world, Barry Young. Let's introduce you to two Brits, ex-Pioneers, SAS: Captain Tony Ford and Captain Norman Aimes.'

They all shook hands. Commander Young turned to the three men.

'These are my Rangers. I got two snipers on the roof, the best in the unit, probably in the United States Army, come to think of it.'

Roberto looked impressed. 'Where are my CIA?'

The commander laughed. 'One let you in, the others are in strategic positions around the compound. The only parts of their body showing are the eyes, I've told them to keep their mouths shut.'

Tony laughed. 'You must have dressed them well, Commander, the one at the gate was like a black ghost. I hope he can handle the MK he was carrying.'

Norman added, 'Didn't think the CIA had the MK in their weapon locker?'

'They don't, but we can't have our defence standing with pop guns on such an operation. These Albanians will be coming at us with AK-47s. Four of your men have an MK, the rest carry M4s. I hope you don't mind but in your absence I placed them in a bull horn pincer formation that I'm hoping will close on the enemy after entering.'

Norm interjected, 'They won't know what hit them.'

Roberto said, 'It seems you've got things moving, Commander, I really appreciate that, but you forgot one important thing.'

'Forgive me, but what might that be?'

Robert adopted a serious look. 'You forgot the bacon sandwiches.'

They had just finished eating the bacon banjos when a man entered, dressed like a walking lump of coal. Agent Stan Grainger, a Chicago friend of Roberto's, was hardly recognisable under his cloak of darkness.

Roberto called, 'That you, Stan?'

Stan lay down his automatic rifle and smiled, his white teeth glowing under his heavily blackened face.

Roberto turned to Barry. 'See what you mean, in asking them not to smile.'

They all laughed at the puzzled look on Stan's face.

'Nice to see you too, Roberto.'

'You've got one heavy call here, man, I've got half of fucking Europe out there in that compound with me.'

Roberto said, 'You're going to need them, Stan, we got some heavy action on its way to us.'

He pointed at Barney. 'We're going to need both of you and the boys. The Albanian killers are close and closing.'

Five miles away the Albanians were approaching Hangar 3 in two vans, the first of which, an eight-seater Transit, held ten men, each carrying an AK-47 with suppressor. Grigoryan shined a pencil torch onto a map that lay across his knees.

A Mercedes box van followed behind.

Grigoryan expected the Transit to receive heavy fire from the guards. If this shooting match went on for too long it could result in delaying the heist. He could not afford the operation to run over the thirty minutes he had allowed. The four guards had to be taken out swiftly, inside ten minutes, for there to be any chance of success. Grigoryan would need to keep casualties to a minimum while Ugly's man blew the containers to get to the gold.

Meanwhile the pilot for their escape aircraft would not wait beyond the agreed cut off time.

Three escape routes from the airport were already covered by Kevin Quinn's gorillas, each reachable via walkie-talkie. Quinn was almost licking his lips at the thought of stealing from a fresh heist. He had already arranged with a sympathiser who agreed to bury the gold on his land until needed. It was imperative they do not damage the transporter because it would be needed to deliver its cargo to its new resting place. All other vehicles were to be destroyed along with their passengers.

With fatherly care, he had protectively put each of the young O'Neil brothers on the road he thought least likely to be used by the Albanians. He did this for his friend and mentor, Peter John, and for his own self-preservation. The last thing he would want to report back to Mayo was the death or injuries of his sons, Ryan and Patrick.

Having first consulted with Liam O'Brian, Quinn was given the all-clear to go ahead with his plans. Kevin thought they would likely use the fastest route, the B road from Gatwick, M23 to M25. Kevin would hit them on the B road.

There was the sound of rolling thunder as the Transit van crept towards the gates of the compound. During a brief stop, the van had attached to its front a V-cut snow plough running bar.

Turning to his men, Grigoryan asked, 'You all set back there? You all ready to go for gold?'

A voice from the back replied, 'Ready as we'll ever be, boss. Let's go get some yellow rock.'

Grigoryan nudged the driver. 'Foot down hard, brother, hit them gates in the centre, we want no shit, pile a clear path through to that vault.'

He shouted back to the men. 'Ready with the rocket launcher. I want them fucking doors open to drive in. We have little time to do this, take the fork-lift from the box van, we need to lift those crates and away.'

He looked at each in turn. 'Our wounded we take, the dead we leave.'

A flash of lightning zig-zagged across the sky followed by a roll of thunder. Rain started to hammer on the Transit roof.

'This rain we don't need, for fuck's sake.'

Behind, the box van followed with only its side lights on, its wipers on top speed. The driver peered through the screen at the Transit's tail lights that were fast pulling away.

The driver turned to his navigator. 'I tell you now, brother, I'm not liking this job. Many of our brothers in London have told us of the dangers. This Fly, he's fucking laughing at us, that is why I'm in on this.' He smiled. 'We should pay him for the vehicle hire, that's all. Well maybe a little for his trouble.'

'I agree, but don't let Tigran Grigoryan hear you say that. He's a nasty bastard when he's angered.'

He snorted. 'That Fly, pay him for his fucking trouble? He has no trouble, it's us that's facing all the shit.'

On the simulated roof of the vault, two Rangers were lying behind sandbags, looking through night vision goggles at the approaching vehicles beyond the gate. Their M24 rifles were aimed at the oncoming targets. The only sounds were the patter of rain and the whine of the generator that powered the fence spotlights and makeshift office lighting.

The senior officer switched on his walkie-talkie communicator and turned to the live channel.

'Visitors at twelve 'o clock, five hundred metres and closing. Over.'

Barney Young received the message and turned to Roberto. 'We have spiders at twelve o' clock, Bob. How do you want to play this?'

Roberto looked to the others. 'Okay, Barney, let's get them inside, then hit them full force.'

Barney pressed the reply button. 'Let both vehicles in, then take out anything that moves. Over.'

He then handed the walkie-talkie to Roberto, and asked him to give an order for the positioned camouflaged agents to disable both vehicles by blowing out the wheels. Then concentrate on taking out the raiding party.

Roberto and the commanding warriors, Tony and Norman together with Barney and his Rangers, all expected the attack to come from a frontal position, but left nothing to chance. The agents concealed themselves in eight pits covered by camouflage tarps in a horseshoe formation aimed at the entrance, the two sides and the rear. A periscope acted as a back-up early warning system.

The Rangers crawled under the two armoured transportation vehicles, while Barney took the three agents to a dug-out on the right side of the vault.

Barney turned to Roberto. 'We go if called upon. We sit at twenty past twelve in our firing direction. We are the last hurdle.'

Norman gave a low hum. 'I know these Albanians, Barney, they'll fight to the last breath, and believe me they're good. Do not underestimate them.'

Barney smiled. 'Appreciate your warning, Norman. My Rangers are good, too.'

The Transit and box van came into view. Joe and Ryona stood in cover as they passed. Joe whispered, 'They've got to go now. See the transit? It's got a ramming bar attachment. They aim to smash down the gates.'

Ryona acknowledged him. 'Think our guys know?'

'Oh, they'll know all right, you can be sure our boys are up and ready. Once they're in, we close the door.'

Out of the silence, all hell broke loose.

It was at that moment the Transit changed down a gear and raced into the gates, which flew off their mountings. The box van brought up the rear. The compound echoed with an onslaught of automatic gunfire as both van windscreens exploded after suffering direct hits from rooftop snipers. The drivers and navigators lay dead across their dashboards, each taking a bullet to the head. An Albanian scrambled out of a door as a series of bursts of rapid fire came from both sides and took the wheel. The van's panels took a row of tracer bullets that cut through its aluminium sheeting like a knife through butter.

More passengers came stumbling out, falling in heaps, after taking more than fifty rounds of non-stop bullet penetration. Grigoryan fell heavily out of the van and crawled in the dirt, seeking sanctuary. The agents slowly walked up to him. His eyes closed; a deep gasp for breath; the man was no more.

Another attacker lay dying by the gate. The man clutched a photograph of a young girl as tears sprang from his eyes, which mixed with the light rain peppering his face.

Two miles away, Kevin Quinn and his men lay in wait on the B road for the return of the Albanians and the gold bullion. They heard the gunfire and held their positions until events became clearer. One of his runners came sprinting down the road, waving his arms frantically. The runner told Quinn of the ambush and the slaughter in the rain of the Albanian raiders by what looked like a small army.

Prudently Quinn decided to withdraw and await further news of the Albanian misfortune. They would have to forget the gold but continue their search for Billy O'Neil and his family. Was this the Fly's work? The Fly had all the answers to the missing Irish commander.

Back in the compound the strong smell of nitroglycerin hung in the air. The bodies of the Albanians were already being gathered and lined in a row against the vault unit. Roberto, Tony, Norman and Barney Young were taking in the carnage.

Joe and Ryona approached. 'How many?' asked Joe.

Roberto said, 'We took ten, no losses.'

He turned to Barney. 'Commander Barney Young had everything planned to perfection. Ten Albanians loaded with AK-47s plus a rocket launcher.' He smiled with satisfaction. 'They didn't get a shot off, we really fucked them.'

'Good job, Commander,' said Joe. 'The Fly's name is going to stink in Tirana, that's for sure. You mark my words, his castle is crumbling.'

Ryona warned, 'But the mole. The leaks, Joe, that's what we got to plug, surely?'

Roberto pointed to Ryona but looked at Barney. 'Ryona Steel, Barney, a peridot amongst the pyrites.'

29

FIVE TO CHECK

It was early morning in Little Venice and Kevin Quinn was explaining the misadventure of the previous evening to Liam O'Brian, who was, to say the least, puzzled with what he was hearing. Quinn related the evidence of his runner who witnessed the slaughter of the Albanians, that they had been ambushed with heavy automatic fire.

'The Albanians didn't get a kick of the ball,' said Quinn. 'There was a strong military presence and American vehicles were seen around Gatwick.'

Protecting the dollar? Possible. Or was there something else, something more important?

O'Brian asked if any of the known gangs had lately taken a liking for gold. Gangs, like themselves, but in desperate need of funding. Quinn thought it unlikely. It disgusted O'Brian that the Fly had to call in an Albanian set-up to do his dirty work.

'I'd like to kick the lot of them in the Baltics,' said O'Brian. 'We could have sorted that. One thing is for sure, we wouldn't have come away empty-handed.'

Quinn reported that no robbery at the airport had taken place and no vehicle had left the depot, so the gold was still secure. Maybe some loose tongue had hinted at the strong military protection of the bullion, and only a fool would partake in such a high risk project.

In Vauxhall, the team gathered in Spicer's office. Joe told them that Lenny Jameson had been in touch to say that Liam O'Brian had moved into the Little Venice home of the O'Neils, and taken Billy's chair. O'Brian had posted a reward of £100,000 for the whereabouts of the mysterious underworld figure known as the Fly. The pot was being rapidly stirred. So many fresh eyes were now looking for the elusive Fly.

Joe wanted his team to probe deeper into the SIS. Was their mole the Fly? Had Sophia DuPont and her son really met this man in Paris and at Davidson's abattoir? Joe didn't think so. He imagined this king of organised crime was happy for them to chase every vague possibility and go on chasing shadows, while all the time laughing at their incompetence.

Ryona wondered if the team should concentrate on reviewing the period before the virus ransom demand, even as far back as the purchase of the *Doonata*, and the major heists of recent years. She felt sure they would discover failures buried inside the success stories—pockets bulging with their triumphs, tears shed for their losses. How many loved this Fly? How many hated him?

Roberto asked, 'Could it be that the Fly, our mole, has a hold on whoever is giving out secrets, for instance threatening a worker's family was a well-known ploy.'

Norman remembered from his years in the Special Forces, a similar situation where one man, known as the Controller, was the king of organised crime.

'Wasn't he caught and executed in Algiers?' asked Joe. 'Must be some twenty-five years ago, big news at the time.'

Norman agreed. 'The Controller was later identified as Franz Wolff, out of Bonn, who left behind a widow and teenage twins, Margo and Ralph. He had dealings with known terrorist organisations who trained in Afghanistan. Amongst his belongings was found two letters from the pen of one Osama bin Laden, thanking him for a three million dollar donation to Al-Qaeda.'

'A major player, then,' said Ryona.

'You could say that. I believe the Fly is another Franz Wolff who's entered the arena.'

Tony said, 'That's all very well but I'm sure the problem of the Fly lies nearer to home than some sand-filled country.'

He asked Roberto, 'Wasn't Bin Laden once funded by the CIA?'

Roberto confirmed that many believed arms and millions of dollars went, along with Saudi funding, to the Mujahideen to help the fight the Soviet–Afghan War, although he himself doubted it. But like Franz Wolff would have been replaced by the Fly, the death of Bin Laden would not stop Al-Qaeda gaining strength.

Joe broke up the history lesson. 'This is not getting us any closer to finding the Fly.'

He began briefing the team on their next moves, at which point Spicer once more absented himself so as not to be party to extra-legal activities. What he didn't know he couldn't veto. Before leaving the room he confirmed he would be available for any necessary assistance.

Joe gave Ryona and Roberto the go-ahead to check out the build and purchase of the *Doonata*. Tony and Norman could chase up the Albanian end, find out anything they could about the vehicles used in the airport raid, their accommodation, and the fishing boat that waited for them in Deal.

Joe stressed they keep vigilant at all times. The Fly would be angry at his failure to take the gold. He would seek revenge, and his supporters would be looking for a replacement if his next ship sinks. So what would he do to regain his lost respectability? The thought sent a shiver through Joe's body.

'I've got to find this fucking mole.'

Ryona said, 'We've got to lure him or her out, Joe, use a sprat to catch the mackerel.'

Of course she was right. Joe placed a folder on the desk and pulled out several photographs.

'These are from Harry Parker.'

The photos showed the scene at Gatwick, before and after the clean-up. They all agreed Harry Parker was a top man. The early morning shots showed the two vehicles looking like scrapyard debris amongst the wrecked fencing; the strewn bodies looked like the remnants of a battle from World War Two. Harry had saved the vehicle's registration plates and also sent Joe the VIN numbers.

Tony and Norm were hoping to take an early morning drive down to Deal, after receiving intel from the Coastguard to the effect that there had been an eye witness to the Albanians' arrival, who said he saw six men get off a boat and get into a Ford Transit. The van had been parked there all day. It was 8 p.m. that same evening when it left Deal and took the Dover road. Tony was hoping for more detailed information, such as who had delivered the Transit, and whether the driver waited to hand it over, and, if so, what happened next? Did he drive them down the Dover road or did he leave by some other means?

The vessel that dropped off the Albanians had returned to sea, so Tony needed to ask his Royal Navy connection to get the Coastguard armed launch to return the vessel to port for interrogation.

Joe had already acquired two service station receipts from the time the vehicles filled up. So the box van was probably picked up somewhere on the A264, Crawley–Royal Tunbridge Wells road. Was there a motel in the area, or better still an isolated holiday house. The two agents should check it out.

Joe returned all the evidence to the folder and handed it to Norm.

Ryona was smiling. Joe screwed up his eyes. 'Okay, Miss Steele, what's tickling you?'

'You say Tony and Norm have to begin at the start, am I right?'

'That's what I said. '

Ryona grinned and winked at Roberto.

'Perhaps Roberto and I have to go back to the purchase of the *Doonata*, which means booking a flight to Monaco.'

'Keep wishing. I'm thinking a phone call to our agent out there would be sufficient.'

Ryona pulled a face. 'Spoilsport.'

Tony asked, 'Should I ask for help from my father-in-law, Admiral Mathews, to facilitate the coastal launch and its crew on a secret operation. It would mean widening the circle of trust.'

Joe replied, 'Sometimes we have to take a risk. If anything did come back that the Albanian fishing boat was pre-warned, then we would need to take action on it. But I know your father-in-law is a true patriot, so yes, get him involved, but stress that it remains top secret, and give the Admiralty only what's required, no more than that.'

Tony shrugs. 'Wish I had Frazier and the boys down in Deal with the launch raider. They sure would have given that fishing boat a heave to.'

Norman said, 'Bet them boys of yours in Scotland have all turned into a bunch of ornithologists.'

Joe wrapped up. 'Let's get to work. Don't let's be running on empty. I'm looking, depending, hoping for some light at the end of this tunnel.'

While the team were out on active duties, Joe contemplated all the evidence in his search for the leak. Pat Taylor and Naomi Randall were the only women close enough to the heart of the service with access to sensitive material. Pat would have received daily reports from Roberto for General Porter. It would be easy to pass on any given message. A quote from Francois DuPont came to mind: 'It's always about the money.' This seemed significant.

Naomi was a typical career girl by all accounts. Highly educated, she began as a simple recorder of domestic issues for Duggie Eliot at MI5, then promoted to work for Colonel Windrush at MI6, which would enable her to record much of the colonel's correspondence. She stayed on when Anton Spicer took Windrush's position. They needed to check out the financial status of both these women.

With regard to the male possibilities, there were three candidates: Anton, Duggie and Alister. Joe could see no obvious reason to check out an old friend... but, to quote his own words, he could leave no stone unturned. Sorry Anton.

Duggie's place in the MI5 domestic anti-terrorist office meant he too had to be checked out.

Last but by no means least was the overall head of the SIS, retired High Court judge, Lord Cummings. Surely not. Sorry, Your Lordship, you also need to be checked out.

The best place to start would be to pay John Barlow a visit in the basement archives. John had a nose for a mystery and he was always near to the bull with his arrows.

The news of the cash reward for news on Billy O'Neil's disappearance was spreading through Kilburn like a virus, and drew never-ending phone calls to the three lines installed at the O'Neil residence. Liam and Kevin were triaging the calls, then sending soldiers out to chase up the leads. Was there someone with the courage to come forward and grass up the Fly? Following the carnage at the airport, maybe an Albanian grass would be tempted out as retaliation, someone who would want payback on the Fly's costly error. The nark Lenny Jameson reported that various O'Neil relatives were racing to London to join the search, especially now the reward money had been increased to £200,000.

O'Brian thought, if this doesn't bring a dog to our door, what will?

John Barlow worked with Joe all day on his probables. He started with Patricia Taylor, finding nothing in her bank account to warrant further investigation. Her international travel was all within the framework of working to General Porter.

Her dossier was an open book compared to that of Sir Alister (Lord) Cummings, and to go deeper Barlow would need access to secret government files that could, if discovered to be investigating Sir Alister, lose Barlow his job. Despite this, Barlow saw no need to worry as Sir Alister spent a lot of his time lecturing on organised crime all over the world. At that moment he was in Bogotá, Columbia, helping to take down a drug shipping cartel. Joe crossed him off the list.

That left Naomi Randall.

Joe knew all about her jump from MI5 to MI6, from Duggie to Windrush, and her subsequent position with Anton. Her bank account was thinner than Pat Taylor's. She came out of Europe after working with Interpol in Lyon, France, while still a rather youthful twenty-one, and came with a vast knowledge of international crime. Now thirty-nine, she was highly respected, having gained the secretary's chair in SIS's top office, one desk down from the director general's.

John told Joe, 'She's a career freak'—and left a pause for effect—'but then aren't all women.'

Out in the English Channel, a Royal Navy Archer class patrol boat stopped the suspect fishing vessel and brought it in to Dover. The skipper and crew were escorted up to Shorncliffe Barracks for detention, and to await the arrival of Norm and Tony. The fishing boat would be given a meticulous search by Border Force officers, followed by a detailed report. Two hours later Tony and Norman drove into Dover. Tony had pre-arranged a meeting with an old ex-naval marine commander, Tod Fisher, at the Border Force. A smiling Tod greeted the two with some good news.

Norman asked the commander, 'How long can you hold these sailors without charge?'

Commander Fisher said, 'Ninety-six hours for crimes such as murder, two weeks for suspected terrorists. Assisting attempted robbery and murder in the hope of gaining funds for a known international organised crime cartel would probably fall in the terrorist category.'

Tony said, 'We need at least a couple of days at them.'

Norman nodded. 'And we need a translator... bet none of them buggers can speak a word of English.'

Hitting the phones, Ryona and Roberto discovered that the *Doonata* was purchased from Bermuda and shipped to Monaco by a German company, Wellenbrecher, which had since gone bankrupt. Roberto was chasing up the ex-company directors in the hope that they could give them a name of the purchasers, but the two listed names—Hans and Lina Noss—seemed to have disappeared.

Ryona was also having little success with her Monaco enquiries, although she did learn that the yacht was purchased with money from a Swiss account, so there was no chance of going any further down that road.

Joe sat in Anton Spicer's office twirling his pen, occasionally jotting down notes. Anton had been called back to Berlin to tidy his office, ready for its new director of SIS Affairs Europe, whoever that might be. Joe had initially been offered the promotion, but turned it down. Following the loss of Stacy Kilmer he felt ready to call it a day. If he was to carry on, he would remain out in the field. He wanted no office chair. He had always been a fighter, never a promoter.

30
DEAD ENDS

Ryona and Roberto were sitting down to dinner in a fine Italian restaurant overlooking the River Thames. Roberto ordered for them both: tortellini agnolotti, followed by *bistecca alla fiorentina*. When the waiter brought a bottle of Fontodi Chianti Classico to the table Roberto placed a hand on his heart and said, 'My favourite meal. I hope you will never forget this.'

Ryona smiled a thank you.

They not only shared a superb meal that evening. They also shared the disappointment of a day of near fruitless investigations. They still needed to know who bought the *Doonata*. There was something hanging in the air; the feeling that they had missed something.

It was a little past 11 p.m. when the naval transport bus arrived at Shorncliffe with the fishing crew from the boat *Ujku i Detit*, later translated as *Sea Wolf*.

Tony was for giving the Albanians an overnight lock-up, and hitting them early the next morning. Norman had other ideas. He thought it best to interrogate them while they were tired.

Before the captain and crew were hauled in, they met the translator, a tutor from Queen Mary University, London, who was dressed in a Bohemian-style flowing skirt and tie-die blouse, and who gave off the distinct whiff of past Greenpeace and CND demonstrations. She seemed unduly interested in the future use of the barracks, which were scheduled to become temporary accommodation for channel-hopping migrants.

Keen to get on with the job at hand, Tony said, 'Let's wheel them in, skipper first.'

Norman escorted the captain to the interview room. Tony handed Abigail a written list of questions he would like answering.

Abigail began with a smile. '*Se e ki Emrin.*'

The Albanian shrugged. '*Gjergi Hoxha.*'

She turned to Tony. 'His name is George Hoxha.'

Norman said, 'Question two, please.'

The translator continued in Albanian. 'Who hired your ship?' Then, 'Who commissioned you to bring killers into the United Kingdom?'

The answers didn't amount to very much. The captain said that he didn't know his passengers were killers or gangsters. He was told they had friends in the UK, family that they had not seen for a while. It was only after he met someone called Tigran Grigoryan that he realised there was something more required. But when he refused and two of his crew were butchered in retaliation, the Albanian gave in.

It all sounded plausible.

The translator had treated him with kindness. Tony was impressed. Nevertheless she pushed for more names. How was the money paid? Into what account? What were the bank details?

Hoxha said the cash was given to him in euros, which he put into the Banka Kombëtare Tregtare in Tirana, with the promise of another 5,000 on job completion. He concluded by saying he was told to lay anchored off Deal while Grigoryan and his men left for the beach in two six-man inflatables. Hoxha was told to give them twelve hours to complete their task. If they had not returned by then, to leave.

The hapless captain turned to Tony and Norman with a hand held out. '*Ne Jenifer por peshkatare te thjeshte, nuk Jedi* gangsters.'

'What's he saying?'

'He's saying they are simple fishermen, not gangsters.'

Tony whispered to Norm. 'It's a waste of time going through the rest of the crew, we need to look into this Tigran Grigoryan account, if at all possible. He's the receiver who delivers for the Fly.'

Norman was not convinced. 'But this Fly's not going to put his name to anything. If it's money, it's cash—hot laundered paper.'

The translator left them to discuss the new information.

'Okay, let's assume Grigoryan had got away with the gold, where would he store it? He couldn't get all that weight to the fishing boat using inflatables.'

He agreed. 'It would have taken him hours, the risk would have been too great.'

Tony considered for a moment. 'That gold certainly wasn't scheduled to leave the UK by some Albanian fishing boat.'

'I think you're right. They'd use a lock-up not far from Gatwick, and then move the bullion at their leisure. With that amount of gold you could afford to rent a castle.'

'Or a cargo plane from some defunct airport.'

Norman said, 'What you saying, brother? One hanger vault to another?'

'Why not? One question, Tony, if that was the case, why use the fishing boat? Why not fly in with the cargo plane?'

Tony said, 'That could have well been their plan.'

Joe Delph's eyes opened on hearing police sirens coming out of Westminster. He looked down at his watch: 5.30 a.m. He'd been sleeping at his desk for ten hours. The sirens faded as the morning hum of traffic rose from the Thames Embankment.

For a moment a recognisable fragrance wafted into the office. Stacy's favourite, Jo Malone's Red Hibiscus. The aroma captured his thoughts. If only he'd been in Berlin to take that surveillance job, if only. The love of his life gone forever. Joe was not a religious man, and adopted more of a scientific approach to how the world came into being. Pray to God. But which God? The world held so many. Would these gods let him see Stacy again? Joe thought not. To remember her, the happy times, her laughter. He knew that he would never see her again, to hold her close, to make love. But the memories remained. Memories that were beautiful yet painful. Where was God when he needed him. Where was God when *Stacy* needed him?

Joe carried these thoughts on an early morning stroll down the Thames Embankment until his mind returned to a plan to find the mole, his main chance of getting to the Fly. Which of the suspected players would take the bait? There were no candidates on his team. Joe knew his people, he was sure nothing had come from their doings. The mole had to come from some other department.

Joe stopped at a newsstand and bought an early edition of a newspaper and the latest copy of *Boxing News*. Rolling the two together, he slung them under his arm like an RSM's baton and headed for Ronnie's for a bacon and egg sandwich and a steaming cup of black coffee. The permanently moored Dutch barge café served the best bacon butty in London. Maybe he'd take on a full English; he'd not eaten for twelve hours.

One thing about eating at Ronnie's, you could be sure to get all the latest gossip, items that no daily rags would print. Ronnie was what you might call a good listener, but if there was news afoot, he'd let his regular customer from the SIS building know.

Ronnie greeted Joe in his usual laconic style. Then, 'I hear the Kilburn Irish have a big reward posted for a name, Joe.' He smiled. 'Looking for some grass to come forward. Offering two hundred thousand smackers for it. One could near on retire on that kind of bread.'

Joe gave a collusive grunt. 'That's assuming the Irish pay up.'

'True.'

'Give me an English, put some meat on these old bones of mine.'

Ronnie didn't move from the counter. 'Could well be right there, man.'

'Right, Ronnie?'

'Yeh, in them paying Joe, the Irish.'

'Got yeh, Ronnie.'

'You're an early bird Joe, six a.m.?'

'Know what they say... early bird.'

He smiled to himself. With me, it's the early bird that's hoping to catch a snake.

'Guess you're right on that, Joe. You want your full on a banjo?'

Joe threw up his arms. 'Why not, Ronnie, why not.'

Joe took a riverside seat, unrolled his papers and quickly scanned the splash in the *Daily Mail*. Government minister fiddling expenses, taking holidays on the taxpayer. Also on the front page an article on athletes taking banned stimulants. He turned to the sports. His team Donny Rovers not doing so well. Could do with some money spending on a few new players, especially forwards. Who can compete with the big boys, Arab, Russian, Chinese owners. Even Americans sneaking into the beautiful game.

Joe put down the *Mail* and opened *Boxing News* as Ronnie brought to the table his full breakfast banjo and a mug of coffee. He pointed at the magazine in Joe's hands. 'Now that's a hard way to earn money.'

Joe smiled nostalgically. 'I was a good middleweight in my time, Ronnie, but a lot of water's flowed under the bridge since.'

'A few more of my banjos and you'd have won the world title.'

Tony and Norman found nothing on the hire of the two vehicles involved in the airport job, except that two vans matching the descriptions had been stolen from a car lot in Watford the day before the Albanians arrived at Deal. This left the two with nothing to follow. Any prints that may have been left in those vehicles would have been obliterated by the Albanians. That's assuming the original thieves were performing without gloves, which was highly unlikely. If on the other hand there were prints, would they have a police record? Harry would have incinerated the Albanians by now, so there was no way of knowing.

Ryona and Roberto were in a similar situation. The road to finding the owner of the *Doonata* was blocked by a non disclosure on the Swiss account from which the money was paid. However they did manage to acquire the name of the yacht's original owner, the deceased multibillionaire

Christoforos Demetriu. Having owned six luxury yachts, the nonagenarian's estate allowed four of them to be auctioned off, one of which was the *Doonata*, at that time named *Callie Aphrodite*. They learned that the five-cabin, forty-eight metre, 491 gross tonnage yacht had a crew of nine, a top speed of 15 knots and could accommodate twelve guests. It went for 20 million euros to Streamline Securities, a front that represented an unknown bidder. Streamline was basically a one-man operation. That man was David Manson, an unfortunate individual whose own security was somewhat short-lived. He was killed in a car accident shortly after the auction. Accident or murder, Roberto would ask for the file from the officer in charge. He and Ryona believed that all roads lead to Rome, that the Fly was somehow involved in covering his tracks.

It was late in the evening when the team reassembled at Vauxhall. Anton Spicer was due to fly back from Berlin the following morning, so the office was clear for what Joe had in mind, which was to propose a revised plan. He told them that he would put out the news that a witness was coming forward with the name of the Fly. The informer had asked for half a million pounds sterling for the information, and insisted that the money be handed over at his given address. The carrier would have to go through a series of calls before the final handover, and that he should come alone, with no police involvement, and that there be no tracers on the bags. Only when these precautions were successfully carried out would he release the name.

The team all seemed rather puzzled at how Joe's plan could possibly work.

Ryona asked, 'Who's going to believe a man phoning in a name after receiving half a mil? Come on Joe, who would release such an amount on a promise?'

Norman shook his head. 'She's right, Joe, nobody's going to go for that. It's too, well, it's hard to take in.'

Tony and Roberto nodded in agreement.

Joe raised a finger. 'You think it's a crazy idea? Then let me tell you it could well panic the mole. He's been digging his tunnels of death for far too long, time for him to come up for some air, where we'll be waiting.' The room went quiet. 'Can he afford to let this chance go by? I think not. If there really is a grass out there, well, he wouldn't want that. We have nothing to lose in giving it a go. But if you've any better ideas, I'm listening.'

Tony said, 'Like Joe, I think we've nothing to lose, and who knows, we could get a surprise.'

Roberto added, 'One thing we have to do, though, is to protest against handing the money over without some better ball in our side of the park. If we didn't, this mole would smell a trap.'

'We can do that,' said Joe, 'but remember, team, we're only giving this information out to our suspects.'

Ryona asked, 'Which are?'

'I've narrowed it down to three. One, and may God forgive me, is Anton Spicer.' The team gasped. 'Reason being, he's been in from the start. Although he doesn't go back thirty years, the Fly doesn't either.' He sighed. 'Let me add, I don't think it's Anton, but we have to eliminate him.'

Roberto interrupted. 'Anton has spent most of his time in Europe. I know the man, he's no mole.'

Joe said, 'That's for us to find out. Like I say, I can't see it being Anton... the two of us, we've been through life together, boys to men.'

He leaned forward in his chair. 'Okay, let's move on to number two: Pat Taylor, another one of the European candidates.'

Roberto said, 'Can't see it, Joe, she's all over the world; when she's not in the general's office she's in the Pentagon. She's well respected throughout our office.'

'I'm sure you're right,' said Joe, 'but this goes for them all. I've only selected those it *could* be, the opportunists.'

Tony couldn't wait. 'Who's number three?'

'Next is top of the tree. The man that nothing goes by without his say so, our chief Sir Alister Cummings. In his position, he's the kingpin. He's not going to like it but we've got to include him.'

Tony said, 'No disrespect, Joe, but it's none of the three. We had Jenny Dilcox, we've had Windrush doing the interplays. They being the long running leaks for near on thirty years, so who took over?'

Ryona answered for Joe. 'I'll tell you who. One that's being threatened, one that's got a gun to the head. Anton, Pat, Sir Alister, they'd be a start, but I won't be surprised at somebody new coming crawling out of the woodwork. Some bank statements that we've not yet looked at, that in these past two weeks or so have suddenly had a win on the lottery.'

Joe put up a thumb. 'Now that's worth thinking about. Tomorrow first thing, go down to John Barlow, get him to check it out.'

Ryona nodded enthusiastically.

Joe said, 'Let's not forget, team. Nothing leaves this office, we know nothing.' He looked at each face in turn. 'Let us remember this Fly has been hurt. Through the mole he probably knows we are responsible. He's going to want revenge by putting out a contract on us, so take extra care.'

Joe went on to explain in more detail how he was going to set the bait, then sit back and watch for any reaction. Tony and Norman would keep an eye on Anton, Roberto on Pat Taylor, while Ryona and himself would take on Sir Alister. He had already arranged Lenny Jameson to act as the informant and put in the pre-arranged phone calls needed for the hoax.

31
THE MILLION POUND PLOY

Two days later the Vauxhall office was back in full flow. Spicer had returned from Berlin with his secretary Naomi Randall, and had begun to examine the files attributed to Colonel Windrush.

The office had been restyled to suit Anton's modern taste. Any hint of Windrush was already history, including the leather chair now replaced with a modern recliner. The office was brighter and fresher than it had ever been.

The door opened and Joe Delph strode in.

'Nice to have you back, Ant. I don't suppose you brought anything like a Berliner currywurst with French fries for me?'

Anton adopted a sad face and slowly shook his head.

Joe shrugged. 'I thought that'd be expecting too much, I could eat a pan full.'

Joe sat in one of the new office chairs. 'Office I like, Ant, never did like the old Victorian dark oak. You've given it a much-needed facelift.'

Anton waved his hand at every corner. 'Shipped from Berlin. I couldn't live with the leftovers of that traitorous bastard. Naomi likes it too.'

His secretary, sorting through a pile of paperwork in the corner, pretended not to hear.

'By the way, Joe, Sir Alister phoned me, something about a male informer. Don't know if he's some kind of nutter or what, he's asking for half a million for the name of our mole. Don't know what to think. Is this guy serious, half a million sterling? He asked for you to contact him asap. He's here in the press lounge with some officers of the counter terrorism squad. They have a load of Saudi princes flying in for next week's Ascot meeting.' He turned to his secretary. 'Give Sir Alister a call, Naomi, he's in the press lounge. Tell him Joe's here.'

Naomi picked up the desk phone and punched in a number.

Joe whistled. 'Half a million. Wow, this guy's got to be serious, he wouldn't dare steer us up a blind alley. This man's for real.'

'I really hope so. To tell you the truth, if this informer has got the name of our mole'—he put up a hand and waved it —'then by God I'd pay it to get the bastard.'

Naomi interrupted. 'Sir Alister can see you over lunch, Joe, you're invited to join him at the Picador on Westminster Embankment. One o'clock sharp.'

'Thanks, Naomi.' He turned back to Anton. 'I'm hoping he's got half a million for me, we need to take this mole.'

Naomi's mind was still on the lunch date. 'Must be nice to get an invite to a top restaurant, especially one used by the bigwigs of Westminster, some people have all the luck.'

Joe walked over to her desk and whispered in her ear. 'That's where you're wrong, girl. My kind of people dine at Ronnie's. I'm one open shirt diner not your Dicky Bow Joe.'

He gently nudged her arm. 'You want a good salad lunch with aubergine and goats cheese, fresh crusty bread, you go to Ronnie's, not yer two-prawn offerings at the Picador.'

Naomi winked at him. 'But I'm a classy lady, Joe, I like a good dresser and a Michelin star restaurant.'

Anton laughed. 'You sure asked for that, boy. Good on yeh, girl.'

Joe finally got to leave the Picador shortly before 3 p.m., leaving the cavalier Sir Alister on his second bottle of chianti, and an assurance that the asking price of half a million would be found. But the deal had to be a fifty-fifty understanding—no arrest from the given name, no half million. There was no way he was going to fall for that old trick.

At his office on the third floor, Joe awaited the arrival of the team. It left them with two down one to go on the suspect situation.

Roberto was first to enter with the news that Pat Taylor was back in the UK, and was due to give a lecture on international organised crime at Trinity College Cambridge.

Joe suggested Roberto give her a call, to keep the kettle boiling.

Ryona had been working down in the domain of John Barlow looking for any new bank balance increases to SIS administration officials. John had found only one, a woman out of MI5 by the name of Alice Freeman. It turned out the lady in question had retired after inheriting a large sum from her aunt. After getting married she'd moved with her husband to Oregon where her aunt had left her a winery. Some folk have all the luck.

She walked in to find the team disheartened and getting nowhere with the investigation. Joe told them that the latest call from the informer was for a midday meet at the tomb of

Karl Marx in Highgate cemetery, where he would find further instructions.

Ryona showed her surprise. 'You're saying you're going to be going in on this false meet with Lenny Jameson at Highgate? That's going a bit over the top on the dramatics don't you think?'

Tony nodded. 'Perfect place for increasing the dead, a winner takes all situation. Joe takes a hit along with Lenny. Our informer walks off with the goody bags.'

Joe smiled. 'Not going to be going down like that team, you see those goody bags Tony is talking of, well they are not being carried by me but left in another hideaway in the cemetery. The mole has to approach us both to get to the money, or should I say Lenny. Oh, I'm sure he'll want both, in fact, all three of us: Lenny, the money and little old me.'

Norman banged his fist on Joe's desk. 'Yes, and he's going to take all, for fuck's sake, Joe, you and Lenny are putting yourself in one hell of a situation, with no back-up you're going to get hit.'

Norman stabbed his finger into his chest, tapping it. 'You need me, Joe, I can take the fucker out from a hundred yards or more, you've got to have me there.'

Roberto agreed, and put a hand on Joe's shoulder. 'Norman's right, you'd be like sitting ducks out there. This mole isn't bothered about the money, he wants Lenny, believing he's got his name. He'll take you as a bonus.'

Joe laughed ironically. 'Do you guys think for one moment that I'd let Lenny Jameson give up his life, a dead man walking into a no-hope situation? Come on now, for a piece of shite to put two more on his list of dead agents. I'm a fucking Yorkshireman—head for thinking, feet for dancing.'

He shook his head. They all laughed.

Tony asked, 'So how're you going to play this one, Joe?'

'I'm thinking, if he's going to come into the open, he'll be looking for a hit and a fast getaway. He'll need to pre-plan his strategy at the cemetery on a busy Sunday morning when there are plenty of grieving relatives laying flowers. The cemetery will have a full audience. The mole will love that. We have to offer him the best time or he won't show.'

Ryona asked, 'And that is?'

'After three p.m., when morning service at the surrounding churches has finished, before tea. That's going to be the peak time for any informer. The mole knows the informer can grab himself a visitor, holding a gun to her head. I say her, as he will probably pick a woman.'

Roberto said, 'You sure this mole ain't going to walk in with a bunch of flowers with some automatic hidden in them?'

Norman answered, 'He could well do.'

Roberto said, 'Can't see it, Norm, he'd want to hit then be away. He'd not be concerned about the money, his job would be to gun Lenny and Joe down.'

Tony asked Roberto, 'So how would you do the job, Bob? Let's assume you're the mole.'

'You asking what I'd do? Well I'll tell ya'll, I'd come in on a motorcycle with one of those Wolves driving. I'd be riding pillion with a loaded Glock ready to aim and fire. I'd take down Lenny, then Joe, then by God open the throttle on that bike and tear myself out into the wooded section of the heath and away, job done.'

The team contemplated the scenario. Joe broke the silence by saying that's what the mole could do, ride pillion and have a Wolf control the bike. No need to stop, do the hits then ride on through, causing panic and confusion in that cemetery.

Ryona supported Roberto's thoughts. 'That's why we should have Norman camouflaged with a view of that tomb.

Let's be honest, he's a trained sniper, he could probably hit a sixpence at a hundred yards.'

Ryona insisted they let Norman take out this mole, and the rider if he comes in as pillion. But they needed the mole to give them the name of the Fly. Joe and Lenny would have to wear body armour as it was unlikely the mole would take a head shot on a moving bike. He'd have to be damned accurate. He'd go for body shots.

Norman agreed. 'Best I take out the bike, the wheels, the fuel tank, the Wolf.'

Joe said, 'That's if he comes by bike. He could call bringing flowers. We've got to be aware of all the possible ploys.'

Norman added, 'If he takes a hostage then I will have to take him down. It's the least we can do to stop the bastard.'

Tony said, 'I think I should double up with Norm on the action. It's not that I feel Norm would miss, but if something goes down that's not expected it would require a second sniper.'

Roberto asked, 'So what part are Ryona and I to play in this set up?'

Joe put his hand on Roberto's shoulder. 'You will be visiting a nearby grave holding flowers that conceal your automatics. You will be in disguise, because I'm sure this mole will otherwise know you. The two snipers will get in position early, remember it's the Karl Marx tomb you will have to have in your sights. Cover all approach roads leading to it. That tomb is a star attraction. Make sure you have a clear shot, we cannot afford any mistakes.'

He turned to Ryona and Roberto. 'You have also to take care, do not hesitate to stop him in any way you think necessary. It would be most beneficial to have him alive, but not at the cost of him taking lives. Meanwhile, let's hope and pray it works, and this mole comes to party.'

32
HIGHGATE CEMETERY

The Friends of Highgate Cemetery Trust had received a top secret warrant for the anti-terrorist squad to enter and set up the hideaways. They were told that a large infiltration of agents would be mixing with the regular visitors, whose admission tickets would be held back between 2–4 p.m. on the forthcoming Sunday. There was to be no public entrance after 3.15 p.m. This would ensure only a light trickle would remain around the mole's expected arrival.

The Home Office put their stamp to the warrant, giving it top priority. Admiral Mathews had brought in sixty naval able bodies who would act out the roll of visitors. Everything had been gone over to the last detail. Joe needed to be completely satisfied with the near certain success of Operation Earthdigger.

Sunday morning, 8 a.m., headquarters. Joe had been up most of the night. His mind was still on overload, ticking like a metronome, gently rocking in and out of the upcoming events that could set Highgate's cemetery on fire. He sat nursing a mug of fresh steaming coffee with random thoughts replaying every possible scenario. And yet, there could still be one he had not thought of. The pass, the hit, the escape. They could all come into play with an armed pillion passenger, close enough to take the vital head shots. Or he could go for a distant snipe, assuming he was a crack shot. Two quick bursts, then dumping the gun before making his escape. Then the thought that Joe feared most. That their target would hire a professional contract killer to do the job.

He was still contemplating this possibility when the door opened and the smiling face of Ryona entered, closely followed by Roberto.

She clocked Joe's haggard appearance. 'And a good morning to you too, Joe.'

Without preamble, he said, 'I've been thinking, we may have a problem.'

Roberto gave a puzzled look. 'We've already dropped Tony and Norman at the cemetery. Do we need to recall them?'

'Only after three thirty p.m. If that mole hasn't showed by then, he's not coming.'

Ryona asked, 'Then what's the problem?'

'No disrespect to your motorcycle suggestion, Roberto, but I've been up all night thinking, putting myself in his place. Would he use contract killers through the Fly's underground network? They certainly have the bread to hire out the kill, like a certain Aunt Sophia did for your family, Ryona.'

Roberto said, 'That'd be a killer, like shutting the curtain, game postponed.'

Joe said, 'You can say that again.'

Ryona stepped over to the window and looked down at the river traffic. 'We've got to hope that it's not gone to contract. Even if it has, we still got to sort it.'

'I guess it's too late to stop now. We take some lunch, then we go as planned.'

At ten minutes to three Joe stood with a large bag a few metres from Karl Marx's tomb. Nearby numerous members of the task force were going full monty by pretending to take photographs of long lost loved ones' gravestones. Lenny Jameson came from the direction of the Chester Road gate. He was playing his part by his slow approach, inspecting everybody with suspicion. Getting to a distance of five yards, he stopped, waved an envelope at Joe who nodded down at the bag. A little further down the path a man in a macintosh was observing the meet with interest. Unknown to him, on the back of the man's coat a red dot was moving up to position itself on his cranium. In a nearby tree sat Norman, camouflaged, and with his rifle sight on the man. His finger poised on the trigger.

Then an unexpected sound. A helicopter appeared low in the sky, coming in from the west. The task force darted and dived in every direction, some raced into the dense wood. Looking up, Joe shaded his eyes with his hand.

'Lenny! Take cover behind the tomb.'

Lenny had already disappeared.

The chopper hovered close, its side door opened, within which crouched a man dressed in black from head to toe and a balaclava covering his head. Across his knees he was nursing an AK-47. The macintosh man on the path put a hand in his coat and brought out a Glock automatic and aimed it in Lenny's direction. He stopped and squared off to make the hit—but not before a shot from Norman's rifle took off his head.

Moments later, Tony fired, hitting the man in the chopper, who fell out of the open door. Further shots from the two agents entered the steel bird's hull. The chopper steered away with a smoking tail. It plunged, spinning, as it fell from the sky, crashing into the pond on Hampstead Heath.

33
THE HURTFUL TRUTH

Monday morning, Joe and his team were called in by Sir Alister Cummings for what they all expected would be the bollocking of their lives. Anton Spicer sat alongside Sir Alister. Both were looking none too pleased at the line-up before them.

‘Well? Is somebody going to tell me what the fuck went off yesterday?’

Embarrassed silence.

'I've got them imbecilic clowns at the Met along with the Scotland Yard mob and the fucking Home Office on my back. I'm expecting a call at anytime from the P.M. himself. What the fuck am I going to tell them?’

Anton added, 'Don't forget the press, Alister. Both the tabloids and the broadsheets are knocking on my door for answers.'

Sir Alister fixed his stare on the leader of the operation. 'Come on, Joe, what goes, and don't you dare bullshit me.’

Joe took full responsibility for what went down in Highgate cemetery, and that his team were simply following his orders. He had expected the assassin to come after Lenny and himself. He never in his life dreamed that a chopper would be employed. But for some accurate shooting from Norman and Tony, he and Lenny would be dead. They had no choice but to take down both the chopper and the ground assassin.'

Anton interrupted. 'Have you managed to put a name to the three individuals in the morgue?'

Joe shook his head. 'Not yet. All we have is that they're imports, probably Romanian.' He gave his bosses a reassuring look. 'I have one call left to make, one card to play.'

Sir Alister growled. 'Well let's not keep you, Delph, get on with it! Let's hope it can get us out of this shite.'

Joe and Ryona sat at a waterside table at Ronnie's restaurant, the barge gently rocking in the waves created by passing waterborne traffic. Joe had dismissed the rest of his team, suggesting they meet up later. He needed a little solitude. Yesterday's fiasco in the cemetery had been hard to take; being taken down a notch by Sir Alister wasn't good either. At least the only casualties were the three dead would-be assassins. He looked out at the water traffic, the cargo carriers mixed with the tourist barges, phone cameras pointing at the Houses of Parliament.

His mind drifted. Whatever happened to Canon, Nikon, Sony, David Bailey with his Leica? The tools of the trade as was. Almost gone, replaced with five quid's worth of breast pocket plastic, costing hundreds of pounds. How easy for us to be had, taken in by the greed of global manufacturers. Every new invention reminded him of his advancing years.

Ryona felt she had to say something 'You're quiet, Joe, penny for your thoughts? It's not the end of the world.'

'True, but I've been thinking about yesterday's cock-up.'

He twirled a fork of spaghetti in the sauce.

'What the fuck went wrong? That could well have been a blood bath. We were lucky, Joe.'

'Whoever he is, he fucking knew too much, that mole could have been one of us for all the inside information he got.'

He stared at her.

'He's close, so close he's wiped our arses for us. He or she's there, standing right in front of us laughing in our faces.'

Ryona put out a hand and stopped him stirring the sauce on his plate.

'Who is that close?'

He shoved his plate away, put a hand to his forehead. He looked up with mouth agape.

'Oh my God. It can't be. He's been in on our plans every step of the way.'

Ryona has followed his train of thought. 'Oh fuck, it's John Barlow. It's him, isn't it?'

Joe snarled. 'It can only be him. We got to get the bastard before he can warn his paymaster the Fly.'

'To think that I saved that bastard's life, saved a man who then goes and gives our secrets, words that kill all our people... Stacy. I want to cut him into little pieces, a bit at a time.'

She tapped the table. 'We got to take him alive, Joe, we need the name of his paymaster.'

Still tapping, she said, 'We've got to set him up, let's think of something.'

'I've got a rain check for dinner at his place. I could call on him and his family, while his guard is down.' Excited now, Joe went on, 'We always do a late-night brandy with coffee. That would be the best time to take him.'

'You sure he wouldn't think something was wrong? You suddenly picking up on the rain check, especially it being so close to yesterday's action? Probably not the best time for you to call.'

She looked to the ceiling. 'Then again, is it John Barlow? He doesn't seem the type. He had a lot of love for you.'

'So he had, like your Aunt Sophia had for you. I don't want it to be him, but who else could it be?'

He remembered that when they enquired about certain files, they weren't available, that they'd vanished from the archives even though John purported to know where every document was. For instance, info on Jenny Dilcox was missing. All the information they'd got on her came from Norman not John Barlow. Why had it been necessary to kill Colonel Windrush? Who had contacted Sophia at her cottage on the Yorkshire Dales saying the colonel had been arrested, that he was being transported to Inverness under house arrest to await trial? Who purchased the train tickets along with those of the two redcaps? He shook his head.

'We should have followed that line,' he sighed. 'I didn't. I fucking missed it, I could have saved a few lives.'

Ryona patted his hand. 'We all missed it, Joe, don't blame yourself. A team of five missed it. We've got to forget the past. If it's John Barlow let's get the team back together and sort him out before he runs.'

'That's one thing he won't do, he won't leave his family.'

'What if he's not the mole, who is it, Joe?'

'There's only one way we're going to find that out. If he's the mole then there's a chance that it's not going to be only us wanting him.' He gave a serious look before adding, 'The receivers that he supplied information to will also want him dead. If Barlow is clean, then he has no worries.'

Ryona gave a weak smile. 'I'm praying he's not dirty. I've come to like the guy.'

‘Me too.’ He clapped his hands. 'Let’s go find out.' He threw a £20 note on the table, waved goodbye to Ronnie and made for the gangplank and back to terra firma.

Joe called in the clan and briefed them on their new hypothesis.

Norman refused to believe it, and advised Joe to think again. Tony uttered that what he found strange was that John would betray a man, Joe, who had saved his life. And that he’d play a part in giving out Stacy Kilmer’s name along with that of new boy David Carter, which led to their bloody deaths.

Joe asked Roberto for his views on the matter. Roberto said it wouldn’t be the first time that brother had stabbed brother, far from it. But in saying that, there had to be a reason to commit these despicable acts on close comrades. He thought blackmailing would be closer to the truth, a gun at his head, or his family’s. If it was John, it was likely he was acting under threat of some kind.

Joe said he felt John could be innocent, but he must still stand a test of loyalty to his country.

Roberto suggested how Joe could handle Barlow. ‘You could invite him to meet with you face to face in some place comfortable for him with a little bit of mystery about it. Enough for him to think. Tell him that you think he knows why you are meeting. You can say that you’ve had a conversation with a man you met in Highgate cemetery. This might make him respond in one of two ways. If he’s guilty, he either panics, comes armed and ready to put a slug in you, or sends a hit to do the job; or proves his innocence by doing nothing, and turning up, asking why the secret meet.'

Norman said, ‘That’s a great idea, Roberto.' He turned to Joe. 'Let’s go with it.'

Tony said, 'It is as good a plan as any, Joe. I wouldn't know how to play it. With you being a close friend of John and his family it might work.'

Joe asked Ryona, 'Anything to add?'

She gave a serious look. 'I should go with you.'

Norman said, 'Perhaps you should meet in a park, open space, giving me a sight of whoever turns up, for a no-kill shot if needed.'

Joe said, 'Now, guys, I'm not looking for babysitters, unless John doesn't show and I get a guest appearance from machine gun Kelly.'

Tony chipped in, 'Which could well happen. If it is John and he panics, he could call for some help.'

Joe said, 'A lonely meet in some park is going to make him aware of something in line with the cemetery job.'

Roberto added, 'Either way, you have to have back-up. We're expecting one, whether it be John or some hired gun, but let's look at it again, it could be as many as four coming at you.'

Ryona said, 'Roberto's right, you've cost this Fly so much to his once prosperous organisation. The Fly wants you out of his face, Joe Delph, he wants you dead and buried. So let's take off the mittens and put on the gauntlet.'

She winked at Joe. 'Ball's in our court, let's play it.'

Joe said, 'Okay, thanks for your concern. Here's what we're going to do.'

He outlined his plan, first by choosing the location. It had to be inviting enough to tempt Barlow into thinking he had an advantage if it came to a shoot-out—him in the castle, Joe in the moat. The two places he'd feel safest would be his home and place of work, which would be advantage John. Somehow Joe had to get the locality to deuce, then advantage Joe. The third choice might give him to question why not at work, why not at home?

What would Joe do if faced with a similar situation? Would he go and see what the problem was? Yes he would, but only if he was innocent. What if he was the mole. Then what would he do?

He could say to his innocent family that through his work there had been a threat on his life.

Joe knew that whatever happened he'd need to keep John alive to get to the Fly. But how to do this if he's pointing a gun at your head. You'd need Norman to take a non-kill shot. If he suspected a trap, Joe doubted Barlow would show.

Norman still couldn't come to terms with the possibility of Barlow being the mole. 'I wouldn't think John would be able to stomach the deaths of friends. People he once fought with shoulder to shoulder in Afghanistan and the Gulf wars. If he is the mole then he wants for a fucking bullet.'

And if that were the case, the Fly couldn't let him live. He'd be in a no-win situation. Having one big problem to solve, he could ask for a deal: the Fly for his life.

Joe had only one answer. A man responsible for the death of Stacy and countless others? Yes, he'd do the deal, then pass on his name to Kevin Quinn after ensuring John had all that was necessary to convince the NIRA that he was the man they sought.

Joe asked his team for their thoughts on a location for the meet.

Ryona said, 'When I was down in the basement I noticed he had a couple of photographs of himself, looking a lot younger, I might add. He was wearing trunks and vest posing in a boxer's stance, bag gloves on. Like you, Joe, a boxer, was he?'

'He was, army champion at light middle, made the finals of the ABAs at the Royal Albert Hall. He represented the Joint Forces. Lost in a close fought contest to a guy from the Fitzroy Lodge on Lambeth Road. He was pretty good, could well have made pro. Believed he boxed for England a couple of times.'

Norman was impressed. 'That good?'

Joe turned to Ryona. 'What's on your mind, what's this to do with a meeting location?'

'Come Saturday there's a European title fight at Wembley Arena, light heavyweight British champion Billy Harper takes on the French champion Marcel Fontaine for the vacant title. There's also a couple of British title fights at feather and welter on the support. Now, if we could get our hands on a few tickets, maybe you could invite John to the fights. What you think?'

'Yes, I'm betting Sir Alister could get us a couple of tickets, he's got a lot of powerful friends, some are sport promoters.'

Tony said, 'Be a great night out, that's for sure. Think he'd get us tickets?'

Joe shook his head. 'Sorry, guys, but we're not going in mob-handed, he could smell a trap.'

Norman said, 'We don't have to sit with you. Opposite side of the arena will do me.'

The rest of the team all agreed. Joe put up a hand in surrender.

'Okay, you can all come. Ryona will accompany John and I, she's been working with him and he'll feel safe with her presence. I'll organise the tickets.'

34
WEMBLEY ARENA

Tickets were scarce for such a high profile fight, but Joe managed to acquire two pairs and two singles. This interfered with his original plan so he decided that he would sit next to John; Ryona and Roberto would be two rows back. Tony and Norman took the singles opposite, eight rows from ringside in the shadow of its bright lights.

As an ex-amateur boxer, John Barlow eagerly accepted the invitation to fight night at Wembley.

The plan was for Roberto to make an approach following the last bout of the night, and take John in for questioning. His cover was to say the CIA had been given his name by an informer, a man arrested at the Highgate cemetery fiasco.

Joe recommended that Roberto use threats to Barlow's family as leverage. If he knew the identity of the Fly, he must tell them, otherwise his family would be turned over to a certain mews house in Little Venice. If John was dirty he'd break.

Forty-eight hours before fight night the team followed Joe into the basement archives after getting the nod from Anton Spicer. He was looking for John's expense sheet and work record. All should be there. Joe effortlessly picked the locks on a filing cabinet, gaining access to all four drawers. He pulled them free from the steel shell and carefully placed them on the floor, putting a number in each, one to six, reminding him which slot they came from. Everything must be handled with great care, showing no indication that they been tampered with. Nothing left to chance.

They soon found the file, filed under Barlow J., section 1, A to D.

Tony asked, 'How long has John been with SIS, Joe?'

'A good ten or more years, why're you asking?'

Tony waved the thin file. 'Didn't you say he knew all that was worth knowing? A mind like that TV guy, the Memory Man?'

Joe gave a puzzled look. 'What's on your mind?'

Tony passed Joe the file. 'His memory seems to have faded, especially when it comes to keeping a record of himself. There's nothing in there. Reminds me of that old Dave Clark Five hit "Bits and Pieces".'

'That bad?'

Tony nodded. 'That bad.'

'Wonder why he stripped it down.'

'Don't need to be a rocket scientist to figure that out, Joe. He pulled out the pages that were for his eyes only.'

'Definitely, but what was it he pulled, and why keep a record of yourself that could be damaging?'

'Maybe he's tucked his expense sheets into some other employee's file.'

'That's something you're going to find out, when he comes in for interrogation.'

Joe patiently worked through the rest of the drawer where he found an envelope of instructions from someone with the initials MRW. He asked his team, ‘MRW?’ They all shook their heads. Roberto added it to the list of questions that needed answering.

Joe had come to the conclusion that John Barlow had somehow been forced into passing secrets to a receiver. A gun to his head—his family’s heads. But knowing John, he would have a safeguard, some protection against the perpetrator. Joe was still hoping that Barlow was innocent. If not, then what an idiot, why didn’t he come to Joe for help?

On fight night, Barlow and Joe found themselves sitting among the dignitaries, the present and past champions, and stars from stage, screen and TV. If Barlow was dirty, he was playing it cool.

What a night it turned out to be for the team to see Billy Harper knock out Marcel Fontaine in the ninth, followed by John Barlow being led from the arena and taken to a waiting car... 8... 9... 10... *Out*!

Barlow sat in the back with Roberto. Tony drove. Barlow angrily asked, 'What am I charged with, what the fuck you got me down for?’

Roberto grinned. 'You’re looking worried.’

'Wouldn’t you be? My family will be too if I’m not home.'

Tony whistled. 'Twenty-five years, fucking long time to be locked away, family visit once a month.' Again he whistled. 'Drive a man fucking crazy, that would.'

'I know my rights, you put a call out for Eric Gates. I’m saying nothing to you without Eric.'

Roberto asked, 'Who the fuck’s Eric Gates?’

He looked to Tony. 'You heard of this Gates that he’s on about?’

‘Don’t know him.'

Roberto nudged Barlow. ‘Criminal mate of yours?’

Barlow was shaking with anger. 'No, he’s not a fucking criminal, he’s a Jag, a military lawyer. I want you to get him for me, now.'

He glanced down at his watch: 12.15 a.m. He looked out through the window and saw the vehicle was entering New Scotland Yard.

‘Why are you taking me to Scotland Yard? What the fuck’s going on? Get me Eric Gates now.'

Roberto asked, ‘Shouldn’t you be asking MCW for help, John?’

Tony noticed that Roberto’s hit a nerve with the question. Barlow, whose eyes closed in resignation, was now a perspiring and worried man. He said nothing more before being escorted into a holding cell. As they prepare to lock the cell door, Barlow whispered, his voice croaking, 'Get my lawyer Eric Gates. I need to phone my wife, I need a phone.'

Roberto said, ‘You look tired, John, so we’re giving you a few hours to think about your problem. You know why we’re here.'

Tony stepped up and spoke softly into his ear. 'The Irish, they have a big money reward out for information on Billy O’Neil and his family.' Tony poked him and winked. 'Maybe we should tell Kevin Quinn where your family lives. Oglander Road, Peckham, isn’t it?’

Barlow avoided his eyes.

As Tony left the cell, he called, ‘Think on it.’

Barlow lay back on the hard mattress with his brain doing overtime, trying to figure out what they knew. He was thinking, how the fuck did they get her name? Who could have known enough to pass it on? Not that wanker Windrush... Sophia... her son? No way. They’d have come for him before his home. He was thinking of his family, keeping them safe. Sandra, his girls Lizzy and Teresa. Oh God, ain't it enough to have one gun pointing at them, without another. They wanted a name. I'd asked for Eric Gates. The lawyer would work out all the necessary, a deal made watertight. Being in a no win situation, I want a deal for that name. Fuck if I ain't risking my life, I'm a dead man walking. How can you win, when you're holding a losing hand? Sandra, the girls, I'll ask for them to be given new identities, a place away from London, but not overseas. No way was he going to let the Undertaker have them.

An hour later Roberto and Tony returned to the holding cell.

Tony asked, 'You ready to talk and no fucking bullshit, John? You do that, we get up and leave, you comprehend?'

'Okay. I want a deal, the name you require for the safety of my family, a guaranteed straight deal.'

'Signed and witnessed by Sir Alister Cummings.'

'Also, I want Eric Gates to witness it. To see that it's carried out to the letter.'

Roberto laughed. 'You're not asking a lot for assisting in multi-murder. You sure that's all you want?'

He turned to Tony. 'What do you think, Tony?'

'I'm thinking we should let Joe Delph hear about this deal, don't you?'

Roberto played along. 'Wonder what Joe's going to think of his saving the life of a no-good scumbag.'

Roberto left the cell and made the call to Joe.

'We're nearly home, man,' said Roberto. 'Barlow's wanting a deal, the name of his receiver for his family's safety. You want to come down and sort it?'

Joe was evidently thrilled. 'Good work.'

'General Porter will also want to question him over our side of the pond, or maybe in Berlin.'

Joe said, 'No worries there, Roberto. That bastard's getting no concessions. I'm on my way.'

Joe ended the call and entered the code for Anton's number on his secure crimson network and awaited Anton's call back.

Joe's phone soon peeped.

Anton, down the mouthpiece, said, 'Joe, what gives?'

Joe explained the news on John Barlow. 'He is our mole.'

Anton's reaction was one of caution. He asked if the team had thoroughly gone over with a fine tooth comb the documentation in the basement. Surely a man of John's intelligence would have put together covering documentation to protect himself in the event of this happening. Maybe a video tape, a bank deposit box.

Joe agreed to send Ryona and Norman back into the basement to continue digging. He, Roberto and Tony would join them as soon as they'd finished with Barlow. Meanwhile Anton offered to send Naomi Randall to help the agents.

During the thirty minute drive to New Scotland Yard Joe's thoughts centred on the horrible butchering of Stacy Kilmer and rookie David Carter. He didn't know if he'd be able to stop himself from strangling the traitorous bastard. But no, strangling him was too easy, he wanted to watch him suffer in a way that Stacy and young David had suffered. Barlow's family, he didn't give a fuck. A man that plays with fire deserves to get burnt.

Roberto met Joe in reception. 'He's asking for a Jag, lawyer by the name of Eric Gates.'

'He gets nothing until he gives us that fucking name. If I ain't got it by'—Joe looked at his watch—'twelve noon, then we give his family to Kevin Quinn. That bastard's got to get it into his head who's driving the bus.'

Roberto smiled. 'Tony's in there with him now, let's give him some shit.'

When it came to it, it was with great reluctance that Joe walked into that holding cell to face the man he once regarded as a friend.

'What's this I'm hearing about this piece of shite?' He pointed a finger at Barlow. 'Well it's like this, you fucking traitorous bastard. I'm giving you till noon to give us that name. You give it or Sandra and the girls get a call from Quinn. You have twenty minutes to comply.'

Barlow shook his head. 'You think I wanted to do this? They, like you, threaten my family. I had no fucking choice.'

'You had no fucking choice? You should have come to me. Instead you went with them. Taking their dirty money, helping to murder our people. You're not a man Barlow, you're a fucking disease. You better give me that name or I personally will do to your family what the butchers in the Berlin woods did to ours.'

He looked at his watch.

'Ten minutes and counting. You're asking for me to give you a deal. A Stacy Kilmer deal, a David Carter deal, and all the rest of the poor souls that you helped dig a grave for.'

He jabbed a finger into Barlow's chest.

'Don't you mess with me, John Barlow... try me, you won't go the distance.'

John cried out, 'It's not for me, my family. They are innocent, they know nothing of this.' He seems breathless as his head hung limp. 'I'm sorry.'

'Bullshit! You have five minutes.'

'Fuck him, Tony, I'm playing no more games, I'm calling Quinn.'

Joe turned to leave the cell.

In desperation, the prisoner begged, crying, ‘Okay, Joe, Okay. You win. She’s going to kill us all anyway, Sandra, my girls, me. We’re all as good as dead.'

Roberto couldn’t withhold a gasp. 'She! It’s a woman?’

Barlow looked like a caged animal, resigned to his fate. 'First it was Dilcox, she was the receiver, bastard threatened my family. When you put her out of business I was over the moon. I thought it was all over.' He gave a short grunt. 'Gone, or so I thought, you’d killed the fucking devil’s advocate. She was finished, and her son, mad Francois, both dead and gone.’ He gave a deep sigh and threw back his head. 'Then she herself appears. Like some ice-pick through the heart. Fucking telling me it’s not over, that *she* was now the receiver, that the threat to my family was still ongoing.' He looked at Joe for a sign of compassion, but there was none.

Tony interrupted. 'So this woman is a receiver?’

John nodded.

Joe pushed him. 'Get on with it.'

Barlow flinched from a threatening punch from Joe.

‘She’s the receiver that has taken over from Dilcox. So young but more powerful than Dilcox ever was, don’t ask me why, but the gut feeling I got was telling me she’s close, close to this Fly.'

Joe’s impatience was boiling over. 'Who the fuck is this woman? Her name?’

John looked at Joe, Tony and Roberto in turn. ‘Naomi Randall. One of the evil fucking twins.'

The name electrified Joe as his thoughts turned to Anton Spicer’s secretary right now in the basement archives with Ryona and Norman.

'You sure?’ he asked. ‘Naomi Randall? Twins?’

Barlow's face showed a combined look of incredulity and pity. 'You all fucking deaf or what? Haven't I said her name's Naomi Randall. She's got a twin brother.'

Joe turned to Roberto and Tony with urgency. 'I've got to go, you better come with me. Lock Barlow up, we deal with him later.'

John shouted, 'I've given you names. I want to see Gates, get me Eric Gates.'

With a look of disgust, Joe said, 'Later, traitor.'

35

A WOLF IN SHEEP'S CLOTHING

Joe raced towards the Yard's reception to sign out and get back to SIS headquarters. Roberto was in pursuit. 'What the fuck, Joe? What's happening?'

'Ryona, she's with Norman going through the archives in the basement with Barlow, looking for anything that can help nail these bastards.'

Tony shrugged. 'So what gives?'

'This morning Anton and I sent Ryona and Norm some extra help. Someone we thought we could trust.'

Roberto gasped. 'You didn't?'

'Yes, we sent Naomi Randall to help them, we have a fucking problem.'

'Can't we phone and warn them, Joe?'

'We could, but would we make a bad situation worse? I think we go in easy on this.'

Tony was worried not only for Ryona, but also for his partner Norm. 'But what if they do find some incriminating evidence? Think Randall's going to let them come away with it?'

'You know I can't answer that, and we're wasting time. Let's get there and get that bitch in cuffs, that's the number one priority. After the damage we've done to the Fly, I dread to think what Randall will do.'

Roberto said, 'Wouldn't it be better to get Barlow to tell us where the information is hidden?'

Tony disagreed. 'No way, Roberto. That secret's the only thing keeping him alive. He ain't going to tell nobody but his lawyer where that's hidden. Some bank security box, probably.'

'So let's get over there and hope there's nothing in the archives,' said Joe. 'Especially anything damaging to Naomi Randall.'

Tony shook his head. 'Another fucking woman! Now you wonder why intelligent men don't get married.'

At Vauxhall they decided not to go into the basement heavy handed. Joe would enter first to size up the situation; Roberto and Tony would be back-up. Come the first opportunity, Randall would be cuffed and locked up.

Joe checked his Glock before tucking it into the shoulder holster under his jacket. He used his pass key to enter the MI6 office sections then the three agents took a stairway that led into the basement archives. There, another pass key was needed, one that Joe had received from Anton. Joe inserted the key and a door slid open. He then passed the key to Roberto. Joe entered, leaving Roberto and Tony to enter later at will. If Joe did not come out in fifteen minutes they were to follow.

Ryona, Norman and Naomi Randall appeared hard at work rifling through files. They all stopped at the sound of Joe's approaching footsteps.

Ryona called, 'Come to help out, Joe?'

'Checking you'd not fallen asleep after such a late night.'

Naomi nodded. ‘I heard about the fight night. Come to think of it, I’d have liked to have gone. I love boxing. Lucky John Barlow getting that spare ticket.'

Joe smiled convincingly. 'Yes, John’s an old friend, used to don the gloves himself. He was pretty good too. Thought I’d give him a treat.'

Naomi sighed. 'Some people get all the luck.'

Joe pulled out the Glock. ‘That’s right, Naomi Randall, and some, unfortunately in your case, are a little too unlucky.'

He unclipped the cuffs from his belt and held them out to Norman. ‘Cuff the bitch, Norm, she’s the no-good receiver.'

Naomi seemed nonplussed. 'So your little bird sang, did he? You think it’s all over? Not by a long chalk, you’re all going to die.'

'Ain’t that what happens to us all, Naomi? Some sooner than others, some who are given a fucking helping hand by the likes of evil satanic bastards like you.'

He shouted to Norman. 'Get the bitch out of my fucking sight, before I fill her full of lead. Roberto and Tony are outside. Take her to the Yard, but well away from the other VIP guest.'

Norman gave her a poke. 'Out you go.'

She led the way through the sliding door.

Roberto entered. 'I’ve told Tony to go with Norman back to the Yard with her. I thought I could be some help in here.'

He turned to Ryona. 'You come across anything of interest, babe?’

Ryona threw a document at him. 'Babe! What’s with this “babe”?’

Roberto gave a sorry look with his hands in prayer. ‘A figure of speech, used all over the States, a term of affection.'

Ryona adopted the tone of a schoolmistress. 'Well we are not in the States, we are in the UK and we say, “Have you come across anything of interest, most beautiful one?”'

She turned to Joe. 'That right, Joe?'

'That's right. Oh beautiful one.'

They all burst into laughter, with Roberto pointing and wagging a finger at her.

Three hours later Joe came across a file hidden in a listing of cartel drug barons. It was the one on Franz Wolff, which mentioned his twin daughter and son, Margo and Ralph. He waved the documents.

Ryona asked, 'You got something?'

‘Could well have, those initials, MCW signed under the order sheets.'

Roberto joined in, 'The ones you found locked in Barlow's draw?'

'They couldn't mean Margo Cali Wolff by any chance?'

Ryona responded, ‘There's one way to find that out. During interrogation call her Margo, see what reaction you get.'

Joe agreed. ‘Good thinking, let's see to that tomorrow morning. In the meantime keep her up all night, get one of the keepers to do a little disturbance every hour, bit of banging, maybe some heavy rock, some ACDC and Motörhead should do the trick.'

Next morning, after signing in, Joe noticed that the guard on reception was not amused. He said one guard had been going party mad playing the Sex Pistols all through the night.

The guard said, ‘I'll be fucking glad when my shift ends, I'm hoping it's only a one night stand.'

Minutes later the interrogation room door opened and a tired looking Naomi Randall was escorted onto a chair. Joe, Ryona and Roberto sat facing her across a large oval table. A microphone was secured to the table, with an overhead spotlight shining on the prisoner's chair, which was bolted to the floor. On its arms were fixed restraints. The windowless room had no other furniture apart from a fixed a one-way mirror on the wall.

Naomi held her face away from the spot's powerful beam. She tried to make out the faces of the interviewers, but could only see three dark images sitting in shadow.

She growled. 'So who are you, the fucking Johnny Rotten fan club? You there, Delph? You and your cronies, your fucking time on this planet is over, man, yeh hear me? You're finished.'

From out of the shadows, Joe said, 'Sid Vicious here, Margo, it's not we that's finished it's you, like the evil loins you came from. Your murdering psychopath of a father, Franz Wolff.'

Naomi betrayed a look of surprise. How come they know of her? Could not have come from Barlow, he never knew, nor anyone else for that matter. Not Lonnie, her boyfriend, they'd hit him in that cemetery fiasco, his head blown away from his body. Brogan and Gough the helicopter soldiers were dead. So who? She gave thought for a moment before it came to her. Ah, those initials, they must have found her mark on the orders she gave to Barlow. The fucking idiot forgot to shred the papers.

Naomi whispered into the shadows. 'Do your worst, Delph.'

Joe had a sudden moment of clarity. It was all becoming clear. The Fly, it's not her brother Ralph Karl Wolff. He'd be too young to mastermind such operations. He decided to give it a shot by firing his name at her.

He tapped the table. 'So how's your brother Ralph?'

Nothing came back from her.

'Must be running out of funds, what with your master's multimillion yacht lost, plus losing out on the gold bullion, the loss of his soldiers. More than a few good reasons for his supporters to want a new manager. I'd say that his castle is crumbling into the sea. It's not us that are finished, Margo, it's you. Your brother, he's next. We will get Ralph.'

He turned his hand into a fist, banged it down hard on the table, making her jump.

'Let me tell you this you psychotic murdering bastard. Your life will soon become a bad memory. I will watch you rot in hell. As for that brother of yours, we will give him to the NIRA. Kevin Quinn will be more than interested to learn his name—and save a quarter of a million pounds in reward money.' He shouted, 'Still no fucking comment?'

She finally broke her silence. 'You underestimate our strength, Delph, you have no idea of our connections worldwide. You think your little building holds all of the world's securities. How fucking far off can you be. Our penetration extends deep. Europe, the Americas, Middle East, want me to go on? My father was a great friend of Bin Laden. You amateurs think you can outsmart the best criminal brain that ever existed, what hope have you clowns got.'

She blinked into the powerful beam on her face. 'You're hiding in the shadows, Joey boy, but that won't stop him from finding you,' she snorted. 'Your luck's ran out. Like I say, you and yours are finished.'

She gave off an hysterical bout of laughter. 'You're all going to fucking die.'

Joe left a pause, then, 'Maybe, but you'll be going first, this I promise Naomi, Margo, or whatever else you want to call yourself.'

'How long do you think you're going to cage me—a couple of months? Could do that standing on my head. You won't hold me. You'll find the Fly has turned into a killer bee. No matter, I can bide my time.'

Roberto decided it was time to inform her that he had put in a request for her extradition to an American state that had the death penalty, and would be charged with planning the murders of at least seven CIA agents.

'You have to get me there first, Yank.'

'Watch how you sleep,' said Joe, 'I may do a sleep-walk and come and strangle you. I'd be doing this world a favour, that's for sure.'

Ryona added, 'Let's give Quinn the name of little Ralph 'big bad' Wolff, give the Undertaker a free first shot at the Fly.'

'You'd be mad to do that, Delph,' said the prisoner, 'Quinn knows better than to go against friends of Al Qaeda. They'd blow Dublin off the map and bring blood back onto its streets and you well know it.'

The agents rose as one and walked out. Joe said to the guard, 'Take her back to the cell, no visitors, no phone.'

The guard asked, 'What about the other guy, you want him?'

'Not required at the moment, but the same applies, no visitors, no phone. Make sure they're kept well apart. Any problems, contact me at SIS headquarters.'

On the drive back to Vauxhall Joe's mind was racing. 'Her brother would know by now that something was amiss, so we have to get to him before things get nasty. Problem is finding him.'

Roberto asked, 'Do you think he's going to come out, show us a face or get help from Al Qaeda?'

Ryona responded, 'I don't think the Albanians will be involved, Roberto.'

'You could be right... oh beautiful one.'

Ryona smiled, gave him a nudge, and winked at Joe. 'He's learning.'

Norm’s mind is on the bigger picture. 'When cash is king, if the price is right, even after their loss those Albanians will come again, trying to win back some respect. I don’t think he’ll show, he’s not to know that we have his name.'

'But have we his name,’ asked Joe, ‘is he the Fly? I’m not so sure.'

'Who’s to say he’s not got a mole in the Yard,’ said Tony. ‘You think he’s not the Fly?’

Joe sighed. 'That wouldn’t surprise me one bit.'

36
TWIN PEAKS

Half an hour later the team were nursing coffees when Anton Spicer popped his head around the door.

'You okay, Anton?' asked Joe, 'you look like shit.'

'Would be if that mob over at Scotland Yard would give my phone a rest. I'm getting a lot of aggravation over our VIPs not being allowed representation or even a phone call.'

Joe told Anton not to worry as charges will be made before the time limit of twenty-one days: espionage and assisting in the murders of agents working for MI5, MI6 and CIA. Anton reminded him that he has a limit of fourteen days for terrorist suspects.

Joe said, 'We've got plenty of time. The interviews were taped and bagged as evidence.'

'Thank God for that, so you broke the bitch?'

'We took a short cut, bit of a risk, but yes she fell for it, and gave us more than we anticipated.'

'Barlow?'

'He wanted a deal, he gave us Randall for a promise to look after his family. Saying that, they were innocent, having played no part in the passing of information. I tend to believe him. Roberto tells me that he and his family could be shipped to the States, given new identities, but only if they were proven to be innocent and Barlow gave us everything when he came to trial.'

'Hope he's going to pay for it all, out of the dirty money he's been banking.'

'I think he'll know that.'

Anton emphasised, 'Make fucking sure he does, because SIS or the CIA won't be paying.' Anton got up to go. 'Better get the Home Office on the blower, get them to quieten that Yard mob down.'

Joe nodded. 'The team and I would appreciate that, Ant. Last thing we want is the Knights of the Round Table involved, i.e. the Human Rights Committee.'

'One more thing, Joe. Think you should pay a visit to the Barlow family. Explain the awful predicament that John Barlow's got himself into and explain to them the seriousness of the charges, warn them against speaking to the media.'

'Don't know what I'm going to tell them.'

'I know it's difficult, but I'm sure you'll come up with something.'

Anton's departure left the team with their thoughts.

After some minutes, a smile appeared on Joe's visage. 'I know how we've got to go with this.'

Tony asked, 'What's on your mind?'

Joe leant back, his hands clasped around the back of his head. 'Our problem is how to get to Ralph Wolff. Margo and Ralph are twins so they have the same date of birth. We can check that in Naomi Randall's file. He could be in the archives under the male registration. He could be the fucking caretaker.'

Roberto said, 'That's always assuming he's made the same mistake, Joe.'

Ryona said, 'Let's go take a look.'

'We have a good ten days to get this bastard,' said Joe. 'Let's go through that file register. Concentrate on the the thirty to forty age group.'

For the next few hours the team sifted through the manpower recruitment system. They found Naomi Randall's birth date: 17 August 1982, making her thirty-six years old, and her place of birth: Colmar in France, on the French–German border.

Joe smiled. 'So let's get a match on our boy, there's a good chance he's in that register.'

Ryona checked the executive staff. Roberto took on SIS Europe, concentrating on the French inputs, followed by the CIA, with the help of Pat Taylor. Tony searched the MI5 files. Norman took on MI6 and anticipated covering the Home Office.

It took the team seven hours of searching before Ryona came up with a match.

'I've got Franco Sauvage, born August 17, 1982, in Colmar, France. Works on undercover organisations, Middle East regions. Small SIS unit operating out of Pakistan. Instructions out of Berlin, overall commander... Anton Spicer.'

A deathly silence hung over the basement on Ryona's disclosure.

Joe's brain was racing. He paced backwards and forwards. He finally stopped and turned to the team with arms spread.

'Will somebody please tell me what the fuck's going on here? Anton! No, no, no. I refuse to believe it. It can't be, he's, he's like a brother to me. There's got to be some mistake.'

Roberto cleared his throat. 'I'm with Joe on this. Anton? It don't make sense, he's not dirty, I couldn't be more sure of his loyalty.'

Tony scratched his chin. 'I don't want to put the cat among the pigeons, but Naomi Randall was Anton's secretary. Be good to find out why he employed her, was it a normal pass up the ladder or was she asked for?'

Joe asked, 'What the fuck you trying to do to me, Tony?'

'I m putting a possibility forward, Joe. He did pay us a visit earlier.'

'True, but he needed to get the Yard straightened out,' said Ryona. 'Didn't he say that?'

Norman said, 'Easy to check that out.'

Joe picked up the desk phone. 'I've got a better idea. Let's get the man in here.' After three rings his call was answered. 'Anton, you got a minute, if you wouldn't mind?'

Joe returned the receiver to its cradle.

'He's on his way. We have to settle this now, we can't afford any more slip-ups.'

The team remained silent until they heard footsteps in the corridor outside. The door opened and Anton entered. 'How can I help, Joe?'

'Take a chair.'

'You guys hit a problem?'

He looked the picture of innocence. Could it really be Anton Spicer?

Joe held up a palm. 'Yes, Anton, and it's a problem that only you can straighten out for us.'

'Fire away.'

'What can you tell us about one of your undercover agent organisers, Franco Sauvage.'

Anton looked unconcerned but the team were ready to eat him alive.

'Franco works the Middle Eastern block, getting back to us information on Taliban movements. He's in a Pakistan house in control of six other agents.' He leant back in his chair with a faint sign of worry showing on his face.

'He's given us quite a listing of insurgents, troublemakers to the United States, Europe and the United Kingdom.' Leaning forward, he asked, 'Am I allowed to ask what this is all about?'

Joe said, 'It's about the man called Franco Sauvage, born in Colmar, France, August 17 1982. Twin brother to Naomi Randall.' He pointed an accusing finger at Anton. 'That's what it's all about. It's about a killing machine who works for you, Ant. That's what this is all about, for fuck's sake. A man who happens to live in a detached nine million pound house down Woodlands Way in Virginia Waters. Not bad for an MI6 agent, wouldn't you say?'

Anton's features tightened as he put a hand to his forehead. 'Now come on, Joe, you thinking I could be involved with these horror shows? I thought you knew enough about me to not give that kind of speculation a second thought.' He took breath. 'Firstly, I was given Franco.' He looked at Roberto. 'Given Franco by way of the CIA office in Berlin, General Porter's office, as it happened. I'm sure if you look more deeply into his file you will see he was originally with the CIA. Ask Langley, Virginia for details. He was, if I remember right, sent over to Europe working out of Germany on the Afghan wars.'

Anton was getting angry with the growing sense of mistrust in the room. He went on, getting angrier. 'We at SIS Europe lost four agents in a Taliban ambush. Being a little undermanned, the CIA offered us Sauvage. He came on a two-year loan. It's all there in those damn files.'

Ryona softened a little. 'I got the date and address you asked for, Joe, but I've not gone through the whole file. He could be the reason SIS lost the four agents Anton's talking about.'

'Okay, Anton, what were we to think, what with all the leaks?' said Joe. 'Seeing his name and your connections with him. '

'Is that an apology, Joe?'

'Yes, Ant, it's an apology. Witnessed by my lot, I'm sorry.'

The whole room seemed to take a collective sigh of relief.

Joe broke the silence. 'So this Franco, where is he now, does he know of Randall's arrest?'

'The man's in Bahramcha working on the Duran line crossing points between Afghanistan and Pakistan, where tons of drug smuggling gangs are operating. His team are also assessing the main crossings used by the Taliban. By all accounts he's still there. He won't know of his sister's arrest. Nobody knows outside of this office, Scotland Yard included. They know her as Randall, not Wolff.'

'So let's say he knows nothing of his sister's arrest, he's going to be worried not being able to communicate with her.'

'Eventually he will realise something's wrong,' said Spicer, 'they'll have some means of contact. We'll have to get hold of her computer.'

Tony put up a hand. 'I'll go to her place with Norman. If she's left it there, I'll get it over to one of our hackers.'

Anton added, 'She also uses one in my office, take that too.'

Joe said, 'That's not all. We need Sauvage out of Afghanistan, we want him to be an easy pick-up, with no Taliban or Al Qaeda interference. How are we going to do that without causing suspicion?'

Roberto said, 'Get him back in to European jurisdiction. There's little trust in countries north of India, where insurgents reign without fear of reprisal. And Pakistan needs a closer look. Even America has had it with the terrorist wars. Won't be long before we're pulling out our troops.'

Ryona looked a little confused. 'But surely to bring him away will make him more suspicious that something's wrong.'

Joe agreed. 'She's right, so what's the alternative? Do we play the game of wait and see by leaving it for him to decide? Letting him crawl away into the safety of Tora Bora in the Safēd Kōh mountains?'

With growing impatience, Anton said, 'Why the fuck are we debating this? Let's get in there and take him out in a box. Jesus Christ he's taken some of our people. Let's get rid permanently.'

Joe said, 'You only have to give the order.'

'Haven't I done that? If you want it in writing then I'll have it drawn up. So let's take it now, an order to proceed.' He stood. 'I leave it to you how you want to play it, Joe. Let me know when you've decided. But let's not wait too long, we cannot let him have too much time.'

Joe told Anton he knew someone on the ground who may be able to help.

Step forward Major Colin Forbes, an old friend and associate from their SAS days in Iraq. Major Forbes returned from his final spell of duty in Afghanistan after the handover of Camp Bastion to the Afghan National Army. He was now back in the Pathfinders brigade headquarters in Melville, Colchester, and riding shotgun over the few British troops remaining in Afghanistan training its army. He also knew the whereabouts of the undercover Afghan unit led by Franco Sauvage, which was giving useless information back to UK headquarters.

37
AFGHANISTAN

In a small mountainous camp north-west of Ghazni, Afghanistan, Franco Sauvage wondered why he could not make any contact with his sister. He had that inner gut feeling that twins get when there's something wrong with their other half. After all the recent setbacks, mainly due to the team of hand-picked mercenaries led by Joe Delph, he was worried that something had befallen her. She was his one and only trusted contact in Europe. Everything of importance had to go through Margo to Colmar. His curiosity got the better of him and he decided to take a risk, which meant contacting one of her moles, John Barlow.

His last correspondence with Margo had been five days ago. He'd been meeting with a Taliban commander to whom he'd given the names of two of his top Afghan undercover agents, brothers Atash and Jahan Stanikzai. They rather conveniently worked for him through SIS Europe, being two of Anton Spicer's little diamonds.

Franco needed to be rid of the brothers. They had passed him information on a Taliban training camp where insurgents as young as twelve were trained in the use of Kalashnikovs.

But he held this information back from Spicer. Instead he indicated another location deep in the mountainous region, which should waste the time of Pathfinder reconnaissance teams. And they would have a surprise waiting for them on arrival. The map coordinates led to a dried up wadi in a dead-end valley, heavily mined with Russian leftovers buried in the desert region of Helmand province, where they would be met by the well-armed Taliban.

A short time later Anton Spicer received a crimson message that caused quite a buzz. More so, kit was coming in from Ghazni, a Taliban stronghold in south-east Afghanistan. It came as no surprise to Spicer that the call came from Franco Sauvage, he being the only operator left working in Helmand. The message requested information on an Afghan translator, name of Abdul Zakir, who Sauvage believed was selling operational information on the Afghan National Army. Could John Barlow forward anything he'd got buried in the archives? He left a number for Barlow to contact him.

Anton smiled at the recorded message. A second later he punched in Joe's number and told him of the strange request from Sauvage. Joe guessed correctly that it was a ploy; he was fishing for information on the whereabouts of his sister. Not to worry, Franco, she's tucked away nicely.

Later that evening, Joe and Anton briefed the team. Anton related the details of the Sauvage message.

Norman Aimes laughed. 'What a load of bollocks.'

Ryona responded, 'Norm?'

'He's got British Pathfinders out there, the cream, why not call them to take this Zakir character down?'

Tony nodded. 'Norm's right, we know what he wants. He can buy a million-dollar super yacht, has an army of killers running all over Europe, and he's asking for a name-check off John Barlow.'

Joe said, 'That's why I don't think this man, Ralph Wolff, is the Fly. He's too weak. He knows he's in trouble and wants to protect his sister by not letting the Fly know of his failures.'

Roberto joined in with his own doubts. 'We know he wants Barlow's assurance on his sister and her sudden disappearance. He's a worried man is our Mister Wolff.'

Roberto put up a finger and continued the thought. 'So let's give him John Barlow's reply. Let Joe act as Barlow. I can't see how Sauvage would ever have met or talked with Barlow, so who's to say Joe can't be him?'

Joe was doubtful. 'I can't see Sauvage falling for the play. Remember what his sister said, that he walked with Bin Laden, that he was a super organiser, and his control of international crime. Have you forgotten the Sardinian mob, the Russian godfather Ivor Stravenski, Sicilian Angelo Rossiano? A pal of mine, Major Colin Forbes, knows Helmand province, and it's no picnic fighting in that sea of sand. In comparison, the Iraq War was relatively straightforward. I can't see how Sauvage would be lured out of his safe zone, despite his worries for his sister. We're more likely to drive him deeper underground, protected by his Taliban friends.'

Ryona asked, 'What's the alternative?'

Joe gave them a précis of what Major Forbes had advised. Helmand wasn't a place for the unknowing and had to be tackled by an experienced team. They would need to employ the help of the Pathfinders that were still out there. He added that times had changed dramatically since the British departure in 2014, so the only way for them to take this man would be to go in like the Americans did in Operation Neptune Spear, when they got Bin Laden. The only difference being that Bin Laden was in a secure compound. It would need two choppers to enter, eliminate the target and away.

Moreover, since that operation by twenty-three Navy Seals, security had been tightened, so what happened that night in Abbottabad was unlikely to happen again. On the other hand, Bin Laden knew he was the hunted, whereas they had the advantage of surprising Sauvage who would likely be accompanied by two young girls, his bed-sharing sex toys.

Joe had already sketched out a plan for a midnight drop by Chinook five miles from the target's last known whereabouts—an upper room on a patio above a grain store. The whole operation could be done in one complete move, in no more than two minutes. Pick-up or destroy, then hopefully out. There would be no WMIK Land Rover to aid a getaway, so the only solution would be to have a Chinook on standby to aid and assist, coming in on a lantern's guidance.

Anton said, 'So what you're saying is we leave it to the SAS, the Pathfinders?'

'No, Ant. What I'm saying is we need experienced help. The Pathfinders know the land, its dangers. We need them if we're to pull this off. I don't care if we take him dead or alive.'

Roberto asked, 'When you say we, do you mean we are all going to Afghanistan?'

Joe shook his head. 'There'll be two or three of us max. Let's say Norman, Tony and myself.' He could see the looks of disappointment from Ryona and Roberto.

'I say this with no disrespect to the two of you, but Norm and Tony, like myself, have had a taste of the desert campaigns. I can't take the risk of losing either of you two.'

He turned to Tony and Norman. 'Major Forbes has given us room on a flight into Islamabad to meet up with Captain

Jim Steed. He'll drive us over the border to an American safe haven on the outskirts of Khost, where it is hoped our operation will take shape.'

Ryona sighed and looked at Roberto. 'Looks like we're out of work, no Taliban bullet dodging for us.'

'Now that's where you're wrong, young lady,' said Joe. 'Who's going to guard the castle while we're away? Don't you think that Sauvage won't find a way of getting the information about his sister's whereabouts? If that was to happen, he would try to get her free. It being his twin, I'm sure he'd put everything into an attempt.'

Roberto accepted his task with good grace. 'You take care, make sure you all return in one piece. When's the flight out?'

'When Forbes gets the green light with a definite sighting of the target's lodging and routine. Then it'll be a go. We should hear something within a few days.'

Tony said, 'Like Joe's saying, it's got to be precision timed. Let's hope it's a quiet night.'

Ryona gave a low whistle. 'Quiet, Tony? Can't see that, what with you coming in a Chinook.'

Joe said, 'I'll leave that side of the op to Captain Steed and his men, but I expect to be dropped by chopper five miles or so from the warehouse downwind. We would then hike to our destination over treacherous ground. That's what we'll be using for transport, our bloody legs.'

Norman had an alternative plan. 'I see us being driven into Helmand Province in a WMIK Land Rover to within five miles from our objective. Then it'll be a walk with our night views and SA80 assault rifles. The Chinook could come in for our pick-up, with the loadmaster wanting a fast withdrawal back to base camp. Am I right, chief?'

'Yes, you're right, it's either the Chinook or a WMIK, there's no other way to do this. Even such a plan can go wrong, it only takes one foot stepping on a mine, being seen on our approach, or the Chinook hitting trouble, and it's all over. Then it's heavy shit flying, in the last place on earth you want it.'

Anton finally got a word in. 'That's all sound. Good work, Joe, and good luck. As far as the other investigation goes, I've sent burglars into the suspect house in Virginia Waters, erstwhile home of our Fly. The guys will be working alongside the Met's anti-terrorist people to comb through the property and take everything that may hold vital information—ledgers, laptops, the built-in safe. If there is one, our guys will open it. Anyone found to be working for its owner will be brought in for questioning.'

Ryona asked, 'What about the sister, sir, is she living there?'

'Afraid not, she has an expensive nest in Knightsbridge. We're on with that too, nothing is being left out. Then there's Barlow.' He turned to Joe. 'Joe?'

'John Barlow had nothing at home, some friends of mine did a full search of his home after his family were taken into a safe house when we told them John had received threats on his life and had been taken into hiding.'

Norman laughed. 'A holding cell in Scotland Yard—can't get any safer house than that.'

38

PATHFINDERS

Two days later Joe got a call from Major Forbes telling him to be ready for a 1 a.m. flight. A C-17 transport aircraft was leaving RAF Brize Norton for Kabul and three permits were ready for Joe on his arrival at Carterton, Oxfordshire. He was to meet 99 Squadron Loadmaster Martin Woodcock, who would see to their needs.

It wasn't easy for Ryona and Roberto to see the three off in Tony's Jeep to Brize Norton. They were both hoping there would be no call for them to go to Oxfordshire and have to drive the Jeep back because Joe, Tony and Norman hadn't made it home.

Ryona shuddered at the sight of Tony waving from the vehicle's window, and Joe's shout of 'Look after the office'. She, in return, shouted, 'You all come home in one piece. Stay safe.'

For the rest of the day Ryona and Roberto followed the team's progress in their minds, converting UK time to Afghan time and wondering where they were at any given moment.

Roberto tried to settle Ryona's worried mind. 'Don't worry, let's hope our target is in Ghazni. If that's the case, our boys should be in his bedroom around two a.m.'

She sighed. 'I'm praying for them, Roberto.'

'Me too.'

'Joe knows what he's doing, he's a survivor that guy.'

That night the three agents were on the ground outside Ghazni. After leaving the WMIKs, dressed in full Pathfinder Special Paratrooper camouflage with night views and carrying SA80s, they were already on their hike towards the town. It was a moonless black night. Visibility was almost zero. Sun up was 5 a.m. The weather forecast was good, with a predicted sharp drop in temperature.

Operation Howling Wolf had begun.

Captain Jim Steed brought his arrow formation of nine into a single file marching several metres apart that followed a well-worn vehicle route in what was Russian land mine country. The lead Pathfinder constantly stopped and steered the column around any suspicious looking ground. Meanwhile two Pathfinders swept with detectors, directing the support vehicles on the slow laborious route. The constant shifting of the sand was like buttering bread, spreading fresh layers over the Russian leftovers.

Even though it had been more than thirty years since the Red Army's withdrawal in 1989, extreme caution was required. Still, to meet with the schedule, Captain Steed insisted the four-mile trek be done in no more than two hours, which would leave an hour to grab Sauvage, bring in the Chinook, and make safely away.

Steed checked his watch and bearing. Progress was better than his first calculations had suggested, so he moved the squad into a track in a dry river bed, knowing that this route had been observed by Pathfinder scouts to be most used by the Afghans, that is, less likely to be mined.

A little ahead of schedule, the Pathfinders found themselves on the outskirts of Ghazni, which looked like nothing more than blocks of high-walled compounds that stood behind a never-ending row of shops along an avenue. Luckily for the hunters their prey was living outside these large enclosures.

Steed took cover behind a pile of cast-off tyres, and pointed out the target property. He then produced a photograph of Franco Sauvage. Each Pathfinder committed the image to memory then passed the photo around. Steed emphasised that the target be gagged, cuffed and taken captive. Only as a last resort was he to be executed, and even then they were not to use their SAs but their sidearm Glock 17 with suppressor.

Joe was impressed with Steed's professionalism. He had a comrade's love for each of his team, which now included Tony, Norman and himself.

Steed looked to each with the silent question: 'Is all understood?'

They all raised a finger and nodded.

He clasped his hands, shaking them, then mouthed a silent, 'Let the show begin.'

The target building had one small, high window, and one entrance, a blue door that had seen better days. Alongside the left of the building was a staircase of stone steps that led up onto a patio, where there was a large living area. Steed pointed to it and took the first step.

Sauvage had found sleep hard to come by that night. His thoughts were with his sister and her absence from the coded correspondence. His messages remained unanswered. Even that imbecile Barlow had not replied to his enquiry for the fictitious Abdul Zakir. He had a strong feeling things weren't right in London, that he would need to get a Wolf to investigate. It would be a job for one of his Romanian brothers. The Albanians were having second thoughts about the strength of the Fly, his uncle, Conrad Wolff, once the most feared man on the planet. The Controller.

By comparison, who the fuck was Joe Delph? The man was a thorn in their side.

Sauvage lay back on his thin mattress. He thought he heard a noise. Probably Razor, the cross-bred Doberman snuffling in his bowl. He stared into the darkness and smelled the hot bodies of his two young companions who lay either side of him on the stone tiled mosaic floor.

The door burst open and three figures entered, bright lights blinding his eyes. He rolled over one of the girls and reached for his automatic when a heavy blow to his head put him out cold. The girls were struggling in their nakedness to find their *payzaar* slippers and *tombaan* tunics. Unfortunately for them a binding of strong tape was stretched across their mouths, hands were being taped around their backs, and ankles securely hog-tied. A sheet was then thrown over the two frightened girls.

The taped and bound body of Sauvage was dragged out of the room, onto the patio, past the anaesthetised doberman and down the steps. The Pathfinders dragged him a thousand metres into the desert where they triggered a pulsating light system to indicate their position for the Chinook. The approaching sound of the chopper was an early wake-up call for the sleeping Taliban, who began running, shouting and firing weapons into the darkness.

Inside three minutes Delph, the Pathfinders and their prisoner were loaded in the chopper and were away, back to Camp Qargha in Kabul province. One hour later Joe and his team were in a C-17 flying back to Brize Norton.

39

CAUGHT AND BOUND

Joe sat in the belly of the jet staring at the hooded prisoner who sat with his hands tied firmly behind his back. A million images, thoughts and plans played themselves out in his mind. Perhaps it would have been simpler to have blown his head off in front of the two girls and be done with him. Problem solved. Such was his need to fulfil a promise to revenge Stacy's death.

Joe now could not kick the desire to hurt his prisoner in some sadistic way. What he really wanted to do was open the passenger door and kick the bastard out, see if a Dragonfly could fly. Now wouldn't that be something for the tabloids to swoop on.

For his part, Sauvage was trying to work out who had taken him prisoner, and how to get a message to Conrad. Whoever these kidnappers were—a British Army Special Unit or mercenaries—his uncle would ensure sufficient funds for his release. He was hoping the latter would be open to negotiation. Money talks a persuasive language and the family had plenty. If these guys were British that would be a problem; a prison sentence awaited him. What he feared was extradition to the USA, the death penalty and a date with old sparky.

While he still breathed, there was always a possibility of escape. There was no place on earth that could hold Franco Sauvage and his sister. Wherever she was he felt her pain, those inner feelings that pass from one twin to the other in times of distress. Escape would not come cheap, but Conrad could call in so many favours he had handed out over the years. Such was the strength of the family Wolff. Conrad had the names that, once called, would have to attend—a marksman that could shoot an ant off an elephant's back, a locksmith who could pick any lock, a driver that could podium in a Grand Prix.

Norman whispered to Tony, 'That bastard's laughing at us, shall I give him what for?'

Tony replied, 'How about you giving him two what fors.'

'Say guys,' said Joe, 'bet Roberto's going to be pleased.'

'How come?'

The name makes Sauvage lift his head. It was the first indication that he had been taken by the thorn that had been embedded in his side: Joe Delph.

'Roberto wants his extradition to the States for the murders of his CIA buddies, he wants to see the bastard and his sister on death row.'

The conversation hit Franco hard. So they do have Margo. Maybe they have Barlow too; perhaps he grassed. He would die for that. Meanwhile Sauvage would need the family lawyer to defend him in the UK. What he didn't want was a military trial. If that should happen he'd want a weak-arsed prosecution that could be manipulated into a non proven, not guilty acceptance. Like his father always said, money talks, use it wisely.

Joe knew that the man sitting opposite was no fool. He came from a long-running criminal inverse bloodline, not the least of which was his Franco's father. If there was money to be got, Franz Wolff could get it. But Franz Wolff was dead. So who had taken over?

Joe also had a father who gave financial advice: remember, son, he would say, nobody does anything for nothing. Whatever it is, it comes with a price, a promise, a favour, repayment... money, money, money. To be without it you're a nobody; to have it you're a king.

Would their prisoner's howl bring the pack to his aid? Joe hoped that his reign was over, but he feared there was more to come. Any aid would have to be met with equal force. Joe could well need one hell of an army to stop it happening. As the flight dragged on, Joe found himself relaxing more. He even smiled, knowing the possibility of going to America's death row was surely troubling the prisoner. Joe decided to push him a little more.

'What state you want us extradite you to, Franco? Shall we say Florida, Kentucky, they say the chair burns the brain. Or perhaps you'd prefer the injection done in Oklahoma or Arkansas. Why not New Hampshire and the noose around that neck of yours. Then there's Texas. Haven't done a hanging there for quite a long time, but I'm betting they'd make an exception. Oh, sorry, they don't do the gas anymore. But let me tell you this... the States I've mentioned all want you, Franco. The bookies are laying odds on who finally gets the job.'

40

MAN WITH NO NAME

It was early evening when the C-17 landed in Oxfordshire, the doors opening to the smell of freshly cut grass from the lawns that surrounded the base. It was raining, making the aroma most inviting after the dry cold of Ghazni.

Joe had papers to sign, a couple of forms that related to entry of the Frenchman. The team thanked Captain Steed and his Pathfinders for their excellent work. No casualties was always a great finish. That, topped with the capture of the Fly's number one, was the icing on the cake.

They walked the prisoner to Tony's Jeep. Sauvage complained that he was already feeling the cold, having only the white robed *kandora* and *shirwal* trousers and sandals. He certainly looked the part of an Afghan camel driver.

'Get into the vehicle,' growled Norman, 'before I take that fucking nightgown off your back.'

In Joe's office, Ryona and Roberto waited for the arrival of the three, Joe having phoned to say they'd put Sauvage into the custody of New Scotland Yard and that his sister Margo had been transferred to Bronzefield high security prison in Middlesex. Her twin would later be taken to HMP Whitemoor in Cambridgeshire. They would both be under guard of hand-picked officers from the anti-terrorist unit. Joe didn't have much confidence in the prison system, knowing that guards and officers could be bought, threatened, easily persuaded to turn a blind eye if the price was right. Joe had secured the full backing of the Home Office, giving him full control over both prisoners' treatment in custody. The charges of espionage and the planning and murder of government agents, robbery with violence, membership of known terrorist organisations would bring several life sentences. In the United States, death row. One thing was for certain, the mob families would have their revenge once they learned the name of the executioner of the Godfather and the silent ones in Sicily not too many moons ago.

Joe personally led Sauvage to his solitude, reminding the Frenchman of how easy it would be to pass on information about him to inmates and imprisoned members of the Cosa Nostra. If he moaned once about his being in solitary, this information would be released to Angelo de Vincato, The Man in Whitemoor—Conrad Wolff's nephew.

Since the black-shirted guards of the anti-terrorist squad could not be bought, paradoxically Sauvage believed the source of his freedom was *the man*. He would have to go through Angelo de Vincato to arrange an escape—and get to him before Delph spilled the beans on the Mafia killings. His price too would be high, but what's money when your life's on the line. He also knew that the idiot Delph believed that he was the Fly. So let him go on thinking it. He would be one day, being first in line for Conrad's throne.

Meanwhile he had to make do with a tiny cell, and food not fit for humans, only Englishmen. He looked at the miserly supper that was pushed through the hatch in the door.

'What the fuck is this shit?' he shouted. 'Cheese on stale bread, tea that looks like it's out of the fucking Ganges and a cooking apple. I'm French, you arse, a coffee drinker, black no sugar.'

Normally he would have thrown the tray's contents back at the guard, but his hunger won.

Again he shouted to anyone that was listening. 'I want pen and paper, I need to write to my lawyer, a phone, I'm allowed a phone call, some reading material.'

He'd no sooner uttered the words when the single overhead bulk light went out, sending the cell into darkness. Franco sat with the apple, his eyes trying to adjust to the unreal world in which he found himself. He tried to orientate himself but noticed his $80,000 gold Rolex was missing.

'What the fuck, what time is it?'

A voice from outside answered, 'It's anytime you want it to be, killer. It's night, it's all you need to know, bedtime. When you wake it'll be day. There's no clock in here, best you get used to it.'

In another more luxurious cell that overlooked the courtyard sat a muscle-bound man of some fifty years, his long, jet black hair showing signs of grey. He sat on a rather nice cushioned lounger watching a 32-inch TV. He was wearing a full length smoker's jacket over black silk pyjamas eating a chocolate finger of Kit Kat. Within arm's reach was an electric kettle and a complete tea service. In the corner was a comfortable bed, above which were rows of shelving filled with books, a collection of CDs and a radio/CD player; under his feet was a thick carpet; the toilet bowl was carefully concealed behind a curtain blind. On the window sill, family photographs took pride of place, while scenes of old Italy were hung on the walls. This was home to no common prisoner. This was the cell of the Man, Angelo de Vincato.

The Man lay back on his lounger with a freshly made cappuccino in one hand while licking the chocolate off his fingers. He was watching one of his favourite programmes *The Sopranos* when, after a short knock, his unlocked door was opened and gangster Baby Bunny Roberts entered. Angelo looked in the mirror at the reflection of the bald-headed little sixty-year-old man.

Angelo snarled, 'Did I say for you to come in?'

Bunny pointed at the television. 'Must have been the set I heard, Angelo, you want me to come back?'

Angelo paused the DVD. 'So what the fuck you want, Rabbit?'

'I come in to tell you, Angelo, we've a special in solitary.'

Angelo waved a hand. 'So what?'

'He's got black shirts looking after him.'

'What's with these black shirts?'

'Anti-terrorist boys out of MI5.'

'So what's his name, this special?'

'Can't find out Angelo, don't even think the warden knows his name.'

'So let's give him one, Rabbit, let's call him... Clint Eastwood, he's the fucking man with no name, ain't he?'

Angelo picked up the TV remote and pressed play. 'You spoilt my Sopranos, Bunny, so you better get out there and bring me his name. You savvy?'

'How do I do that, Angelo? He's isolated, no one can go near him.'

'Get Nicky McFee in here, now.'

Moments later Bunny returned to the cell with McFee.

'I want you to get me that special's name,' said Angelo, 'and don't come back here with Clint Eastwood.'

McFee scratched his chin. 'Clint who, boss?'

Bunny said, 'Eastwood, that right Angelo?'

Angelo shook his head at the chandelier.

'You two fuckers brain dead or what? You never heard of Clint Eastwood? Man With No Name, where the fuck you been these last ten years?'

'We've been in here boss,' said McFee.

'Fuck me, so you have, well go get me that name pronto and try to find out why he's getting the full treatment, the no-talk-no-see.'

41
SOLITARY

The team gathered in Anton's office. Sir Alister joined them to offer congratulations for a job well done. He said that Barlow and the twins would likely be going down for a long time with no chance of parole. Their lives would be spent behind bars till the day they died. He asked that they be reminded that each was as guilty as the other. No deals would be entertained, even though Barlow wanted to give the Crown Prosecution damaging evidence.

Sir Alister turned to Norm. 'For outstanding service, Captain Norman Aimes is promoted to Major, the rank to take effect immediately. Well done, Aimes, or should I say Major Aimes?'

The room was filled with applause. Sir Alister looked at Joe. 'Although holding the army rank of major, Joe Delph is promoted to Lieutenant Colonel. Well done Delph, soon be getting my job.'

More applause.

'Thank you, sir.'

With that, Sir Alister quickly left the meeting and Anton took over the chair.

'Don't think for one minute that it's all over,' said Spicer, 'we have to guard against the flak that's going to come from these arrests. Sauvage or Wolff, whatever you'd like to call him, will be planning an escape.' He tapped his desk. 'We know his type, coming out of a billionaire family. I can assure you he has powerful friends. He will demand their help, and believe me they'll give it. Joe, I know, believes that the so-called Fly is still out there, that Franco Wolff is what you might call the supervisor, his man out of office. Franco and sister Margo are merely knights. The Fly is king. I tend to agree. So take care, you are all in his sights, and he knows all our names, thanks to our traitorous Barlow, who's asking for a deal.' Anton laughed. 'He must think we've all just fallen out of a walnut tree. A man responsible for God knows how many sadistic killings wants a deal for his family... is he the full shilling?'

Early morning, Whitemoor prison. A disembodied voice said, 'Pass the tray back if you want breakfast.'

The tray was handed back and quickly returned with a bowl of porridge, a slice of cheese and ham, a round of toast, a small pot of strawberry jam with a mug of black coffee.

Franco shouted, 'I see the chef's arrived!'

He placed the tray on his mattress.

'When can I wash? I need to shower.'

A towel and prison uniform was presented at the tiny window and unceremoniously pushed into the cell. The voice told him that he could shower in an hour. After washing he should ditch his Arabian dress and don the prison uniform of a high risk prisoner common in the USA. If he wasn't already in America, surely this was a sign of future extradition.

He was told not to speak with his guard. To do so would lead to him having no dinner. The window was quickly closed.

'What about my pen and paper,' Franco shouted, 'my reading material?'

No answer, just the sound of heavy boots receding.

He sat on the bed. The tray had a stamp on it: "Property of HMP Whitemoor", the first indication of where he was. But still, where the fuck was Whitemoor?

He felt naked without his Rolex. Delph or one of his cronies must have taken it. Bastards. His hands went to his neck. The necklace that once belonged to his father was also missing. His heart and spirits plummeted, which sank lower when he looked at the tray of so-called food. A man would have to be starving to face it. Which Franco Sauvage was. Several days of this and his body weight would drop like some Auschwitz intern.

Breakfast was over and the door to his cell was opened by an athletic six-footer dressed in police black. From his belt hung a heavy baton. The man pointed to the towel and the red trousers and shirt. Franco picked up the bundle and walked out of the door, with the silent guard pointing to the right of a corridor of six steel doors. At the end was a glass-frosted door. The guard, now with his baton gripped in his hand, tapped Franco on his shoulder to stop, and pointed to a small bench. He indicated for him to undress and put his desert clothes on to it before entering the broom cupboard of a shower cubicle. Inside, the shower emitted a fine spray of cold water. With a bar of industrial soap in hand, the shower lasted no more than three minutes before the water was cut off. He dried himself off, quickly dressed and returned to his cell. He wanted to scream out in protest at the treatment, but the thought of losing a meal held him back. They were playing a game with him. Trying to break him.

He thought of how many opportunities for escape would be offered. Not many. He would have to take the guard on some shower break. With no sense of time, he would be dependent on the light in his cell to indicate night and day. He was hoping for an exercise period. But he knew there was little chance. He was here to suffer to the edge of insanity.

What of his sister's situation? Where was she? Would she be able to take similar treatment? He needed help from someone, somewhere. And while he wasn't shackled, there would always be a chance. He would bide his time.

His thoughts alighted on the incompetent John Barlow. He imagined him to be close by in Whitemoor. Was he in solitary too? If so, was he within earshot? Would he hear him if he yelled? He could call out now. No, after dinner would be best. He couldn't afford to lose that shit. He was hungry and needed to keep his strength.

Back in the comfort of Angelo de Vincato's cell, Bunny and McFee were telling the Man that they'd had little success finding the name of the special one, at least no other than the one Angelo had given him, Clint. The solitary wing was blocked, taken over by the black shirts.

Angelo firmly reminded them that Whitemore had room for only one special, that being Angelo de Vincato. The two drudges quickly nodded. He thought for a moment before laying out a plan—to put a man into solitary and find out who this Clint was. Tomorrow morning McFee would cause a rumpus by striking a guard with one of his famous Glasgow kisses at breakfast. The mess would erupt into a free for all, with no punches pulled. Hopefully that would be enough to get him into solitary, where he may be able to make contact with Clint. He was to be told that the Man would like a word in his ear. That he wanted to know his itinerary.

McFee scratched his chin. 'What's this itinerary, what's it mean?'

Angelo shook his head. 'Nicky, did you ever go to school? Perhaps you ought to visit Rabbit in the library and learn something. I want Clint's fucking life story—why he's in here, what makes for him having the special treatment.'

Bunny and McFee made for the door.

'And one more thing,' said Angelo, 'before you start tomorrow's entertainment, make sure Nobby Howard brings my breakfast. Now get the fuck out, the pair of you, *Scooby-Doo* is on in a minute.'

42

MOVING THE SPECIAL ONE

Following the breakfast riot started by Nicky McFee, two guards dragged his bruised and battered body into a holding cell while the warden negotiated with the anti-terrorist unit to put the troublemaker into solitary. The ATU immediately contacted Anton Spicer, who firmly replied that there was no way such a move was going to happen. His prisoner was not to be mixed with regular prisoners or staff. He suggested they either moved McFee to another prison or kept him in the holding cell. This would be confirmed by an order from the Home Office. In any case, the trial of the high-profile prisoner will be coming up soon after which Whitemore could return to normal.

What Anton and the ATU could not control was prisoners being released on parole. One such parolee was Declan O'Reardan, who'd served eight years for robbery with violence. O'Reardon had followed the recent news of the missing Billy O'Neil and his family, and taken a special interest in the reward being offered by Liam O'Brian. Could it be that the man with no name in solitary knew something of Billy's disappearance?

Meanwhile, news of the special prisoner was spreading through the prison system like some jungle telegraph. Wasn't the talk going around that he was a top dog, rumoured to be a life-taker by most violent methods. He certainly was one for serious consideration. On release, O'Reardon planned to get himself up to Little Venice and put it to O'Brian. Quarter of a million smackers. New start, new life. Or was he dreaming? Even if it came to nothing, Liam might give him a few quid for his trouble.

Anton Spicer got word of a possible leak about his man at Whitemore prison. What he and MI6 didn't want was for this thing to go public. That would open the floodgates to all the human rights activists, the international do-gooders, nutcase supporters of serial killers, the bomb makers, and all the criminal dirt that could open the way to the European Court of Human Rights. That meant Anton and the team had to move fast to get Franco Sauvage and his sister extradited to the States. He called a meeting with Joe and his team to assess the problem. Sir Alister was present and they brought in Sir Philip Cranwell from the Home Office. Cranwell's main concern was whether they had used the correct procedure to arrest and hold the prisoners. If not, Strasbourg would set them free.

Sir Alister was quick to reply. 'We are talking about a pair of mass murderers. For God's sake, man, set the fuckers free? I'd sooner put a bullet into their sick brains, man.'

Anton said, 'Alister is right, Philip, we can't let these bastards go free.' He pointed a finger at the Home Office man. 'If you do, the killing, the robberies, their demands will continue to terrorise our world.'

Alister cut in. 'I'm sure you would not want that to happen, Philip, would you?'

Sir Philip looked at the faces around the table and shrugged. 'Then what do we do? I'm open to offers, but I've got to take something back to the Prime Minister. He won't want an international backfire on this.'

Sir Philip Cranwell was no novice to the rule of law—close to sixty years High Court Judge of some standing, respected by his peers, a voice in the courts of Europe. He could not, would not, allow any breach that could damage or turn a good apple bad.

Joe said, 'We will hit obstacles if we try them here in the UK, what with our ongoing political wars with many of our European neighbours. Wouldn't it be best to let the CIA have them. We could get them on a flight to the US tonight.'

Roberto liked the idea. 'No one need know. My team could act as escorts, fly them on some flight out of Leeds Bradford.'

Sir Alister shrugged. 'Leeds Bradford, Philip?'

'General Porter's just flown a party of Japanese into Yorkshire. Private jet job out of New York. I'm wondering if we could use it for extraditing the twins.'

He turned to Roberto. 'What says you, my CIA friend, think we could persuade him?'

'We could well do that, sir, shall we give it a go?'

'Yes, two arrows fired are better than one, let's go for it. Better to go first class than a troop carrier box, don't you think?'

Sir Philip wagged a finger. 'Now, just to make it clear, I have not heard Joe's suggestion, I know nothing of this. I can't be involved. I'm not saying it's a bad idea though, and it would make the P.M. rest a little easier.'

He stood and made for the door. 'You'll keep me informed?'

Declan O'Reardon gripped the hem of his jacket in nervous anticipation as he entered the mews house. Although he had never met the New IRA, he had heard through the grapevine of the men to whom he was brusquely introduced: Liam O'Brian and Kevin Quinn were men of great power in the new army, men to be feared. O'Reardon wondered—too late—whether this was a good idea at all, mixing it with the Irish Republican Army.

He had come with news about the man with no name, expecting to receive some reward. But the thought soon left his mind on hearing that a woman on a visitor's pass to Whitemoor had already passed the information to O'Brian.

Declan stammered. 'Sorry for wasting your time.'

Quinn replied, 'Nevertheless, we appreciate your efforts to bring us information on this prisoner Clint, whatever you want to call him. That was good of you.'

He looked to Liam. 'We know of you as a bomb maker who worked with my grandfather on my mother's side, Brendan Hunt.'

Declan nodded. 'Brendan was my mentor, a born leader. Nothing got by Brendan, that's for sure.'

Kevin put a hand on Declan's shoulder, squeezing it. 'Thanks for that, Dec. So let's get down to business here. We need you to draw us a map of the inside of Whitemoor Prison—gates, guard strength, who has keys, the kitchen, solitary cells, who's weak, who can be worked on, what gets delivered, what's taken away, what type is it a bin lift or a bin drop of empties and a pick up of full.'

Declan O'Reardon had just been offered steady employment.

'Have I missed anything?' asked Quinn. 'Think you can do this, Dec?'

Declan nodded emphatically. 'After five years in that hole, I know every fucking brick.'

O'Brian shot a self-satisfied look to Quinn, who stuffed a bundle of notes into O'Reardon's jacket pocket, after which he was led to a side table on which was laid a selection of writing material. 'So let's get started.'

O'Brian shouted towards the back kitchen. 'Connor, get coffee and a meal knocked up for my man here. He's wanting to get back to fine dining after five years of prison shit.'

A voice came back. 'Nice slice of sirloin coming up, boss.'

The meeting in Little Venice was not as secret as the NIRA might have wished. Back at Vauxhall Anton received a call on crimson from Lenny Jameson, who told him that the NIRA know of their prisoner in Whitemoor and are busy looking into it, and that Kevin Quinn has called a meeting with some of his soldiers.

Events were moving on apace. Anton called Joe to his office. What with the press a worry, and now the Irish, they had to move quickly. His immediate thought was to move Franco and his sister immediately. Then he reflected: Why didn't they shoot the bastard in the first place? Left him buried in the sands of Afghanistan? They would have avoided all this shit and expense. And the thought of him coming to trial was another headache. No, they had to be flown out to the States, to the waiting arms of the CIA. Anton was not a drinker, perhaps the occasional glass of wine. But he found himself taking out a bottle of Johnny Walker Black Label that he kept for distinguished visitors. He poured out a near full tumbler and virtually threw it down his gullet, gasping and shivering at its effect. He was contemplating another when he heard a knock on his door. Joe entered.

Joe stopped at Anton's desk, arms on hips. 'Things ain't that bad are they, Ant?'

'If they don't get any better I'm going to fuck off, go to some desert island, like some modern day Robinson Crusoe, away from all this shit.'

Joe smiled empathetically. 'Then things must be bad, so come on now, let Man Friday help solve these problems.'

Anton, glass and bottle in hand, told him about the call from Lenny and the Irish interest in their man.

'You know something, Joe, Sauvage has got the luck to get a not guilty verdict.'

He poured another glass of scotch and gulped it down.

Joe said, 'Then let's get him out to the States tonight. Tony, Norman and myself will take him gagged and hooded in the Jeep down to Menwith Hill, leaving Ryona and Roberto to see to Margo Wolff. They'll take her in the Land Rover. Then it's a flight to Langley, Virginia. Tony will come back to sort out Barlow.' He smiled and pointed at the bottle. 'Give you the chance to become an alcoholic while we're away.'

'Now that you mention Barlow, what's the plan?'

'For what we have on him we can hold him for whatever's needed to sort out his trial in closed court. He's looking for a deal, well we'll give him one. He does what we ask and we see to his family, he's not to know we've removed their problem.'

Anton, still a little unsure, put the bottle away.

'What do I do about informing the two Sirs, Alister and Philip?'

'You heard what Sir Philip said... he doesn't want to know. As for Alister, I suppose you ought to let him in on it.'

'I hope this works, Joe, it's tricky without signed and sealed extradition papers.'

'You know the alternative, the trials and the risk. We can't go down that road, there's no way I'm going to allow

Stacy's killers to go free. I'd sooner kill the bastards myself than allow that to happen.'

'I'd still like to get some kind of nod from Alister, with his support, well... I'd feel a lot easier.'

'Then give him a bell, and if it's a green light, then we go.'

'What if it's a red?

Joe smiled. 'Then it's which island are we looking at, Mr Crusoe?'

Anton picked up the receiver and called Sir Alister and laid out the predicament, and all the options and potential pitfalls of each plan of action. Anton warned him that if it was a no-go, then SIS had better start preparing for an onslaught from all sides and think of a substitute for Joe's plan.

Sir Alister asked for an hour to consult a few people before giving a firm decision.

He turned to Joe, arms spread. 'What the fuck, Joe, what we going to do?'

'He's not got the balls, Anton. He's passing the buck around the fucking table, he'll want some CIA backing, a firm commitment to get on with it from General Porter. Now there's a man with a pair in his crotch. Porter is a soldier first and will sweep the shit off the floor given half a chance.' He scowled. 'I've a good mind to give the general a buzz and tell him of my plan.'

Anton nodded. 'Believe me, I know what his answer will be.'

'"Let's have the bastards".'

'Yes, those exact words. I've worked alongside the great man for over five years, he won't let us down. If anybody would back us to the hilt it'd be Norbert Porter.'

'Let's hope Alister gives him the story like it's being played, with no holding back. We have one hell of a problem if the answer is no-go.' He added, 'Hope this island of yours has fresh water, fruit on its trees, fish in the sea, because Anton, my friend, I can see us both going there.' Joe's tone turned serious. 'That's after I've executed those evil twins.'

Anton said, 'I know how you feel, I feel the same way. I'm thinking Alister and Philip will be more than happy if they can get them off this island, but we need all the boxes ticked.'

After an hour and a half, Sir Alister rang. Anton puts it on speaker-record.

Sir Alister said, 'Who is in the room?'

'Just myself and Lieutenant Colonel Delph, sir.'

'Okay. You don't know what a fucking roundabout I've been on with the P.M. He's had to contact the head of CIA... yes, the President himself, who must have had a nod from Langley to say that they'd very much like the twins in. So my dear Anton, the answer is "go". Get those pair of bastards over the pond tonight. We are working this minute on your clearance papers, allowing four British agents to accompany them. By the time you get them down to Leeds, all should be in order. There's a special flight out set to leave around four a.m.'

43

LEAVING WHITEMOOR

Word reached Liam O'Brian that the prisoner with no name was being prepared for a move. This information came from the Man, Angelo de Vincato, so it was reliable. What more could this prison God, De Vincato, know? Had Clint been arrested on suspicion of the O'Neil murders along with the Thomas Coyne restaurant massacre? This man would have to be taken and brought to court—not with judges in wigs and a jury of his peers, this would be a court unlike any other, held by the NIRA, where a guilty verdict was a sentence of death.

Lenny—in his undercover role as NIRA sympathiser Sean Nolan—had been getting valuable information back to Joe and was taking dangerous risks to gain more. It was not that Lenny wasn't capable, but was it worth it? Did Joe need more? Joe thought not, not enough for Lenny to lose his life—and for him to lose a valuable source of information. Joe's most urgent need was to get him out from a situation that could put his life in danger.

Lenny shrugged. 'It's part of the job, Joe, let me handle it.'

'For God's sake, I've already met my quota for buying flowers. You don't have to go the whole hog.'

Lenny ended by saying, 'If I run and hide, then it's game over. I'd sooner take Quinn out, so if he comes a-looking, then I will.'

'Not without back-up, you know they don't come alone. I'll get Tony Ford and a few of his water babies to give you some help. Don't you fucking dare refuse me now. You hear me?'

'Okay, Joe, you win. Best you tell Tony Ford, remind him these Irish ain't your koala bears, but the other end of the family tree, the grizzlies.'

Joe laughed. 'I'll be sure to tell him what you've said, it'll be fun to see the reaction of a bunch of commandos who've done campaigns in Bosnia and Afghanistan.'

Lenny said, 'Forget what I said, that's some backing you're giving me, thank you.'

'No problem, but you listen to me good now, you inform Tony on all future operations. He's a top man, you share your thoughts, work together on this, okay?'

He nodded and shook Joe's hand, but not before getting Captain Tony's contact crimson number and code. Joe watched Lenny Jameson walk away as Sean Nolan. 'Stay safe, Lenny, stay safe.'

It doesn't take long for information to make its way along the prison telegraph. So it came as no surprise that the mystery woman in solitary confinement was being moved without notice. Inside an hour every inmate would know. But who was she? Big Mama Grimshaw didn't know, which in her case being the prison queen, was most unusual.

A chance visitor heard the news and consequently relayed it to the ears of Kevin Quinn, who shook his head and turned to O'Brian. 'What in hell's fire is going on?'

O'Brian ordered him to gather their cockroaches, a bunch of interns at various prisons throughout the United Kingdom. Unlike Quinn's men, they did not have the respect of the NIRA. They had been caught, overpowered by the British Army and therefore looked weak in the eyes of the commanders. O'Brian felt sure they would go all out to get back into his good books by digging up the information required. He also gave instructions for Declan O'Reardon to return to his home of the past five years and set up a watch on Whitemoor prison's comings and goings.

The door to Franco Sauvage's cell was flung open and two Blackshirts manhandled him off his bed and presented him with orange overalls. They did not need to speak for Sauvage to get their drift. His hands were pulled around to his back and he was cuffed with double tie-wraps. A black hood was placed over his head. In darkness he felt their grip on his elbows as they led him out of the cell and down the corridor. He counted three doors being unlocked and locked behind him before he felt the cold night air fanning his body.

He felt gravel underfoot, and then heard the rattle of a gate being opened. His brain worked overtime counting the steps, sixty in all, before they held him at what he believed must be the final gate. His exit from Whitemoor prison.

He then felt the presence of more bodies, and the sense that he was being handed over to a gang of men.

He was not wrong. Joe, Norman and Tony stood waiting to receive him. Not a word was spoken, but the elbow grip had now increased its pressure. He could feel more drag in the grip from two different hands. He was thrown into the back seat of a waiting vehicle, diesel, its engine ticking. A man slid in next to him on both sides. He was the meat in the sandwich. The vehicle began to move and pick up speed. Still not a word had been spoken.

Some distance away, O'Reardon sat in a dark blue Ford Escort watching the Jeep pull away from Whitemoor. He took out his phone and made a call to the mews house in Little Venice. O'Brian ordered him to follow the Jeep, and to update him on its destination.

Meanwhile, Joe had commissioned Captain Frazier and six commandos to watch their backs during their journey to Leeds Bradford, which would take a few detours to spot any tails.

O'Reardon's phone beeped. It was Quinn. 'Where the hell are you? What's happening?'

On hearing the ferocity in Quinn's voice, he nervously stammered a reply. 'They're driving towards Stamford, the man Clint with three escorts. I'm on their tail, don't worry.'

'Okay, any change you let me know. We're on the M11 heading north. Don't you dare lose them.'

His reply was far from convincing. 'I'm on it, Kevin, to be sure I'm on it.'

'You better be, O'Reardon. You fucking better be.'

O'Reardon took his sweaty hands one at a time from the steering wheel and wiped them on his jeans. He passed the road sign "Stamford A1 North 10 miles", with an arrow pointing right. Up ahead he could see the Jeep's right-hand indicator flashing. He immediately called Quinn, who was still around thirty miles away. O'Reardon noticed his fuel tank showed a quarter full. Not good if the Jeep had a full tank scheduled for a long journey. He was by no means a mathematician but what to do? Fill up at the next filling station and risk losing sight of the Jeep or keep going, hoping the Jeep's destination was not too much further?

He shuddered, which seemed to be a permanent condition with Kevin Quinn relying on you. He made a decision. He would take the next opportunity to fill up and hope to catch up with the Jeep.

Meanwhile the Jeep cruised along under a strict code of silence. Joe texted Frazier to say they would be taking a detour at the village of Tickhill, outside Doncaster, before rejoining the A1.

His thoughts were on how Ryona and Roberto were making out with Franco's twisted twin. He sent a message, asking if everything was going to plan. He suggested they use the detour through Tickhill, where Frazier had men watching their tail. He gave his position as nearing Grantham. Roberto texted back that they had passed Pontefract, Tickhill was next, then added, "Seems we're winning the race, want us to put the kettle on for a nice cuppa Yorkshire Tea, Joe?"

Joe could smell the heavy body sweat soaking the clothes of Sauvage who was trying hard to speak through the tape across his mouth. The prisoner took a moment to think of where it had all gone wrong. It had to be the killing of the agent Stacy Kilmer. That was a mistake. Her death brought in Delph. His sister Margo told him that Kilmer was Delph's woman. This surely was the main reason for finding himself in one awkward situation. But still, his captors were no nearer to the truth than when they started. Delph believed that he was the Fly. Let him go on thinking that, he knew that the Fly was already working on his escape. Delph didn't know who the fuck he was dealing with. All SIS agents, along with their CIA bureaucratic muddle-headed leaders were no match for the Fly. They would feel the vengeance, experience his wrath.

The silence and the darkness under the hood sent his thoughts back to his teenage years when his father had trained both his children in the art of survival. Many of his sayings returned to him now. Never enter a room you cannot walk out freely from... In the world of international crime, you have no friends, only acquaintances... The only friend is the Glock you carry in its holster... Don't ever hesitate to use it... Better to be wrong and live, than to hesitate and die.

Wasn't his father Franz Wolff the Controller, king of his domain? Wasn't it his father who, on passing his legacy on to them, had instructed the Fly to prepare them? For the day would come for the dead to rise again.

His mind began racing. Why the silence? How many in the vehicle? Where were they taking him? Was it day or night? This was England, not Afghanistan, they don't do this kind of thing here. He needed to pee. He nudged the bodies that sat either side of him. Only to feel the cold steel of an automatic against his head.

There was one thing that he knew for certain. He would play the game of being the Fly. He would protect Conrad Wolff—if it meant his life then so be it. Paradoxically Conrad had been brought up to respect the law. At one time he'd thought of becoming a lawyer, but all that was swept away when his wife and son were murdered by a car bomb meant for him. The police were not interested in investigating the incident, so Conrad's life changed overnight. He became the king of Europe's underworld and one of the most wanted men on the planet. His name of the Fly was known only to three: Franco, Margo and his second wife Claudia. Even his two children to his first wife, Julianna, did not know of their father's business.

Fuck them, let me stink their meat wagon out, I'm having a piss. Which he did, causing the vehicle to stop in a lay-by. He was dragged from the Jeep and his jogger bottoms and shorts were pulled off him. He didn't expect the blow to his head that rendered him unconscious.

At that moment O'Reardon came speeding past, and to his horror realised he was overtaking the vehicle he had been pursuing. Tony clocked the speeding Escort, and thought, *Where's the fire?*

O'Reardon re-evaluated the situation: the stopped Jeep, the lay-by, the next petrol station, Quinn on his case. His cellphone lit up and rang, on the passenger seat. He was driving at such speed that he tried to ignore it, but the constant beeping pushed him over the edge. It was probably Kevin Quinn wanting an update. He momentarily closed his eyes and swore aloud, 'Fucking Christ almighty, what a time to phone!'

He re-opened his eyes and peered at the fuel gauge, to the phone, then back to the road, but too late to see the articulated lorry merging from a junction onto the motorway. He pulled violently on the steering wheel to avoid contact, but only succeeded in hitting the lorry's near side, then ploughing the Escort head over heels into a roadside tree. O'Reardon was dead, while, in the footwell, the phone beeped.

The lorry with German plates continued without stopping.

Fifteen minutes later the Jeep drove by the accident scene. Tony could see two cars parked, and people attending the crushed Ford. He shook his head, thinking, *On every highway rides an idiot. If he was on our tail, he's no worry to us anymore.*

In the people carrier, Quinn was losing his mind with anger. The seven soldiers look to each other, saying nothing. They know to keep silent when Quinn got angry.

'O'Reardon's fucked the job up, something's gone wrong.' He turned to the men behind. 'You lot, you be keeping them eyes of yours open, we're looking for Reardon's dark blue Ford Escort, last known to be approaching Stamford.' He looked to the driver, Brendan Collins. 'Let's move, put that fucking foot of yours down to the board.'

Quinn was worried why Reardon didn't answer his phone. He was not far from calling the mission off, his experience being to never enter the cage of a hungry lion. He didn't want to give Liam O'Brian a buzz, but felt that Liam would want to know the situation in which they'd found themselves. O'Brian responded as expected—go find out but stay incognito. He then said that he'd got a tail on the woman in the other car who was a few miles outside Doncaster. She too was being driven up the A1.

O'Brian added, 'I'm hoping they're not going to the land of the fucking Jocks.'

'Wouldn't fucking surprise me. These are two important animals, Liam.'

O'Brian growled. 'Don't you think I've not worked that out? I'm thinking they could be terrorists.' Kevin smirked. 'Whoever, whatever, I'm going for them... if they're that high up the ladder and not involved in our missing O'Neils, I'm reckoning they'll be worth something. Our man O'Donald is on the job, he won't let us down.' Liam sighed. 'You and your boys take care, don't let us be running with our tail between our legs. Nobody gives funding to fools.'

Meanwhile Ryona, driving, was also leading a journey of silence. Roberto sat behind her with Margo Wolff gagged and hooded next to him. Ryona took the detour through Tickhill, and flashed her headlights to a stop-go man dressed in baggy trousers, check shirt and flat cap, for all the world looking like an Irish navvie. He waved her through. Moments later he stopped the car following, the Volvo being driven by O'Donald. Two commandos stepped out of the bushes on each side of the car, dragging him out. A gun from O'Donald's overcoat fell out, clattering onto the road. His hand reached for it but a heavy boot came down, crushing his wrist. He was taken away. Frazier sat in the Volvo and wound down the window.

He shouted to his stop-go soldier. 'Captain Ford is coming soon. If there's a tail, you know what to do.'

Frazier then drove the Volvo off the main street and into the car park of a public house.

Ryona rejoined the A1 at the next junction. She didn't want to be letting her prisoner go to the Americans. To drive into a remote woodland and put a bullet into her brain was what she wanted.

Despite the hood and the silence, Margo Wolff knew who was in the car. She knew her perfumes and could smell Ryona by the strawberry Jo Malone, Roberto by his Paco Rabanne.

She was going over the last few days. First chance she got, Barlow would be a dead man. Conrad would want his family too, a betrayer had to suffer. They'd let Barlow live long enough to watch his family's executions. As for Mari Bambella, she'd finish the job that Sophia failed to do all those years ago.

Margo still had these vibes, those feelings that were passed between twins in times of stress. She had a deep feeling of sadness that Ralph was having problems, a dark cloud having descended, telling her he was close by, suffering. She felt sure that he was getting the same vibes, telling him that she was in trouble too.

She had failed to send in her weekly report to Conrad, who would be concerned. For if there was one thing her uncle insisted on, it was punctuality. Her delay would instantly alarm him. Once known, her uncle Conrad would inflict whatever was needed for their safe release. In his little blue book were the names of many of the most powerful individuals under his control. *If you lose control of these disciples, you lose an arm and a leg of your business*, he would say

Sometimes you have to remind them of your power by taking out someone who was no longer useful. A demonstration by the strong over the weak.

They all knew him as the Controller, never the Fly, the name made legendary by her father Franz. Now Uncle Conrad was continuing to endorse it. In the few years since her father's death, the business had eased off, mainly due to a time of mourning and the priming of her father's younger brother. For her uncle had insisted on knowing everything needed to bring the business back up to speed.

Now the Wolffs were back, and the world of international crime was feeling it. By taking out the major mob and cartel leaders, like some ravenous vampire, Conrad had sucked the blood out of all who opposed him.

44

LEEDS BRADFORD

The mobile lit up on the front passenger seat, next to Tony Ford. A text from Captain Frazier. "R and R OK, tail eliminated, you no tail."

He gave a thumbs-up to Joe, and passed him the phone, who read the message and handed it to Norman who passed it back to Tony. Franco Sauvage snored.

For the first time on the journey Joe spoke. He whispered in Tony's ear. 'Let's forget the Tickhill turn off, head straight to Aunt Betty land.'

Tony nodded.

Meanwhile 120 miles south at Stamford, a section of the A1 northbound was blocked by three police vehicles positioned across the dual carriageway. Two officers directed the traffic to take a slip road, and follow the diversion signs.

Brendan Collins brought the people carrier to a stop alongside a young officer. 'Say, what's the hold up, officer?'

'Some guy shed his Escort, hit a tree back there, car's a wreck, he's a wreck.

Brendan shook his head. 'That bad, eh?'

'The man didn't make it, engine caved his chest in, must have been going eighty plus. Waiting for the fire department to cut the poor soul out. Follow the diversion signs, come on, move it now.'

Quinn leant over and tapped Collins on the arm. 'Fuck if I know what to do next... Stamford, Grantham, fucking Scotch Corner, we've lost them. Best I give Liam a call, tell him the news.' He turned his fist into a hammer and smashed it down onto the dash. 'Fuck, fuck, fuck!'

Collins said, 'What about the woman, Kevin, ain't we got a tail on her?'

'That we have, Brendan, my boy, Paul O'Donald, and last I was hearing she was near Doncaster. Fuck if I be forgetting all about that. Good thinking, Bren, I'll put money down that she and the man are destined for the same location. Follow her, we get them both. Get us back on the A1, I'll give O'Donald a call.'

Collins added, 'I think you should give Liam a call too, Kevin. Let him know about O'Reardon, that he's dead.'

He should have kept his mouth shut. Quinn reared at him. 'You think I should what? You doing my fucking thinking for me, Collins? Well do you, Commander fucking Collins?' He showed him a fist. 'You don't think for me ever again, not fucking ever again, you hear?'

Brendan stammered, 'I didn't mean to ever upset you Kevin, I'm truly sorry, please forgive me.'

Like a Jekyll and Hyde character, Kevin Quinn smiled as his fist turned into an open hand, and he gently rubbed Brendan's shoulder. 'Just remember who's the chief and who are the fucking Indians.' He turned back to the rest of the crew. 'That goes for all you lot, if I want advice I'll ask for it.'

Quinn tapped Paul O'Donald's number. But the phone lay in the driver's door pocket of the Volvo parked in the military garage, its ringing heard by no one.

'Don't tell me that fucking idiot's also run into a tree. Something's going down and we're blind to it.'

He killed the call and pressed Liam's number. O'Brian sounded angry.

'Oh, somebody's decided to call me, hope it's good, Kevin, because I've got two imbeciles who've lost all communication.'

Quinn got to the point. 'Declan's dead. Crashed his motor on the A1 near Stamford, cops are everywhere... tried O'Donald, he's not answering, everything's gone to shit, we're driving blind on the A1 Grantham. The last communication with O'Reardon said the Clint character was last seen at Stamford. Can't say if he left the motorway there or continued on. He could well have left at the Grantham junction. What do you want us to do?'

Alone in the quiet of the Little Venice mews, Liam O'Brian tried to put himself in the shoes of the anti-terrorist squad. Why travel north? Seemed stupid to take the two away from the country's most secure holdings, the lock-ups at Whitemoor and Bronzefield. He was beginning to wonder was it worth it, pushing further into a no-win situation that had already lost them the O'Neils, Tommy Coyne and God knows who else. Maybe it would be better to ease off until the fog cleared. To carry on this wild goose chase could lose him more men. Kevin Quinn he was not prepared to lose.

O'Brian came to a decision. 'Kevin, you try to get O'Donald, give him another half-hour to reply, if no further response, then return to base. We've got to give this some thought.'

'If we could get hold of the motorway CCTV footage, we could see where they left the motorway.'

'That's for tomorrow, don't go poking till I finds me a man who could help us there. Let me check who we've got north, leave that with me. Somehow I feel we haven't heard the last of our two mysterious prisoners.'

With no word on O'Donald's whereabouts, O'Brian and the team returned to London.

Franco and Margo Wolff were safely hooded, cuffed and gagged in separate parts of the jet.

Despite the offer of Tony's help, Lenny Jameson wanted to protect his cover so preferred to work alone, which left Tony to join Joe and Norman to guard Franco; Ryona and Roberto's charge was Margo.

When it was safe to speak, Joe said, 'You know, Tony, I've been thinking a lot about these twins. I don't think Franco Wolff could be our Fly. I'm thinking he's from the right blue blood group, but not our man.'

Tony whispered, 'What makes you think that?'

'It don't fall right for me. That man's too young to be the brain of a worldwide crime consortium, one CIA-cum-SIS agent working out of Afghanistan.'

Tony scratched his chin. 'So who's he protecting, who's the twenty-four carat controller?'

'I've an idea, Tony, let's play one against the other. We've two to one on getting a result.'

'I think I know what you're aiming at, and it could bloody well work. Just say when.'

Tony returned to the prisoner and handed Norman a written note explaining the matter. Norman read it and gave a thumbs-up. Meanwhile Joe briefed Roberto.

Roberto said, 'I know you'll probably not believe me, Joe, but I too was having my doubts about our friend Franco being the kingpin. Let's hit the bastards with it. I think we'll get something out of it.'

Joe put his hand on Roberto's shoulder. 'I'll leave you to put Ryona in the picture. Let's make them sweat a little longer, loosen their resilience.'

He asked, 'You got Margo sweating? Brother Franco is running a river.'

'She's more or less pissing rivers.'

Roberto returned to Ryona and put a finger to his lips. Ryona mouthed a silent, 'What's going on?'

Roberto mouthed back, 'Later.'

Eight hours later they landed at KLFI Langley Air Force Base in Hampton, Virginia.

Joe and his entourage were escorted to a high security section; the prisoners were taken to separate interrogation rooms.

With the hood off, Franco Sauvage looked a beaten man, tired and drained, his eyes drooping, desperately in need of sleep. The tape over his mouth was unceremoniously ripped from his face, the cuffs taken from behind and reset around the front.

Joe was ready to put his plan into play. He'd purposely left a tap dripping into a sink that was fixed in one corner. The constant drip was having the desired effect on Franco's already fraught state of mind. He lowered his head, cowering away from the blinding light.

'Can you turn that fucking tap off?'

Joe replied, 'Needs a plumber, washer's gone.' He glanced at Tony and Norman. 'Water's brown, can't even get a nice cool drink from it.'

Franco lost it. 'You taking the piss or what, Delph, where's my lawyer? I want that phone call.'

Tony answered. 'Why, you want to contact the controller? He can't save you, you're on your way down the fucking river, Wolff. The ferryman is waiting for you.'

Franco looked up into the powerful beam.

'Don't know what the fuck you're on. Who the fuck are you, another of Delph's tossers?'

Norman emitted a laugh. 'Your lovely sister Margo don't want to see Mister Ferryman, she's not going to sail across that lake with you.'

Tony added, 'Sensible girl, opting for a life sentence in the hope your controller will come to her call, which I'm sure he will. Such a big man, pity he had a squirrel brain like you working for him.'

Joe stepped up. 'Do you really think we'd believe you to be the Fly?'

Tony said, 'Your acting wouldn't get you a fucking B movie part. Oh yes, welcome to the United States, Franco, you're here to face charges of multiple murders.'

Franco sat back, eyes still shut tight. 'In that case I need a lawyer. Think you can get me one? Not some jumpy old has-been, no-win wanker?'

'Texas wants you for four of their citizens that you cowardly put to death in 2018, remember? George Shaman and his family, who just happened to be in the wrong place at the wrong time. The Dallas bullion robbery, innocent people you gunned down along with the security guards.'

Joe slammed Wolff's head onto the table. 'Oh, Franco, baby, they're waiting with a loaded needle in Texas. No fucking millionaire top of the tree lawyer's going to get you free.'

Wolff reflected on what had been said regarding Margo, her wanting to do a lifer, in the hope that at some future date Conrad would come to her rescue. Surely she knew, like he did, that Conrad would not be far away with a plan to get them out of America. He knew the Wolff family would never betray or give hurt to the business, even if it meant sacrificing their lives. They'd never have got his sister to do anything to jeopardise the family business, a never-ending road of crime that stretched across the United States, with strong ties in Chicago, New York, Atlanta, Vegas. Even a face or two in the corridors of power, Washington DC.

Executions were soon to be abolished. But Conrad would not take too long in securing their freedom. It was therefore imperative to give the family lawyer all the necessary information that Conrad would need to free them. Franco wanted his father's trusted lawyer, a sixty-eight year-old French advocate, Michel Laurent.

Joe broke into his thoughts. 'Give me the number of your lawyer.'

Franco, relieved, said, 'I do not have his number. Michel Laurent is his name. He lives in the seventh arrondissement in Paris, near the Quai d'Orsay.'

Joe whispered, 'If you give me the controller's number it would be so much easier to correspond, don't you think.'

'I'd have thought Margo would have given you that, why not ask her. No, Delph, maybe that's because you and your tossers here are giving me nothing but a load of bollocks. So why don't you all go fuck a turkey.'

Wolff calmed himself. 'This torture you're attempting will all be added to my defence, it won't look good for you, refusing to supply food or water, denying me a phone call to my lawyer. All will go against your feeble attempts to find an innocent man guilty.'

Joe brought his head forward into the light. 'Now's the time to find out... we're going to see Margo soon, maybe she'll give us a little more. When it comes down to giving a little to avoid losing your life then it's a different ball game. She'll know her brother has chosen the needle by failing to contribute.'

'Keep trying, Delph. You're in a fucking dream world, man. Tell you what, I'll put money down, name the bet, that you and your fucking tribe are dead before I get to trial. Your final curtain. No encores for you, Delph.'

'Now who's dreaming?'

45

IRISH HEADACHES

Over the pond in Little Venice, the name Paul O'Donald lit up the screen on Liam O'Brian's cellphone.

O'Brian showed Kevin the name of the caller. In an exaggeratedly humble voice, he answered, 'Who's calling?'

O'Donald, unsure of Liam's tone, said, 'It's me, it's Paul, Paul O'Donald.'

'Paul O'Donald is it?'

O'Brian's voice changed to one angry snarl. 'Back from the fucking dead are we? You taken a fucking week's holiday, O'Donald? Where the fuck are you? Your answer better be good.'

O'Donald now understood the sarcasm. 'They stopped me, Liam, locked me up they did, been drilling me on and off these last two days.'

'Who are "they". Who locked you up?'

'The military! Fucking army commando unit, asking why I was following that woman.'

O'Brian mouthed to Quinn, 'Military.'

'Hope you kept that mouth of yours shut, O'Donald?'

'I ain't no grass. They got me for driving a stolen vehicle, the Volvo I nicked in Stevenage, and for carrying an unlicensed weapon. Told them the Glock had been left abandoned, and that I was driving to York to visit some old mates. Course they didn't believe me, said they'd watched me following the woman, every detour she made, pure coincidence, says I.'

'Where the fuck are you anyway?'

'Doncaster rail station, waiting for the Kings Cross train. They took the Volvo off me.'

O'Brian laughed. 'Why, were you expecting them to let you keep the fucker? Get yourself back here, pronto.'

'Could be a while, Liam. I've got a date at Stevenage Magistrates' Court at two thirty. What with my previous convictions, I'm looking at six months.'

Liam was furious. 'You know what, O'Donald, I hope they give you ten fucking years, because you're finished. You hear me?'

Liam tapped the red button and screamed, 'Why did no one check him out? He's a fucking liability, that man.'

Kevin agreed. 'He was one of Billy's boys. That's why he was kept on. But he did say the military are involved... fucking Doncaster! What's at Doncaster besides the racecourse?'

O'Brian said, 'I've got a friend of a friend in traffic control looking into those CCTV cameras. I'm hoping he'll come back with news that could well answer that question, Kevin. Let's wait and see.'

Sure enough, it was barely noon when he received a text to say that a red Jeep had left the A1 at Leeds. Further to that, city cameras spotted it heading towards Leeds Bradford Airport.

'For fuck's sake, Liam, they've flown them out.'

'Yes, but to where?'

'Who have we at Leeds? Who'd know which flight they've taken?'

O'Brian took out a ledger from a desk and scanned the pages. 'We have Cillian Brady. He runs the Catholic Club on Huddersfield Road, he's sure to know someone who could answer that for us.'

'Cillian Brady,' said Quinn, in recognition. 'Now that's a name I've not heard for quite some time.'

'Sure enough, he was on that big arms fuck-up, remember? That cache we had coming into Castletown-Bearhaven.'

Quinn took a minute to recall. 'The AK-12s were supplied but never received from those Black Sea pirates. We came out all shit on that shipment, cost the pirates two hundred thousand dollars, if I remember right.'

Liam sniggered. 'We never did pay those chancers, Russian, Albanian, Romanian brothers in arms, known as the *iliac i keq*, bad medicine. They're not wrong there! Billy O'Neil negotiated the deal, cash on delivery.'

'But you know our Billy, he'd pay for nothing till he held it in his hand.'

Quinn shrugged. 'So Billy never paid. Could there be some connection between that and Billy and his family going missing?'

'Who knows till we get to the bottom of this mess. What I'd like to know is where's the two hundred thousand dollars. Billy was the banker, he held the payments. I've searched high and fucking low for it.'

'Could be they hit Billy and his family. What puzzles me, Liam, is what's Tommy Coyne got to do with all this?'

'Unless Tommy was holding it. Would Billy do that, let him look after the cash?'

O'Brian was clear. 'No, it's not that, Kevin, Billy would sleep with a machine gun tucked under his bed before doing anything like that.'

'Suppose it wouldn't hurt to look,' said Quinn, and pointed up towards the bedrooms.

'You gonna cut up Billy's bed?'

O'Brian does a friendly spar and jig. 'Yes, Kevin, I'd cut the fucker up if I thought for one moment that he'd shoved the cash in there. I think he's dead and gone, Kevin, the money, it's gone... whoever has Billy, dead or alive, has the bread too.'

'Whatever, don't let Peter John know any of this. I've sent his sons Ryan and Patrick to the prisons to see if there's anything else we should know. If anything should happen to those two.' Liam drew a finger across his throat.

46

LANGLEY AIR FORCE BASE

Joe and the team were given a warm welcome at LFI Langley by the Delta Force acting officer, Colonel Scott Brady Jones, who had come from Fort Bragg especially to interview the twins on some Afghanistan matters. Franco Sauvage/Wolff just happened to be around at the time various American agents were ambushed by the Taliban. Scott was aiming to get his piece of cake before the twins were moved to Dallas, where the trial was scheduled to take place where he would answer multiple charges of robbery and murder. District Attorney Vincent Mawray was appointed to work on the prosecution.

Meanwhile Wolff had finally got his phone call to Michel Laurent, who brought in one of America's star defence lawyers, Barry Nelson, from Chicago. Nelson had recently enjoyed great success in court cases played out on nationwide television, not the least of which was a not guilty verdict for Sonny Graham, the film director charged with the murder of his beautiful wife. The prosecution had made one small error which Nelson pounced on. That's all it took for a not guilty verdict. If the twins were to have any chance at all they would need such a man in their corner.

Michel Laurent would be close by to report back to Conrad who had insisted on daily updates, and who was already planning their escape in the event of a guilty verdict. But unbeknown to Conrad, of course, important news was coming into Little Venice from a pub in Leeds. Cillian Brady called O'Brian to say a Gulfstream G650 refuelled at Leeds Bradford on the night in question, destination United States. News was that it was boarded by seven passengers, two of which were cuffed and hooded, and looked to be one male and one female. The other five looked like plain clothes cops.

O'Brian said, 'We've got to go to the States and finish the job. Didn't we hear that those two were responsible for Billy O'Neil? Between you and me, Kevin, we're going to have to kill the bastards.'

Quinn, his mouth agape, shook his head. 'Now come on, Liam. You're not suggesting we're to fly to the States ourselves, are you? That would be fucking crazy.'

'We both don't need to go.'

'Thank God.'

'Just you.'

Kevin pleaded. 'Now come on. You can't be serious, I've no knowledge of the States. You need a fucking contract killer, a top shooter. Someone out of New York City or Chicago. Buddy O'Dell, he'd know of one.'

'You frightened of America, Kevin? Never thought you'd want to miss Disneyland.'

'No fucker frightens me, Liam, as you know, it's just that I was thinking... well, Buddy, didn't he have Joey Malfonso done in Vegas?'

'I'm wanting you to organise it, to see it's done clean with no comebacks. I'd rest a lot easier knowing you were there.'

O'Brian's mind was made up. No matter what more he said, Quinn knew he wasn't going to change it.

'Let's get your trip sorted,' said O'Brian, 'I've a few calls to make. Best let Peter John know what's gone down.'

With a note of resignation in his voice, Quinn said, 'I'll be needing the best team of Paddies—Chicago, Vegas, New York. Make sure of that, don't give me no wankers. If I could take Conor Maguire with me, I'd have someone I could rely on.'

'I can arrange that, but then you do realise you're asking for Peter John's nephew... don't lose him. If you do—'

Quinn patted Liam on the shoulder. 'Conor's top of the tree, Liam. You should be asking *him* not to lose *me*.'

Meanwhile news had reached Conrad who was quickly organising the rescue of his nephew and niece by securing the services of Milo Du'Fort and his eight-man squad of ex-Legionnaires and mercenaries.

With the promise of $20,000 a man for the rescue and safe return to France of the twins, they entered America via Canada and set up base in two rented RVs on a trailer park thirteen miles east of Dallas. Milo, their leader, had arranged all that was required for a month-long stay and a successful operation—arms and ammunition, refrigerators full of Kronenbourg, bottles of Beaujolais and Milo's favourite tipple, Calvados.

The rescue would need to take place during the trial, when security was at its weakest. Unknown to his squad, Conrad had offered a bonus of an extra $100,000 for the successful completion of the mission. With his squad on $20,000 a man, and a $160,000 starter, Milo was expecting to come out with $120,000. Quite a haul.

Dallas District Attorney Vincent Mawray received a fifty-page file on the two prisoners, faxed over by Pat Taylor from General Porter's office in Berlin. He believed it was more than enough to secure guilty verdicts, in spite of their opposition, the young LA upstart Barry Nelson.

Roberto invited Joe and the team to stay for the trial. DA Mawray wanted Joe to act as a prosecution witness, at the expense and courtesy of the CIA. Anton Spicer agreed, believing the extra support would be useful in any unforeseen problems that may occur.

Kevin Quinn and the athletic Conor Maguire had already returned to Ireland to board the Aer Lingus flight to Boston Logan, from where they were taken to a safe house in Scituate. There, they met a large gathering of NIRA sympathisers, only a few knowing the reason for Kevin and Conor's visit. Patrick Campbell, their host, was a sixty-year-old whose family emigrated from Armagh in the time of the great famine, who had organised a party for their arrival, on the lawns of his large house. A cèilidh band was playing, the Guinness was flowing and the Jameson was going down the hatch.

Kevin and Conor were overcome by the exuberant welcome from fellow Irish who treated them as returning heroes. After the introductions, and with a drink in hand, Patrick Campbell took the two aside. 'Tonight is for drinking, dancing, so have fun. It's in your honour. I've already booked our flights down to Dallas. Tomorrow we discuss business. We have some of the finest triggermen in America, so there's nothing to worry about.'

Back in Langley, the twins had undergone Colonel Brady's interrogation. The result? 'No comment.' They refused to answer questions without the presence of their lawyer. By this time Brady was ready to transport the twins to their new abode, the infamous Walls Unit at Huntsville State Penitentiary where the electric chair was waiting.

Meanwhile Joe got word from Lenny the nark via Spicer that Kevin Quinn plus one other was on his way to the USA.

Before they arrived the team took a much needed break and went out to sample Boston nightlife. They dined at Rino's on Saratoga Street, one of Roberto's favourite Italian spots. It came as no surprise to Joe that Roberto was trying hard to impress Ryona. Love was in the air now that they had become more than just a team. What with Tony and Norman working in harmony, Joe had one excellent squad.

Still, he'd be glad when it was all over. Stacy's gruesome death had left him thinking seriously about retiring, like a boxer approaching his final fight wanting to retire a winner. Then again if the twins walked free, knowing the Fly was still out there, there was no way he'd call it a day. But then again, those twins would not walk free if he had anything to do with it. They would go down like the *Titanic*.

Two days later, Joe, Tony and Norman found themselves in Dallas, leaving the two lovebirds time for a well-earned break before they pick up the trail of Quinn and Maguire's imminent arrival in Boston. The agents would all meet up later in Dallas as the trial wasn't expected to take more than two weeks.

Conrad secured passes for Milo and two of his lieutenants to gain entry to the court room under the guise of being French newspaper journalists. The room was full and sweaty. The six overhead fans working all out to bring some relief from the forty-degree heat that that seeped in through the open windows of courtroom one.

Milo could see that five men in the crowded room were still wearing jackets, a sure sign they were FBI agents. All were sweating profusely.

Heads turned as Franco and Margo Wolff entered the court. On one side was Prosecutor Marshall Packard, a man blessed with the good looks of a mature Cary Grant. His opponent was the new kid on the block, defence lawyer Barry Nelson. In a nod to the Dallas crowd, he wore a purple shirt with half-moon embroidered pockets and a white silk kerchief over white chinos.

Let battle begin.

The media had named their confrontation David and Goliath. Joe was reminded of the old Mongoose Archie Moore fighting the cocky Cassius Clay in Los Angeles in '62, when the young twenty-year-old upstart stopped the forty-eight-year-old Moore in the fourth.

One thing the prosecution did not want was a repeat of that result.

The court bailiff roared, 'State of Texas versus Franco and Margo Wolff. Judge Mary Beth Sloan, presiding. All rise.'

After preliminaries, Judge Beth invited Packard to call his first witness.

'Prosecution calls Joe Delph.'

Joe was questioned about the murder by garrotting of Frank Bitten, a CIA agent and native of Austin Texas. Joe listed the murders ordered by the twins, and the messages from Margo Wolff's iPad and cellphone sent to her brother. Fighting off the never-ending shouts of 'Objection', he nevertheless got his message across to an open-mouthed jury.

'Your witness.'

The first full day in court was a disaster for the defence. A combination of cockiness from the defence lawyer and savviness on Joe's part brought regular sniggering from both judge and jury.

Franco Wolff was furious. 'What the fuck, Nelson, you're losing the case. You better get this trial turned around fast. You understand?'

To compound matters, the trial, while not videotaped, was being reported closely by the TV show *A Day in Court*, which milked the defence's efforts to regain control. The press too were enjoying the spectacle: "A bad day at the office for Nelson" and "Defender Nelson runs into a Packard Tornado" were two of the kinder headlines.

That night Michel Laurent had to listen to a tirade of abuse from one of Conrad's top aides, who was phoning from Monaco. Conrad was none too pleased at the day's weak effort. He ended by saying that it would be best if Laurent did not make a court appearance the following day. Call in sick. This would be his one and only warning. Clearly, plans were already in place, wheels were turning.

The voice on the line was cold and determined. 'You keep yourself safe, old friend, stay away tomorrow.'

The lawyer did the only thing that would help him get through his predicament—he drank the mini-bar dry.

He had read in detail the damaging evidence that would put the final seal on the twins' fate. There was no way Nelson could save them. He was holding a losing hand.

How Laurent wished he was back in France, that tomorrow wouldn't come. He knew that it was essential that he appear in court tomorrow, to stand alongside Barry Nelson. He hadn't any choice.

Conrad had everything arranged for the safe return of the twins. Milo had earlier wrapped weapons in waterproof bags and concealed them in the high water tanks of the men's rest room that was situated across the corridor from courtroom one. The hit would take place at the break for lunch, when the twins would be escorted back to the holding cell. The ex-Legionnaires would storm the court, release the prisoners and take them to a helicopter waiting in a secluded spot in the Great Trinity Forest, from where they would be flown to Venice, Louisiana to take a yacht over the pond to France.

Based on today's observations, Milo was expecting no more than four guards, plus the FBI presence in the public gallery, who had to be eliminated first. Earlier that morning Milo had tested the police response time when he phoned the police to say he'd seen a man carrying a gun enter a café in downtown Dallas. It had taken the police seven minutes to respond. Milo was looking to rescue the twins in a maximum of four.

Once the job was done, and the twins safely on board, the rest of the Legionnaires could fly home.

In the Crafty Irishman public house on Main Street, Kevin Quinn and Conor Maguire sat across the table from Patrick Campbell who had brought Tommy Hunt and Davie McCane, two Irish-American courtroom guards sympathetic to the cause who guarded the holding cell containing the twins.

A large envelope was passed over the table.

Tommy Hunt whispered, 'I'll not be checking it, Mr Quinn, I can see that I'm looking at an honest man.'

Nevertheless, Patrick confirmed what was in the envelope. 'There be ten thousand dollars you be having there, Tommy Hunt. Another ten thousand when the job's seen to be done. So's best you two not to be throwing that kind of money around, now.'

Kevin Quinn leant forward. 'If you fail me. I'll be wanting my money back, you understand?'

Patrick answered for them. 'They understand, don't you be worrying yourself now.'

Davie McCane was a little excited. 'You brought us the mixture, Pat?'

Kevin answered. 'We've brought enough to kill a thousand fucking elephants. Treat it with respect, you get any inside your body, as much as a tiny drop and you're a stiff, dead in a couple of days. It's what you call bad medicine.'

Conor asked, 'How're you thinking of doing them?'

'We have it in pearls not unlike olive oil capsules, and two loaded syringes. If the pearls should break in the mouth they'll get a burning sensation. They'll try to spit it out, but the damage is done. The syringes? A stab while they're sleeping.'

Tommy shook his head. 'We was thinking in their food, their breakfast. They have that continental shit cheese and ham, hot rolls and coffee.'

Conor shrugged. 'Whatever you choose, but make it work.'

Kevin added, 'You guys have only one chance, so make it pay, if you give the full Molly Malone they'll be dead in hours not days. You think you can do this?'

Davie McCane said, 'For your dollars, Mr Quinn, many a man would kill his mother.'

Tommy Hunt said, 'I heard that defence fellow Nelson speaking to a colleague in the ante chamber, he was carrying the thought that they'd be found guilty. They'd be making death row. So why not wait, Mr Quinn? Let the great state of Texas do your work for you?'

'Let's just say I likes to be sure. No fucking maybes, and you see, Pat my friend, to my chief this is what you might call a family matter. Davie and I would find it hard to return to the motherland on a maybe. He wants to hear that the job's done.'

47
EXTRA STRONG COFFEE

Joe Delph was watching a TV report on the trial that, encouragingly, suggested it was going favourably for the prosecution.

His cellphone rang. Anton Spicer. He warned Joe that he had received reliable information that the Undertaker, Kevin Quinn, was in America for only one reason—that being the trial of the Wolff twins. Joe was not surprised, and in any case he had already detailed Ryona and Roberto to stay on his tail. He reminded Anton that MI6 did drop a few hints to the NIRA, with regard to the missing Billy O'Neil family and how the twins could have been involved. He wondered if the courtroom was big enough to hold all the interested parties.

Evidence in the trial moved on to the Dallas bullion robbery and the murder of two guards. Joe believed the evidence of those crimes would put a final nail in their coffin. Unfortunately no reference of any involvement by Margo could be found. But there were plenty of other crimes to nail her on.

Pat Taylor sent further evidence of Margo's involvement in the Berlin forest murders. Pat had found a text that had been sent to the Berlin killers, that read, "Get all all the information you can. Use the Butcher." Her order to butcher the two agents, along with John Barlow's taped interview, surely meant the woman was doomed. And that was before the horrific photographs from the sawmill would be shown.

Meanwhile Joe gave Colonel Jones the heads-up about the NIRA killers in their midst. He assured Joe that Delta Force would be looking out for Mr Quinn who would be arrested on sight and deported.

Meanwhile in the courthouse holding cell, breakfast was served.

Sitting across from the twins was Barry Nelson and Michel Laurent. Nelson held a copy of the file handed to him on his arrival, by the clerk to the prosecution.

'How come you never mentioned the fucking bullion robbery, the killings of a Texas family, the murders of George Shaman and his family, his wife Monica, his sons, or the two security guards.' Barry heaved a deep sigh. 'Jesus Christ, Michel. What do you expect me to do? Tell me because I'd like to hear what a French advocate would do!'

He slammed the file down in front of Michel, who picked it up and skimmed through it.

'I'm waiting, Mr Laurent. Give me a clue. Because to be quite frank with you, we haven't got a cat in hell's chance of pulling this off. Tell me now if I'm going to get hit with any more surprises because, if there's more, you can find some other pigeon to take your shit.'

Suddenly Franco, who had been unusually quiet for the last two minutes, grabbed his throat, gasping. He shouted, 'My throat's on fire, burning. Water! Give me a drink, Margo.'

She poured out the coffee and handed it to him. He gulped it down. Again he shouted, 'No, no, it's worse, it's bitter. Water! Give me water, quick!'

Margo took a mouthful of coffee, and immediately spat it out. 'What's with this food? My throat's on fire. That coffee tastes like it's just been drawn out of the Mississippi.'

Marcel shouted for the guard. Moments later the face of Tommy Hunt appeared in the cell door window. He unlocked the cell door. On the floor was the writhing body of Franco Wolff, his hand gripping his throat, hoarsely pleading for water. The guard picked up the breakfast tray and left the cell, letting the door self-lock behind him. Michel Laurent banged on the cell door, demanding a doctor for his client.

Tommy raced back to his fellow guard in the kitchen, where he carefully put down the tray and told Davie of the fiasco inside the holding cell. Tommy ended by saying the coffee was like Mississippi River water.

'Didn't know how to tell her that it was fucking poison.'

Davie asked, 'How much of that Ricin shit did you put in the breakfast?'

'I put the lot in, emptied the syringes too. Can't have dangerous stuff like that lying about now, can we?'

'You what! It's supposed to kill within a couple of days with just a little drop,' Tommy said. 'They'll be fucking dead in minutes with the load you've fed them.'

'Just making sure we get our bonus.'

'Their insides must be like shovelling coal into a steam train's boiler. Best I get rid of the evidence, flush it down the drain and put some bleach down with it. You better get hold of Doc Wallis. Get him to take a look. Keep us in the clear. Tell them the doc's on his way.'

Tommy nodded. 'Will do, Davie. We're fucking rich, man.'

Tommy stopped and asked, 'Davie, where did you put the syringes?'

'I was only born green, brother, I ain't stupid, they're securely wrapped. I put them in the sanitary bin in the ladies' rest room.'

'Good thinking, man. I was on a cliff edge for a moment. Sanitary bin, nobody puts a hand in those that's for sure.'

Carrying a jug of water and a glass, Tommy returned to the cell where a senior guard was trying to console everyone in the cell. The twins looked like they had been tossed around in a tornado, their eyes were rolling and they were sweating profusely.

Nelson shouted, 'Get that doctor here now. My clients need a doctor!'

He looked at his watch. 'Shit, we're due in court in ten minutes, where's that doctor?'

Tommy answered, 'The doc is on his way, sir. Here's the water you asked for.'

'Give it to me, let me try it. I can't trust anything you give us.' He tested the water. 'Yes, that's okay.'

He took the tray and passed it to Michel Laurent.

To Tommy's surprise, the doc entered the cell accompanied by Davie who was carrying his bag. As chance would have it, the doc had been entering the court to assist the prosecution. He asked the lawyers to leave him to examine the patients. Davie stayed.

Three Legionnaires entered the men's room and moments later reappeared with the pistols unwrapped and firmly tucked into their belts under full-length sweaters. They entered the courtroom, shortly followed by the prisoners who were dragged there to prove they were both unable to stand trial in their condition.

The judge took a cursory look at the prisoners and, to the great disappointment of the public gallery, banged her gavel. 'Court adjourned.'

There was some confusion as the guards went to return the prisoners to the cell but were held back by Michel Laurent who suggested they wait for the ambulance as stretchers would be required. The guards looked to the bailiff who merely shrugged.

At that moment Milo stood and shouted to his two accomplices, 'Go, go, go!'

He stepped forward, took out his weapon and popped the two guards with head shots. Another took out two of the suits in quick succession; the third saw a man going to the aid of a fallen suit. He shot him too.

The judge was glued to the spot. Joe Delph raced across the court and dragged her under the bench.

Norman Aimes leapt from his seated position at a Legionnaire, taking him from behind and snapping his neck. He took the automatic out of the dead man's hand and fired two accurate head shots at another, who was dead before hitting the floor. He rushed over to Tony who was on the floor with blood soaking through his light blue jacket. He sank to his knees and gently turned his friend over. He held him in his arms until he faded away. Only now did Norm realise that Tony Ford had rushed to help two elderly family members of victims, unaware that the assassins were shooting at suits. Everyone else was on the floor.

Milo, in the meantime, put a bullet between the eyes of Barry Nelson. The young lawyer fell dead over the desk, his files soaked in his blood.

Milo took a moment to express his disgust. 'You were shit, Nelson.'

He forced Michel to help him get the twins out of the courtroom.

Michel shouted at Milo in his native French. '*Los song maladies, ils ont besoin d'stress hospitalises.*' (They are ill, they need hospital). '*Ferdinand il sera en colere.*' (Ferdinand, he will be angry.)

Milo responded. 'You do your job! Let Milo do his, okay? '

In the corridor a panic stricken crowd raced to the exit where two uniforms lay dead. A Legionnaire waved them to hurry.

Milo turned to Michel. 'You help us to our vehicle, then you can fuck off.'

Norman lay Tony alongside the dead body of a boyish-faced FBI agent. He picked up the agent's Glock and made his way to the judge's bench, stepping over two more dead agents. He banged the gavel. Joe popped his head up and Norman passed him the Glock.

'Leave the judge, Joe, she'll be okay. There's only dead people left in here. We lost Tony.'

There was a creak of a door. They both turned. A frightened looking bailiff entered.

'They all gone?'

Norman nodded. Joe lifted the Judge to her feet and told the bailiff to escort her to the safety of her quarters.

She turned to Joe. 'Thank you, Mr Joe Delph. Now you go and get them killers, you hear?'

Joe, loud and clear, said, 'Ma'am you bet.'

He approached the bailiff. 'Over there amongst the dead lies a very brave man, a dear friend of ours, in a powder blue jacket. I'm asking a favour of you. Look after him for us, till we return. Treat him with respect.'

The judge answered, 'Consider it done, Joe.'

Joe and Norman shared a moment to assess the situation. Joe said, 'Thank God Ryona and Roberto weren't here.'

‘Could have been a lot worse if they had been. What with Roberto being a jacket and tie man. But then we’ll never know.’

‘What you say we go finish the bastards off, Norm?’

‘Sure, but... what we gonna tell Ryona and Roberto?’

‘Don’t want them worrying especially when they’re chasing Quinn. You need a clear head when dealing with that animal.’

Joe and Norman left the courtroom into the corridor of death, where bloodied bodies were lying everywhere, with a strong smell of cordite in the air. Delta Force had arrived in full battle dress, pointing their automatic rapid fire rifles at the two agents. Joe flashed his SIS ID and they passed on by.

Outside, Colonel Scott Brady Jones was giving out orders to his squad.

‘What a fucking mess, Joe. First count: six FBI agents dead, two wounded, four courthouse guards, plus Barry Nelson.

Joe held his gaze and sighed.

‘What! have I missed something?’

‘We lost Captain Tony Ford.’

There was a moment’s silence before Scott spoke.

‘Jesus, I’m sorry guys, I liked the man, I feel for you.’

He saw the colonel looking at the pistols.

Joe raised a MAC 50 automatic, known as the preferred tool of the French Foreign Legion.

‘Got this off one of the assassins. Joe has a Glock automatic I got off the young FBI agent still in its holster, man never got to pull it out. The pistols we got from the dead.’

Scott held out his hand. ‘Let me take them off you, save any awkward questions that may arise. Let me issue you with a couple of Beretta M9s on my note, if that’s okay with you.’

Joe asked, 'So what's the plan, Scott? We want them bastards, Colonel.'

Scott pointed down the street. 'An ambulance driver who saw the getaway said they left in a Ford Tourneo, heading east towards Highway 20, probably making for the state line. Let's get you them pistols and go take these killers.'

48
TRAVEL SICKNESS

In the back of the Ford, the twins were gasping for breath. Milo opened the windows, hoping the fresh air might give them some relief. If they died there would be no pay day.

Milo was confronted by his driver. 'They don't look good, Milo. We can't take them far in that condition. We should pull in somewhere, get help.'

'You fucking serious or what? You want the electric chair?... cause that's what we get if we're caught. Just fucking drive.'

Franco was coughing up a vile smelling vomit, his eyes rolling to the back of their sockets. Margo was trying hard to speak. She managed to stammer something out.

'Get... my... broth... er... some... help... N...ow... he... s... dy... ing.'

Victor tried again. 'Come on, man. We have to stop. If we lose them... oh fuck, if we lose them, Milo, we're in deep shit.'

Milo hit the dash in frustration. 'Okay, next town we stop and grab a doctor, we take him with us.'

Victor's expression was a question mark.

Milo smiled. 'He will have no choice. You should be wanting this. The money. You've increased your wages... We lost two men, so their cut will be divided among those who remain... Ain't that good of me... doesn't that encourage you to see this job done... At whatever cost?'

Milo's mind had already been made up. He'd been calculating just where their $20,000 was going. Into Milo's account.

He looked back at the twins whose eyes were now shut, their breathing a wretched wheeze. He told the driver to take the next exit, signposted Longview.

'Put Longview Hospital into the sat-nav. If there's a bug house then it'll be in there.'

They quickly located a clinic a couple of miles away.

Milo nodded. 'It's sure to have a doctor.'

The driver smiled, as if to a private joke.

'What's so fucking funny?'

'You, Milo. *It's sure to have a doctor*.'

'So?'

'That's usually where they work, doctors.'

'So, ain't I right ?'

'You're right, Milo. Of course you're right, silly me.'

Following a few miles behind the Ford Tourneo was a Delta Force Hummer. Joe, Norman and Scott were on the back seat. The front seats were occupied by two elite soldiers. Above, in the east Texas sky, Colonel Brady was sweeping the highways in an MH-6 Little Bird helicopter.

Scott said, 'I know they'd take the twenty. It's their best route. I'm thinking they might hear that chopper and take cover.'

Joe said, 'Or they've made a stop. The twins were in need of some serious medical attention.'

'Joe's right, Colonel,' said Norm. 'They'd need hospitalisation. The doc at the court said their temperature was sky high and needed intensive care. Without it, they'd die.'

The realisation that they may be entering the end game concentrated Norm's thoughts. 'Look, Colonel, I've lost a dear friend in Tony. Joe's loss too. Our girl, Ryona, her whole family. I hope that pair of bastards die screaming in agonising pain. Those two are the devil's spawn.'

Scott said, 'Gee, Norm, I didn't know about this. Ryona, her family... and you too Joe? Fuck if I ain't beginning to understand you guys.'

Joe said, 'Those photographs of the sawmill in Berlin, Scott, the butchered bodies... that woman was my soul mate, Stacy Kilmer, the man was a young recruit on his first mission, a good friend of Ryona's.'

Scott patted them both on the shoulder. 'We've got to find those twins then decide on what to do.'

In Boston Logan's departure lounge, Kevin Quinn and Conor Maguire were waiting to board their return flight to Dublin. A man and a woman approached, accompanied by two armed members of the US counterterrorist force.

The woman said, 'If you two gentlemen would kindly follow me.'

Kevin hissed, 'What the fuck's going on? We robbed a bank?'

One of the armed men shouted, 'Get off your asses and do as you're told, big boy.'

Conor pleaded, 'What we done? Where you taking us?'

The officers took out handcuffs and quickly secured them, before marching them away.

Ryona turned to Roberto and asked for a high five. 'I think Anton and the boys back home are going to be over the moon when they hear the Undertaker Quinn and Maguire are locked away, Robbie.'

Roberto smiled. 'Robbie? Now that sounds almost affectionate. Think I'm going to call you... let's just see now... think I'll call you, err...' He put a finger to his brow.

Ryona jumped in with, 'Rye?'

'No... yes, that's it, Mabel. What you think girl, er, Mabel?'

Ryona gave him such a wack. 'One can easily go off someone, you know, er, Uriah.'

Roberto laughed. 'Let's give the boys a bell, er, Mabel. You want to tell them the good news?'

She squinted at him with a fierce expression. 'You have been warned, Mr Veneto, you're getting close to another slap.'

Joe's phone beeped and lit up with the name Ryona. Joe put his phone on speaker. She shared the good news that Quinn and Maguire were being transferred to Langley for interrogation.

Norman whispered to Joe if he was going to mention Tony's death. Joe mouthed, 'No.' He then told her about the car chase and that he'd call her later. He finished, rather curiously, by asking her to watch CNN news.

The Ford Tourneo turned into the Longview Clinic Hospital car park. The twins lay huddled together on the back seat, their breathing shallow. Milo and his driver were feeling increasingly concerned.

'Lets go find ourselves a doctor.'

They searched the corridors and treatment rooms until they found a consulting room that announced the name of a professor on the door. They entered, only to be stopped by a receptionist. Milo pulled out his pistol. Her scream was cut short once Milo shot her with a bullet between the eyes. The inner office door opened and a middle-aged man rushed out.

'What on earth have you done? Why?'

Milo smiled. 'The bitch wasn't hospitable. Get your medicine bag because you're coming with us. I have a couple of friends who need your expertise.'

'Then take them into emergency admission,' said the doctor. 'There was no need for you to kill her. Why do this when you have all the facilities in the clinic?'

'Because she was annoying me. Just like you are beginning to. So do as I ask. My friends will need oxygen. If we could put them in your clinic, we would. But you see, Professor, we are wanted men, desperate men. So the choice is yours. Do or die. What we want, we get. You, doctor, we want.'

The doc felt a trickle of perspiration running down his face, soaking his shirt. These two men before him were clearly insane.

'What do you want?'

'Now we seem to be getting down to business. I want you to make my two sick friends well. They're sweating, burning up, vomiting, shitting themselves and God knows what else. They're down in the parking lot, and unless you treat them right away they're gonna fucking die. And it will all be your fault.' He squeezed the doc's shoulder menacingly. 'If you do, we'll let you return to your experiments and microscopes. What could be simpler?'

The doctor turned back into his office to gather some supplies. On the desk was a photo of him with a woman and two boys, not yet in their teens.

Milo pointed. 'Family?'

'Yes.'

'Nice. You play ball with us, you get to see them again.'

Back in the Hummer, Joe was frustrated that they had lost sight of the Ford. He turned to Scott.

'Where the hell are they?'

'They're on this route somewhere, they probably heard that Little Bird so went under cover.'

Norman chipped in, 'I'm thinking they've gone looking for a doc, Colonel. Those twins had been got at. Someone else has an interest. Can't be Quinn, Langley has him in a lock-up.'

'Then why was he here?' said Joe. 'That man wasn't here for Disney. I do believe you have a point. Someone else is involved.'

On balance, they decided to head to the nearest hospital on Highway 20.

Joe's phone beeped. It was Ryona. He put her on speaker.

Ryona said that she and Roberto had watched CNN and were now up to speed on events at the courthouse. Joe also filled them in on the twins, their apparent sickness and how two of the killers escaped with them.

'How did they get pistols into the court, Joe? Jesus. I think Roberto and I should join you. We have Quinn and Maguire jailed, so we're just sitting here worrying about you three. Five is better than three, if you catch my drift.'

Norman whispered to Joe. 'You have to tell her about Tony. They're going to hate us if we don't.'

Scott agreed.

'Thanks for the thought, Ryona. You stay with the Irish. We have Colonel Jones with us and men from Delta Force.'

Norman nudged him.

With a deep sigh, Joe said, 'Got to tell you both, it's fucking heartbreaking. You watched the news about the casualties being FBI agents, courthouse guards, civilians, lawyer Barry Nelson—'

'What is it, Joe?'

Joe could hardly bring himself to utter the words.

'Has something happened? You don't sound good.'

There was a moment's silence before, in a voice just above a whisper, Joe said, 'We lost Tony today, he was one they counted a civilian death. The assassins shot at everyone wearing a jacket, thinking they were FBI agents. He took two shots in the back and died in Norm's arms.'

The line went silent.

Roberto swallowed hard. 'It's me, Joe. Ryona... she's overcome right now. Norm must be feeling it too. Ryona asked me to send him her love.'

'Norm's with me now. He took down two of the killers in the courtroom. Snapped the neck of one, took his weapon and to put two head shots into the other. He's one fucking hero.'

The doctor could see the twins were in critical condition. He fitted them both with masks connected to oxygen bottles they had carried from the clinic.

The driver fired up the Ford and drove out of the parking lot, and headed towards Highway 20.

While the doctor worked frantically on the twins, Milo pushed his pistol into his neck.

'Get to work, Professor. Get that knowledgeable brain of yours working.'

'Are you both mad? You need to turn back. These people need to be admitted into my clinic now for urgent specialist care.'

He pointed to the clinic that was slowly disappearing from view.

'You need to take them back. They're in a near-death coma situation.'

'Then you'd better keep them alive, Professor. Your fucking life depends on it. That's why you're going to cure them two babies. So stop babbling on. You're wasting precious time. Savvy?'

'Won't you clowns listen?' said the doctor. 'I need to take samples that will have to go to a lab to be analysed to see what the fuck they've caught to see if it's contagious. If you want us to catch whatever they've caught, then let's just sail along till we catch it.'

'Then we die... you and me, we die in pain together.'

The driver was getting anxious and driving erratically. 'We have to listen to the prof, he's a specialist. Knows what he's talking about. Fuck's sake, Milo, we don't want to catch whatever they have. Look at them, man, I don't want that bug in me. Let's dump them. I don't want what they have at any price. Fuck the money.'

Milo put the pistol up and under his chin. He growled like a sore bear, and shouted, 'Shut the fuck up! Dump them? We do that and our lives won't be worth living. Ferdinand will put us both in cement boots and toss us into the River Seine. We have to save the fuckers. We have to find our professor here a laboratory.'

The doctor couldn't help laughing at the absurdity of the situation. 'You've just left one! Go back! All the facilities are there, doctors that could help them.'

Milo was working himself up into a frenzy. 'Listen to him, he still can't get it into his head that if we return we get to sit the electric chair. You better select a safer venue and fast.'

There was little more the doctor could do for the two patients with such little equipment. His mind turned to how he could find this animal Milo a safe place, a place that would not put other innocent people at risk. These killers would not leave witnesses. Then it came to him. He had a remote cabin in Pineywood Forest that he used for family vacations. Nearby was a cabin that belonged to Henry King, one that old Henry hardly ever used. It was sure to be unoccupied until the hunting season two months away. Once he got them to the forest—a region he knew well—there was always the possibility of escape, more than being cooped up in a people carrier.

He put the cabin idea to Milo, who accepted it without question.

49
HENRY'S CABIN

The phone in Colonel Scott Brady Jones's lap lit up. It was Bill Edwards from Delta headquarters. News had come in from the Gregg County Sheriff about a shooting at Longview Hospital Clinic. A secretary had been shot dead in the office of a professor of tropical diseases, Professor James Fask. Fask was missing, after taking two bottles of oxygen out of storage. The professor's car was still in the parking lot.

The Colonel turned to Joe. 'It's got to be our killers. They now have medical help for the twins.'

Norman added, 'And clearly don't want to leave any witnesses.'

Joe said, 'Longview, Gregg County... why's the Little Bird not seeing them? Surely they've got to come back onto Highway 20?'

Scott was glued to the Google map on his iPhone.

He began to think out loud. 'So that's where you are... the forest. That's where I'd go. You have the professor, oxygen, the twins, two passengers that are valuable cargo in need of urgent medical help... then you have to hole-up, best place.'

He tapped Leo on the shoulder. 'Take us into Pineywood.'

Back in Boston, Ryona sat watching Roberto twirling a spoon in his coffee. Their depressed thoughts were on the same subject, having lost a unique friend and colleague.

Roberto said, 'What puzzles me is how the assassins got the pistols into that courthouse. They had to have had help.' He looked ready to make a decision. 'Since Joe and Norm are busy, why don't we get over to Dallas to do some digging around?'

'Let's do just that, Robbie.'

'I'll give Mr Joe Delph a call.'

Roberto shook his head. 'Best text him, girl, just a simple, "We're on our way" is enough.'

In the speeding Hummer, Joe glanced at Ryona's incoming message, and showed it to Norman, then Scott.

'I knew we couldn't keep them away,' he said.

Norman said, 'I'm sure they're coming to say a final goodbye to Tony.'

Joe sighed.'I'm not going to stop them, Norm. They'd never forgive me if I did that.'

The vehicle approached Longview Hospital.

Colonel Jones said, 'Lets call in. I'm hoping they will have CCTV that might help us see who's in that Ford.'

In the car park they found themselves in a phalanx of police activity—highway patrol vehicles, flashing lights, taped-off areas. Two men in suits were talking to a woman who seemed to be giving out instructions. The Hummer drove up to her and they wound down the window. Colonel Jones took the lead. He explained to the police lieutenant who they were and why it was important they check the hospital CCTV footage, and its implications for the Dallas courthouse killings.

After a few preliminaries, they gained access to the communications room. The footage showed the Ford entering the car park, and two men leave the vehicle. Joe recognised one from the courtroom.

The footage was forwarded to the point where the two suspects reappeared in the car park with Professor Fask and the oxygen cylinders. All three got in the Ford and left.

Joe said, 'It's a big risk to drag a civilian with you. The twins must be real sick, could well be on their way out.'

Norman uttered, 'I hope they are Joe. I really hope they die in pain.'

While not quite dead, the twins lay motionless, their eyes closed, in the Ford. Their faces were covered with oxygen masks. Dr Fask had administered heart stimulants and antibiotics along with morphine. He knew that if they died, so did he. He could hardly feel a pulse on either of them, their bodies having gone into a comatose state. Their signs were critical. If they were to survive they had to receive immediate intensive care. Without more sophisticated diagnostic equipment, his best guess was that they may have been administered with a deadly poison.

Milo leant over the front passenger seat. 'How's my two sleeping beauties doing, Professor?'

Fask replied with a lie. 'Oh, come on now, you're asking for miracles. They'll be needing some time to rest.'

'Okay, but you better fucking remember, we ain't looking for no holiday stay. I'm wanting for you to get my friends here back on their feet. I've a deadline to meet, a boat ready to sail.'

They were deep in the forest now, and soon passed a sign "Henry's Place one mile ahead". He told Victor to take the second exit right. The cabin was a quarter mile up that road.

Fask pointed to a cabin standing back from the road. 'Our cabin... our holiday home.'

Milo waved his pistol. 'Just be careful, Professor, I'm not to liking fucking comedians. You know what I'm saying?'

Fask nodded. 'I've got your drift, mister, I know where you're coming from.'

The nineteen-year-old daughter of Dr Fask's murdered secretary was alone at home, trying to come to terms with the news of her mother's death. Her murder in cold blood at the hospital, the two sadistic killers, the courtroom shootout in downtown Dallas. Kirsty Johnston's mind was spinning.

The screen of her cellphone pinged a message from Professor Fask.

"In Henry's Cabin, Pineywood, held hostage by two killers who killed your mother... will kill me if police don't find me. Help, Fask."

The teenager called her brother Ralph and told him about the professor's message.

He dropped everything and was on his way.

Soon after, the girl's phone rang.

Dr Fask was on the other end of the line, whispering urgently but so softly she could hardly hear him.

'They murdered your mother... I'm so sorry... they've kidnapped me to attend to two people. The man is already dead. The woman has only minutes left... Don't ring me back on this number, they'll hear. Please get the police. I can't hold out much longer... help me—'

The line went dead.

Kirsty Johnston took her father's revolver from a bedside drawer and filled the barrel chambers. In the driveway outside, her brother Ralph was waiting for her on his Harley Davidson 117. Strapped across his back was a Ravin R29X sniper crossbow.

The news of their mother's murder was still a visceral thing. Adrenalin coursed through their bodies, and they were both overtaken with an overwhelming desire to right this terrible wrong. Her killers were still out there, holding their mother's boss. These dogs had to be stopped.

She slipped onto the pillion seat and slapped his back. She shouted, 'Pinewood Road, Henry's Cabin.'

Ralph tapped his sister's knee then gave the 117 full throttle.

Colonel Jones received a call from Bill Edwards at headquarters.

'Thought you should know, just in from Little Bird... we have a biker with pillion passenger heading into Pineywood. Could be nothing, but then again, it's worth checking out. Also, some woman who didn't leave her name called HQ to say the killers were in Henry's Cabin in Pineywood holding Professor Fask prisoner.'

'Thanks, Bill. We're just off the twenty, entering the Pines now.'

Norman commented, 'It's probably another part of their team.'

Joe said, 'That's feasible, those two with the doctor certainly didn't do this job without back-up.'

It wasn't long before they were on the slip road onto the narrow dirt track that ran through the pine forest.

The driver said, 'Looks like we've caught up with the bikers, sir.'

Up ahead the Harley cut its speed and was casually cruising.

Ralph Johnston saw the Hummer in his mirror and shouted to his sister, 'We've got company.'

'Take us into the wood,' said Kirsty, 'go past Henry's place... it's just ahead. If the killers are still there, we can park up and make a detour on foot back through the wood.'

Ralph understood.

Norman had second thoughts about the bikers up ahead. 'Aren't they more likely to be tourists? With long flowing hair and an arse like that. The pillion rider's a woman. I'll stake a month's pay on it.'

Joe laughed. 'Not tourists, Norm. They had no back pack... But then again, they don't look like killers either.'

The driver said, 'Looks like we have the cabin up ahead, sir... sign saying "Henry's Place".'

The navigator cried out, 'Henry's just ahead... Ford Tourneo parked across its driveway. Can't see the Harley.'

Norm turned to Joe. 'Seems that biker and his girl were tourists after all. I think this is far enough, soldier.'

The driver slammed on the brake and shut off the engine.

Colonel Jones laid down his plan. 'Two go to the rear of the cabin... take the the stun grenades, the blasting caps. Take out the rear door.'

Joe added, 'The stun grenades should force them to exit by the main door.'

Jones smiled. 'Where we will be waiting... synchronise watches... it's 16.36... if the back door warrants a hit, then we go at 17.10.'

Norman asked, 'What if we hit a snag, we still go?'

'We've lost enough of our people and I'm not looking to lose any more, therefore we hold.'

Colonel Jones looked to the east, the sky was darkening.

'Nightfall will soon be upon us, giving us more of a chance, we have our night views. I doubt that they'll have them.'

Meanwhile Ralph had parked on a path that led to the rear of the cabin. Kirsty was clutching her father's revolver; Ralph shouldered the crossbow and its quiver of arrows.

'Say, sister K, that revolver of father's, you sure it fires?'

'I'm sure going to find out now, ain't I.'

Ralph affectionately pushed her shoulder. 'Guess so, it's just the wrong time to be finding out.'

He walked on, mumbling to himself, 'Can't remember the last time Dad pulled the trigger. Must have been a lifetime ago.'

At the rear of the cabin, Norman and a Delta Force soldier crouched in thick gorse bushes ten metres from the cabin's back door. All was quiet.

'So what's your thoughts, Major. Think it's a go... we on?'

'My thoughts are to stop it with this "Major"... I'm Norman, Norm if you like.'

They both heard a rustling coming from nearby undergrowth. They quietly spin and see a young couple slowly coming towards them. The woman was carrying a pistol that looked like it was out of the Wild West. The man held an impressive crossbow.

Norman whispered, 'We have a problem. We've got to reorganise this play.'

'What about Colonel Jones, Norm?'

Norman gave a sigh. 'They've got to hold. Fuck me if it ain't Sunday morning.'

Kirsty and Ralph were approaching in a duck-like crawl. Norman slowly rose from the gorse and gave a firm order. 'Drop your weapons... On your knees, now!'

Brother and sister froze.

'Drop your weapons and tell me who the fuck are you?'

Ralph let go of the bow and turned to find himself looking down the barrel of an MK46 assault rifle.

His fright produced a rather comical, 'You're not one of those killers, are you?'

Norman smiled. 'If I was, you'd be dead. But it's me asking the questions... who the fuck are you?'

Kirsty dropped the revolver. 'We know those killers are in Henry's. They murdered our mother. Barbara Johnston... Professor Fask's secretary.'

Norman told them to take cover as he explained the gist of the operation about to take place. Once the op was completed successfully, then and only then were they to reclaim their weapons.

Kirsty asked, 'What about the professor?'

'Not to worry, he'll be good.'

Back in the cabin, Milo was pacing the floor and growling like some caged grizzly.

'Make sure the doc's working on them twins... We've got to get a move on out of here.'

His sidekick nervously replied, 'You been hearing what he's been saying? What if what they have is contagious... we're gonna catch their dog shit, we have to be careful here, brother.'

'Dog shit! That's what we'll be fucking eating if we don't get food. My belly thinks my fucking throat's cut. It's food I'm wanting, and a drink.'

Milo walked to the refrigerator and kicked it. 'We're all going to be dead if we don't eat soon.'

For want of something to kill time, he entered the bedroom—two single beds with bare mattresses on which the bodies of Franco and Margo Sauvage showed little sign of life. Milo kept his distance. The professor, masked and wearing surgical gloves, was taking Margo's temperature.

'They're not dead are they?' asked Milo.

The doctor laid out the facts. 'She's barely got a pulse. Her temperature is 105 and will soon die. He's no better.' He nodded towards Franco's prostrate body. He was dead but the doctor kept the news from his kidnapper. Milo edged towards Franco's body, trying to get a closer look.

'Keep back,' said the doctor. 'The fever they've got is contagious.'

From the open door, Milo's sidekick called out, 'Do what the professor says, didn't I tell you. We catch that virus, then it's goodnight Vienna.'

Milo backed off and waved the doctor to follow him out of the room. Once they were in the lounge area Milo stabbed a finger at him. 'Go with Victor to that store, get some food and drink.'

He pointed to the cooker. 'That thing runs on bottled gas, which is fucking empty, we need gas to cook. So get me some grub, bacon, eggs, beans and anything else you can think of —fresh milk, coffee, sugar. He knows what to get.'

He thumbed over his shoulder at the bedroom. 'Get those two something to open their eyes. Wake the fuckers up.'

Outside on the approach driveway Joe was inspecting the far side of the parked Ford. The sound of the cabin door opening sent him into a crouched position. The man who was evidently the doctor was being unceremoniously prodded by the barrel of a gun into the passenger front seat. The gunman then came around to open the door on the driver's side.

Joe silently stepped back to the rear of the vehicle. The driver's door opened and the killer prepared to climb in. Joe sneaked up and took him from behind, plunging his

Fairbairn-Sykes fighting knife into his neck and slicing his throat. Unable even to cry out, the gunman fell to his knees, toppled over and died.

Joe put a finger up to his lips, and whispered to the doctor, 'You okay, Fask?'

The doc briefed him on the situation inside the cabin, and their intended drive to the store.

'Not to worry, you're safe now.'

The dead gunman was put into the back of the vehicle, then driven onto the road, and parked out of sight.

Once completed, Joe moved back up with his Delta Force point man, who was covering the cabin door with a CAR-15 automatic.

The colonel's phone alarm flashed 19.10.

'Time to blow that door. You ready, Joe?'

'After you, Colonel.'

At that moment they heard an explosion and the crashing sound of the rear door being blown off its hinges, followed by the sound of stun grenades. Amongst the shouting there were two pistol shots.

'I think they've got him.'

Inside the cabin, Milo, who was masked up against the stun grenades, fired two shots into a Delta Force soldier, who lay on the floor with a night vision scope attached to his head. Norman entered and soon felt the warm steel of a recently fired gun barrel on his neck.

'Think I didn't see you fucking parading about out there, soldier boy? That I wouldn't be prepared for you?'

Milo pushed the barrel deeper into his neck.

Norm replied, 'You're gonna die... You're surrounded, there's no way out...You're in a fucking hole, man.'

Milo pushed him towards the front door. 'If I die, then so do you. Open that door. Let's find out just how much your comrades fucking love you.'

He did as he was told. He walked through the fog and out onto the cabin's driveway as a human shield for the killer with a gun to his head.

Milo shouted, 'You out there... I want your vehicle... Get it here, now!'

He grabbed the Norman's night views and placed them on his head. There was no answer. He dragged Norman back into the doorway, and again shouted his demand.

'I'm wanting an answer! I can't hear no engine running. You out there, don't you dare fuck with me... If I die then so does the soldier boy here.'

Scott was not sure how to play the situation. 'Fuck! We have a problem, Joe. We're dealing with a do or die maniac here. How're we going to play this?'

Joe screwed up his face. 'I ain't losing Norm. We'll have to bring back the professor. We need to buy every second.'

Joe discarded his helmet, and rubbed his scalp. 'Need time to think. We've just got to fix this deep shit we're in.'

Jones said, 'Those shots we heard, he must have hit Mitch. Fuck!'

Suddenly there was another shot. They both turned back to see Norman step aside, to allow the gunman to fall to his knees. A moment later an arrow from Ralph's crossbow entered the gunman's neck. He rolled over, his eyes staring.

Joe gasped. 'I'm not a religious man but where did that angel come from?'

Norman shouted, 'Get the medication. Mitch has been hit. Where's the doctor? Mitch needs help back here.'

Jones ran to the Hummer for the first aid kit. He phoned Leo to bring the professor. Joe rushed to the cabin, stepping over the lifeless Milo. Through the smoke he saw Norman kneeling over a shallow breathing Mitch.

Joe shook his head in bewilderment, and looked at Norman. 'So where the fuck did that arrow come from?'

'The Johnstons—the professor's secretary was their mother. They need decorating for saving my life and getting us out of a heavy duty situation.'

He looked down at the Delta Force soldier. 'And here's another one. He has two shots in him: one in the shoulder and one in his back. Let's hope Doctor Fask can do some magic.'

Within an hour the soldier was safely airlifted to hospital.

Colonel Jones said, 'At least we won, Joe. The killers are dead and so are the prisoners. We're saving the state a lot of money.'

Joe shook his head with a deep sigh. 'We lost Tony, along with some agents, yours and mine, not forgetting a fine lawyer in Barry Nelson, the professor's secretary... hardly a victory.'

The following morning, Ryona and Roberto finally got to team up with Joe and Norman in the coffee lounge of the Marshall Hotel. Joe filled them in on the events of the previous day that had cost them their friend and companion, Captain Tony Ford.

Joe had spent much of the night speaking to Anton Spicer, and giving him the good news of Kevin Quinn and Conor Maguire's arrest.

Norman made an official request to Admiral Mathews to be considered a replacement officer for Tony's squad. Not for one moment did Norman think he could ever replace Tony, but he had been the man's friend and work partner from day one of their mission to catch the Fly. Anton promised

Norman he would pass on the message and try to get his wish granted.

EPILOGUE

Margo Wolff lasted one day longer than her brother Franco. Their bodies were cremated and ashes shipped to Paris. Anton placed the address under surveillance, hoping to see who would collect the remains. But Conrad was one step ahead. He had instructed Ferdinand Cortez to pay somebody to collect the urns and pour the ashes into the River Seine.

In Dallas, Kevin Quinn and Conor Maguire were tried in the same courthouse by the same judge that presided over the Wolff affair. Charge: murder. Verdict: guilty. Sentence: death. The two bent guards were also tried: one was sentenced to death while the other, McCane, received a life sentence in return for helping the prosecution convict Quinn, Maguire and Thomas. Three weeks into his sentence McCane was found dead in a prison washroom.

John Barlow got twenty-five years without parole, courtesy of Her Majesty's Prison Service.

The names of Ralph and Kirsty Johnston got lost in the police investigation into events in Pineywood, thanks to Norman suffering a convenient memory loss.

Ryona Steel reverted to her original name of Mari Bambella. She had become more than attached to her partner, CIA agent Roberto Veneto, and was soon to change her name to Mari Bambella-Veneto. They quit their roles with their respective government agencies to live six months each year in their two homes—in Bowling Green, Kentucky, and Aunt Sophia's cottage in North Yorkshire. They began a private investigation office called Under Cover that mainly dealt with insurance fraud.

They adopted two young Turkish sisters who attended a fine girls' school on the outskirts of York. The first words of English they learned were 'God's Country'.

As for Norman, he was offered Tony's old job. Captain Frazier and the men welcomed him with open arms.

Joe considered retiring, but Anton wouldn't hear of it. He granted Joe a month's leave, after which he was sure he would return to his role as a double o agent, with one evil Fly still to catch.

In a large house in the picturesque town of Colmar on the French–German border, Conrad Wolff sat drinking coffee with his personal aide, Ferdinand Cortez. They were putting together final plans for their next moneymaking scheme, one negotiated with the Russian Bratva that involved stealing nuclear torpedoes from the storage facilities at Pantex, South Carolina—after which, there would be just one more operation to finalise: the execution of agent Joe Delph.

In a quiet MI6 office in Vauxhall, Anton Spicer received a crimson call from an old friend asking a big favour. To agree, he would have to bring Joe back from leave.

Lightning Source UK Ltd.
Milton Keynes UK
UKHW012236040123
414806UK00001B/30

9 781916 081987